Young Silas

By

Robert William Jones

Copyright © 2022 Robert William Jones

All rights reserved.

ISBN: 9798354630127

To Harry and Jenny, back together again.

Foreword

Many of the characters within the series are based on one or more people I encountered and came to love during my long career and the character, Silas was autistic from the first word written. Translating that into sixteenth-century culture has been both fascinating and difficult although those who are familiar with the series know that, amongst other things, these are tales of triumph over adversity as well as stories of redemption.
If this is your first 'Micklegate' experience, it is worth noting that any mysteries that remain seemingly unresolved in this book are unravelled in the others.

Young Silas

Table of Contents

Prologue *1*

1 The Commission *4*

2 Mary Cooper *11*

3 Three years old *29*

4 Six years old *48*

5 The rain *79*

6 Forest Adventures *91*

7 Monkgate *117*

8 York prison *137*

9 The ambush *153*

10 The trial *165*

11 The thieves and the poor *189*

12 Sixteen years old *205*

13 Skipton castle *226*

14 The conspiracy *238*

15 The office *254*

16 Desperate measures *276*

17 Cawood Hall *287*

18 The Cottage *303*

19 Reflections *322*

Epilogue *328*

Special thanks to David Griggs for
his dedicated proofreading.

Thanks also to VisitYork for their support.

Young Silas's Adventures
1525-30

Prologue

Throughout a tortured and blessed lifetime, Silas would have had so many dreams, fantasies, illusions and other imaginings. His obsession with hierarchy, pageantry, heraldry, knights of the realm and even King Henry the Eighth had him relentlessly wondering how he too could become a person of note. But most of the time, he contemplated an existence like that of other people. He desired to have worth, be loved and feel that there was a sense of purpose to his somewhat narrow existence. Sadly, during his formative years, he had to learn how to negotiate life as that odd person around the city of York who became constantly lampooned and made to feel as if he did not fit into Tudor society. And, despite those many dreams and fears, I am sure he would never have thought for a second that hundreds of years later a book would be written about his life. So important was he to me, his peers and those who loved him that I was left in no doubt that his story needed to be told, although it was not something I took on willingly.

I am Dr Nick Douglas, and even though I write this book so many years later I was, believe it or not, Silas's companion, ally and friend. Even as late as the 20th century, let alone in my time, there was no doubt that Silas would have benefited from a diagnosis and some understanding of why he was, how he was and, although I record this so many years later, I was his peer, ally and friend and loved him dearly, as did many others. It didn't matter how many mistakes he made, how many times he fell down, or simply misunderstood what was said, or even what the facial expressions and nuances of others meant, there was something remarkably endearing about his character. Certain of his worthlessness, his journey was unquestionably that much more difficult than that of his peers. He languished in an age when people would laugh at others without any filter whatsoever although often they would laugh with him, for he too recognised his vulnerability and individuality. He is still alive in my heart and my mind and I smile whenever I think of the many things he said and the innocent errors he made. Ultimately, his story is one of a young man overcoming huge hurdles and barriers. A tale of someone who, at times, was extremely isolated, who failed to understand other people and particularly what they expected of him. Certainly, at a very early age, he was certain that he was inferior to others and this stayed with him even throughout his eventual triumphs. Silas famously became an integral member of the Agents of the Word, and no matter how many times I question and reconsider this notion, if you took him out of the equation, so many adventures during those years between 1541 and 1547 would have been altogether different and, yes, may well have failed. More than anything, I admire my friend Silas for his heart. That integrity came above all other things. His ability to see the best in others and want the best for them too. 'What more could you ask from a fellow human being?' I ask myself. I also have to add that in any written Tudor history, or for that matter Tudor fiction, you won't find many people like him. Why? Because stories are written about heroes and villains, often those on the extremes of society or simply those who were in power. For me, Silas represented a young man with special needs in an age where the phrase just wouldn't have made any sense. And he was also someone who would persevere, not only to find ways in which to fit in with Tudor society but succeed within it.

Yesterday I returned from York. How it pains me to walk the streets and see so many buildings that I knew so well destroyed or only half visible and I still yearn to be back there with my friends.

What you may find even more curious is how I came to write this unusual, warm and delightful tome so that is where I shall start.

1 The Commission
Tilbury, August 1588

If it wasn't for his unique gait, you could hardly distinguish Francis Walsingham from any other senior member of the court. Seen from behind, his stiff ruff rode high, almost touching his cap. Now in his mid-fifties, his breathing was that much more laboured, exacerbated by the urgency of his business and a series of health issues that left him in almost constant pain. As he entered the queen's chamber, in the West Tilbury blockhouse, he found her writing at her desk but then suddenly stopped, realising that she had not heard him enter. There were only a few that would have been afforded such privilege, but the relationship which had developed over decades between the two of them merited one or two concessions, and it had even been rumoured that the queen had once been a guest at his house.

Walsingham stood still and took advantage of the situation, resting his eyes upon the back of Queen Elizabeth I for a few moments. He considered that, although they had disagreed on many matters, his loyalty was as firm as it had ever been, and then he thought for a moment about his feelings. 'Could the queen's personal spymaster allow himself feelings?', he asked himself. He had been one of many who had found themselves constantly exasperated in an attempt to get her married, but now he thought, she is getting older and that ship had sailed. It was then that he conceded, just for a moment, that he may once have desired her, but on the subject of affection, he could not discern between the love of a subject and that of an admirer. He found himself staring at her ridiculously huge laced ruff and the faux dry curls of red hair that topped it.

'I know you're there, Moor...' she said without breaking from her writing.

'I seem to be losing my stealth, Your Majesty…', realising that he was being teased.

She shuffled her billowing dress as far to the right that her farthingale would allow and faced him. Every day, the makeup seemed to appear more and more white and her black eyes even darker. A bout of smallpox just a few years earlier had rendered her complexion scarred and she was determined to mask it.

Elizabeth wagged a quill at Walsingham as she spoke.

'I admire you for joining me here in our hour of need, Francis. Some of the others are still in hiding.'

He nodded to acknowledge her compliment but was, all the same, very aware that as both he and Burghley had insisted on Mary Queen of Scots being executed just one year before, they had found themselves somewhat distanced from their monarch. The whole affair had caused the queen a considerable degree of displeasure.

Still, he was silent, unsure of how forgiving his queen may be.

'Oh Francis…tis done with! If it wasn't for your meticulous investigations, it would be your queen that would be dead. As for this…'

'I would be happy to advise Your Majesty...,' said Walsingham.

'You have always served me well…,' said Elizabeth.

Walsingham raised his eyebrows, surprised to be in such good favour once more.

'The power of your pen has seen off as many Spaniards as my soldiers. It is fitting that you join me here today.'

As they spoke, the Armada, by and large, had already been

defeated, although they were worried about a further invasion from Dunkirk. Elizabeth had bravely decided to rally her troops at Tilbury, and Walsingham had followed her.

'You are too kind Your Majesty. Would you like me to look over your speech?'

She gestured for him to come closer but just as he was about to look down at the lengthy proposal, the quill used to write it caught his eye.

'Looking a little worn now Francis, don't you think?'

He chuckled.

'…seen better days methinks' added Walsingham smiling.

'Do you remember?' asked Elizabeth,

'Aye, that I do Your Majesty. The Agents?'

'It was one of a few quills given to my father by one of the very first Agents of the Word. Who would have thought that it would lead to your network of over fifty spies, avoiding wars and uncovering sinister, clandestine threats?'

'I believe that much of their intent was simply to please God himself,' said Walsingham.

'True. Mostly a bunch of misfits and yet…'

They mused and smiled together at the many tales they had heard of the Agents of the Word.

Elizabeth continued to stare at the quill throughout the conversation.

'He was an errand boy. Used to call him "Sillyarse" in York', she said.

'Because his name was Silas as I remember', added Walsingham.

'Yes…yes of course…'

She paused. Francis said nothing as he had seen that same expression many times. She turned the quill between her thumb and forefinger for what seemed like minutes.

'Are there any records?' she said almost in a whisper.

'Much of their work was indeed absolutely secret, Your Majesty. After your father's concession, they became known as the Royal Secret Agents of the Word.'

'I'm surprised they could remember the name alone!' she said and they both laughed.

'Are any of them still alive?' she said now looking directly at Francis who had knelt and, in doing so, was now in the queen's eye-line.

'Just one I believe, although their tales live on in living memory.'

'No one writes histories of such people do they, Francis? I would find such a record most amusing!'

The queen's face lit up and Walsingham had that familiar but unsettling feeling that he always had when asked to achieve the impossible by his queen.

'Well…um…about your speech…'

'Oh, I'm bored with it', said the queen. 'Who do we have that could write this story?'

Francis could feel his heart racing.

'Erm…we have Marlow. I'm sure he could…'

Elizabeth stood up so quickly that she almost knocked her Secretary of State over.

'That ungodly snake! A spy! Usurper!'

Walsingham was frantically waving his arms in an attempt to calm her.

'Of course, Your Majesty, most unsuitable…most unsuitable…'

Then silence.

Walsingham's breathing became heavy as he measured whether to offer anything else.

'Although it was a little rough, I did see a play by a fellow from Stratford on the Avon…' he said nervously and then he started to chuckle to himself, clearly amused by the plot of the performance in question.

'Well…out with it man!'

'It is most amusing Your Majesty. A tale of how to tame a disobedient woman…'

If ever a man had wanted to swallow his own words instantly it was poor Francis at that moment, for then he heard his last statement endlessly echoing around the chamber.

'Actually, Your Majesty, it was appalling. Also most unsuitable…'

She glared and then impulsively said,

'How about that doctor? He knew the agents.'

So startled by this comment was Walsingham that he was almost tempted to return to talk of Shakespeare. He even thought to remind her that the grandfather of this unknown writer from Stratford was indeed an agent himself, but then thought better of it. He knew exactly who the doctor was, but did not know how much the queen knew.

'Nick Douglas!' she said as if she had discovered cake for the first time.

Desperately trying to find a way out of the conversation, England's smartest man chose to glare at the pearls along her sleeves and the bows that punctuated them every five inches.

'Where are you at man?!' she said growing impatient.

'Your speech? Your Majesty…'

'How well do I know you, Francis? Why are you avoiding my query about the doctor?'

'He is very difficult to get hold of. He comes from…'

'I know,' she said 'I believe he is from some arcane and distant land, but I also know that if anyone can find him it is you.'

Walsingham did not know how to find me and so made further attempts to distract her from her intent, but it was to no avail. Whilst Queen Elizabeth made the speech of her life later that day, he was dispatching spies, diplomats, and adventurers in all directions to track me down.

At least Francis Walsingham knew the truth about who I was, but was somewhat at an immediate disadvantage as we hadn't met in almost five years.

However, long after the Spanish were defeated, I was approached by a stranger in an Irish inn. It was only when he began to drop many a familiar name that I agreed to sit and listen to him. He showed me Walsingham's seal and handed me a letter that was evidently not new. I questioned him in return, wondering how he was so sure that he had the right man.

'My father knew you, man and mouse' he said leaving me in no doubt that he knew enough.

I read the letter whilst he awaited my reply. It was clear that he did not know its content by his surprise when I laughed aloud at Walsingham's request.

I told him that I would meet Walsingham one month later and give him my answer personally.

When that time came, I was taken aback at how gracious the Secretary of State was.

'Aha! The elusive traveller who never ages!'

This was followed by a somewhat unwelcome embrace.

So desperate was he to fulfil the queen's wishes that he was ready to offer gold cups in return.

'It so happens that I have kept a log, a diary of all my interactions with the Agents and the deeds of Lord Silas would make fine reading so, you see, Her Majesty's request isn't as unusual as you may have thought…'

He slumped into his chair and gave the longest sigh. I could see that he was in pain.

'So, what of it, Douglas? Will you do as she commands?'

'I will, but you and the queen will have to be patient. I have business here to deal with first and then I shall return to my homeland where I can access all my logs. I shall have it with you in no more than six months.'

'Most agreeable Mouse! Her Majesty will be most grateful. What do you wish in return?'

'That you don't call me Mouse, even in fun, and that I will never again be asked to pursue Catholics on the queen's behalf.'

I half expected a negotiation but he immediately grasped my shoulders with both hands and thanked me and with that

I went to my lodgings, trying to work out, not only how I would get home, but how I could return within the time frame I had referenced. Nevertheless, with some difficulty, it was exactly six months later that I managed to deliver the following account to Walsingham.

2 Mary Cooper
York, 1510

Still a girl in her teens, Mary Cooper was as welcome a sight in the narrow streets of York as was sunlight each morning. Not that everyone knew Mary. It was simply that she regularly exhibited the same habits and mannerisms, and those traits were readily noticeable. Yes, she was pretty, but it wasn't that alone that caught the eye of citizens who frequented Coppergate. She was blessed with an innate joy for living which could not hide itself, and if you were to ask her neighbours to describe her, it would be more likely that they would describe what she did rather than describe her looks.

She skipped. Mary skipped and danced and smiled, and even sang to herself as she went about her daily chores. And, it made no difference whatsoever if people took notice of her or not. The smile was offered and if it was not welcome, she would happily breeze by. Her name gave something away about her origins, as Mary had come from a long line of Coopers (barrel makers), although her grandfather had also been quite expert at making quills, something which had fascinated Mary from being a little girl. Doug Cooper, her father, was now an old man. There was as much chance of him making a cask as there was of him flying out of York now that his best was behind him.

However, his dignity was intact, but his very sinews ached from a lifetime labouring in the dim and chilly snickleways of York. Most people knew Mary or at least knew of her, but it would be a little bit more difficult to say who she knew in return. She could certainly describe most people within a half-mile radius of her home, but only because of their crafts and trades, although she did know a few by name.

However, by the time she was sixteen, it did not escape

her attention that as she narrowed by a small blacksmith's forge each day, two brothers were looking out for her. Neither was she naïve about what she was experiencing. She understood that she was attractive and was picking up on the idea that her natural ebullience was especially appealing to boys and men. But jaded and buggered as he was, Doug Cooper did a damn good job of talking Mary through some of the imminent dangers for young women in his home city. I should add that whilst he did this, he was anxiously wishing his dear wife was still there to do the job for him, but all the same, he knew how desirable his daughter had become and also how young men behaved. After all, he told himself, I was once one myself.

Beyond that, her sex education consisted of those odd few times when she had walked too close to Grope Lane on dark winter afternoons. Truth be told, Mary could not distinguish from the grunts and groans whether assaults were taking place or the fruits of lifelong passion were being explored. She did know that she didn't like it, and the idea that, during any part of her life, she would be expected to behave in that way, terrified her.

Raven

Raven Smith, one of the two young blacksmiths, seemed so much quieter than his brother and Mary particularly liked his smile. She was becoming wise to the ways of the world and knew that a few glances, exchanged smiles and perhaps a now and again greeting was the very first drop of that waterfall from which lifelong love and marriage flowed. As her father was surely nearing his end, it was important to him that Mary sought out a stable and secure life. Marrying a tradesman was an ideal solution and by the sixteenth century, many women took part in domestic businesses, although by and large it was still the province of men. If she were to remain a spinster, her options would have been very limited.

Mary was absolutely sure that it was sinful to approach a

young man without there being a business agreement, a previous arrangement or being in the presence of a chaperone. Added to this was the conundrum that Raven seemed almost incurably quiet. Glances, smiles, blushes and heavy hearts remained for many months, and soon those months turned into years. During that time, Raven's brother, Clifford took it upon himself to become the go-between and had no reticence whatsoever in approaching Mary as she passed by. In the beginning, this seemed completely innocuous. Clifford would pay her the odd compliment and ask about her business. Bravely, she managed to talk about her father, where she lived and where she was going on any given day but, even with the best of efforts, Clifford got little else out of her. Raven knew that this was taking place and so challenged his brother about his conversations with the pretty young girl.

'You should be thankful brother. If you are ever to do more than glare at that poor girl you need to speak to her. Can't you see what I'm doing? I'm acting on your behalf,' said Clifford.

'Really?' Raven hesitated, 'really you would do that for me, brother?' He breathed heavily, thought for a moment and then, overtly excited about the prospect, fumbled over his words,

'What did you say? what did she….? is she coming again? what is…?'

Clifford laughed.

'Steady, steady brother! She'll be back here most days. I promise I will relate to you anything that is said, but for some time it will just be idle conversation. Be patient, these things take time.'

Raven could not sleep that night. Raven did not sleep for weeks. Every time he saw his brother walk alongside the slim and effervescent brunette his hopes were further raised. Every day he is singing my praises, Raven told himself. I have a brother who is an ambassador! 'God bless him,' he said out loud and his heart beat even faster.

The following day was the start of June, and almost before Mary appeared on the horizon, Clifford had leapt up from his anvil and then met her in the street. Not that his father approved of him casually abandoning his work, but he accepted that, one way or another, he needed to get his sons married off, and for the time being conveniently ignored the fact that both his sons seemed to like the same girl. She smiled and skipped a little and for the very first time, the two of them managed something close to a conversation. It did not escape Mary that Clifford could talk the talk.

He looked strong, was boastful, confident and, although not as good-looking as his brother, Mary found him acceptable. As the church bells of All Saints, Pavement rested a while and the smoke from the foundry dissipated, he began his first real conversation with Mary.

'I will walk with you but a short while, maiden' said Clifford 'I would not wish to embarrass you and I do have to return to my chores.'

She thought him to be charming.

Then, whether he had instigated it or not, they both stopped and, for the very first time, spoke face-to-face.

'I must apologise for my brother for I did know, kind maiden, that you had an eye for him but he simply does not like girls. I would not wish to say more, as some men are just not interested in that type of thing, and I wanted to save you the embarrassment of holding any unnecessary affections for him.'

Mary held her hand up.

'No, kind sir. You have been most gracious and honest with me. You are a good man and a good brother. At least I have made a new friend in you, and you are correct, I had wondered why he had never spoken to me himself.'

Clifford hesitated, excited that his plan had worked, but was, even at this stage, left discontented that Mary may only be his friend.

'Well, that will do for now, although I must say, dear Mary, if I may use your name, I barely sleep at all, waiting for that moment when you cross by the threshold of our blacksmith's shop.'

She blushed. Mary may have been temporarily red-faced, but neither was she green. She knew that Clifford had designs on her, but never expected him to be so forward so soon. She gave him a smile that was as good as a small deposit. A slight promise, perhaps, that something more may evolve with time. Then, just when she thought their engagement was at an end, he started to talk again. Mary found this somewhat strange as his attempt to woo her had suddenly developed into a mighty boast. Many boasts in fact. He told her that already he had made armour for dukes, earls and knights and that it would only be a matter of time before his skills were recognised by the king himself. She listened intently, and as he became more and more persuasive she was quite impressed. There was absolutely no question that the work carried out at their humble smithy was of a very high standard. The family had a very good reputation in York and, of course, on a daily basis, Mary had personally been able to observe many of their products. Perhaps it was simply that Mary was quite inexperienced, although she had had fleeting conversations with young men here and there, she had never met anyone who was so keen to impress. Dumbfounded, she did little more than nod and smile.

He then walked no more than another ten or fifteen yards and bade her farewell whilst she carried on singing, skipping and smiling to the confused populace of York.

'My, you look happy today brother,' said Raven.

Raven had caught Clifford off guard and he realised that he needed a moment or two to think.

'I'm happy brother because I believe that young lady might well become friends with our family. Is that not good news? But no more. I assure you that I believe she would, at some stage, regard you almost as a brother but nothing beyond that. Please forgive me. I've tried so hard to win her for you, but sadly you have no experience of these things. There is no explaining the intricacies and mechanisms of a woman's heart, and I won't even insult you by trying to do so. Please put this fanciful notion to bed for good. Take solace in the hope that she may befriend us, and in turn, she will no doubt introduce us to more young maidens.'

Clifford noticed that Raven began to shake. He was sure that he was about to weep too, but then he threw his hammer, picked it back up and started to beat a half-forged adze head over the anvil almost as if he wished to destroy both. There was a flicker of guilt in Clifford's heart, but it was a very faint flicker that came and went in less than the time it took him to think about what he had done. In fifteen minutes, it was extinguished completely, with only the slight whiff of his deceit in the air.

The difference between the two brothers was probably most exemplified by the fact that Clifford would also lie awake at night, but only to brew his dubious and devious scheme in which the somewhat simple Cooper's daughter would become his wife, although romance, weddings and children were the very last things on his agenda.

Sadly, Raven would never forget this girl. Any feelings he may have harboured for her remained deep-seated in his soul. It was a love that never dissipated. To add salt to the wound, he had to witness, almost daily, his brother wooing the very girl he had set his heart on. Neither was this just base jealousy. It was the incurable irritation that his brother could appear so attractive to anyone beyond the forge; a place where he was known for his wickedness.

Clifford

Clifford barely smiled, or would even pass on a kind word to anyone. He was regularly ill-tempered, violent and struggled to grasp those basic Christian values that got most people through the drudge of sixteenth-century life. His father knew. Almost disinterested by nature, Harald the smith was the engine room of the forge but spoke very little. He could chastise his sons when necessary but had long since acknowledged the chasm between them. 'My very own Abel and Cain,' he had once said and presumably people wondered whether he had been blessed with the gift of prophecy, for you would be hard pushed to find any two brothers in York so different to one another. Sadly, Raven had grown up doting on his older brother, but this most recent affair would eventually drive a wedge between them for all time.

To give Clifford the respect he deserved, he worked hard on the courtship, and one can only presume that somewhere deep down, the performance he offered must have come from somewhere inside his soul. Something in years to come he would struggle to locate.

Mary's father, with some reluctance, agreed to the wedding. In many ways, it was a blessing, for he knew he would be not long in the world. He told Mary that although the humble house in Dead Alley in which they lived was rented, the couple could live there and that it would be hers when he died. Unfortunately, she was foolish enough to pass this information on to Clifford well before there was talk of marriage, but failed to mention the part about not owning the property.

There would always be rent to pay on the house and, unbeknownst to Mary, it would be three times what it had been when her father died, ending a mutual decades-old agreement with the landlord.

Weddings for the likes of Mary Smith were extremely simple affairs, with barely a handful of people in church, a few wildflowers in her hands and hair, but vows would be made and for her, those were absolutely sacred. Any wedding was indeed entirely about those vows made in the sight of God and little else, being one of the most serious oaths one could make in Tudor society. There was a brief feast and celebration at which Clifford became embarrassingly drunk and for the very first time, Raven spoke to Mary. Graciously, he gave her his blessing and she clasped his hand and said,

'I am so happy to have you as a brother. I feared for so long that you wouldn't speak to me at all. Please, please regard me as your sister and visit us anytime.'

He then looked very nervous. So much so that she commented on it.

'Are you well brother?'

'Oh…I'm sorry…I do not know whether it is wise to mention it or not. No…no it is fine…sorry…sorry on your wedding day as well, I apologise…'

But Mary was smart. She was changing, becoming increasingly incisive and perceptive. There was something afoot and she wanted to know what it was.

'Tell me, Raven, what ails you?'

'Oh…I still feel so embarrassed, ashamed. I well…you know…I…I tried to woo you through my brother. How weak was I? Please forgive me…'

Mary stared at him, dumbfounded. At first, she was clueless as to what he meant. What did wooing through his brother represent? She thought.

Her head went down as she mused.

'Do you mean? Raven? are you saying that you had designs on me?'

'Why, yes. Please forgive my forwardness then and now.'

Then Clifford appeared as if out of nowhere and pushed his brother to one side, so violently that he almost fell over.

'Aha! dear brother, dear wife! What a day!'

And then he fell over himself.

Raven and Mary picked him up and put him in a chair. Harald Smith soon appeared and insisted that both Mary and Clifford go home and get to bed.

Mary's heart was heavy. Confused by the brief conversation with her new brother-in-law, she was already seeing a version of Clifford that she knew had always been there but had denied its existence. So drunk was he that his own father had to get him into bed and then leave the marital bedroom. Mary's father was still downstairs, too poorly to even attend the celebration, and little more than a nod was shared between the two fathers throughout this debacle. Mary tended to her father for a while and then took a little supper herself, eventually carrying up a candle to the bedroom. For what seemed like an eternity, Mary sat on the side of the bed acknowledging that things were not as they should have been on her wedding night when he suddenly jumped up and informed her, in a most ungentlemanly manner, that he needed to empty his bladder.

Five minutes later, he returned and threw Mary onto the bed. Any dreams she may have harboured of gentle seduction, romantic whispers and a lifelong love birthed went down the alleyway with his urine, for the next few minutes would be something that would scar Mary for her whole life. She wasn't completely naïve but knew very little of the mating process. It wasn't enough that she was nervous. She was very willing to please her husband, but as she awoke the next morning she regarded the encounter as more of a vicious assault than anything to do with love. Her wrists hurt, her legs hurt, her head hurt and she was ruined inside, both figuratively and literally.

Even allowing for the fact that a woman was expected to do a husband's bidding, this was brutal, and any decent man would have regarded it as so. Ironically, it was also incredibly unlikely that any other man would ever know of it. This became her private shame, and no one would ever be aware of the mortal dread she faced day in and day out as this man gratified himself. The charmer who had walked alongside her so many times, promising this and promising that, had disappeared. If someone had told Mary that Clifford had a twin brother and they had swapped places before the wedding she may well have believed it, for she would never see that person again.

However, despite her desire to maintain her dignity, word did get out. Following an attempt to reason with Clifford whilst Mary was out one day, her father bravely challenged him, although he was ill-prepared for what he got in return.

'This will be my house soon, you old bugger and if you interfere again, it will be sooner than you think. I would think nothing of doing you in one night. Have some respect. What goes on between man and wife is none of your business!'

He waved his fist so close to the old man's face that old Doug could feel the air move.

Wisely, Mary's father said nothing, leaving Clifford still ignorant of the fact that he did not own the property in which he had lived for forty years and in which he had just been abused.

This was Clifford's modus operandi. Threats generally worked for him and he was happy to see them through. As far as he was concerned, that was an end to it and Mary would never know anything about the conversation.

Clifford continued to work at the blacksmith's foundry alongside his brother and father, and one morning found them both waiting to confront him. Clifford may have appeared tough and known to be a complete and total bastard by neighbouring tradesmen, but he would never challenge his father. Harald the smith did all the talking.

'Isn't it enough that you got what you wanted?' You've got your own way despite the fact that I had someone lined up for you to marry. I gave into that. I let you work here and take money from this business…but I'm telling you now lad, if I hear anything about you mistreating a woman ever again, you'll have me to deal with. Am I clear?'

Of course, Clifford denied everything. He did a decent job of appeasing his father and reassured him that there was absolutely nothing to worry about. He had ways of getting around the old man, and now Mary was pregnant. That did the trick. Nothing works better on an angry father than telling him he's just about to be a grandfather. This completely took the wind out of his sails, and so Clifford's father left the two brothers working alone for hours whilst he delivered goods in Knapton.

'This had better not have anything to do with you' said Clifford angrily.

Raven said nothing.

'Yes, I see it now, it's written all over you. Bloody jealous, aren't you? You'd love a taste of that tender meat. You drool at the very thought of it. Mine though, brother and I'll do what I want with it! Oh…and if I find out it is you who has been worrying father, I will pay you back.'

Raven said nothing.

Mrs Tumble

Mary enjoyed being pregnant. It wasn't simply the joy of knowing that she would have a child; there now seemed to be a point to the marriage and, as women are wont to do, she believed that her husband would change once the baby arrived. However, there were many nights when he never returned home at all. She didn't complain, as those were the happiest days she had known since being single. It also gave her the chance to tend to her ailing father.

Come Christmas, Clifford's appearances became fewer and fewer, and when he did show up, he was drunk. Very drunk. He was rude, abusive and violent towards Mary and her father. Now, she was thankful for his absences and she didn't even ask where he went on those nights when he did not sleep in the house. She eventually cared little for him or his habits but prayed nightly that the baby would live, be well and that, at some point, Clifford would acknowledge his duty as a father.

Thank God for Mrs Tumble. Mrs Tumble also lived in Dead Alley and had an air of mystery about her. When Mary was a child, Mrs Tumble's name was mentioned only in whispers. Huddled women in corners starting sentences with 'don't tell anyone…' and 'I hear Mrs Tumble had to fix it' and 'if it wasn't for Mrs Tumble…' Mary acknowledged that she was the local midwife but had also heard rumours that she had probably helped young girls get rid of their babies. Desperate for her own child, Mary mulled over this one night and prayed for those women, the babies and for her child to arrive intact.

Six weeks before the baby was expected, Doug Cooper hobbled up and down the snickleways to find Mrs Tumble, who promptly rushed around to help the delivery of Mary's child. Once he was born, Mary lay there still and white, the blood draining from her body. Mrs Tumble was useful, efficient and punctual but she had no social graces whatsoever.

'Baby will live and, if mother is not dead in an hour, she might recover completely,' she said to Mary's father and then buggered off, presumably to the next job.

For an old man who could barely negotiate the stairs, her father did an astonishing job of swaddling both Mary and the child, and where she was bleeding he took care to pack sheets of soft hessian. When all was done, he held the noisy baby and lay it next to Mary to keep her warm. As an hour passed and Mary had barely regained consciousness, he realised that the baby needed feeding and so attempted to get the little boy to suckle. Miraculously, he did so and the colour slowly came back into Mary's cheeks too. Her father broke down in tears.

Silas Smith was born on the Nineteenth day of February 1514, and was loved. At least, throughout his life, he could boast that. He was born and two people loved him, although amongst that modest number he sadly could not count his father. Although neither of them commented on it, as they looked at the skinniest child ever seen, tuffs of red hair erratically sprouting from various parts of his noggin, he immediately seemed different to other babies. If he became angry or indeed needed anything, he cried like a banshee and would flap his little arms. They also noticed that during those early months, he remained quite expressionless. However, he was flawless in Mary's eyes and in him she saw a miracle. She, therefore, decided to name him after one of the earliest followers of Christ; a missionary. He would now forever be, her Silas.

It would be another two days after the birth before Clifford saw his child. Mary had hoped that her prayers may have worked and that Clifford would find something inside him akin to affection for his son and then stay home for good.

'Why has he got red hair?'

Mary's mouth dropped. She didn't have an answer. She didn't know why the baby had red hair. She realised that she was starting to panic. Why am I panicking? she thought. I haven't been with anyone else, but why has he got red hair?

'Your father has some red hair. More than anything it is grey,' she said, 'but he has some red hair.'

Clifford grunted, perhaps acknowledging that this was a reasonable explanation.

'He is feeble and docile. I believe it to be an imbecile….'

He looked directly at Mary.

'I come from good stock. If there is anything that ails him, it has nothing to do with me or my kin.'

She could not hold it in any longer. She broke down completely. Had he not realised that she almost died giving birth to this child? He was beautiful. He was perfect. He was her Silas and he was the most important thing on God's earth.

Unsurprisingly, Clifford then lost his temper and stormed out of the house, although it wasn't long before Mary had calmed and was glad that he had gone.

One month later life was seeming a little better for Mary. The little boy became her entire world and now she could get out and resume her walks, but this time with her beautiful boy. She even happily acknowledged that he was different to most other babies but, if anything, she loved him all the more for it. The better people of York would reserve comment, but others, usually older women, would ask why he could not make eye contact or smile. Mary knew the answer. Inside, Silas was working out the greater mysteries of life and would save his deductions and deliberation until he was an adult when he would astonish the world and make her proud. He was a thinker. That's what she told herself. She still sang and she still had a slight skip in her step, but those who knew her could see that some of the life had seeped out of her, and rumours had spread that this was because of her difficult marriage.

During one fine spring morning, she bought bread and vegetables from the market and then ambled back to Dead Alley. She had a habit of talking to Doug, her father, long before she had actually opened the door. Once inside, she was still relaying a tale of who she had met and how Silas had impressed the people of York, but when she eventually looked up, she saw her father sitting there in his chair with his eyes open, looking back at her. Sadly, no matter how much she stared at him, his eyes did not move, and neither did anything else. Mary knew immediately that he was at an end. The only person on God's earth besides Silas who loved her, and whom she loved in return, had now left her. At that instant, Silas closed his eyes and went to sleep. She turned to him and couldn't help feeling that his soul was spending a little time with that of his grandfather. She put him down and went over to wrap her father in a blanket. There was little common sense to this as the blanket was unlikely to do anything. This was solely an act of dignity. She closed his eyes, kissed him and then sat holding his hand.

'Since mother died, you have been everything to me. You have dedicated your whole life to me and I've been so happy that you got to meet your grandson. You have had a smile on your face day and night since, and God help me, father, I am so sorry I married that man but I will be alright. I know that you will oversee me always. And I pray for the peaceful and safe passage of your good soul this very day... Dear Lord in Your mercy, bring my father close to You for all eternity taking my love with him.'

Tears gently meandered down the length of her face and then onto her apron. And then she simply sat in silence holding the old man's hand and Silas in her other arm. She wasn't to know it, but it would be almost an hour and a half before she got someone to help her lay Doug out and, although every fibre of her being was willing her to remain stoic, her heart was heavy.

Just two days later, Doug Cooper lay on his bed ready for burial, but there was still no sign of Clifford.

Mary chastised herself, for one of her very first thoughts was about her financial security. Doug had had a long-term agreement with the landlord which meant that he paid very low rent and Mary knew that this would end with his death. Now, the rent would be three times as much and the money that Doug had saved would only pay it for a few months. Sadly, his Christian funeral was that of a pauper and few mourned him, many of his contemporaries already having trodden that eternal path before him.

Hard times

Clifford's response to Mary's bereavement was not at all sympathetic and she didn't expect it to be. Her father was dead and that was that, in fact, he was probably glad to have him out of the house. Nothing more needed to be said. Four days passed in which Mary became more and more anxious, as she knew that she would have to tell Clifford that her father did not own the house in which they lived. It wasn't necessarily that she had deceived him but the subject was never broached. He had moved in, contributed nothing and little else was said.

Eventually, she had to tell him. For a man who suddenly gave his wife the impression that they were now destitute, he did a good job of destroying many of the few private possessions that they already had, but by now, Mary knew how to deal with his tantrums.

There was a small annexe beyond the living quarters where she would place Silas, and then she would habitually brace herself up against the wall. If he were to hit her, she chose not to retaliate or show any response. On this occasion, she watched him berate everyone he had ever met, including Mary, her father and his son and when exhausted, he collapsed in the same chair in which Doug had died, Mary drew in a deep breath and decided to speak although her voice trembled.

'For once I will not remain silent. I've put up with your long absences. I put up with rumours of what you get up to when you're not here. So please, please can you just be reasonable for one moment? Let me presume that you are telling me the truth. Is it not true that you are forging armour for the Duke of Norfolk? And did you not tell me that this would give your business much prestige and that he would pay well for it? I cannot imagine for a moment why you cannot pay the paltry rent on such a small property in one of the poorest areas of York.'

One thing that everybody knew in the sixteenth century and also in every century since, is that if you chose to lie to people, you have to become very good at it. You have to maintain those lies and bolster them up with even more lies, so this little intellectual prod from Mary actually silenced him for a few moments. He stood, waved his hand at her as if to dismiss her logic and then stormed out of the house.

It would be two days before anyone else came to the house and, not surprisingly, she presumed it was him returning to vent his disgust once more, but as she opened the door there, standing before her, was Clifford's father, Harald Smith.

'May I come in, daughter?' he said.

'You are always welcome here father. I wish I could see

more of you.'

He went straight to Silas and asked if he could pick him up. Once inside the modest property, Clifford's father appeared huge and the scrawny little dot rested comfortably in his left hand. Mary stood behind him and was sure that she saw a tear drop down onto Silas's cheek. Harald then sat down with the child and rocked him. So cathartic was this moment, no one said anything for a while and Mary found the peace, no matter how transient, extremely welcome.

'No need to worry about the rent daughter,' he said, as if he was saying 'please shut the door.'

She started to protest but he stopped her.

'Mary, I can easily afford it. You have no idea how much he shames me, and if he didn't have a family he would be gone from my business and my life. I have tried. I've tried so very hard to make him see the world as others do, but he seems endlessly embittered and ambitious. I can pay your rent, you needn't worry about it, and he won't mention it again. Also…I need to put the other matter to bed. I am sure you have already uncovered the fact that Raven wished to marry you? And that Clifford deceived you both? I apologise, for I did not see what was happening right before my eyes…'

He sighed.

'I wish I could control him, but, as a father, I feel I have failed. Don't get me wrong, I would think nothing of coming round here and give him a bloody good hiding, if that's what you wanted but I'm guessing that you, like myself, would think that it would only make things worse.'

Mary took Silas away from him, put him in his box and then turned to give Harald an affectionate embrace.

'Your kindness will save us father, and you must call to see your grandson anytime you wish,' said Mary.

'He's an odd one, isn't he?' said Harald, 'but that much more lovable for it. No one like him, I'd say. Our Silas. One in a million,' he whispered and then chuckled, proud of his somewhat unique grandchild.

The difference that this single visit had made to young Mary Smith was immeasurable. A financial burden lifted and a renewed family bond had her singing all afternoon, and Silas burbled and gurgled in harmony with her. Apart from the few irregular drunken visits by her husband that punctuated her peaceful routine, Mary was as happy as she had ever been on that side of the marriage.

She would rarely walk by the forge, but continued to enjoy Harald's visits. This pattern continued for some time, and during that spell others were quick to remind Mary that her son's movements were limited and that he seemed to ignore their attempts to catch his attention, even when pulling the silliest faces at him.

Silas was slow to walk and even slower to talk, but by the time he was three and a half years old, none of that seemed to matter. He was happy to sing, dance and play knights along with his mother, and the pair became inseparable.

3 Three years old
1517

No one seems to know when Silas's obsession with lords, knights, pageantry and jousting began but women in the marketplace reported Mary calling him 'my Lord Silas' whilst he was still an infant. There is little doubt that this notion was exacerbated by the fact that Mary had decided that Silas was to have a father even in his absence. Although there cannot have been any intent on her part to collude with Clifford's tall tales and downright lies, that is unwittingly what she did. The domestic appearances of Clifford Smith became further and further apart and the last she heard about him was that he was working in the armoury at Hampton Court. Unwisely, she informed the neighbours of this, which also resulted in Clifford's fantasies being passed on to an increasingly obsessive Silas.

It was on one such day that there, at the end of Dead Alley, St George had hunted down a dragon in his own living room and the creature squealed and giggled as he moved in to slay it. This, however, was abruptly interrupted by a loud bang on the front door. Not a tap, mind you, but an authoritative bang with the metal end of a stick. Catching her breath, Mary opened the door to find a constable standing before her. A dozen scenarios ran through her head, although the one which portrayed Clifford as dead was the one that came to the fore.

'Mrs Smith…I am sure you know why I am here?'

'Why…no constable…' she stopped to get her breath, 'no…no…what is afoot?'

Silas tried to stab him with a stick.

'Die ye greasy beast!'

The constable looked down at a bundle of rags with a fire-red head sticking out of them, two determined eyes glaring back at him. Mary told Silas to go sit on his throne in the corner, a wobbly stool with two good legs and one broken one.

'I shall be plain. You are now two months in arrears with your rent and if you cannot pay today....'

'Dear constable. Please let me explain...' she smiled, relieved that there must have been an oversight, possibly that Harald was simply late with the payment.

Silas see-sawed on his stool, waving his branch at the enemy.

'You see, my father-in-law, the well-respected blacksmith, Harald Smith, pays the rent on this...'

'No signs of him,' said the constable.

'What?'

'Gone. You have one more week and then you will have to be out.'

And with that, he was gone.

'Smelly bobgoblin!' shouted Silas but neither the constable nor Mary heard him.

Within minutes she had bundled up her son and marched around to the forge to remedy the issue. As she turned the corner and set eyes upon the all too familiar workshop, she saw that there were two people busy at work, but neither were members of the Smith family.

'Employees,' she muttered to herself, 'business is doing so well…what with Clifford's income from the king…'

But in her heart, she knew that something was amiss. Desperately she asked after Harald, Raven and even Clifford. The business had been bought in good faith, said the owners and even showed her what were newly drawn up bills of sale. To make matters worse, the owners told her that it had been bought as a lapsed business and that they had no knowledge of the previous proprietors.

She remembered her manners and thanked them but was imploding thought by thought. She could think of no explanation for what had happened. Where was Harald? Why had he stopped paying the rent and…why hadn't he told her? He had doted on Silas, she thought, her mind now a storm.

That was when a deep panic set in. She immediately felt completely alone in the world. Mary grasped Silas and picked him up, carrying him all the way home.

'Wan a sheeld! Wan a sheeld!' cried Silas pointing back at the forge.

Once home, Mary asked him to play alone whilst she went upstairs to "see to a few matters." As she awkwardly ascended the uneven staircase, Silas stood and stared at the only thing he really loved in the world. But Silas strained to understand the cues. When mother cried, something was wrong, he told himself, but why didn't he understand that? Should I be crying too? he thought. This would be the very first time that Silas would question whether he was different from others, but it was far from the last. Mother had gone upstairs to sort things out, so they would be sorted out. That was what he had learned so, content with that, he prepared the order of combat for the upcoming tournament.

Mary sat on the side of the bed and took almost the whole of her apron and screwed it up so that she could use it to muffle her weeping. This was one of those occasions when she questioned her sanity, let alone her faith. This was an extra straw after the last straw, leaving her sure that her misfortunes were that much worse than that of others. All sobbed out, her head came up as the last grain of common sense tried to find a solution, although neither the blurred view through the tiny window nor the expanse of the floor or the ceiling, would offer any answers. She told herself to carry on with the rest of the day as she did not have to pay immediately, and so cleaned the house and the few possessions within it, twenty times. As he grew up, Silas would remember his mother's habit of constantly rearranging objects when she was upset and also noted that they always ended up back where they had started.

Exhausted, she stopped and turned to look upon her son. Putting aside that deserved bias that a parent has for their child, she assessed that, whilst he was indeed slow to respond to nuances, whether physical or verbal, he had a very intelligent imagination, and where she wasn't able to inform him of every detail of king, court, dukes, earls and barons, he seemed to fill in the rest. She sat and watched him discuss his latest quest commissioned by the king. Then, he became the king.

'Afore ye venture forth...'

"Venture forth," thought Mary. Had I taught him that? It was then that she realised that both her father and Harald Smith had probably furthered his vocabulary.

'Afore you venture forth,' repeated Silas, in as deep a voice as a young child could manage, 'the Pope and the monks must give you a letter...'

Mary watched on astonished as Silas once more became the knight and went in search of the monks who were actually just around the corner. Not that there were many corners in the Smith household, there was barely more than one room, but the haphazard late fourteenth century construction, if you could call it that, meant that one part of the room was larger than the other.

She waited for him to return but all had gone silent. Doing what you would expect her to do, she stood and peeped to see what he was up to, but was left dumbfounded. He was on the floor and on his knees scratching a message into the crumbling plasterwork, and even more disconcerting was the reality that he was using and ruining one of Mary's quills.

She reprimanded him immediately and took it out of his hand. Not that Silas could write, but he had seen others doing so.

He stood staring at his mother. She was upset again.

'Where did you get this Silas?' she said, now calm.

'They are under the big bed.'

'My bed…you know you are not meant to go in there…'
She took care to retain eye contact with him.
'It's my room and you are not allowed in.'
She saw him frown and it broke her heart. Silas had got it. He had disobeyed his mother, had hurt her and that hurt him. Although immediately Mary was wishing she had not scolded him, she had taught him more at that moment than in all the telling of her knight's tales. But then he started to flap his arms. He did this when he was confused and she had never seen it in any other child. She had noticed too that sometimes he did not respond when his name was used, but then she turned her thoughts to the matter at hand.

The quill was ruined and she could tell that he had played with it many times before. She ran upstairs to check the others but they were all untouched.

Downstairs, she sat again and told him that he could keep that one quill to play with, as long as he did not disobey her again. It was then that she realised she still had five quills in her hand. They were dusty but perfect in their craft and design, but even the fleeting thought that there may be an answer to her dilemma amongst those discarded feathers left her sure that no one would buy them off a woman, let alone a poor woman.

The quills

Although she would never know it, this skill had been passed down through many Cooper generations, and there had been a quill maker in the family as far back as the eleventh century. It had been something that had fascinated Mary from being a child and her father had told her that she should one day teach her own children. In infancy, Silas had watched his mother fashion the pens and this became part of his fascination with hierarchy and the structure of medieval and Tudor society. It was no easy task to source large feathers, particularly as they had to be ones that had been gathered naturally and honestly, and they lasted longer and functioned better if they were from geese, swans or turkeys although she would, now and again, practice on feathers from smaller birds.

When Mary was in her teens, her father had been given what was possibly the most important commission of his life. York Minster's cellarer had stumbled upon twenty casks of wine that were seeping and, as a consequence, the whole batch had to be discarded. It was decided that the fault lay in the commission of sub-standard barrels. That place, the Minster, beyond the Liberty Wall was almost another world. A mini-city with its own set of rules and even its own constables, and this, of course, meant that they could also indulge as much as they wished. Doug Cooper was recommended as a cask maker, but almost immediately lost the commission when his humble existence was uncovered. Nevertheless, he agreed to make one cask complete with stamps and engravings of the keys of St Peter and challenged them to test it. Later, rumours suggested that in addition to being heated, cooled and kicked, it had been dropped four feet to test its integrity and, having fared so well, Doug was given the task of making twenty barrels in five weeks.

Doug enlisted labour and transport to take them into the Minster yard and a cleric made a thorough check of every cask before parting with God's good money. It was just one week later, whilst a humble monk was taking stock of the seemingly excessive volume of the blood of Christ, that he noticed a small scrap of battered parchment sticking out from the bottom of one of the barrels. He removed the one on top revealing a small note and a quill.

"wie gd wshes"

It had been written by Doug himself, and whilst this was possibly the complete repertoire of his literary skills, it was well-received by the monk who decided to keep the pen for himself. Months passed, but apparently, not only was the monk very impressed by that quill, but others noted that it was unique, and as such didn't stay in his illicit and clammy palms for long. And it would be another two years before Doug received a compliment and a thank you.

This tale had been indelibly stamped into Mary's psyche. It would be even fair to say that she was able to relate the whole story verbatim, and sometimes with embellishments, and it left her in no doubt that people would now pay for good quills.

However, as she stared at her tired five quills that lived under the bed, she told herself that they were nowhere near as good as her father's. That night she lay staring at the cracked ceiling of her bedroom. Silas was asleep and it was deathly quiet inside and out. Visions of knights and monks flashed before her; the forge and the whole Smith family, the rotund constable and her own little knight in dirty armour. Birds, barrels and bishops. Cathedrals, clerics and casks. Demons, debts and disgrace. And, in all of it, she was homeless and practically a beggar, a tremendous sin in the early sixteenth century. For the greater part, she was ashamed to tell anyone about her husband, although every anxiety she had should have been his instead. She prayed. She muttered petitions and would then get out to kneel by the bed to pray once more. She asked for wisdom but remembered to give thanks for her beloved son. Bless her, she even prayed for the welfare of Clifford Smith. At almost three o'clock she sighed and turned on her side and noticed that the moonlight was highlighting the quills on the floor, and it was then that she went to sleep.

When she awoke, she saw Silas with his back to her standing still as stone. He was wearing what he always wore in the house. Mary had fashioned a tabard out of an old apron and very neatly painted a red cross on the front. It would be some years before Silas understood that everyday Tudor knights no longer dressed like crusaders, but it really didn't matter. For now, he was a knight: Lord Silas. All the same, Mary didn't have a clue what he was doing.

She stretched out a hand and caressed his hair. Still, he

did not move.

'Silas…. Silas…what are you doing?'

'I am gardin' my keen until she is well. I project her from the smelly bottomed cernstubble…'

Mary smiled knowing that he would stay for days if she let him.

'Let us break fast my love, you must be hungry,' said Mary.

There wasn't a second when she did not think about the six days remaining before her eviction. Neither was she selfish. Her concerns were for her son. She had gestated grand plans for him during his first few years on Earth, many beyond the imagination of most ordinary folk, and none of them included throwing themselves on the mercy of the parish.

She would repeatedly find herself frozen to the spot, usually staring at the front door, presumably in the hope that her saviour would walk through it at any second. Almost all her senses had taken leave of her when she was rudely startled back into reality by a sudden banging on that door.

Unsurprisingly, her first thoughts were of the constable, but no, she told herself, this was a different knock, much more muffled. Mary threw open the door to find Mrs Tumble standing there.

'Oh Mrs Tumble, thank the Lord it is you…I have but days before I lose our home…constable you see…all of the Smiths gone….where have they gone?…what will become…the rent was paid I'm sure…Mr Smith…it was him, but the forge…well, six days left…do you want any quills?…do you know anyone who would buy any quills?…Oh…what to do!…the constable was banging it so hard he almost broke…'

Mrs Tumble raised her hand to stop her and it was only then that Mary realised that Mrs Tumble's hands were dripping with blood as was her apron.

'God's teeth girl! What has got into you? I need help.

Throw on your oldest apron and run with me.'

Mary told Silas to sit and play quietly and promised that she would not be long. Before she knew it, Mary was inside the first house along Coppergate, which was grand and unlike anything Mary had ever seen before. For a moment she wondered what people would do with so much space and so many possessions that seemed to be just sitting there and doing nothing. Silver plates and flagons were displayed, gold crosses and tapestries, and the room was filled with light from the finest windows, she had only ever seen the like in church. These observations, however, were fleeting as, within seconds, she had followed Mrs Tumble into an anteroom and found herself looking down upon a girl, possibly as young as fourteen years old, barely conscious and soaked in blood from her chest down. There was a still, bloody object on the floor that reminded Mary of the offal that ran down along the Shambles, but on closer inspection, she noticed that it was a lost child, many months premature of full term.

'I need to sew her, it's the only chance she has. You put pressure on the bleeding here,' demanded Tumble.

Mary did what she was told to the best of her ability, but then noticed that there was another woman in the room, beside herself with grief and clearly incapable of assisting Mrs Tumble. Every so often, she would check the door and sometimes peep out into the street before closing it once more. Mary deduced that the older woman was terrified of anyone knowing about the incident and that, more than likely, would have included her husband.

Once the stitching was complete, Mrs Tumble took over again without even getting out of breath. Mary was spellbound and left wondering if this is what the poor woman did day and night all year round and how she would ever have had any sleep.

Tumble's imposing figure loomed over all present and said more or less the same as when Silas had been born.

There was hope but only if she survived the afternoon.

'I will be back in two hours and I will help you to get her abed and clean all this up. Burn these rags before then. Think of a reason to give your husband as to what ails her,' commanded Tumble.

Mary kindly offered to stay and help. She noticed ashes out the back of the house where there had been a previous fire so hurriedly took everything out including the lost child and started a fire.

'I need to go now.' said Mary 'Make sure there is nothing but ash outside and think of a reason why you struck a fire. Can you afford meat?'

The bewildered woman stared back at her.

'The smell.' said Mary 'You will need to cook some meat, no matter how small, to disguise the smell.'

Although no one would look twice at the state of Mrs Tumble as she hurried to her next job, Mary knew that she would have to run home if she was to avoid suspicion. She had already burned her old apron but still had spatters of blood on the rest of her. Numb, she remained in awe of the overbearing Mrs Tumble, but never once thought to judge. It was quite obvious that either the child naturally miscarried or someone had tried to force it. She told herself that there were things of the world that she did not want to concern herself with and thought no more on it.

The Ouse
Whilst she had been away, Silas had carried on playing downstairs, but eventually, his curiosity had got the better of him. The door slightly ajar, he thought to look outside and so wandered out into Dead Alley. I can joust much better outside than inside, he told himself, so galloped around in the mud, announcing his allegiance to king and country only to stop in his tracks when he heard the sound of laughter. There was only one accessible end to Dead Alley, and as he looked along the length of it, Silas could see three boys older

than himself, and their behaviour mesmerised him. You could well imagine just how protective Mary was of her only child, but you may also be surprised to hear that this was the first time, ever, that Silas had been outside on his own. As they continued to dance, make faces and laugh even louder, something moved inside of him and he began to pull faces and laugh too. He quickly decided that this was a very good idea indeed as it made his new friends even happier.

Silas hopped up and down, his torn tabard completely sodden and his face caked in mud. Friends. He had made friends and thought that he had understood the concept at last. However, they moved away as swiftly as they had arrived leaving little Silas momentarily lost. Then, his mother appeared. Horrified, she bundled him up and took him inside to wash away the filth. Jaxon and his band had scarpered when Mary appeared and Silas told her that he had made new friends, and was so enthused by the experience that he did not even comment on her state. Relieved that her ghastly ordeal was over with and that her son had not come to any harm, she listened to his disjointed tale. Not knowing what to think, she told her son that she was pleased that he had met other boys, although neither of them yet knew that those boys were making fun of him and nothing more. It would be some time before Silas understood such cues and nuances, which meant he would endlessly be at the mercy of others.

Exhausted, Mary slumped in the chair, unwittingly mimicking the posture of her deceased father, and then she cried. Soon, she felt a little hand on hers. He whispered, thinking it would soothe her.

'I yam thy nite and thee ma kween. Kween of hole ingland and we wul be togetha fur all time.'

He kissed her hand.

'I love thee and will die fur thee fur midden…'

She looked up and cast her eyes upon an angel, for that is how she saw her innocent child, and there is little doubt that she may well have given in to the darkest thoughts during such a difficult time if it hadn't been for him.

Later that week, with only three days left until the eviction, Silas had persisted so much about playing with his friends that Mary finally conceded. Jaxon's heart-warming promises did the trick, although she insisted that Silas was to be out no longer than an hour. However, he had been gone but five minutes when she started to panic. Why didn't I ask why that boy wasn't working? She asked herself, and then rearranged her few possessions, an activity which would be repeated several times over the next hour.

For children from poor or modest families, there was no school and children were put to work as soon as possible. Normally, you wouldn't see groups of boys playing in the street on a daily basis, although it wasn't unheard of either if their parents allowed it. Boys, in particular, would have obligations at an early age, and as they grew this would include archery practice commanded by the king, at least once a week, for which Dead Alley was ideal. But Jaxon had won over Mary, despite the alarming cut that he had across his neck, yet another detail that she wished she had quizzed him about. And, by the time she was endlessly traversing her living space and had started to panic, the four boys were almost at the river carrying Lord Silas on their shoulders, although in her mind she saw him no farther away than the next snickleway. Keen to avoid as many adults as possible, Silas could be heard chanting his usual mantra with the others joining in except they were not entirely echoing his declarations. "Lord Siliarse!" they pronounced, "fool of York!" "lad in a dress!" "stinks o shite!" and "maiden in distress" became their alternative battle cries. Oblivious, poor Silas was having the time of his life, at the same time as completely forgetting his mother's wishes. Soon they were on the Ouse Bridge, a most curious part of the city. Over time, people began to build houses on the bridge, and although they were all timber structures, there was no thought given to the integrity of the bridge itself. So overpopulated had it become that it was becoming difficult to see the river as you crossed, and the busy passageway was becoming narrower. One could easily imagine that mathematicians, engineers and scientists would daily hog the rope ferry as they were possibly the only ones sure of the total collapse of the houses and perhaps even the bridge itself, although it never happened. It would only be replaced in the 1550s. However, the streetwise Jaxon knew where the gaps between the houses were, and also where the wall could be found, and so he led his merry train into one of those gaps without being detected.

Making it clear that Silas was now their leader and that he should start to rally his troops, they stood him upright on the wall inciting him to speak to his soldiers beyond.

'No, no,' said Jaxon, 'face the river, imagine your army is afore you.'

Silas obliged and no sooner had he opened his mouth than he felt a sharp push in his lower back. He began to fall but something was holding him back. At that instant, he was completely confused. He could hear them laughing, although he was also sure that he was in danger. Then he heard a protracted ripping sound and instantly plunged downward at such a rate that it stopped his breath. Jaxon had pushed him off the bridge whilst the other boys grabbed at his tabard which did exactly what they wanted it to. The light was dimming as Silas went down and down, wearing nothing but ill-fitting and much-repaired hose.

Certain that he was to drown, he felt himself crash, and although his fall had been broken, it was harsh. He heard cracking and crunching, but still, he had not stopped his downward trajectory. All sound dissipated as the boys ran away and his collision deafened him. Before Silas could see anything, he became aware of pain. Sharp, stinging pain everywhere and the more he tried to settle and then move, the worse it got. He had been purposely thrown into bushes of stinging nettles which consumed him for almost five minutes. When he saw daylight again he didn't even notice that he had also lost his tights, so not only was he naked but every bit of his flesh was raging. He could just make out the river and thought to throw himself in but was wise enough to know that it would have killed him as, like so many other citizens of York, he could not swim. He did splash water onto his naked torso but this offered him little relief. He was howling so much that it was a wonder no one heard him, but he didn't know what else to do. He called out for Jaxon and then for his mother. Any mother would have done, for he truly was a pathetic sight, but no one came. Eventually, he managed to scramble up the steps and back onto the bridge, but he had no clue whatsoever as to how he would get back to his dear Mary Smith. To one side of the Ouse Bridge was darkness and to the other were church and cathedral lights, so this obvious contrast made his first choice for him. He ran blindly, screaming in pain toward Coppergate. A woman was returning home after relieving herself before bedtime only to see a small fiery red demon heading towards her. Now, she was screaming as well, and doors already shut for curfew were open once again.

With thoughts only of home and relief from his pain, Silas was oblivious to the ignorant of York falling to their knees and genuflecting.

'An Imp! Sent from the bowels of hell itself! Dear mother Mary, pray for us!' said one.

A burly tanner prostrated himself in the filthy street proclaiming, 'A banshee! The marks of Satan on it from head to toe! Lock your doors and send for a priest…'

It would take just another two days before half of York was certain that this diabolical entity also flew, and spat fire at the church rooftops. Ten people had been killed with their bodies or souls never to be seen again. Even more shocking was the news that all the women of Coppergate were now pregnant with Beelzebub's babies.

This ridiculous misunderstanding did at least mean that

no one apprehended Silas on his quest to find Mary, but eventually she found him. Already halfway toward Coppergate, and hearing the commotion, she knew that it must have had something to do with her son.

With no family or friends to speak of, Mary remained ignorant of a solution to her son's predicament, and that included some of the more popular and bizarre remedies of Renaissance England. Leaves. She had heard something about nettle stings and leaves, and also managed to mentally reference the poultices that had been applied to her as a child. Half an hour later she beheld a sobbing and squealing nose protruding from a woman-made bush that had been beautifully crafted by spreading animal fat all over his skinny frame and then sticking on anything she could get hold of from the part of Dead Alley that was blocked off by the graveyard. Having risked being detected beyond curfew, she grabbed at anything that grew, and truth be told, some of those were probably nettles as well. An orange bush topped a long thin, green one and, as he stood in the corner shaking and crying, he resembled a poorly sunflower.

Her heart was broken. Throughout each recent calamity, she had worked so hard to protect her precious son, but now he was suffering so much, and she struggled to deal with it. Neither of them slept that night, but in twenty-four hours he was healing. Mary questioned him about the incident until his mind was blank, but Silas could not understand what had happened either.

However, as mothers do, she slowly put the puzzle together and told Silas not to play with them again. This left him even more conflicted as he wanted so much to have friends.

Seemingly, at the point where she was devoid of tears, Mary sat in her father's chair for the last time before it was to be taken away. She had resigned herself to the reality that she would lose the home and thought to take herself and Silas to St Mary's Abbey in the hope that they may help. However, deep down she understood the severity of begging in Tudor England. If found out she would be lucky to find herself in the stocks, and the other options terrified her.

Eviction day
Mary realised that, as she started to feed her son, he was becoming too old for her to do so, but he still struggled with eating utensils. She then decided that it didn't matter as long as others did not know, but pondered once more about his future on a day when all the world was already collapsing about her. He put his face close to hers and in an instant she forgot about it.

At twelve noon, she stood with her arm loosely embracing her son and awaited the metallic bang on the door. The constable was on time and she cooperatively opened it wide.

'I put up no defence constable, let your men in and we will leave…'

The huffing constable took a deep breath to reply when he was unexpectedly pushed aside. Mary could not believe her eyes and was already trying to tell him that the impromptu assault had nothing to do with her. He wobbled and grunted and managed to stay on his feet but it took him some moments before he was able to recognise his assailant.

'Out the way, you blocked bowel!' boomed the voice of his attacker.

More than anything, Mary noted the fear on the constable's face as he weighed up whether it was worth engaging with such a fierce opponent.

'No business here today, Lily…'

The constable's name is Lily? thought Mary and then observed that his rotund figure had been replaced by a similar one.

It was Mrs Tumble.

'Two months' rent here Lily liver, so you can be on your way!' demanded Mrs Tumble.

'I must protest!' started the constable, 'I carry the authority….'

'Was that you I saw visiting Mrs Prostrate's gentleman's house yet again yesterday?' said Tumble.

'I must protest!' he said once more 'and she isn't called Mrs Pros…'

'Be on your way, and be sure to give this to the landlord.'

He grumbled, huffed and shook all sorts of body parts that looked as though they hadn't been mobilised in decades, but did eventually, sod off.

'You can imagine who the coins are from?' said Mrs Tumble, 'but you are never to say a word about what you saw that day. Do you understand?'

Mary was astonished that the lady from the large house in Coppergate would give her money for what she had regarded as her obligation as a good Christian, and she told Mrs Tumble the same.

'It would not be right and…I would never have said anything...' insisted Mary.

'Well, tis yours,' said Tumble abruptly, 'and is already spent.'

'Perhaps…' said Mary and she turned to go upstairs, but Silas tugged at her dress holding her back.

She looked down and found him grasping the small bundle of quills.

'Oh, very well!' said an increasingly impatient Tumble, 'don't know what she will do with them, but I will pass them on and say you have taken the rent money as payment.'

Business-like, Mrs Tumble then turned to leave, only to find two arms around her neck and another two skinny ones around her leg.

'Dear Mrs Tumble,' said Mary.

Once Tumble was over the shock she giggled, something she very rarely did.

'First time I've ever been called that…' and then she left.

The French armourer

Over the next few years, Mary managed to keep her home. The lady who had paid her rent, and effectively saved her life, was the wife of an almoner at the Minster, leaving Mary wondering why they had so much money, but was, nevertheless, grateful for it. Her daughter had completely recovered and the incident was never spoken of again. She had told her husband that the quills were a celebratory gift, but he did ask about their origin, which led to a few serious enquiries about their source, although Mary sold only one or two more.

Six months after she was almost evicted, Clifford walked in as though he had left that same morning. Silas, slightly taller and even thinner, hopped on the spot and shrieked with delight, although he was most careful not to touch his father. It was just something that just was not done.

'Who's this?' he said as if asking the time of day.

'It's your son. You know it is.'

Mary wanted to say and ask so much more but thought better of it.

'Mm, what's wrong with him?'

This time she refused to take the bait so said nothing. Silas claimed the silence.

'Pater! How is the king? Do you have to go to war, fatha? Where is…?'

Clifford Smith glared at his son. Mary had the measure of him, she knew he was either ready to raise his fist or possibly rise to this accolade.'

'The king is busy building a palace.'

That was it, nothing else. Mary wanted to ask about his missing family, where he had been and desperately wanted to admonish him for almost having her thrown out of her home but instead, she said,

'Do you need food?'

'Yes…food'

She had some bread and cheese and it was then she

thought to say, "Why are you here?" or "Where did the business move to?" but instead said,

'Silas, please play upstairs for a few minutes whilst I speak to your father.'

She then sat and stared at a man who, by now, was almost a stranger. She thought of how she had constantly prayed for him, despite his shortcomings. She had also prayed for him to return, and there he was.

She looked up and spoke quietly,

'I have no money for rent'.

The way he ate was as ill-mannered, as was the way he spoke and behaved. She patiently sat through a myriad of disgusting noises. Eventually, without looking up, he spoke.

'I can let you have some money.'

All those many other questions came to the fore once more but she told herself to be thankful for what he had just said.

She examined him whilst he ate. He didn't look like he worked for the king, but neither did he look poor. She knew that people had seen him about York, but she had no idea where he would be living.

'It is good for Silas…he aspires to such things,' she said.

'Who?'

'Your son, Silas'

'Mumph?'

'Your…work with the king…it is good for him to hear.'

'Oh…can't talk about it…mumph… buurpp…secrets.'

'Of course,' she said.

'I will pay rent to the landlord, but you bring…belch…him…up and you don't talk to other men.'

Audacious as this was, Mary thought that she had been offered a good deal. He seemed to have visited and left within less than an hour, and that would be the last she would see of him for some time. She personally visited the landlord a month later, who confirmed that an arrangement had been made.

4 Six years old
1520

In 1520, by the time Silas was six years old, he had only seen his father a handful of times but revelled in the knowledge that he made armour for the king. During his most recent visit, he had told Silas that he was off to France and the boy did not doubt it for one minute. Silas was taller but scrawny, pale as a Minster gargoyle and now sporting a huge bush of orange hair. His mother, his home and his imagination were his complete world and, beyond that, he had no self-worth and was sure that he was inferior to almost everyone else. Never again would the boy play with Jaxon or his friends but they seemed ever-present both around that part of York and in Silas's psyche and he was of course, mostly responsible for Silas's lack of confidence. Added to that, was the endless rhetoric about how he "wasn't like other boys" which would only have been avoided if his mother stopped visiting the market and church and kept him indoors which she was not willing to do.

If anything, Mary became even more protective although Silas was allowed to play outside the front of his own house. There was something curiously paradoxical about Dead Alley in that, as a Cul de sac, it offered some security but it was also a dark and secluded place where people could easily get trapped. At the end where it wasn't open, it was blocked by overgrown tree roots and bracken, the graveyard of All Saints, Pavement Church beyond. This was their church but no one tried to negotiate a way through the overgrowth, always choosing to walk all the way around. At six, he still jousted, went on quests, fought monsters, tended to his steed and had audiences with the king and would often sit in the dust and mud and play with whatever was at hand. Jaxon often appeared at the end of Dead Alley to goad and insult him. On one occasion, he pelted Silas with stones just for fun. One hit him so hard that blood gushed forth from his forehead. Now, he was getting the gist that not only was he different from others but that no matter how hard he tried, he could never depend on anyone being his friend. But that is what he most wanted and it was admirable that throughout his life he never stopped trusting people.

Mary tried not to think of him growing up. Everyone had to work but not Silas, she told herself. Quite how he was to be a favourite of Henry the Eighth at the same time as never leaving Dead Alley she never seemed to work out.

Now, his favourite pastime was to watch his mother making quills. In doing so, she would explain the process and why different writers preferred different quills and she would embellish the instruction by explaining the Norman Conquest, the feudal system and the Wars of the Roses. It is only fair to add that, in each instance, these were Mary's versions and therefore it was no wonder that Silas was confused so often. But it did give him aspirations no matter how distorted. In contrast, Silas's Christian education was a wonder to behold. In a time when almost everyone in England followed the faith, one's Church and family would be their only moral reference point. However, even long before The Reformation, that supposedly singular creed could well be interpreted in many ways by different people as it was in years to come. If you wished to wage war you would completely ignore all the teachings of Christ and find some Old Testament reference that would support such madness. Possibly because of the way his mother was, but more likely because of his own good spirit, Silas was more fascinated by the bearded, awkward hermit who had been sent with a completely unique message for mankind. As he grew, his personal passion for putting others first, forgiving, seeing with his heart and even loving his enemies was to further disappoint him as he met very few people who lived that same message. Having said that, the moral rigour of

Christianity did offer structure to both Silas and Tudor society and with it came some sense of security for most people.

Mary did take pains to share all of her skills with Silas. He marvelled at how she made scents giving every quill its own aroma and it was this, in addition to the fine quality of her produce that started to get Mary Smith noticed. She had also become aware that if she could get near enough to a potential client, the sale was much easier and even the monks had been known to mellow at Mary's smile.

This is when Hugh came into Silas's life, a junior cleric who at first thought Mary to be a widow, was a recipient of one of the quills that had been handed to Mrs Tumble. He too lived nearby and was a modest cleric at the Minster. He suggested that she gave a few quills free gratis and he would have them passed around. In turn, this helped to popularise her work.

Silas didn't take to Hugh. Even as a child he was aware of his mother rejecting his advances but he did offer to market her quills. He made an arrangement with Mary that would set her up as a supplier of quills although she saw little return from it. All the same, it did give her a sense of purpose and enhanced confidence that periodically put Clifford Smith at the back of her mind. She would only see Hugh now and again as an intermediary and was thankful that he was doing all the leg work.

Ironically, this was a time when Mary and her son spent much more time indoors, partly because of the demands of her work but also because of a local threat. The women in Dead Alley had been made aware that a young woman had been gruesomely killed in a nearby alley, although no one was told that she was the third. Besides the perpetrator, only two other people knew that the three women were also victims of a sexual assault. Such a serious occurrence was rare but would always warrant the visitation of officials. On this occasion, the sheriff, the constable, a priest and two lawyers were present around Dead Alley. None of the locals would learn any further details from them or anyone else, relying entirely on rumours which, as you may imagine, made things worse. During that same visitation, one of the contingent, a legal notary from the Minster, found himself seeking out the popular quill maker of Dead Alley.

Silas remembers standing behind his mother as she opened the door and he also remembered that she was nervous. The man was dressed in a full-length gown but it was his cloud-white collar and the fur trim that fascinated the boy. On their rare expeditions beyond Dead Alley, Silas became obsessed with the fineries of well-to-do folk and now he had one in his house. The man was polite and Silas decided that he liked him. They sat and talked. The boy was aware that men smiled and were quite gracious when speaking to his mother and presumed that they must have liked her in the same way as he did. Throughout the conversation, Silas's only point of reference came when he heard the man say "fine quills…" but then Silas started to play with a horse that his mother had whittled out of a branch and much of the conversation was then lost to him.

This man was the young William Fawkes.

'It has come to my attention my dear lady, that whereas we used to acquire thirty quills for a farthing we now only get twenty for that amount.'

Mary instantly got into a flap but he insisted on continuing,

'And…I have already presumed that you are not seeing that profit?'

She became very upset, resorting to rearranging her ornaments before William took care to reassure her. She sat again and Silas would later recall that he saw William touching her arm.

They both agreed that Hugh was embezzling the profits and so William Fawkes promised a new intermediary on better terms. And, that would have been that, a foggy conversation beyond the castle walls of Silas's retreat until he heard the words, "the boy" and then "work" but it was the third one that brokered the deal.

Completely oblivious to his mother's reticence to have him work, Silas jumped up when he heard the word "errands."

His face became flushed and his knees began to wobble inside his baggy hose. Errand, he thought. That is what I am going to be. A knight errand! He muttered to himself. Of course, he was wrong. A fourteenth-century poem about Sir Gawain and the Green Knight, called the knight errant, had found its way into popular culture and Mary had offered Silas her very own Dead Alley version. Where he wasn't wrong was that by doing errands for Fawkes and his associates, he could possibly start to find his way in the real world and get himself known.

William Fawkes promised that these would be short errands and that the boy would never be alone and would also be looked after initially by him. It was at this juncture that Mary dithered. Not because of the issue at hand but because she was worried that the handsome Fawkes may have had designs on her. She had never told anyone that she was a widow but acknowledged that it helped if people believed it. The stigma of having an absent husband was far worse than being a widow or a spinster and society would, of course, presume that an unhappy husband would only be so because of his wife. She decided not to say anything on that subject but then agreed with some stipulations.

One thing that helped to seal the deal was that he offered to clothe Silas. For some years the boy had sported a whole array of tights with holes, stitches and stains but none had fit him. Mary would replace his Knights Templar tabard every year or so (or when it got lost in a nettle bush) and he had been gifted a used jerkin that he wore to church and market. This was also too big. When his new clothes arrived, they were magnificent in comparison but, of course, they were too big as well. Although Mary had been very reluctant to agree to his scheme, she realised that this would probably be as good an opportunity as Silas would ever get and she was admirably very honest with Fawkes. She told him that her son was given to fantasies, lived in an ever-present daydream and didn't seem to understand when people made jokes. He also struggled with changes in moods, sometimes never seeing the signs at all when someone was becoming impatient with him. She added that it was extremely likely that he would get lost at first.

'But sir, beyond that, he is the sweetest and most loyal little boy and I have no doubt that he will work very hard.'

William Fawkes made Mary many promises and was as good as his word. As soon as his new clothes arrived, Fawkes walked him to the Minster and took him inside. This was his first visit and he remained speechless throughout the tour, his world already thousands of times bigger than it had been the day before. William Fawkes was kind and kept asking Silas if he understood what had been said but got little more than a nod in return as the boy was spellbound. The Minster interior seemed endless and the effigies, especially of Knights, astounded him as did the magnificent stained-glass windows which related endless, wonderful tales. He was then taken through some of the offices before again finding himself at the gates of the Liberty Wall. Here, he met David who was to tutor him in the role of errand boy. David seemed civil enough and, before Silas knew it, he was back with his mother.

'Oh, thank you so much, sir, I have been beside myself…,' said Mary.

'He has only been gone just over an hour' said a smiling Fawkes 'he has been attentive and well behaved and there is nothing to suggest that with some guidance he wouldn't be ideal…although I feel it has been more than enough for one day.'

'May the Lord go with you' he said.

'And also, you' replied Mary.

Of course, as soon as he was gone, Mary sought reassurances from her son but barely had the chance to ask. He rambled, demonstrated, gesticulated and babbled endlessly although in doing so, the Minster and its environs became a fantasy land where God himself rescued the righteous.

There was not one second that night in which Silas succumbed to sleep. Etched on the ceiling were towers that climbed to Heaven, pictures in coloured glass that moved and Jesus healed the sick and then approached and prayed over Silas who would then go on a brave quest to avenge all the dead knights, maidens and bishops that lay within the Minster. He would scale the outside of the central towers, one hand on his sword and the other carrying the flag of St George, his feet alone scurrying upward and upward. Even his imminent errands featured in his imaginings, each one a matter of life and death and now that he was practically indispensable to the city of York, his mother lived like a princess.

Bolt

When Silas had started work just two days after William's visit, the reality was somewhat different. David offered some advice but thought Silas to be an idiot. He had even heard his nickname used frequently leaving him wondering why someone would have employed him at all. Furthermore, David set traps for him. At first, Silas was lost in every sense of the word and the city may as well have been the whole world. He had heard the names of the many gates, bars and streets but they had no bearing on his reality. William Fawkes was considerate. Even if he had been somewhat won over by the innocent charm and natural beauty of Mary Smith, he meant well and wanted Silas to succeed. One day he followed the two boys, horrified to discover that David was literally leading Silas astray and admonished him for it. Within the hour, Silas found himself standing in William's office.

'I want to help you boy but you will need to learn the Minster precinct and the city beyond. You do realise that they are both different?'

'The Minster is… err… the province of St Peter and York that of our blessed king, Henry the Eighth of that name.' answered Silas.

'My, my! So, it's not all fantasy in that little head…' said Fawkes acknowledging that the boy's obsession with both rule and rulers had birthed some sense.

A dog appeared from behind Fawkes's chair.

'Bolt' said Fawkes and it hobbled toward Silas.

Silas gawped, confused by the name.

'He used to move a lot faster' said Fawkes with a wry smile.

'Where's his leg?' asked the boy.

'When he was young, he chased an intruder who slashed his front paw with a dagger. He had to have it removed. As I said, he used to move a lot faster…'

Bolt sat on Silas's foot which made him smile.

'Stroke him' said Fawkes realising that the lad needed to be constantly prompted.

Bolt then rested his head on Silas's foot. Fawkes turned around a huge piece of paper that was on his desk.

'Do you know what this is Silas?'

'It's a map' he answered 'is it of York?'

William nodded.

'It is beautiful…'

Then, Silas started to ramble. He pointed out where the defences were poor, where to position archers to send off the Lancastrians and a likely landing area for dragons. The admirably patient Fawkes tutored the boy on the many distinctions between fact and fiction.

'York is no longer under attack and certainly not from the Lancastrians. The bars are guarded and we take care about who we let into the city and also who can visit the Minster but I need you to become familiar with street names, buildings, addresses and people or you won't be able to do your job.'

He understood the last part and so began to study the map.

'Is that...Dead Alley? And that...um...Coppergate?'

'Yes,' said Fawkes, quite astonished.

'I think it makes sense,' said the boy.

'We are here' said Fawkes pointing to the Minster on the map 'this is the door where you came in, you will leave that way. Here, as you leave the Minster yard is Petergate and there is Stonegate. There is a large townhouse here called Mulberry Hall. I need this document to go there and the owner will send a reply. That's your next job.'

Without saying another word, Silas turned to leave and Bolt followed him.

'That's alright' said Fawkes 'he will help you get there and back.'

Four minutes later, young Silas knocked on the door of Mulberry Hall.

'Yes', said the maid.

Nothing.

'What do you want, boy?'

Bolt barked; Silas trembled.

'I am…err at your very…Master Faw…the map…you are a princess. My lady!' and he bowed.

She giggled.

'Are you meant to deliver that document?'

'Aha! Yis… dokeremint!'

She disappeared and Silas turned to walk away, Bolt tugged so hard on his baggy tights that they nearly ended up around his ankles.

The penny dropped and so Silas turned back, stood and waited. He felt as though he had waited all day but, eventually, a new document was placed in his hand.

Soon, he returned, handed it to Fawkes and said nothing.

'Just as I thought...' said Fawkes almost forgetting that the boy was still there.

'Thank you, Silas. That will do for today. Can you find your way back here for first bells in the morning?'

He nodded. William Fawkes had been astonished at how quickly Silas had memorised the map and, in years to come, he would acknowledge that there would be no one who would know the city streets better. However, he had to concede that this seemed to be the limit of his abilities. Silas remembered to thank him and turned to leave. Bolt followed.

'The dog stays with me tonight but you will see him tomorrow.'

That evening he described the wonders of York to his mother which helped to minimise the stress that the changes had caused her. It was a wonderful opportunity for both of them and now, she would not have to worry about income. And, for the very first time, she broached the issue of his awkwardness and how he seemed to others.

'I do not care, for you are my queen and I am Lord Silas, knight errand to St Peter!' he exclaimed quite fluently and at that moment Mary learned, as Fawkes soon would, that when he was comfortable he could speak well although every other situation would forever be a challenge. Mary decided to leave it there not knowing if she had made things better or worse.

Each day, his obligations became slightly greater and William Fawkes accepted that the boy would make mistakes, often. Silas became more and more familiar with the streets but would mix one house up with another and, more often than not, completely forget names. Mostly, he would forget to wait for a reply and found himself being sent out once again. But day by day, he learned so much about York and the people in it. As Monday of his second week ended and he sat down to eat with his mother, he heard a scratching at the door. She hurriedly opened it to find the scruffiest three-legged mutt panting at her. Without invitation, Bolt wobbled in.

'Master Fawkes will be furious!' said Mary but Silas didn't hear it and, as expected, fifteen minutes later, Fawkes was at the door. There was a conversation but all Silas remembered was,

'The dog stays with me at night but you may do what you will with him during the day.'

Delighted, Silas was accompanied on his errands from that day on by his very first steed, the bold, brave and athletic Bolt.

Of course, Silas continued to attract glances from passers-by. As the months passed, Silas wobbled almost as much as the dog. Jaxon and his associates would lay in way for him and thought nothing of hurling abuse, ensuring that the catcalls of "Lord Sillyarse" were catching on with the citizens of the city.

Bolt's appearance did little to help. During one of his deliveries, a man asked Silas to show him the dog's best aspect. Silas walked around the dog three times and declared,

'I don't think he has one, sir'

In an age when the upper breed chose thoroughbred greyhounds for hunting and for prestige, Bolt was definitely at home amongst the poor of Dead Alley. Silas never found out why Fawkes kept him but it became immaterial as he soon became the Smith's beloved pet and assistant in affairs of state. Neglect, poor diet, a bad accident and more in and out breeding that the Plantagenets had led to Bolt's unique appearance. One of a kind you may say and Silas liked it that way. It seemed as though, even when washed, there were no two parts of him the same colour and his hair would grow different lengths on different parts of his body but would only moult around his backside. But, to Silas, Bolt was the finest hound ever to stand by his owner and, in time, they would not be separated. Mary became aware of the effect Bolt had on her son. She knew that, even as an adult, he would forever struggle with people but now, at last, he had a real friend. A dependable one who loved him for who he was and Silas was offering the same in return. Now, Lord Silas could talk fantastical gibberish from dawn to dust with an attentive audience by his side.

The Queen of Sheba
One winter's afternoon as the light was fading, Silas realised that he had walked the full length of Micklegate only to find that he was at the wrong Holy Trinity church, he should have been at the one in Goodramgate instead. As Bolt led the way back, an elderly woman who was already drenched from the icy sleet tripped and fell into the mud. No one seemed to take any notice as she lay there quite helpless. Silas approached her.

'May I resist you in your hour of dire... er... dangerousness?' rambled Silas.

Although she could not have been expected to understand fluent Silasese, she did raise a weighty arm in the hope that he would grab it. Silas had never encountered anything as heavy in his whole life but, eventually between the woman, the dog and himself she was once more upright or at least as upright as she could be as the old lady had a crook in her back so severe that, as she walked, her face could not have seen anything but the street below her. Silas instinctively insisted on helping her home which, as it turned out, was in Gillygate, not far from the Minster but on the other side of the city wall. Eventually, he would be given permission to exit and enter the city with William Fawkes' authority but on this occasion, he assisted the old lady through Bootham Bar and none of the guards even flinched.

Her home was little more than a shed and its roof no more than heaps of straw so, unsurprisingly, it was almost as wet inside as out. She rummaged around her sparse possessions hoping to reward him. Silas, as he simply did not know what to do, just watched her.

'Oh…a curse on it' she said 'if you return tomorrow, I will give you something in payment boy. Truth be told, if you hadn't passed, I'd be no doubt dying in the street.'

As best as he was able, he told her that he did not want anything in return. Already, Bolt had dozed off and the woman realised that Silas seemed fascinated with her humble trade once he noticed what was on the table.

'Queen of Sheba' she said.

'Pardon?'

'That's who I am. The Queen of Sheba. Fallen on hard times, I grant you but that is how you will address me.'

Yes, Silas had found someone as barmy as himself with only the small matter of sixty years to distinguish between them.

A queen! Silas thought to himself. I have met a real queen at last. He then stared at the materials that were laid out on a small table near the fire, which was yet to be lit.

'Do you know what they are boy?' she asked in a tired, thin tone.

'This is for a notary like my master and this…a chorister or a Precentor. That one is for a commoner and this…only the mayor would wear this…'

Although he was not to know it yet, this little speech showed, yet again, that when he was at ease, he could speak without pausing.

'Goodness' said that Queen of Sheba 'where did you learn all of that?'

As best he could, he related his passion for pageantry, his mother's talent for quills and then told her that he was a lord. She chuckled possibly acknowledging that, at long last, Court was quorate.

'Well, Lord Silas, the queen is in your debt and you may call upon her anytime. Would you like one of these? As you say, it would have to be one of the more common ones as you are an errand boy about the city.'

Silas jumped with joy and then kissed the old woman which was some feat seeing as he could barely find her face.

He was to have his own white collar.

Collars, strangely, had already started to be a thing. Firstly, as an addition to one's chemise, an undershirt worn practically by all, which would rarely come off even when dead and in winter there would be no chance. Small, frilled collars emerged as a fashion statement and already these had developed into ruffles around the neck, a kind of folded cloth. Eventually, these would become the ever-expanding ruff, so ridiculously huge by the end of the century that it was a wonder anyone could move in them at all. Looking at this impressive array of collars, Silas would, in later years, wonder if the Queen of Sheba had prophesied the creation of the said silly ruff.

Eventually, Silas returned to the ever-patient Fawkes who, by now, had only the last few wax drips of candle left to keep him company. Silas apologised and Fawkes reminded him that he still hadn't completed his errand to Holy Trinity in Goodramgate.

'Twill do tomorrow.' He said patiently and sent him on his way.

Regardless of the promised collar, Silas would check on the queen's welfare almost every day for some time to come, often finding himself chastised by his gaffer for the very same reason.

The following day was the one and only time that William Fawkes considered that he may have to let the boy go. As he sent Silas off, he left his desk and his many other duties to follow him the short distance to Monkgate. Almost as soon as he had left the Minster precinct, all manner of abuse was being hurled in the boy's direction. Over less than a quarter of a mile in distance, this persisted although Fawkes also noticed some who greeted him and there were even some who felt apparently sorry for him. For a person who would be renowned for his stiffness in years to come, Fawkes found himself touched by what he saw. As Silas turned and dawdled back, he was once more set upon by Jaxon who, on this occasion was about to assault him.

'You boys come here at once!'

Silas jumped so far that he almost fell onto Jaxon, he had no idea that Fawkes was behind him. Jaxon and his thugs thought to leave but knew that this man represented the law. So, they stood, mouths agape, staring back at him.

'This boy is in my employ and, as such, in the employ of both the Pontiff and the king. Any offence against him is an offence against them, carrying the harshest of sentences!'

Fawkes was on very good form that day. The whole street had stopped to acknowledge his authority. This was the best show since Bayard had been in York and it left no one in doubt as to who was in charge. Of course, the abuse would never subside. As he grew, his looks and his speech became even more awkward and his job made him known to almost everyone in York.

All was not well. Despite his clear gift with maps and places, his propensity to become forgetful, fanciful and simply live in the moment meant that he was not getting the job done.

One evening, just two months after Silas had started his job, William Fawkes stood in front of a huge stone fireplace analysing a document. Between the spits, crackles and wheezes of the burgeoning fire, Fawkes would umph, sigh and sometimes smile and yet he read it over and over again. On his desk was a list of the duties that Silas had been expected to fulfil but this was altogether a very different list. For each entry, there was a date and then a comment. David, despite his flaws, was an apprentice and Fawkes insisted that he had learned to scribe and it was he who had been responsible for the document Fawkes now held. In it, David has documented every reason given by Silas for his tardiness:

Young Silas

Returneade layte
Returnaede layte
Returneade layte agin
Dyd not retuorne at ayll: got loste
Dyd not retuorne at ayll: endede up in Londone
Dyd not retuorne at ayll: was wit Queen of Sheba
Dyd not know from wither he cometh
Dyd not know from wither he goethe
Loste satchele
Loste satchele and documentes
Loste satchele documentes and dog
Layte: looyking for dog
Loste a shoo forasmuch as it neer returneade
Loste both shoos
Layte: dog was looking fur ownere
Forgetteth whome he workede fur
Culd not sayeth 'honoureable'
Culd not sayeth 'judgemente'
Culd not sayeth 'recompnse'
Culd not sayeth 'Silas'
Muddied Holy grownde
Manned battlements to lookout for French.
Loste in multitude
Layte: 'feeding five thousande'
Stoppt to releeve his bladere and forgott hose
Dispaired and did nowt
Fell into bushe
Fell into mud
Fell into ponde
Fell into publik latrine
Trespassed on mayores propertie
Temptd by Devile: sat downe and restede
Beykame loste: dysfunctions of his bowelle
Returneade layte: 'called to jowst'
Returneade layte: 'defendeth woman's honore'

And on it went. He then heard Silas slosh in behind him.

'Is that another document to deliver sir? I do not mind going out again.'

Without turning around William paused and said nothing. Politely, Silas repeated himself but Fawkes still did not move. With his back to the boy, he casually tore up the document and threw it onto the fire.

'No, no. That will do for today. Thank you, Silas, I shall see you in the morning, first bells.'

The Alehouse

On reflection, anyone would be hard pushed to say whether Fawkes ever got value for money out of the boy but during the next six months he showed some improvement. Mary naturally wove into her busy schedule the regular stitching, repairing and cleaning of Silas and his clothes. Before she knew it, she was also cleaning and feeding the dog but, by and large, life was good with heart-warming future prospects for them both. She only saw Clifford once during that period. One Tuesday morning, Fawkes visited simply to review the terms of Mary's contract. On this occasion, he was there no more than ten minutes but, as she opened the door to bid him farewell, a dark figure loomed in the doorway. Taken aback, Fawkes looked the man up and down and once outside of the property, turned to reprimand him as a notable official of the Minster was wont to do,

'In God's good name man, you have succumbed to drink this early in the day? Shame on you...'

He turned to Mary,

'Do you know this man?'

Meekly, she declared that the foreboding figure in the doorway was her husband. Fawkes thought to say more but then thought better of it although Mary was left wishing that he had stayed. Surprisingly, the furious husband also stormed off leaving Mary sure that she had committed a cardinal sin. She had spoken to another man, moreover, she had made him welcome in her home. She spent the rest of the day pacing up and down, anxious about what retribution may be in store for her but as the rest of the week passed, she did not see Clifford again.

'You often speak of your father, but you do not speak of him to me' said Fawkes assertively to young Silas.

Silas didn't know what to think of such an observation but was sure that it wasn't a question.

Fawkes slumped into his Romanesque leather-seated chair as if he was awaiting a sermon and then repeated the question and Silas answered.

'He makes armour and weapons and... erm...is with the king in France. Best blacksmith in all of H'ingland sir.'

Silas's delivery was so perfect that William Fawkes was left in no doubt that the boy had said this many, many times. Fawkes said nothing more, concealing the fact that he had bumped into his father that same morning and was definitely not in France when he did so.

Eventually, Silas's tasks became a little more adventurous and he was allowed to wander further, once or twice legitimately even venturing beyond the city walls. He would rarely see David who had been of little help and Silas was much happier running errands with Bolt instead. Although time after time he would be stopped at the Liberty Gates to the Minster precinct as well as both leaving and entering the city, he would show the archbishop's seal with pride. However, he had never been inside a public house before. Silas would never know why Fawkes had a message for the owner of Ye Golden Fleece but he was excited to see what went on beyond the mysterious walls and its single opaque window. November had once more come around and he found himself up to his knees in snow and he could hear the din long before he had turned into the Pavement. He had passed alehouses many times and was intrigued by the diverse noises that emanated from them, conjuring visions of medieval battle in his mind. Shouting, cursing, laughing and even singing; he could not make sense of it at all but he found it simultaneously frightening, thrilling and overwhelming.

In years to come, depictions of the old English pub would suspiciously become more and more quaint although there was nothing particularly picturesque about Silas's destination on that deep winter's day.

During the Middle Ages, people, sometimes to supplement poor wages, would brew beer and sell it at the front of their dwellings, often through windows. Over time, those businesses would take over the whole house and, as such, there was no specific template for what became known as the ale house and later the pub or public house. There are possibly two good arguments for the benefits of such establishments, one being that they were, of sorts, community hubs. The second more dubious excuse was that ale was healthier than water, which it most definitely was.

They could sometimes be small, squalid places and from the time of Henry the Seventh onwards, they became a cause of constant concern for local authorities, due to the growing habitual sinning, which included drunkenness and brawls as well as accessing prostitutes and gambling. In York, whilst Silas was still a child, there were more alehouses than there had ever been previously and an open war waged between the alehouse culture and that of the Church. However, where priests may well have been loathe to frequent such premises, they would make arrangements for alcohol to be delivered to them, sometimes in an arcane manner and, no amount of drinking within a monastery or the Minster quarter seemed to cause any moral outrage.

York had a thriving history of beer making, born of mixed cultures. There were still many sweet, pale-looking ales that were as opaque as honey that the York Vikings may well have enjoyed hundreds of years earlier. And, intriguing names were already in existence during the sixteenth century, a favourite being "dragon's milk." Producing poor beer or watering it down was deemed to be a serious offence and was punishable. Habitual drunkards were sometimes put in the stocks or may well have been made to wear a drunkard's cloak. This is something that Doug Cooper would have been very familiar with, not because he was a drunk but because the cloak was in fact a barrel. This was to be worn in public to shame the offender and must have offered much light relief to those parishioners who regarded themselves as law-abiding. Silas had wondered many times what the drunkard's cloak was.

Few alehouses had windows but almost always had a good fire and, in years gone by, this is where customers would start to congregate, some of the earliest domestic ale gatherings being in the kitchen. This was a time when serious legislation came into play but there were no official licences until 1552. The king, Henry the Eighth, was more concerned with whether drinking was interfering with regular archery practice which was mandatory for men. Where the alehouses did come into their own was when they became a go-to place for the very poor. If the monasteries failed the worse off, it was rumoured that alehouse owners would let them sleep in the cellar for free, asking for recompense when the individual found work. If that failed, they would put them to work and, for women, as you can imagine, that could be a very slippery slope.

Hesitating for just a moment and telling a tired and shivery dog to stay, a dirty, drippy Silas bravely crossed the threshold only to be slapped around the cheek by an itinerant drunk who then pushed him onto his backside and into the snow. He brushed himself off and once more pushed the door open but this time thrust forward his seal for all to see. One man shouted,

'Landlord! the Pope wants an audience with ye!' and his friends laughed.

So, he got inside but Silas still felt adrift as bodies seemed to crush him from all sides. He had learned to avoid making any protest when in the presence of adults but his face was now pushed so far into one man's arse that he could barely breathe, reminding him of that day when he fell into the public latrine. At the end of his rope and almost ready to complain, he was forcibly squeezed out of this small but abhorrent crowd leaving him with a better view of those customers who were seated. He managed to retain his fascination for wonder, adventures and tall tales told and it was this that had all his senses picking up on the boasts of one man in particular. Perhaps it was the volume or possibly the tale itself but certainly, Silas thought he recognised the voice. Forgetting all about his quest, he then made his way toward the table only to discover that the man in question had his back to him. The boy stood and then listened intently, trying to make sense of what was being said. Amused, a second drunk alerted the storyteller to the curious child that had crept up on them. Then, the man turned and everything immediately made sense to Silas.

'Pater! Oh, Pater, you're back from France!' he shouted.

So delighted was Silas that, for the first time in his life, he moved to embrace his father but, as he did, he realised that everyone was laughing at him.

'Why are they laughing father? Are you unharmed?' he continued 'is all well with the king?

More laughter ensued but not even a smile was offered by Clifford. As his father's face neared his own, it became bright red with fury and everyone except Silas realised that he just did not know how to react.

The crowd grew as word of the encounter spread.

'Is there an alehouse called France then?!' said one of his drinking buddies.

'Make me a shield, Smith, to carry these tankards on!' said another.

'Make way for sir Clifford!' came a voice from the fireplace.

'Good news lads, this round is on 'enery!'

Some of them laughed so loud and so childishly that they

were starting to fall on top of one another.

Clifford's head was now spinning and, as he could not bring himself to laugh at the situation, he decided to confront the boy head-on. Realising that he now had an audience, he believed that a public rebuttal would suffice. He told Silas that he did not know what he was talking about. As Silas managed to eventually get his arms around the large, pungent and cold-hearted Clifford Smith, he struggled to make sense of what was happening. Perhaps he is on a secret mission, he mused and that thought was so thoroughly convincing that he continued to press his father further.

Clifford, now angry, held Silas at arm's length. He shook him and, as he did, water and snow splashed everywhere, Silas's ruddy head now like an oversized paint brush being shaken.

'Now listen here urchin, I don't know what you think it is that you know. I've never met you, never seen you before and I don't…have…any…children. And you can tell that to your soft mother too!'

As much fun as they were having, combined with the supposed camaraderie of pissed men, the atmosphere suddenly turned sour as he had given himself away to his drinking comrades. Drunk as they were, many of them were skilled craftsmen, their forefathers having built the Minster and they otherwise thought themselves good Christian men and did not like what they had just heard. It had become silent almost instantaneously. However, it was the landlord who chose to rescue the boy. He took the message sent from Fawkes, threw it behind the bar and then took him outside where the boy broke down in tears and he stood and flapped his arms, his eyes rolling. Silas wasn't given to crying and, in years to come, it would be something he did rarely but the whole experience had been completely overwhelming for him: the noise, the smells, seeing his father after so long, the loud and threatening drinkers and, added to that, another mission failed. For some minutes, he remained in denial so the landlord helped him to fill in the blanks.

It would have been too much for anyone to take in, especially someone who rarely doubted the word of others but, for Silas whose imaginary world had revolved around his father's deeds, the experience had been almost surreal. Still, he tried hard to believe that his father was on some clandestine mission but it was the comment about his dear mother that had hit home and would not go away. As he wandered aimlessly, that part would not stop replaying in his mind. Silas had never seen how brutal his father could be with his mother so as he ambled and sloshed home, he struggled to understand any of it. As best he could, Bolt tried to nuzzle his sodden nose into the boy's spongy legs. Instead of going straight home, he found himself trudging the increasingly darkening streets of York trying to make sense of it all.

Even when he had concluded that his dad had been deceiving him for so long, he could not understand why. When I knew Silas in later years, his ability to always see the best in other people was, besides many other attributes, something that touched me deeply. Had my mother known? He thought. Why would she lie? Am I not going to be a knight? As the light completely left York on that afternoon, it left Silas too.

When he returned, Mary was already beside herself. For years he had never left her sight and now she feared the worse every time he was late. He decided, in a quite forthright manner, to ask her when his father would be back from France. Mary stiffened, smiled, rambled and then set about moving around wooden and pewter cutlery, shoes, brushes and soap only to put them back where they had once been. She attempted an answer then changed the subject and, at that moment, he understood that she was trying to protect him. Silas would never see his father again and, within a few years, would think of him no more.

The good years

Silas counted his blessings and those blessings would be his go-to place for the rest of his days. Despite the almost constant abuse that he still suffered on a day-to-day basis, he loved his job and he loved York. As time passed, he accepted that his father was a rogue and loved his mother that much more for it. He would remember the few months that followed his visit to the Golden Fleece as happy times. He delighted in watching Mary refine her craft and was proud of how well received her quills were. Despite his shortcomings, he was learning more day by day and already had a map of York in his head which he could access at any time. However, it would forever be human beings that created problems for him and he had already deduced that Bolt was better company than almost all adults. He regularly visited the Queen of Sheba, no doubt because they could share each other's fantastical nonsense but also because Silas was able to naturally offer kindness and love wherever and whenever it was needed and he had recognised that the queen was very frail and vulnerable. His mother knew of the visits but he did not tell Fawkes despite it being recorded as one of the many reasons for him being late.

Neither did it bother him that the old woman was almost at a right angle when she walked, her head practically facing the floor. All he saw when he looked upon her was the Queen of Sheba and there is little doubt that, in return, this eccentric sexagenarian fed the boy's already fertile imagination. He would marvel as she received court each morning. The court consisting of just one courtier.

Rising from her rickety chair, she would place a shawl over her head and her back and would then begin to parade, waving with one hand and using her stick with the other and announcing,

'The Queen of Sheba!'

Silas would join in, revelling in the cheers from his nearby admirers. This in itself was a measure of Silas's fertile imagination as, in reality, it was her neighbours telling him to "bugger off home" and "quieten down."

The queen would allow her vassal a spoonful of beer each day and then remind him that he was late for work although Silas would not leave until a fire was struck and he had rubbed balm into the old lady's agonising neck. This would repeat day in, day out but one morning she stopped him.

'You are such a good boy Silas. Why do you keep coming back here?'

'Tis my duty, you are the queen.'

And, with that, he left. Truth be told, he was quite ecstatic that he now served two queens. One day, I will definitely be one of the king's knights, he told himself and he believed it, if only he had known what was to come in his adult years.

Around those snickleways which had become offshoots to the busy branch that was Coppergate, there were endless whispers and rumours. Much of this bypassed the boy as it was mostly mother's talk. No wonder, as the now-infamous predator had still not been caught. Constables marvelled at how obedient the local public had become as curfew fell and so made it their business to put an end to the threat.

Petty crime was rife in York as it was elsewhere in England but murder was relatively rare. So abhorrent was such an act that the general public would make it their business to have a culprit arrested and punishment would be unrelenting and severe. Add to that, the insinuation of rape and you would have three-quarters of the city looking for suspects. Nevertheless, the perpetrator had not been caught. Silas simply wasn't aware enough, or even old enough for that matter, to pay much attention. Even his mother's priorities lay with his continuing occupation and employment and, as there were periods where it seemed as though the killer had either left the city or had died, there were spells when some almost forgot about it altogether.

There would have been some expectation, at around seven years of age, that Silas would have been offered an apprenticeship although, as yet, it had never been mentioned. Most boys would be employed around that age and Mary would often reflect on her good fortune for it was by chance, and chance alone, or as Mary would say, by God's Grace, that Silas was in such a favoured position with William Fawkes. And, he was learning day by day as he came face to face with the realities of sixteenth-century York.

That summer, on one of the hottest days the city had ever known, he found himself leaving Goodramgate and ambling behind a large middle-aged woman who was pushing a cart carrying several plants. He strained to see what they were and marvelled at how green they looked. Admirably, the woman had been trying to grow one of those quite new but also quite alien lettuces. Silas had never seen one before.

Just as his imaginative ventures began to take him to the new world where there were fantastic creatures and wonderful fruits, he saw her tumble. She dramatically fell head first into the trolley with her legs unintentionally reaching skyward revealing that she had nothing on under her skirts. His immediate reaction was to help the poor woman but so startled by what he witnessed was he, that he rushed home instead with Bolt dutifully following.

'Silas! Whatever is the matter? Are you hurt?' asked a distraught Mary Smith.

'Oh mater! Oh, mater! I have seen the most dreadful thing…'

Stumbling over his words, he went on to explain about the woman, the cart, the lettuce but also what he witnessed thereafter.

'It was the most dreadful injury, mater. Methinks suffered in battle! Oh…. poor woman!'

He looked at his mother realising that she had become transfixed. At first, there was no expression at all although she was unquestionably holding her breath and her eyes widened. And then, she laughed so loud that she frightened the bloody life out of him. She stood, walked away and laughed even louder whilst he sat desperately trying to work out what was funny. She turned back again and clasped his small cheeks in her hands.

'Oh, my dear, beautiful, innocent little boy. Promise me you will never grow up' and she kissed him.

He never asked again about the incident and the intricacies, delicacies, complications and nuances of the stronger sex would be as foreign to Silas as the new world for some time to come. Neither did he want to know although, now and again, he found that some of those realities were unavoidable. He too had become familiar with Grope Lane but had returned home to tell his mother that men and women went there "to do battle" and this obsession with conflict of his was to protect him from many realities for some time. However, he had arrived at one certainty whilst still a child and that was that women were kinder. He found women more understanding and patient with how he was and, they almost always looked and smelled nicer too.

As a means of trying to give the boy more responsibility, William Fawkes returned to more important matters and set up a schedule whereby Silas would pick up a whole day's commissions at the Liberty Gate and return to the same location at the end of the day and, to some degree, this did improve his general performance and punctuality although it also gave him the opportunity to take advantage when it suited him. Just beyond the Liberty Wall of the Minster was a large clearing. Silas wasn't to know it but it but it was being prepared for building and, although it would be a few more years before works started in earnest, the new build would become the Church of St Michael Le Belfrey which would be the preferred place of worship for William Fawkes and where his son, Edward and, in turn, his son, Guy would be baptised in years to come. Children even younger than Silas were constantly being reprimanded and chased off the land but it was to be a much older delinquent that would take full advantage of it. To be more precise, it was a quite specific location just beyond the clearing that, every so often, a gruff and portly peasant would set up a small stage and then perform twice a day for the discerning unwashed of York and Silas made sure that, on each occasion, he caught at least part of it. Some of the subtleties as well as the adult humour completely bypassed him but the people laughed and jeered and he loved to take part too as well making sure to keep himself half-hidden.

Years later, Silas would recall that the first show put on by Bayard, and the first ever that Silas watched, had something to do with monks. In the performance, the Pope had travelled to England to inspect its fine monasteries. The drunken monk welcoming the said pontiff swayed back and forth, hiccupped and attempted Latin in a Yorkshire accent. He had a huge backside and, unseen by his holiness, was a second monk using it as a pillow. As the Pope became more impatient, the first one tried to back up but as he did so, the second fell to the floor and two young maidens ran out from beneath his habit.

'We tend to the poor…err…hungry and homeless children!' he protested nervously.

Already the crowd was not only laughing but hurling faux abuse at the characters.

As the Pope toppled too, he farted, a testament to sixteenth-century special effects, and, as he did, a mini-Henry the Eight appeared from his rear proclaiming 'I am the defender of the faith!'

It was, of course, a child dressed as Henry but if you could say one thing about Bayard it was that his skits were always current. That very title had only recently been awarded to Henry leaving many feeling that he was in the pocket of Rome or if you prefer, its backside.

The crowd bawled with laughter and if they hadn't known better, they may well have presumed Bayard to be a prophet as the questionable practices of monks, friars and nuns would soon find themselves at the fore of English reform. Vulgar as they were, Bayard's performances lifted the spirits of the overburdened populace and rather than break it up, officials were often found to be at the front, fully participating.

Of course, Silas would forget to break away and fulfil his duties and was often seen scurrying toward the gate just before curfew.

Three weeks after that show, Silas realised that his tasks had made him late for Bayard's performance but nevertheless loitered a while just to watch them packing up. He looked down at his feet which were idly kicking stones although he hadn't previously been aware of it. When he looked up again, Bayard appeared right in front of him. Silas jumped and then squeaked.

'So, you're here at last?' said Bayard.

Silas knew not what to make of such an unusual introduction so prepared himself for a bollocking, for that was what adults usually offered.

'Of course…' said Bayard 'this is exactly the right time…'

'My name is Bayard and this is Dunstan, he's my…err…apprentice. Do you know what an apprentice is, Silas?'

'Oh yes sir, I am hoping for a harprentersherp myself, I believe it to be himinent…'

Bayard smiled. Northerners spent so much time dropping the letter H that they presumed it was good English to add them back in, usually where they didn't belong. A practice that lasted for hundreds of years.

'Stay strong lad…' said Dunstan 'challenging times are ahead.'

Bayard poked his protégé.

Silas wasn't listening. Instead, he was full of pride, the entertainers had spoken to him no less and called him by name. He also decided that he liked the two shoddy showmen and became particularly fascinated with Dunstan. He was slightly older than Bayard which left the boy wondering how he could possibly be an apprentice but he smiled a lot and looked kind. That was the top and bottom of Silas's assessment and it was never to change.

Over the next few weeks, Silas was to see Dunstan pop up all over York, never close enough to speak to but he always waved. A smile and a wave offered were like balm to Silas. William Fawkes liked him, or so he presumed, he served the Queen of Sheba and now one of the king's own entertainers was his best friend. How Silas thought that Dunstan was employed by the king or even that he was his friend, no one would ever know but it gave him renewed confidence. However, as with all good news, it was measured against another completely new experience.

The day after that first show, he believed that he saw a jester behind Bayard's stage and, at first, thought nothing of it. However, for a while, the jester was to appear and disappear in almost every place that Silas frequented and that included his bedroom. He had even tried engaging with this jester but every time he appeared, he faded away once more. This troubled him so much that he thought to seek counsel. The next time that Dunstan waved to him, he gave chase almost frightening the life out of him. Initially, Dunstan gave the impression that he wasn't allowed to talk to him but Silas insisted on telling him.

'Oh….' said Dunstan 'no….no….no…that's not good. Do not have anything to do with him young Silas. Do not look and do not try to talk to it. Just be yourself and it will go away.'

That was the sum total of his advice. Silas got the bit about not talking to the jester but was clueless about being himself. I'm an idiot, he thought. Some say the village idiot. People laugh when they look at me, I'm worthless. He found himself muttering and this was possibly the first time that he had verbalised his low self-esteem, reciting an itinerary of how others had measured him. In those first few years of his life it had been so constant that he was bound to absorb it, he was certain to believe it. He wondered too how he even managed to secure a job but "be yourself" meant nothing to him. However, Dunstan's heart-warming albeit erratic presence in York was enough to give him strength and there would be much more to come.

One night he could not sleep. Now that he had responsibilities, he rarely bothered his mother at night but on this occasion, he walked into her room to tell her that he was troubled. She was sound asleep. He looked upon her sure that he had the dearest and most beautiful mother in all of England but, as he did, he saw the jester above her. He could well have believed that the fool was actually floating for that is how it seemed but it was dark. Silas was almost always scared. The constant teasing, berating and being told that he was not good enough made him nervous before each errand and every engagement with another soul but he did not fear the jester. He would never know why but he simply did not and during this most unorthodox confrontation, he remained calm and self-assured.

'You have no power over me or my mother. Begone dark one…' he said quietly, eloquently and confidently.

The jester seemed to flicker as a dying candle would and was then gone.

'Ruff!' said Bolt and followed Silas out. Mary did not wake. Silas would never remember those words but, for the time being, the jester was gone.

5 The rain

Therefore, for some time, all seemed well. No one around Dead Alley knew anything at all about the local celebrity quill maker and neither did Mary bother to tell anyone. This was one thing that she absolutely had in common with her son, they were both happy to be solitary. Neither of them particularly liked the idea of loneliness but they usually felt better in their own company or in each other's. Her clientele was centred mostly around the Minster Quarter so it made sense that, now and again, Silas could add some deliveries to his duties. He had also revelled in the ancient craft that had excited and now consumed his mother. By now, Mary was turning out bespoke quills as different scribes had their own personal preferences. She would show these to Silas and explain how the shape affected the speed and fluidity of lettering. Carefully, she would show him the calamus, the part that was originally attached to the skin of the bird, and how it could be carved for many specific and desired outcomes. Over time, although she could only write a few words, she would also show him chancery italic hand and he would jump ecstatically as he recognised the calligraphy he had seen so many times at the abbey and at the Minster.

'Learning is the answer to everything, Silas' she would say often 'listen to your betters and masters, the more you know, the greater chance you will have of getting on in life.'

She would also apologise to the boy not just because the rest of his family seemed to have disappeared but because she could not offer him an education. She was grateful for the Church. They would attend and then go home without a word being spoken to anyone unless it was in confession but Mary knew well her New Testament and it also increasingly intrigued Silas. Come what may, and that would include The Reformation, Silas would refer back to the teachings of

Christ always and would remember to follow them no matter how others behaved.

Although still infrequent, there were more visitors to the house than there had ever been before but none were family. Silas now had no family to speak of besides his mother and the dog, which one could suppose he only half-owned.

One spring day in 1521, Silas had all but delivered the quills and had also completed several errands. By now, he insisted on calling these "missions" and that would not change throughout his life. Quite often, as he zigzagged the city, he would bypass Dead Alley but, on this occasion, he found it full of officials. He stopped to assess the situation but became mesmerised by what they wore, and how they carried themselves and he even started to count them. This was his obsession kicking in again. Hierarchy, people of importance, legal matters, honour and duty. He recognised the sheriff, Roger Geggs but, initially, no one else. By now, Bolt had adapted to the erratic way in which Silas would circumnavigate the city. Silas, he had learned, seemed to have three speeds and he would change from one to the other seemingly without reason and always without notice but Bolt was very obedient. If Silas stopped, so did the dog.

For a while, with the dog sitting on his left foot, Silas just watched but it didn't take long before he worked out that there was a drama unfolding. And soon, he was sure that they were all congregating around his house. He ran forward but was stopped. A firm but compassionate grip stopped him from going any further. Bolt stopped too and stayed by his side. When he looked up, he saw that it was his boss, William Fawkes who had hold of him.

'Can't go in there Silas. Just stay close to me' he said.

He let Silas stand in front of him but had draped his arms securely but considerately over the boy's arms. Silas then realised that the door to his home was open and inside was Mrs Tumble but she was crying. He had seen Mrs Tumble a few times but had never seen her cry before.

His attention then turned to the sheriff who was insensitive enough to mention the spate of murders that had taken place in York.

Silas was, and would forever be, slow to pick up, especially on emotions displayed by others but as Mrs Tumble came running out, he knew exactly what had taken place although he so very much wanted to be wrong. She hugged him and told him that he could not go into the house. When asked about this many years later, Silas would recollect that no one actually said that his mother was dead or that she had been murdered but he knew it in that instant. It was Mrs Tumble's out-of-character embrace that had informed him. Bolt had slipped past all of them and into the house and he whimpered as he looked upon his mistress slumped on the floor in a foetal position. She had one large wound to her head under which was a pool of blood. Bolt lay down and pathetically put his head next to hers.

Silas could barely hear above his own heartbeat. Panic had set in and, as he looked around, he noticed that the targets had not been put away from the morning's archery practice. He politely asked the bemused William Fawkes if he could tidy up but he did not reply. Then, his arms started to flap and Fawkes gently secured them. The scene outside the house was somewhat chaotic but Silas did not notice that Fawkes, another church official and a monk were furiously falling out with the sheriff.

'Whether this is the work of the same man or not, the people of York will not live with such evil any longer!' said Fawkes.

The sheriff argued that they had arrested, tried and sentenced someone four months earlier.

'Well, it's quite clear you had the wrong bloody man!' protested Fawkes.

Silas was oblivious to it all and would never recall any of the detail but to anyone else present, it was clear that William Fawkes was invested in this particular case and he must have surely thought that it could have been prevented.

'Must be an outsider' proclaimed the sheriff.

'If only that were true' said Fawkes 'this is the darkest of deeds. This man lives amongst us.'

Everyone present reeled back in horror at such a suggestion although in their hearts they knew it to be true.

At that moment, they decided to add more watchmen to secure the city after curfew but came up with little else in the way of a solution.

Eventually, Mrs Tumble told Silas that he could not go into the house and took him to her home nearby. No one would ever know what Silas may have envisioned as a home for the tireless Mrs Tumble but it was as equally humble as his own if not sparser. He caught a glimpse of her husband although he didn't speak and then he tried to sleep on the floor downstairs whilst Bolt anxiously whimpered outside. The time between Mary's death and her pauper's burial was fleeting. Mrs Tumble attended and Fawkes stood in the distance but did not speak. Neither did the priest have anything to say to the boy as he didn't even recognise him. Silas had worshipped in the same church four times a week since birth and yet the priest did not know who he was and possibly didn't care. Silas had one very brief conversation with Mrs Tumble who made it clear that he now had to make his own way in the world.

Little Silas and his dog stood looking down at a rain-soaked grave that must have had more than ten people in it already, trying to make sense of it all. The very thought of his pure mother being with one stranger was too much to bear let alone so many especially having been dead so long already.

The relentless rain noisily spattered and plopped into the mud and dirt becoming so overwhelming that it soon drowned out everything else.

His head seemingly weighing three times what it usually did, he slowly looked up, saw the Minster in the distance and then eventually up toward the heavy black sky above

Yorkshire, the piercing rain stinging his face.

'I know you are with Jesus, mother and… the Saints will be in need of your very fine quills… I will see you again one day. I will be a good boy. Your…Silas. Your Lord Silas. I will forever be at your side and you by mine. Do not leave me altogether mother, for I am nothing without you. Ye that giveth me life, I owe you everything.'

He then knelt in the filth and said the Lord's Prayer. When he turned to his right, Bolt's head was down too.

As you can imagine, once the prayer was finished, he had no idea what to do so he sat down in the soil as the rain drowned out all that could be seen or heard. What a pitiful sight that skinny boy must have seemed as he lay there drenched with only the dog and the sound of torrential rain for company. Hopelessness, loneliness, grief, guilt and worthlessness took turns to wash over and through him. What a disgrace this was as well as a poor testament to Tudor society that in his misery he was entirely alone apart from a three-legged mongrel.

Minutes passed, perhaps even hours but, eventually, he stood and thought to make his way to the Liberty Gates but he could not leave her. Certain that his mother was in Heaven, even he could not understand why he found it so difficult to leave the grave where only her mortal remains lay but he was to linger there for some time.

Eventually, Bolt tugged at his clothing and he took this as a sign to turn to practical considerations and so plodded toward the Minster. Still numb, he awaited his contact and, when he appeared, Silas simply said,

'Am I still in your employ?'

Which was, for once, exactly the right question to ask.

'Master Fawkes has said that you are to be here in the morning at first bells' said the clerk.

He knew too that this wasn't good news. It was then that, inexplicably, he decided to return to Dead Alley. For some time, Silas stared at his home except, it wasn't his home anymore as Mrs Tumble had told him that the landlord had taken possession immediately. Silas wasn't bothered about any of the few things that remained inside, he had kept hold of some of his mother's quills and that was enough. If only he had known then that those quills would remain with him until 1542, half a lifetime away, it may at least have given him some solace on that darkest of days.

The Shack
He was aware, as he stood in the rain and gawping at his former home, that people were watching him. They were also making comments about him although, on this occasion, they would be mistaken in thinking that his head was empty. All that experience of mapping York in his noggin was now coming to the fore. Silas had always known that adjacent to the property was a lean-to, no more than a dilapidated shack. It was run down and neglected and there was no way into it even from his former home. It was almost as if it had been forgotten about and, no wonder, as it was also impossible to get to. However, Silas had an idea. An idea in which his stringy frame would be to his advantage. At the end of Dead Alley, you could more or less make out the graveyard to All Saints Church beyond. Trees, bushes, bracken, roots, brambles, nettles and weeds had knitted an unsurpassable barrier between the church and the street. Not that anyone would have accessed the church from that direction during the previous hundred years, but all the same, Silas was aware of it. At that moment he carefully explained in detail his battle plan to his trusty steed, a detailed and complex quest which would ultimately provide shelter for them both.

'Unto the enemy, Bolt! Whereunto thy will secure yonder castle. I beseech thee abide and victory will be ours!'

Bolt, cross-eyed, looked at his master as if he were now speaking a foreign tongue but dutifully stood.

This was an almost impossible feat and one in which Silas's little frame was left in a condition not much better than when he had fallen in the nettles. It took him almost ninety minutes to get through the foliage and then do a U-turn and get close enough to touch the shack and, to his amazement, it was still there as he had imagined. Unfortunately, it too was held hostage by nature and the old door was barely visible, the rain only making matters worse. He had continued to instruct Bolt throughout although it was only at that point in the journey that he realised that the dog hadn't followed him. Now he was stuck, unable to go forward or backwards and it was also very dark. Silas tugged, pushed, pulled, stretched, fell and then started again but could go no further. It was likely that Bolt could have made it to their intended destination but, instead, went to sleep on the narrow entrance made by his master. Within half an hour, the boy had given up and slept where he was.

The dawn chorus woke him well before the church bells started and, almost as if there hadn't been an interval, he started wrestling once more with mother nature for whom he was no match. However, even the most stubborn of roots eventually began to fall away and he found himself suddenly upright and free.

'Just needed a little help from my friend here' said a voice from behind him.

'Yapp!' said Bolt who had now caught up.

Although Silas still wasn't in a position to turn around, he recognised the accent, if not the voice immediately. They were the reassuring, albeit southern ones of Dunstan.

'Oh…err…at your service…good sir…thank ye…'

Silas wasn't sure how to address Bayard's apprentice but was relieved that he wasn't to spend the rest of his days on the wrong side of a grave. Dunstan was wielding an adze, a long-handled tool with a downward pointing cutting edge attached. In minutes, they were both directly in front of the door, still without any explanation as to why Dunstan was there. The door was unquestionably the best feature of the hovel. It was strong and possibly dated from the twelfth century meaning that whoever first lived there would have seen the Minster being erected. It was made of solid oak so, although it was well weathered, most of it was intact. The same could not be said of the surrounding wattle and daub. Where the branches and roots hadn't consumed it, they had punctured it instead. Neither was there much of a roof and, on first inspection, it was hard to distinguish between what was an inside and what wasn't. Dunstan told him that he would have to throw Silas through one of the holes as it was the only way in. A beam of sunlight illuminated what there was of an interior and the sudden jettisoning of a boy into it had rabbits scurrying everywhere. If anything, Silas was upset that he had disturbed them for he couldn't care less whether they continued to live there or not. He stood and peeped out through the rutted hole only to find that Dunstan was gone leaving the adze behind. Given the almost impossible task of accessing it, you would easily be convinced that the heap of wood, straw, hair and animal dung was worthless but not to Silas. Not only had he convinced himself that this would be his home, but he was also already thinking of it as an extension to where he had lived only days earlier and the truth was that it may well have been at one time. It was this that had him facing a damp wall that was overcome with ivy and wildlife, acknowledging what lay at the other side. Mary would forever be awaiting him there, just feet away, he told himself.

He found the adze awkward but soon understood its diverse applications and so set about trying to clear the doorway. Meanwhile, his brain was doing what it usually did. A fantasy about this, a memory of that, a conversation that never took place, an altogether different fantasy, a chat with an imaginary friend and so on. Real life was bound to intervene at some point although it would be anyone's guess when. Bolt had become a very obedient dog and was only given to making sounds when he was hungry, when he was being a guard dog and also when he was answering Silas.

However, inexplicably and out of nowhere he lifted his head to the sky and said,

'Haroo!'

And this had Silas jumping up, struggling to hurriedly negotiate the way out again when he wondered how it could have been possible for Dunstan to fit through. When he got to the Minster, over two hours late, there was no one there. He could not possibly lose his job. Everything was now about survival in every sense of the word so he waited. Eventually, he leaned on the gate post of the Liberty Gate as he was already attracting unwelcome glances and comments. He looked down. Almost every garment he wore was ripped and parts were missing. He had scratches and grazes on all the exposed parts of his body. He was dusty and bleeding. If just one person suspected him of being a beggar, all would be over.

Truth be told, he knew not what to do so wisely stayed. At around five o clock, he saw a tall figure crossing the precinct and he was sure that it was Fawkes. He cried out. It seemed as though everyone stopped and turned except for William Fawkes. Silas tried once more, Fawkes turned and saw the boy and anyone who witnessed this would tell you that he seemed both indecisive and evasive. He continued walking only to hear the call once more. It was then that he marched back toward Silas, furious. Fawkes grabbed the boy's arm and took him to one side. At that moment he would have been entirely within his rights to chastise the boy and no one would have looked twice if he had beaten him. After all, he had hardly been the ideal employee and his eccentric ways had reflected poorly on Fawkes as an employer. He had heard every rebuke, insult and lampoon regarding the child but he had put up with it. Why? No one would ever know. As brusque and business-like as he would become in later years, he had also won a reputation for compassion. Maybe it was his respect for the boy's mother or even something more but, at that moment, he pitied him.

'Sir…I am…this…it is so…of such importance. I…'

William Fawkes could tell that the boy was shaking.

'Calm down boy. I know why you were late'

Silas said nothing but understandably looked confused.

'The ragged showman, yonder'

He pointed toward the rickety stage.

'A fool's errand I would say. If you have anything there it will not be worth having. However, if by God's Grace you can sleep within what remains of that shack for five nights or more, legally it will be yours.'

The sun had come out. This was manna from Heaven. Silas almost wanted to rush back straight away but, instead offered an explanation.

'Twas Bolt'

'I beg your pardon,' said Fawkes.

'I was completely lost in my task. Then…Bolt said "errand!"'

'I doubt very much…oh very well. Listen, boy, if it wasn't for your mother's misfortune it is unlikely that I would tolerate your tardiness, your strange manners, lack of discipline…'

The sun had gone in again. Silas was sure that he had found a home and lost a job in less than a day.

'I cannot in clear conscience keep you in my employ…'

What Fawkes was really saying was that there would be increasing pressure for him to provide an employee of Silas's age with an apprenticeship, something he, or the Church, could ill afford.

Unintentionally, Silas became all puppy-eyed and limp but Fawkes didn't notice.

'However, the last thing I would want is for York to have another beggar on its streets so, I may have a solution. There is an acquaintance of mine…someone who by marriage will soon be my brother-in-law…'

'Oh yes, sir…I am...'

'Please listen boy and, take heed, he will not tolerate ill-manners. He is a businessman and nothing more. He is intent on making himself wealthy by…well…almost any means. Your work will change. Nevertheless, he will have many an errand for which you will be useful…'

Silas then spluttered out the world "apprenticeship" or as near as he could manage.

'There will be no apprenticeship, he will be your master and you will do his bidding but…he will pay you… something.'

Yet again he tried to interrupt but to no avail.

'He lives at the house with a red door on Goodramgate, there is only one. You must report there today before curfew. His name is Master Robert Hall.'

Silas nodded.

'I wish you well. Do not return here again unless doing business and do not ask for me again.'

Fawkes turned to walk away but saw, in the corner of his eye, the boy slump to the floor. His inquisitiveness got the better of him and so he looked back over his shoulder.

Silas had taken to his knees so that they were across the border that led to the Minster precinct whilst his feet were still in York. He then began to pray.

'Dear Lord. Accept my prayers for your agent, Master Fawkes for his good Christian soul and for all he does for those less fortunate…'

Fawkes pretended not to look although he had stopped in his tracks with his back to the boy. Others looked on.

'…. he saved my good mother from ruin and ran to her aid in her last moments. Neither would I be alive without his charity. Dear Lord, may your blessings rain down on him and his family for all their days. Amen.'

Passers-by were dumbfounded for there was no doubt that his petition was sincere. It would have been way beyond Silas's wits to feign such a performance to gain favour and neither did anyone suggest it. Momentarily, William Fawkes had considered that perpetual paradox, the one in which Silas could not, and never would, be able to string two words together but sounded as if he was possessed by an angel when he prayed. William's heart began to swell. Even at such a young age, few were so genuinely innocent, and as he slowly began to walk away, Fawkes knew that there was something about the child that he would miss.

6 Forest Adventures

That night, Silas and Bolt slept amidst the bracken in the church graveyard although this time, he was up before first light and knocking on the Queen of Sheba's door. She welcomed him in and gave him a small cup of watered-down wine. He looked even worse than the day before. Although Mary had owned only a few possessions, she did enjoy the luxury of a large half barrel that had been fashioned long ago by Doug Cooper. The hours Silas had spent in there, often finding the day's water filthier than he was. Unbelievably, the Queen of Sheba would limp to the river every few days and so offered her friend a reasonably clean cloth dipped in not very clean Ouse water. He looked a little better after rubbing a hundred varieties of bacteria into his cuts but there was hardly anything left of his clothes. The queen had found out about his mother's death but did not say how. Many years later, Silas would confess that if it hadn't been for William Fawkes, Dunstan and the Queen of Sheba he would never have survived and, unsurprisingly, no one had a bloody clue what he was on about when he said this. Almost as if nothing had happened, he welcomed the queen into court with the usual routine and he then headed toward Goodramgate. He had been down there a few times before but this was the first time that he noticed a quaint church half-hidden behind some medieval cottages. This was Holy Trinity, possibly half the size of his own church.

He told Bolt to wait near the church in case his new employer was not fond of dogs.

The house with the red door clearly belonged to someone with means and, he observed, they even had a maid.

'I am…attending on…. the behalf. Haha! The Queen of Sheba!'

Even Silas was startled at the gibberish that came out as

the sentence had sounded very different in his mind.

'Are you quite sane?' said the haughty young maid.

'Master Robert Hall' he managed to say in one breath.

Then, a handsome young man around twenty-four years of age peered over her shoulder.

'Haha! What have we here?! Are you Fawkes's boy? What a bloody mess! Take him into the kitchen.'

Silas was glad to find himself inside but was already certain that he was way beyond his station in the scheme of things. I can't even say what's in my head he thought, chastising himself once more.

A thoroughbred greyhound bounded in and jumped on Silas and then licked his face but then Hall sent it out.

'God's buttocks lad! What on Earth have you been up to?'

Silas opened his mouth to speak but was immediately interrupted, which was possibly just as well.

Robert Hall was now walking around the petrified child presumably weighing him up.

'I can see you're filling your hose boy. Don't be nervous with me, if you can do the job, we'll get on fine' he said stopping and then leant backwards.

'Haha!'

Silas almost jumped out of his rags.

'Been in a bear fight lad? What a bloody mess!' he said again.

'I'll make this a bit easier for you. I'll ask questions and you either nod or shake your head. Can you manage that Silage?'

Although he nodded, his heart suddenly weighed twenty pounds heavier as someone had found yet another derogatory derivative of his name.

'Silas sir…'

'Yes…very good…what I said, Silage.'

'I am a businessman and I'm getting very good at it.'

Silas nodded.

'No, no, no, lad. I haven't asked you anything yet!'

'I make money in the wool trade and also the growing glass industry. Anyone who matters desires glass and the bigger and more ornate it is the better. That's the future boy. Just think…'

And then Hall rambled for five minutes about his latest obsession during which Silas was nervously trying to work out when he should and should not nod. This sudden condition became so bad that his knees started to knock and this, in turn, succeeded in stopping the over-enthusiastic Robert Hall in his tracks. Hall looked bewildered.

'What are you doing now?'

Silas nodded and then shook his head. Hurriedly, Hall pulled over a stool and pushed the boy down onto it.

'Relax lad…we'll start again.'

'I do business with people in the city and beyond. Some of it is private and some…is very private. Do you understand what I mean?'

Hall found himself nodding in the hope that Silas might recognise the prompt and nod back.

'Sometimes you will deliver letters and items that must be signed for and no one else besides the recipient must see it.'

Nothing.

'The recipient means the person you are meant to give it to...'

Silas nodded so hard that the stool wobbled.

Six questions later, during which Hall had thrown back almost half a pint of mead to help his nerves, Silas sat there not knowing what to do with his little head and his neck soon became very sore.

'That door…there…is the back entrance. Never come to the front again. Sometimes I will give you an errand, sometimes it will be the maid but do not come to the front.'

How his heart started banging. Was this a nod for yes, I will come to the back door or, a shake meaning no, I won't come to the front door?

Fortunately, Hall didn't wait for an answer.

'You can stay here and Jenny will feed you and then she will order you new clothes and…was that a satchel?'

Silas nodded.

'She will get you a new one of those…oh…and…new shoes.'

Silas threw himself at his new master's feet.

'Oh, good God! No, no lad. No need for that. It's business. Do your job well and I'll look after you, even pay you I will, but no questions, do you understand?'

Silas liked the idea of no questions. A world without questions seemed ideal to him as he never had any answers. How different this man was from his previous master but Silas did not think to make comparisons, he was quietly giving thanks under his breath, sure that his mother up above was still looking after him.

Robert Hall also told him that he wouldn't be needed for a few days and that he should call around the following Friday. As he was still in rags, it made sense that he got to work on his home and keep away from the public eye. He had even found a few edible berries at one end of the graveyard but took care not to take chances with anything else. If only he had known that, one day, he would become an expert on all wild plants and fungi as well as maps.

Bolt slept most of the time and, at first, Silas did more damage than repair to the shack. Determined to move the door, he hacked away at what must have been a hundred years of roots and overgrowth. In less than a day, the door was exposed but the hinges were solid, it simply would not move but undeterred, he used the hole in the wall to get in and out and began clearing the interior. Every inch that was recovered had Silas giving thanks once more and he acknowledged that this was the most rewarding work he had ever done, remembering to chat to his mother throughout. He set about layering the cut branches so that the hole in the roof could be covered and although this was an improvement, it still let in daylight and rain. After two days, he could see a room, the possibility of an entrance and also a roof. He had a home. He remembered what Fawkes had said so made sure that he slept there overnight, Bolt keeping him warm. On the third day, he used the adze with increasing expertise to clear a path from the shack, through the graveyard and into Dead Alley and Silas was very careful to make sure that the entrance was just big enough for the dog who was still slightly wider than he was. Not only was the entrance difficult to detect but, by and large, people were not interested. They could not see the shack from the alley and, even when word had got out that there was a dwelling beyond and that Lord Sillyarse was living in it, all sorts of rumours spread. It was nothing more than a hole in the ground or, a box in which he slept. Over time, these would become so much more elaborate. Reputedly, Silas was harbouring witches and some said that he guarded the entrance to hell itself. He would never care. After the fourth day, he stood back and admired his handiwork.

'Castle Cooper' he whispered.

Why he had given it his grandfather's name no one would ever know but this would add to the delusion which eventually made Lord Silas notorious amongst the people of York.

Eventually, Castle Cooper would be a home with a secure door and roof, a borrowed table and stool and cartoons with stick figure drawings appeared on the plaster. This was the boy's record of good times spent with his mother and they were never to be erased.

As Silas arrived back at the house of Robert Hall, he knocked on the back door. The greyhound barked and Bolt replied. Surprisingly, Robert opened the door.

'God's teeth lad! You look even worse. What hour is it?'

Silas didn't know whether they were still doing nod or shake or not but presumed it to be a rhetorical question.

'Ah yes! Good and early. Jenny!'

Jenny came running.

'Got his things?'

'Yes sir' she replied.

'Go with Jenny lad, when you are done, we will talk.'

Silas was very keen to obey but was taken aback when he walked into the living quarters to see a tub full of water before him.

'Everything off and get in!' said Jenny.

Silas stared at her. Surely, she couldn't be serious. I had a wash in December, he told himself. But Jenny was as insistent as he was hesitant. He may well have been more cooperative if she wasn't so young. Silas guessed that she was around nineteen years of age but it was probably that she was quite pretty which worried him. She thought nothing of it. He was a dirty child and her master wanted him clean and that was the top and bottom of it if you'll forgive the expression.

Reluctantly, he peeled off the sticky garments, folded them and put them carefully in a pile on the floor. Jenny walked over to the pile, grabbed the lot and threw them on the fire.

'Oh…. oh dear…what am I…'

'Just get in!' she barked.

He tentatively immersed himself in the water. It was extremely cold and his ridiculous performance left her in no doubt of that fact. Five minutes later, he was still only up to his knees and she was furious.

'Bubble…..ips…soo…coold. Ips…unberabubble…..'

She thrust her hand on his left shoulder and submerged him.

'Either you wash yourself… properly or I'll do it' she said wielding a brush that was obviously made for scrubbing the floor. Reluctantly, he set about washing himself with one hand only and the water turned a dark burgundy colour. His other hand protected his modesty throughout although Jenny reminded him that his thumb alone would have sufficed.

Then she left.

He looked around nervously, got out, dried himself and, as he did, he could see woollen and leather objects on the chair. They were quite magnificent and the new satchel was far superior to the one he had used previously. Proudly he stood, clean, whole and dressed.

'Lord Silas', he muttered whilst thrusting his chin into the air.

Then, Robert Hall walked in but, at first, said nothing.

'Well, tis an improvement I suppose but nothing fits. How is it that nothing ever fits you Silage? Never mind, to business.'

He then outlined the type of errands that Silas would be expected to do with more names and places than the Doomsday Book. Of course, Silas didn't retain one word of it. When he had finished, Robert opened the back door and, for the first time, saw Bolt.

'Haha haha! This has to be your dog. What a pair! You two should be on the stage!'

Silas took no offence and promised to return the following morning for his first errand.

Nut errant

Days, months and years soon passed. Working for Robert Hall was nothing like working for Fawkes. Silas no longer had his seal and therefore could not boast that the Archbishop of York was his boss. He soon got used to Hall's clandestine methods but did not understand them. There seemed to have been so many messages that had nothing at all to do with glass or wool but, by and large, he managed to do his master's bidding. Come March 1524, Silas was ten years old and Robert had married. What was most astonishing to Silas was that Robert did not marry any of the women he had seen him with but never asked why. Hall made good in supplying the boy with clothes but, of course, they never fit. He now resembled a string bean with a flurry of orange hair on top and his nose was already moulding itself into an upturned point. Bolt was slowing down but, nevertheless, went everywhere with Silas and the Queen of Sheba was now confined to her house. He still visited regularly and he would happily run any essential errands for her. He never once asked if she really was the Queen of Sheba and still held court every time he visited.

On two occasions, once when he fell down a dry well and another when he got stuck in the portcullis at Micklegate Bar, Dunstan seemed to appear out of nowhere. Curiously, this was something else he never questioned, it simply became an expectation. By now, Silas had turned falling down holes into an art form and some would follow him in the hope of seeing such an incident. His home was the queerest domicile on the planet but it remained home and it remained his. Silas had started to deliver messages beyond the walls of the city and had been assured that, soon, he would be expected to travel. Of course, he was excited. His head was still full of castles, palaces, kings, queens, knights, dukes and earls, demons, dragons, jousting, pixies, damsels in distress and marching armies. All of which could be found just beyond the city walls. At least that is what he thought.

Thanks to the strange home in the graveyard, the plethora of either mistaken or made-up names for him added to his enigmatic existence and thanks to all sorts of new rumours, Silas had been labelled. And, there were many labels ranging from village idiot to Lord Sillyarse and nut errant. A few even got this wrong and actually addressed him as Lord Silas and, as he was wont to do, never corrected them. He was almost constantly in a daydream which was wonderful for him as well as great entertainment for everyone else. He would catch a Bayard show whenever he could but rarely saw Bayard and Dunstan together again.

Silas had found a quite comfortable routine with Robert Hall but, one morning, all that was to change.

'Aha! Morning Silage! Time to venture forth at last! Time

to get my money's worth out of you…'

Hall then started to mumble as if he was calculating something.

'Mm…Where to start…Easingwold? Rosedale?'

He turned to Silas who was screwing up his eyes whilst his mouth was lopsided and wide open.

'Yes. Yes, you're right Silage, bit too much to begin with but I bet you are ready for an adventure in Galtres Forest. Hey?'

Realising that the boy had stopped breathing, Hall sat himself and Silas down and started again.

'You've been as far as Bootham and seen behind the Minster?'

Silas nodded and started to breathe again. Something familiar at last.

'You must have seen the treetops from the walls?'

Another nod.

'Every boy's dream I would say. What goes on in your mind when you think of the forest?'

This time he received an answer. Silas rattled off visions of fairy tales, knights, goblins and, of course, Robin Hood. What he didn't know until Robert Hall explained was that there was a vast and quite dense forest north of York and, to some degree, he was right, it was the stuff of fantasy and adventure.

Silas soon became most invested and excited, even when Hall started to reveal more about his business dealings.

He sat back and told him that the Yorkshire wool business had been thriving since the Bronze Age and was renowned for its quality. During the Middle Ages, monks kept sheep and would either sell the wool or process it themselves. There were also many very small but successful domestic concerns. Richard the First had introduced laws regarding standardisation and by the fifteenth century, an influx of Flemish weavers brought new methods. In Robert Hall's time, domestic wool manufacturing evolved into small industries but the tax was high. Robert had learned that by using monasteries, priories and individuals that he could evolve an almost hidden system of manufacture avoiding any tax or constraints. Of course, this meant a lot of connections, people who could keep quiet and wool changing hands in the middle of the night.

Almost bored with the tedium of such double-dealings, he had recently taken a keen interest in the production of glass thanks to a friend. Technological improvements meant that pieces of glass could be bigger, more ornately decorated and, where needed, less opaque. And, people with means wanted it. During the sixteenth century, chimneys and glass would be the ultimate sign of prosperity.

Unsurprisingly with his aspirations regarding glass, Hall could not resist the temptation to cut corners and save money where possible. To be clear, many citizens of York respected him because of his success but not so many members of the cloth as his love of money and how he acquired it seemed quite immoral. Later in life, it would be said about him that he was no lover of the faith. Perhaps they should have added that he was, at least, a great lover of his purse. And, whatever it was he was doing, it eventually paid off as he became very successful when he was a middle-aged man as he became the Mayor of York and a member of parliament.

Like you, Silas slept through all that stuff about sheep and glass awaiting his new assignment but perked up again when he once more boasted of the breathtaking forest north of the city. Common sense having prevailed, Robert said that he would have Silas go no further than the second village in the forest.

'There are villages in the forest?' he asked.

'Oh yes, lad. Some are hamlets as many of them don't have their own church but, yes, many settlements are under the same rule as York. In fact, it would be fairer to say that York is in the Forest of Galtres rather than the other way around. But they are free of the noise, smells and general bloody nuisance of the city, haha! You know all those pigs you see killed in the Shambles?'

He nodded.

'They are bred in the woods on a special diet of nuts and acorns and then brought to the city when they are fat enough. Pannage…'

'Eh?'

'It's what it's called when you ready stock in the wild, pannage. It is the most beautiful forest in England Silage, but…remember, forests are the king's land. If I were you I wouldn't even squish and eat a bug unless the wardens or regarders deemed it to be hunting…'

Robert was hoping, in vain, for a laugh. None came so he continued.

'But…all the timber you see in York…the gates, supports for the walls, the grand buildings…they all come from Galtres. That along with Henry's ships and all…'

'There'll be none left sir…'

Whenever Silas was brave enough to make a contribution, he awaited a retort or insult but, on this occasion, Robert Hall complimented him as he was completely right. Deforestation was already a problem and those who loved the woods knew it. In the sixteenth century, it was not out of the ordinary for many people to still live in the woods but slowly and surely their homes would be taken away from them.

For years, even if you were to ask both Silas and Hall, you would be hard pushed to define their relationship. There was no doubt that he was using the boy but he did eventually, start to grow on him. In return, Silas knew that he would never have the security of an apprenticeship or a trade, but was regularly employed and was paid. In his head, he was a knight errant, an emissary, a diplomat and an adventurer and this wasn't altogether nonsense as there did not seem to be any limit to what Robert Hall would ask him to do. You could suppose that for a man with no parenting skills and little real knowledge of how some adults could abuse a child of his age that Robert Hall would be the nearest thing Silas would ever know to a father. And, thankfully there were times when he would offer some caution,

'Leave the city via Bootham Bar. To your right you can see the forest entrance, it grows right up to the city walls. At first, there is a broad track, almost a road. Can you count boy?'

'I can count up to ten' he said.

'Count up to ten, thirty times. Then do the same five times over. Take that many steps'

Hall wanted to continue but could hear murmuring.

'One two…three…four…ten five time…'

'Not now! I need you to listen! Up to ten, thirty times. Then do it all again four more times.'

It was a blessing that Robert could not see his protégé's face as he was hurriedly recalculating which soon became a dark and heavy fog in the boy's mind.

'There, the track thins and then splits into three…'

'Times…four after thirty…times…. splits…'

Hall ignored him.

Take the one on the left until you see a straw-roofed cottage. That is Brint. Not many people live there. Ask for Isaac. Give him this and he will give you something in return. Turn around and come back here before curfew. Easy! You got all that?'

'Oh yes sir'

'One more thing. You know that I don't like you asking questions…well, neither do I wish to keep things from you if it's not necessary. Look inside the package.'

Silas hesitated, unsure as to whether he really had permission. Hall nodded and so he looked. He gasped. He had never seen so many coins.

'Look after it, show the coins to no one except Isaac and return safely and…never steal from me.'

'I swear sir. My mother would… er… weep in …

well...Heaven if I were to do such a thing.'

Robert Hall was never again to question it.

Outside, he looked down at Bolt wondering whether he could make the journey but realised that he might well need him for support and perhaps even the counting. Numbers were reverberating around his little cranium whilst constantly repeating the names he had been given. Everything seemed that much easier when Fawkes was his boss despite his didactic manner.

Often it was down to chance whether Silas could get in and out of the city but on this occasion, the guard knew Robert Hall. It would be years until Silas realised that many officials in York were in Robert Hall's pocket. Eventually, he would trust him with a seal that would grant him passage almost anywhere.

Galtres

The contrast between Silas's romantic idea of the forest and reality could not have been greater. Forest land was important to the economy and precious as it belonged to the king. Although Robert had been bursting to elaborate, he wisely kept many of the details of the mysterious woods beyond York, to himself. Although they were now somewhat depleted, there were once almost sixty townships within that vast area labelled as Galtres and they enjoyed many rights as well as allocated pastures. Pilgrims and travellers would often use York landmarks as signposts to guide them north and into the forest with All Saints, Pavement itself ensuring that a lantern burned day and night. The owners had the same rights as city dwellers and, depending on their location would have benefited from a bureaucratic hierarchy like no other. The natural resources and the "beasts of the forests" were most precious to the crown and as such, wardens, gamekeepers, riding masters, riding foresters and bow hunters had been employed on and off since the days of the Norman conquest. Some of those would have special duties if the king chose to hunt however infrequently that was. And, even if Robert had mentioned this in an attempt to put him at ease, there is no doubt that he would have kept the many dangers well hidden. A fox or a doe may well seem innocuous to Silas but the aforementioned beasts at one time also included wolves and wild stags and reports of bears and wild cats were frequent. Added to that were the almost cliché reports of bandits who reportedly lived in caves. Travellers were often approached by guides at Bootham Bar who would charge to take them safely to their destination although many of these were bandits as well. Amongst the many surprises in store for them was that this stunningly aesthetic wood had bogs and marshes that punctuated it and they had taken many a pilgrim victim. One of the details that Robert did emphasise was that practically all of it, even the wildest areas, were owned by someone. Historically, kings had granted lands to Holy Houses and individual churches, something which was being brought into question even as early as 1525. The fact that Silas was growing up in changing times did little to make his mission easier. The king wasn't as distant as one might presume, the Council of the North having been held deep in Galtres Forest for many years. Having said all that, Silas was to see everything in life as much brighter and more innocent than it actually was and it was his naivety that not only got him lost and in trouble so often but also had him questioning why others were not the same as him and did not enjoy the world as he did.

As soon as Silas set off into this compelling hinterland, he started to count but the counting did not go well. He asked Bolt to help but his maths was only a little more advanced than his own. And, he hadn't been in the woods more than fifteen minutes when he stopped to marvel at his surroundings. Looking back, he could see the Minster peeping over the trees and the city was slowly disappearing. Around him was wildlife of every variety. God's good Earth lay there before him in all its forms and where nature's magic became commonplace, he filled the rest with his imagination. There were clicks, cracks, snaps and creaks. Howls, tweets, whistles and hoots. Shuffles, scratches and scurries but, in the daylight, it merely informed and excited him. Silas would stop to examine a plant, a mushroom or squirrel whilst Bolt was having the time of his life chasing sticks and exploring the dense overgrowth which had laid out a verdant carpet as far as the eye could see. The canopy reminded him of the Minster, convincing him that both had been carefully crafted by God just for him. The weeping branches brushed over him much like a priest's blessing and he soon became calmed and somewhat distracted by the dappled light that was cast all around. Gradually, the path became thinner and Silas remembered what he had been told about counting except, of course, for the detail. Suddenly, he didn't even know which was forward and which wasn't.

He had lost the memory of his mission altogether as, no more than four hundred yards in front of him was a fierce dragon spewing forth flames and destroying the forest, devastating all life before it. Or, to be a bit more accurate, he saw a small clearing where woodsmen had started a fire. Collecting himself, he paused and measured, possibly for the first time, just how much he was given to fantasy and also deduced that it was much more interesting than reality. Without realising it, he had now veered northeast on what was barely a track. There were trees all around him and now, he was very much in the thick of it and yet it did not dawn on him that he was lost as he was still counting. If I'm still counting, the mission must be going well, he told himself. It was then that he decided that he was exhausted because of the counting so stopped.

He thought that he could hear a sudden wind but it very soon became louder and louder. Then, he presumed that it was a horse. Moreover, it was a horse travelling in his direction but it continued to thunder and shake the ground and become increasingly louder. The dragon! He thought. I didn't imagine it after all! Then he saw a granular cloud of dust that quickly rose in front of him although, through it, he could see the flared nostrils of a steed. It was a horse after all. He had never seen a horse move so fast. He braced himself against a tree and it flew past except that it was two horses. No, three. He counted eight horses snorting and breathing steam and their riders shouting as they chased through the woods. One had a bell and its tone rose and fell as it sped by although in an instant they were gone. When his breath had returned, he was so excited that he jumped and then ran up and down hoping to feel what the riders felt although he just looked like a prize twit. This was something he would never forget. On his return, Robert would explain to him that he had witnessed one of the very regular forest races, the previous winner marked by the bell it had been awarded.

When his senses eventually returned, he chose to start counting once more but decided that he didn't like counting and had no use for it so ditched it for good. He sat down, resting his back on a tree and soaking up the wonder all around him. There was nothing about nature that offended or even frightened him. Here, where there were no people, it was serene and Silas could be himself. Perhaps that's what Dunstan meant, he mused. Neither the hares nor the deer would call him names, the bluebells would not laugh at him and neither would the puff balls shout. He looked up at the canopy which seemed to stretch forever Heavenward and considered that he was now in a part of the woods that was dark.

He stopped, certain that an even smaller path was branching away to his right. As he looked along its length, he could make out the silhouettes of three men. Behind them was a cart with one horse and beyond that was a barrow. They were moving objects from the barrow to the cart although Silas could not make out what they were moving. Some objects were clearly heavier than others and they seemed to be in a variety of shapes although the last two were very big and heavy. Although Silas remained still, hiding behind an oak, he noted that the men were moving silently and quickly. He sensed danger and so quietly continued along the path he was on. It was then that he observed that he must have been in a very dark part of the forest.

The more he thought about it, the darker it became. And then, it went completely dark.

'Ah…that's why it's dark…' he mused.

Dunstan

It was night-time, he was lost and despite his encounter with the silhouettes he still did not panic. Instead, he went to sleep. He fell into a peaceful but incredibly vivid dream. In the dream, he was laying there calm but the sun had come up again and sitting next to him was Dunstan. He had with him some sticks, a bow and an axe. In fact, all sorts of paraphernalia.

'Good morning good fellow' said Silas without even a stutter 'tis the finest of days. God has breathed new light into our beautiful forest.'

His eloquence alone should have informed him that he was not awake.

'That it is my fine friend…to work. There is no time to waste' said Dunstan.

Then, they both ate a breakfast of mushrooms, roots and berries before wandering deep into this new found paradise. Even in this deep dream state, Silas was smiling, enjoying the best of days.

'Will you teach me everything today?' asked Silas.

'As much as I can while I am with you' replied Dunstan.

He started by showing him how to make a fire. Dunstan started to demonstrate how a spindle, stick or arrow could be utilised for this purpose. He put the spindle in a loop of the bowstring and, by thrusting the bow back and forth, the spindle became a drill. The friction of the drill against a stable fire board and dry leaves eventually gave a spark.

'What if I cannot access a bow?' said Silas fluently.

Dunstan then took the time to show him how to make a bow and then how to achieve the same results without the bow. Then, they took archery practice.

Suddenly, the forest faded and Silas was in the office of William Fawkes looking at maps but was still alongside Dunstan.

'Why are we doing this?' asked Silas.

'Today you have started your travels. Year by year you will be expected to go farther and farther. You need to learn how to survive, alone,' said Fawkes.

Silas was aware of his smile getting bigger and, as it did, he found himself back in the forest again with Dunstan. He walked him through almost every plant, bush and tree, one by one, explaining what was edible and what was poisonous. Silas fell over as a deer brushed by him at speed and Dunstan pulled him out of harm's way. When Silas looked up, he could see every creature that lived in the forest. They lined up in front of him like an audience.

'If the king, or any of his courtiers, likes to kill it, then it is out of bounds' proclaimed the teacher.

'Even the squirrels?' asked Silas.

'Deer, foxes, boar, rabbits, squirrels. Even badgers and mice. Never risk it. Some of those who live here have a licence to keep and kill for food or, for their table. If they offer you meat then you should take it. Besides that, you would be committing treason if you ever gave way to temptation. Creatures of the earth will sustain you if you have nothing else to eat. If you set out on a long journey, take along those things that do not perish easily...'

The lesson went on and on. Dunstan issued warnings about foul ale, stale meat and water.

'A stream coming down from a mountain will give you the finest sustenance of all but always check that neither man nor beast has fouled it.'

Dunstan then pointed to the sky. It had suddenly become dark once again and yet when Silas looked at the earth beneath them, he could clearly see a large parchment. Dunstan started to draw on it.

'You thought that London was in York. You think that York is almost all of England. See…this is the shape of England…if you looked down from the sky, that is. This little circle is York.'

He then explained what was meant by north, south, east and west.

Then, his voice became distant as the throng of morning birdsong overpowered it. Calmly and happily, Silas came out of his slumber. Bolt stood and stretched so much that he ended up falling over whilst his master stood and, in seconds, all traces of his dream had dissipated. He too stretched believing he had awoken in paradise and it was almost ten minutes later before he even thought about where he was, let alone why. Reality hit home. He should have been back at Robert Hall's grand house long before it had gone dark. Where others would contemplate the mood that Hall may well have been in and the retribution heaped upon them, Silas then thought only of his errand but, for the life of him, couldn't remember the name of his contact. He looked at his feet and decided to walk in the direction that they were pointing. Strangely, he carried on looking at his feet as he continued along what was barely a path and his dog dutifully followed.

For a moment, he contemplated imminent terrors, after all, this was all unknown territory. Robbers, murderers, trolls and ogres. Giants, mythical beasts and snakes. Sadly, he would soon be confronted by possibly the most unpredictable of creatures and understandably the most difficult for a ten-year-old boy to negotiate. Still contemplating his feet, he collided with his nemesis. A ten-year-old girl.

'Ulloo' she said in a soft tone.

'Oh…,' said Silas.

She stared at him wondering whether he could speak and then quite boldly, but considerately stretched out her hand and touched his hair.

'Same' she said.

Although stretching the point she was, more or less, right. If you discount the minor detail that, by now, Silas's hair looked like a wild bush erupting from under his cap and was barely distinguishable from a forest nest, it was indeed bright orange like hers. However, in contrast, her hair was long and soft. Silas stared endlessly at her hair.

'Can you speak?'

'Oh…my…maiden…I…ham…very…at…your…hair…knight errand…'

'I'm Annie'

'Oh…Silas'

'Hullo Silas'

His shoulders dropped and he gave forth the biggest sigh. Someone, at last, who said his name correctly back to him. Although it wasn't true, he thought at that moment that this was the first time it had happened since his mother had died.

'Will you kill me?' she asked.

'Why….err no…I never kill anything…'

Her question said more about how forest dwellers viewed their city counterparts than any of Annie's previous experiences.

She smiled at him which made him even more diffident.

Neither knew what to do until, seemingly out of nowhere, two men appeared behind Annie. Silas grabbed her and pulled her alongside him. He drew his sword, a rather tired and chewed stick that Bolt had been playing with. Bolt started to growl but ended up choking and spluttering leaving all four of them watching him and waiting until he either stopped or succumbed.

Silas then looked at his enemy. Both were huge and very diffcrent from city folk. The general fashion for men was to be clean-shaven but these two were very hairy.

The taller one looked at Silas, he had a stick in one hand.

'What have we here?' he said.

'Oh…err...I yam Lord Silas of Cooper Castle and I will... depend... my lady's… '

At that point, he ran out of ideas.

'Haha!'

They both laughed very loud. Silas remained both expressionless and motionless.

'Well, well, …. you do good service to our ladies in distress and our king but you, young lady, what are you doing so far out?'

'Sorry father, just collecting berries.'

'In a world of your own again, Annie, c'mon, we'll make our way home now.'

Poor Silas always took some time to grasp even the simplest of events so the man explained.

'I am Annie's father, your Lordship. You are both safe and well and you are invited to eat with us.'

Not only was he relieved but he realised that when the man had said "Lordship" he did not intend to humiliate him. He gave Silas a friendly pat on the back and they headed deeper into the forest. The other man did not speak but wielded an axe as if he was ready to use it at a moment's notice.

After a ten-minute walk, in which Silas, Annie and Bolt followed the two men without speaking, they arrived at a circle of quaint but primitive dwellings with a wooden church in the middle. Outside there were a few people about their work and Silas thought it to be a wonderland particularly as the forest offered a backdrop in all directions.

On entering the largest building, Annie's father made an announcement.

'Look what we found along the path. Our dear daughter astray once more and she hath captured a troll!'

Everyone laughed except Silas who did not know that he

was being teased.

'Actually' he continued 'this is Lord Silas of Cooper Castle.'

'Well, we'd all be on our best behaviours then, hadn't we?' said the kind lady who was surely his wife as she had already kissed him.

Silas made a somewhat unique and clumsy courtesy but no one reacted and then he didn't know where to look. At first, it seemed as though the house was full of children but when he had calmed, he managed to count seven including Annie. Thank God there aren't more than ten, he thought. They all made a fuss of Bolt and he happily settled on his back having his belly tickled.

The other man, the one who hadn't spoken did little more than grunt and went back to one of the other houses swinging his axe.

'Well, young Silas' said Annie's father as he sat down 'this is my family. The Croppers.'

Instantaneously, Silas thought that this was similar to his grandfather's name. And, it wouldn't have been a great stretch of the imagination either to presume that they might have been kin. In the sixteenth century, there was no standard spelling and the pronunciation of words depended mostly on accents and dialects. The Croppers and Coopers could well have descended from the same stock. It could also be said that Silas was possibly too keen to seek out a family, having none of his own. Annie, he worked out, was the second eldest. As everyone took seats, he noticed that the mother played with the youngest son for a moment and then picked him up. His heart stopped as he was instantly transported back to his former life with Mary. Eventually, somewhere beyond his daydream, he heard his name being repeated.

'…you still with us my Lord? I was just asking what it is that brings you out here?'

The panic returned as he realised that, since awakening,

he had never checked the satchel. He looked down and it was still around his shoulder. He peeped inside. All the coins were still there.

Gathering his senses, he told them that he worked for Hall. A chilling silence followed although Silas barely noticed.

'I am on a mission but…I cannot…remember where it is…. I am meant to go…'

'Well,' said Master Cropper 'how about we start with some names of settlements nearby?'

He recited the names of every village and hamlet within five miles and the third one mentioned was Brint. Silas jumped up

'Yes, that was it…oh…. thank you, kind sir, I was…'

'That's ok. Be seated and eat. So, I'm guessing you'll be looking for Isaac?'

He couldn't believe his luck so again he thanked the man.

'My, you've wandered off track, lad but we can show you the way. Once fed, I will go with you.'

As he stood in the doorway to leave, he made sure to thank everyone in the house and learned that Mrs Cropper was called Agnes. Rarely did he spend time in the company of others without being lampooned and he felt as if he could have stayed there for days. Finally, he wished Annie goodbye but found himself tongue-tied. Then he just stared at her. Fortunately, the Croppers found this quite sweet but then had to prompt him out of his trance before Silas lost yet another full day.

They walked for almost half an hour and then Cropper pointed along a very thin track telling Silas that he would find Brint at the end of it.

Peace be with you,' said Cropper.

'And also, with you' replied Silas.

Silas felt warm inside. He had made new friends and they had even said that he was welcome back anytime. So overwhelmingly consumed by Annie's presence was he that, then and there, he chose to write an ode, a ditty just about her. He thought to consider what the right words would be before fully committing himself but it wasn't long before Silas Smith's very first work was ready for publication. He could not read or write so sang it out loud and this is how it sounded:

> *I wunce appened cross a maidin fur*
> *Annie witte red ure*
> *I ad their bread and sat ont chair*
> *I luked pon Annie wit red ere*
> *Anging up were a ded hure*
> *It ad red red ure*
> *I wusnt as if I ad no cur*
> *Fur Annie wit red ure*
> *I'd say we'd make fine pair*
> *Me and Annie wit red ure*
> *Bolt wur thure*
> *He dint ave red ure*
> *I was int forest….*

And then his prose ran dry for before him was Brint. He would recite his award-winning sonnet many times but it was never the same. Each time it changed slightly and sometimes he even forgot her name.

'About time I'd say!'

He could see that a man was shouting at him and, presumably expecting him much earlier. Silas and Bolt picked up their pace but were astonished that, however much closer he became, he didn't seem to get much bigger. Finally, they were face to face.

'Before you speak lad, I'm thinking that you have never seen a dwarf before?'

'I thought…'

'Don't think and don't speak until I've done, as I'm guessing you are about to offend me and all my kind.'

Isaac went on to explain why he was different to Silas and

that, otherwise there was no difference whatsoever. They were not "creatures of the wood" or "people in fables" or "elves, goblins, hobgoblins or even fairies" and, he was quite emphatic that they contributed as much to society as anyone else.

Silas accepted the rebuke for Isaac was right. Few other cultures had had so much nonsense written and spoken about them as his kin and Isaac had proudly served the king in battle more than once. So dumbfounded by the reprimand was Silas that he handed over the satchel immediately.

Isaac took Silas and the dog inside. His wife, Geraldine, wasn't a dwarf but their daughter was and Silas was wise enough not to comment. Isaac counted the coins, three times.

He took Silas's satchel and placed in it; a thin but very heavy object wrapped in coarse cloth.

'You are not to look, do you understand? Hall will be furious if you do.'

Silas was on his way before he had said anything more but after walking less than a furlong, he heard Isaac call after him.

'Come on back…'

In just a few strides, Silas was busy working out what else he had got wrong.

'My wife is right. I have been too harsh with you Lad. Not always easy dealing with your master or city dwellers. You are welcome here anytime and, by the way, you're going in the wrong direction.'

Once Isaac corrected him, Silas peered into the distance.

'You are quite right sir; from the end of this track, I need only travel directly south.'

Isaac was impressed but not as much as Silas was. He had no idea how he had learned what south meant but, he definitely seemed to have an improved sense of where he was although, as yet, he could not remember that it was Dunstan who had taught him, albeit in a dream. However, his adventure was not quite at an end. He once more passed the men he had seen the day before, making the fire, and could not resist looking closer. This looked more like a small encampment than a hamlet although he noticed at least one platform amongst the trees. On the ground, close to the fire, were sacks, boxes and heaps of cloth or clothing, he couldn't tell which. Then he saw their weapons. One had a bow across his back but other bows and accompanying quivers lay next to him. One of them stood and then Silas ran. He had, on his very first journey, discovered Robin Hood. Leaving out mere details that he would have been centuries old even if he had ever existed and that bows were still the weapon of preferred choice for woodsmen (and that not everyone was allowed to carry them), his fantasy may have had some credibility. Nevertheless, it made his day. By the time he had returned, he was certain that they were all dressed in green and that a tipsy friar was singing to them all.

7 Monkgate

He was back in the city before he had properly contemplated the consequences of his actions. He was almost a day late. This realisation dawned on him so suddenly that he stopped at Bootham Bar.
His shoulders dropped and he gave forth the greatest sigh.
'He will be furious' he muttered to himself 'I will lose my position and no one will employ me again.'
For one fleeting moment, he thought to lie. Mary immediately intervened. Her voice was as clear as the birds above him. Silas would never lie and it was probably fair to say that he wasn't capable of doing so. He even understood the distinction between his wild and uncontrollable imagination and the act of purposefully misleading someone. Neither could he think of a lie worth telling.
'I will make haste to Goodramgate and be honest with my master.'
This was said a little louder and so attracted the attention of passers-by who, in acknowledging that it was him, just carried on regardless. However, by the time he had knocked on the door both he and his dog were trembling. Jenny opened the door.
'He's ere sir!' She bellowed.
Hall came running into the kitchen. He then stood on his own back step and let loose on the child. This was, to date, the greatest roasting that Silas had ever had and, he had encountered a good few. So fierce was the mead and cheese-breathed tirade that Silas held his breath throughout. He shivered, blinked, farted and made squeaky whimpering noises but heard nothing that was said. Internally, he was just praying for it to stop.
'Give it here!'
This was the last thing he heard before Robert Hall snatched

the satchel and slammed the door shut. Silas stood there still shivering, blinking and making more squeaky noises but had no idea what to do next. He looked down to find Bolt but he was hiding around the corner. Then Silas heard voices. One of those voices was still ranting whilst the other was calm. To him it sounded something like:

'Hurumph bloody…grumph God's bollocks! Good hiding… grunt… Never again…idiot…I've a mind too…imbecile…spent all my money on…hurumph!…the stocks!…cut off his bal..'

The other was much clearer.

'Don't be too harsh dear. It was his first time beyond the city. He may have found himself lost.'

Then once more it became indecipherable except, he heard the woman say,

'…who else would do it.?'

Then silence.

Silas, with no ready alternatives, waited and waited. An hour later, the door was slowly opened by Jenny.

'Mrs Hall has saved your bacon, she has. Wait here.'

Another fifty minutes passed and a much calmer Robert Hall opened the door.

'Be back here at two of the clock, prompt.'

He didn't know what to think so he returned home, ate, started to plug a few holes in the wall of his house and then went back to Goodramgate.

This time he had to wait another twenty minutes before Hall opened the door. He strode straight past Silas.

'Follow me and…keep up.'

Off he went at breakneck speed along Goodramgate, through Monkgate Bar and along Monkgate itself. Eventually, they turned right and followed a muddy track where, at the end, there were some old gates, one almost off its hinges. Hall scraped open the one that would move and then turned a corner where there was a barn. Silas looked around but Bolt was nowhere to be seen. Taking a second glance, Silas realised that the barn had been converted into stables and within it were four horses. Silas loved horses and this wasn't solely to do with his obsession with knights. They were beautiful, graceful and usually obedient creatures and it hadn't escaped his attention that people who rode them around the city looked quite grand even if they were not necessarily superior.

The second stall along seemed at first to be empty. However, Robert went straight to it and opened the door. A most beautiful white colt sprang up and walked toward Hall. Silas, until this point had said nothing as he was still reeling from his reprimand but he could not resist commenting on such a fine animal.

'Oh sir, he is so beautiful, fit for a king…is he yours?'

He saw his master's face and, for a moment, thought that he should have kept his comments parked, at least for the time being.

Robert Hall glared at the boy.

'Yes, she is and I have kept her for one purpose and one purpose only but I do declare that I am very much regretting it today.'

This meant nothing to Silas so he indulged himself by stroking the colt's nose.

She was a sight to behold and although Hall would often describe her as a Spanish horse, it would have been unlikely. She was a fine palphrey and anyone would have been proud to own her.

Hall suddenly went around the back of the boy and grabbed him hard around the waist. In that instant, Silas was sure that he intended to do him in there and then where no one else could see so he wriggled, kicked his legs and yelped only to suddenly find himself astride the horse. The colt stayed still whilst Silas, dumbfounded, momentarily posed like a king as he was now even slightly taller than his master. Still, he had no clue as to Robert's intentions. Silas looked between his legs.

'Aye…you might well look! Cost me a prince's ransom that did…'
The saddle was very fine, noticeably very small and yet too big for the boy. Then, Bolt appeared, hobbled into the stables and stood next to the horse as if they were kin. Hall grabbed Silas again and put him down. For a lad who was confused by default, this was possibly the most perplexing situation he had ever been in and he still had an inkling that he might meet his maker in that isolated barn.
Why would he bring me to a barn to sack me? Or to hurt me? What is the horse for? Then, he remembered hearing about those people who had been hanged, drawn and quartered. Did Robert Hall mean to have him drawn on a pallet throughout York and then dismember him?
He considered that notion for a moment and as he did, his knees knocked and his tongue made an eerie burbling noise. Silas began to plead with him, offering excuses for his poor performance and even promising that he would work for nothing.
'I beg you master do not hang, draw and shorten me! I will tend to your horse, I can…'
'Get a grip Silage! What in God's name are you talking about? You have the rest of the week…'
He then whistled so loud that Silas almost shit himself.
A boy, possibly three years older than Silas and much bigger ran into the barn.
'Yes, master' said the boy 'good God, is that him?'
'Tis too. Nothing of the little bugger is there?'
Silas looked upon his executioner in awe. He had run out of promises, petitions and excuses.
Once more raising his voice, Hall told Silas to keep still.
'Yesubble mastuurr'
'You have one week. Turn up here every morning. Daniel will teach you. Your afternoons this week are free…do what the hell you want. Show up here first light Monday and sort out that bloody map in your head!'

Then he left.

'You don't understand, do you?' said Daniel

Silas was sure that this was a shake of the head.

'You're his errand boy and he wishes to send you further afield so…you need to learn to ride her.'

Daniel had to rephrase and explain this simple concept four more times and when, finally, the groat plopped in the well, tears flowed down Silas's cheeks.

'Oh…and he says you have to name her.'

'Annie' said Silas without any thought given to the task 'Annie, she will be called Annie.'

'All the same to me,' said Daniel.

Not only was Daniel a good teacher but he was impressively patient and treated Silas fairly.

Silas was as bad at horse riding as he was at most other things but it didn't matter. Even after many years had passed, he believed himself to be completely in command of his horse and his dog but it was forever the other way around. Annie and Bolt spent their lives taking care of Silas and as such became his devoted family.

As you may imagine, once he could ride, he became even more fanciful and unbearable but Robert would not put up with it. He derided him for his "faux airs and graces" and commanded him to get to church and learn some humility. All the same, at ten years of age, Silas believed that he would now become a knight in no time.

That wasn't all that Robert Hall had said. Still debating the wisdom of keeping the boy on, he had told his wife that the lad "couldn't help making a tit of himself" and on this subject he was right. Just when he had the opportunity to impress the commoners of York with his admirable steed, he rode around in circles with his nose in the air, offering increasingly affected waves to them. On the cusp of gaining some respect, he just wound everyone up. Both "Lord Silas" and "Lord Sillyarse" became that much funnier overnight although he would be the last one to notice.

However, he was to be disappointed in his new role as he was sent time and time again into the forest on foot. On one occasion he dared ask why he could not use the horse and was offered a reasonable answer. He could ride the horse when he was to be sent beyond the forest which, unsurprisingly, had him begging daily for ventures afar. He did at least become more familiar with Galtres Forest and, despite being ordered not to, would visit the Croppers and Isaac. Silas had been told that the man accompanying Annie's father when they first met was his brother but told him nothing else almost as if there was an embarrassment or a family secret. Silas doted on the young girl called Annie and there was no doubt that she welcomed his illicit visits. On one such call, he spent time with her siblings and a boy called Arxe, the son of Cropper's brother. Silas guessed he was about two years his elder and he liked him very much particularly as he did not wield a deathly weapon. He tried so hard to make a joke about the fact that the man's son had a name similar to his father's weapon but no one understood. Soon, Silas was tasked with transporting an even greater variety of objects, sacks and letters to and from Isaac and never once thought to look at what they were. Some weighed hardly anything and others were a burden. Once, and only once, Isaac laid out some food for Silas although it was clear that he did not usually welcome outsiders. Nevertheless, it was good for Silas's education, offering him an early understanding of other lives lived. It didn't take him long to realise that, inside, most people were similar, had similar desires and fears and they were vulnerable to varying degrees. There were many times when Silas and Bolt found themselves wandering aimlessly, whistling with the birds and loving woodland life only to find themselves late yet again.

The sisters

Finally, in 1525, in his eleventh year, it looked as if Silas would, at last, be given the chance to take Annie, the horse, into the woods and beyond. However, the good news came at a price, something was awry with Robert although Silas could not at first put his finger on it. All at once, the business seemed troubled as did Robert Hall's family life. It was probably as well that Silas didn't ask questions but it did leave him clueless as to the foundation and development of Robert's businesses. He understood that it had something to do with windows or sheep, or both, but that was the extent of his knowledge and his curiosity, Silas would be forever content doing whatever he was told. The bit that often escaped him was the remembering of it.

As ever-increasing responsibilities were bestowed upon him, the less sense he made of it. Whether he liked it or not, his role was one of a messenger and, from time to time, this also involved conveying packages or objects. During 1525, Robert had tasked Silas with regular visits to one of the most respected leather-smiths in York, a huge man by the name of MacManus although however much Silas tried to get a smile, greeting or any response from him, it was sadly effort he spent in vain. Silas saw MacManus as the archetypal Viking. This wasn't necessarily fanciful on his part, the man's Nordic genes spoke volumes and, yes, he did also fit the stereotype. He was huge and blond with the finest of beards but seemingly he had no manners. If nothing else the boy had the opportunity to wonder at the astonishing crafts that had been mastered there, MacManus possibly being the best whittawer, tanner, cutter and embosser in York. He gawped and marvelled at the creations that came out of the workshop. Pouches, and purses, all detailed and decorated. Satchels, reins, bridles and harnesses. Scabbards and sheaths, saddles and straps and, of course, shoes. Even things he did not recognise, MacManus once gave him a kick up the backside for picking up a codpiece and asking what it was for although once, he did let him watch with some amazement whilst he fashioned a turnshoe, a shoe that was made inside out.

Then, almost suddenly, this changed. Silas was sent only on Tuesday mornings with a note and nothing more. This was to be handed to Mrs MacManus for, on Tuesday mornings, her husband was never to be seen. Naturally, he presumed that the letter would be for her husband based only on the general notion that some men could read and most women couldn't. Silas had also suspected that they had children although he had never seen them except for the baby she carried when he visited and, if there were any, they certainly weren't there on Tuesday mornings. But the MacManus couple did have other children and Silas had seen them. Sometimes, around the marketplace or the castle keep, he would notice a young girl of around nine years of age, her hair so blond that it was a wonder that Silas did not make a connection with the Viking tanner. Her sister was very young, perhaps only three years old although they appeared inseparable. They would giggle endlessly, point at passers-by and take part in pretend sword fights, a pastime that would have been deemed unseemly for young ladies of York but nevertheless was exactly what Silas thought everyone should be doing. This alone would have been enough for them to stand out except it was also noticeable that the little raven-haired girl struggled to walk and when she shouted out in play, her speech seemed affected. This sparked Silas's curiosity but, when he stopped to stare, they just pointed and laughed at him and his dog. No doubt he had already been labelled by their parents and so the girls in turn also ridiculed him.

In Silas's little life this was all by the by, a series of interesting coincidences that meant nothing except indirectly this would very soon impact him and his master and as an adult, the girls would become an integral part of his existence.

He returned one Tuesday to Robert's house in Goodramgate

to find his master addressing him directly at the kitchen door.
'You found a place for the horse lad?'
'Yes sir.'
'Tomorrow you will ride out, much farther than you have before and this time you will have much to remember.'
Silas was a little nervous as he knew that this would test him but he desperately wanted to ride Annie and in doing so project himself ever nearer to his knighthood. He nodded presuming that it would do as an assurance.
Robert started to draw a route and it was indeed so much farther than he even knew existed. Surprisingly, it made much more sense to him than his first forest visit and, subconsciously, he was thanking Dunstan although he had no clear recollection of why his sense of direction had improved so much or when any teaching had taken place. Robert sketched out the route to where the Croppers lived and then to Isaac's house. He told Silas that, this time, he had to remember the words as they were said to him. Already he was muttering the phrase over and over in his head. Robert then drew a castle and Silas gasped.
'You must pretend it is not there' said Robert 'it could be dangerous for you and dangerous for me. Do not, ever, go near that castle.'
'I believe I have seen the battlements peeping out…err…in… over…'
Just as Silas was about to wax lyrical, he had yet again lost his wick.
'I know what you are trying to say' said a calm and understanding Robert Hall 'it is the stuff of romance. To be free, in such a beautiful woodland with the castle rising high above the treetops makes the heart rush but please…please do not go near to it.'
Robert then emphasised a track and one track only that stretched for miles.
'Here, you come out of the woods and into moorland. There is quite a climb but here…'

He scribbled a large cross on the parchment,
'…this is your destination. You will have something to deliver and something to bring back…'
At this point, Silas was almost bursting with confidence and sure that he could easily handle the mission. As it was, Robert had no one else or it may be more accurate to say that he could not risk sending anyone else.
On all future excursions, Silas would be much better equipped. He had a blanket, a dagger, an axe and a rope all thanks to Robert. On his first venture on horseback, he would find himself with cargo that was a large irregular bundle. Silas could not make out what it was and neither was he inquisitive. It was soft, not too weighty and fit comfortably behind the saddle.

Little Harry
Uncannily, over those weeks in which he stayed in York, the boy had managed to find a route to and from his abode for the horse. It would be ridiculous to suggest that he did so undetected but no one even seemed to care. He wasn't intruding on or damaging church property and there was little interest in his rickety shack beyond the targeted regular abuse and old wives' tales that had been shared locally. There was just about enough room for Annie to graze but this latest modification left him with a domicile that was poorly covered. Even this did not bother him. He could work on his home anytime, he told himself and presumed that he would be there for life anyway. That evening, he had with him the saddle. He spent an hour admiring it before putting it on the floor and then sitting on it. Bolt and Annie looked on wondering what the hell was up with him. Neither did he sleep that night, ever new adventures rushing in and out of his somewhat fanciful imagination. And, in between each fantasy, he rehearsed over and over what Robert had told him.
The next morning before even the first slight ray of sunlight

appeared, he walked Annie and Bolt into Dead Alley and waited at the end. His master had told him not to take the dog and for good reason, he simply was not fit enough to make the journey. Silas, of course, ignored him.

He waited until there was movement, until the busyness of York was in full flow so that he could preen his way along Coppergate and then into lower Petergate. He was Lord Silas and no amount of derision or catcalling would take that away from him. Never in the history of transport had a horse been guided slower through the city, as its master milked every last drop of admiration. What was most interesting was that mouths opened and jaws dropped on so many who could not fathom why the mad child from Dead Alley had been given a horse. A quite fine one at that. Given a few days to get over it, they would restore their mocking, horse or not.

The forest looked different from the saddle and it made Silas much more conspicuous. Many years later, when he would relate such stories, even he could not work out whether Robert Hall had been his saviour or had just used him. Undoubtedly, Robert had given him an incredibly dangerous errand. Silas's ignorance was indeed bliss. He was told not to take the dog, go straight to Isaac's, not visit the Croppers, bypass the castle and then ride without stopping toward his destination. Silas ignored all of it. He had a horse and everyone was going to see it. Admittedly, the Croppers were well impressed with his steed although when asked about the horse's name he avoided the question. To be fair to him, he did also avoid staying long although Silas would have loved to have been with them all day as, by now, he was doting on and had become completely besotted with young Annie. As he left their cottage, he saw Cropper's brother looming over him yet again, axe in hand but then, out of nowhere, came his son, Arxe, who greeted Silas like a long-lost friend.

Insisting that he had a deadline, he was soon with Isaac who reeled backwards when he saw the colt.

'My! He must think well of you lad. You giving Hall rub

downs n'all now?'
Silas did not know what this meant but suspected that it may have been vulgar. Then he began to recite his message.
'This is…you are…on payment…err…off…'
'This is your last payment,' said Isaac.
'Yes…oh yes!' said Silas astonished that Isaac knew his lines better than he did.
'What I expected' said Isaac 'glad to see an end to it all.'
Isaac checked his final payment, nodded in approval and then offered Silas food and drink.
'I know where you are going lad' said Isaac 'the dog won't make it. If you wish, you can leave him here until you return, I will look after him.'
Bolt seemed content and this time Silas knew better than to argue so he thanked him, checked that he was pointing the right way and then set off once more.
Half an hour later, he could see the turrets of the castle at Sheriff Hutton nestled between the treetops. Annie was walking slowly but confidently along a quite well-worn path, one from which it would have been unwise to deviate. But then, he saw some flags. As they fluttered and flapped in the breeze they called to him, their bright colours promising all that he had ever fantasised about. Percussively, the ropes snapped against the poles inviting him in. Kings, queens, princesses and princes. Horses, jousting, knights and noblemen. Bowmen, crossbowmen and swordsmen. Banquets, jesters and dancers. It all seemed quite irresistible so he stopped. Silas had developed an uncanny gift of seeing what wasn't there. Still, he had only seen three flags but he had filled in all the blanks below with his imagination. Then, he detected movement. Following Robert Hall's orders, he thought to flee but realised that someone was calling to him from one of the towers.
'Ho pilgrim!' came the call.
As he responded to this, Silas was left in no doubt that it was a child.

He waved back.

'Ride to the bridge' the child insisted.

Feebly he replied,

'I can...I can't...not allowed...'

'I'll allow it. Hehe...,' said the little voice.

This was all it took. Silas's resilience had dissipated and already he had forgotten his mission and so he wandered in a haphazard fashion toward where the towers were.

It was a while before he saw much more but eventually, he came to a small clearing and beyond it he beheld the full scale of the castle. It was huge, both impressive and foreboding and he was certain that he had detected a royal standard amongst the flags. Now, the tower where the boy had been seemed to stretch forever skyward but the boy had gone. But in front of Silas was a stone bridge over a broad moat and beyond, a portcullis. Seemingly out of nowhere, this audacious child, a boy of no more than five years, was running across the bridge and towards Silas. He then grabbed the horse by the bridle and pulled it into the overgrowth.

'I'm Harry' he said sounding pleased with himself.

'I'm Silas....do you live in a castle?!'

'I do now. Won't...be here always. Do you want to play?'

Silas could have easily been included in the five most naïve people in England although now and again he did have a sense of responsibility and was learning to detect danger. Surely this child cannot be allowed to roam beyond the castle unattended? he thought. But, as he persisted, Silas decided that a few moments' play would not harm him or the child. Harry took him further into the clearing and, thankfully, got Silas's name right.

It was there, in the sunshine, that Silas had a chance to see him properly. The boy was wearing the finest of clothes. Even as a person of privilege, these were not play clothes. He wore hose but it was of fine wool and clean, no holes to be seen. Above he wore a skirted doublet although it reminded Silas of the tabards he had worn when he had played with his mother. Everything was so pristine and new. Silas had never seen the like on a child. In those few moments whilst Silas was once more gawping and daydreaming, he mulled over the innocence of children giving no thought to the reality that he was still only eleven years of age himself. He then considered the emphasis Christ had placed on the innocence of children and was left with no doubt that such purity really was indeed that which paved the road to redemption. Then he thought of Jaxon. Perhaps Jesus never met Jaxon, he mused.

Harry opened up a small leather bag which had a rose embossed in it and pulled out two miniature swords. These were unique. The hilts were gold and there were rubies inlaid on the pommel and the cross guard although Silas presumed that they were also pretend. Snake-like patterns adorned the grip and were coloured like a rainbow. But they were wooden and this alone completely confused Silas.

'Toy swords…I have two…' said Harry in a matter-of-fact fashion.

Why would anyone go to such trouble for a toy, thought Silas? A thought which he was hurriedly snapped out of as Harry lunged and stabbed his opponent in the foot.

'Ooha ouch!' said a quite startled Silas 'they…sharp!'

Harry giggled and Silas fought back. Seconds into the battle no one would have guessed that there were six years and a foot in height between them as they danced around Annie proclaiming their just cause to one another. Soon Silas was giggling too, it had been so long since he had been able to simply enjoy himself. Graciously, he fell on purpose and yielded.

'I forfeit…my life…oh great knight…'

And Harry giggled even more.

'I spare thee…as thy are…'

For a moment two of them searched for a word that would suitably end this spectacular melee but, as you may imagine, there was quite a pause.

'…. noble!' shouted Harry.
They laughed again but as it subsided, they could hear a trumpet. Harry panicked and hurriedly gathered up the swords and tried to brush off his clothes. '
'Please come again Silas' he said.
'I cannot…I err…may…'
'Pleeaasse.' Silas nodded and then offered to help but Harry was emphatic in his dismissal. So close were the castle guards that he could hear them bustling and clanking over the bridge and calling Harry's name. Silas retreated as far as he was able. Undetected, he watched the drama play out fearful of the consequences for Harry.
'How many times?!' said the sergeant picking him up 'you will make quite an adventurer, Harry...' and the two guards laughed.
'Look at the mess. I will personally get you cleaned up but you cannot keep doing….'
Then his voice faded and Silas was relieved that the boy was not punished. What Silas didn't know was that if he had been caught with the young boy, the consequences would have been quite severe for him.
As he made to mount Annie, she looked upon him in disgust. The prince that had left York was now a muddied pauper and once in the saddle dripped mud, leaves and all variety of woodland life over her, once beautiful, white form. It was minutes before he broke from his daydream and realised that he was, yet again, lost. On this occasion and on many future occasions, Annie bailed him out. She remembered the diversion from the original track and took him back there. So, he thanked his horse for, without her aid, he would have truly been in danger. Not that the forest was any less foreboding but the remaining daylight gave him confidence as he ambled along the seemingly never-ending trail.
So enamoured with his new found friendship was he that he decided to add to his catalogue of ditties by writing a new one.

I com cross a castle int wud
There wus flags und walls
It ad a mote
I playd at swords wi arry
I lost
And wus full of shite

Admittedly he struggled to put a tune to it so resorted to the one he had used for Annie's song which was just as well as he had forgotten the words to that as well.
There was just one place where the road had become both waterlogged and blocked due to a fallen tree. Silas didn't know as yet whether Annie could jump and if she could, how far, so he chose to use his axe to pare down the branches that had ended up standing upright. This simple act, without him knowing it, was possibly his biggest mistake to date.

Celeste

Eventually, he came upon some marshland but detected horseshoe prints that led away from them. Although this added another hour to his journey, he was happy to discover that they did bring him out on the other side of the marsh. However, part way around, he saw men moving bundles from one cart to another and he was sure it was the same ones he had seen before. This time, they stopped as Silas was much more conspicuous on a white horse. He pretended that he had seen nothing and carried on his way content that they had ignored him. As the forest became patchy and then slowly disappeared behind him, he found himself amongst North Yorkshire moorland. And, as he started to climb, he experienced northern terrain as he had never before. It was rocky, with steep climbs. Some of the ground was marshy and most of it was covered with heather. The wind, even in summer, was so fierce that he had to stop and dismount at times to guide Annie and, he could see for miles and miles.

He presumed that this was what the rest of England looked like, the wild lands beyond the somewhat civilised haven of York.

He became increasingly anxious. He had never been so far from home. He had hardly been away from home at all and, as he climbed even further, he could just make out York city in the distance. It sent chills down his spine; he had come such a long way and it looked so small.

Thankfully, a path of some sort remained and he thought he could see his destination ahead. Neither could the contrast have been greater; he had spent the day surrounded by a cornucopia of wildlife and an array of God's creatures but now, even the forest pigs had been replaced by sheep and sheep only. He had never seen so many sheep and thought to dedicate an ode to them but then thought better of it.

As he neared, he was sure that he was almost there and the feeling of achievement it gave him was immeasurable. However, forty minutes later on arriving at the priory, he was left somewhat deflated as, apart from sheep, it seemed quite deserted. His heart sank once more as he presumed that either he had made a mistake or that there was no one there to greet him but he was in the right place; this was Rosedale Priory and nuns had been in situ there since 1158. Moreover, they had been graced many times with royal concessions ranging from lands to building extensions. They had also gained a reputation for wool manufacture embracing modern methods from both England and abroad. As he took a better look, he was overwhelmed by the complexity and beauty of the place particularly set against those wild environs.

He led Annie to a stream to drink and then took some himself. Everything out here is pure, as God intended, he told himself.

'Hullo…hullo! … I seek Prioress Matilda' he shouted.

Amazed that he had remembered her name he continued calling.

'Prioress Matilda Felton!' He screamed to no avail. Silas

approached the property and although he thought he heard movement; he could not be sure that it wasn't just the wind. He then saw a corridor which was lined with cloisters and found a large oaken door slightly ajar. He could smell smoke which gave him some hope that his journey had not been wasted.

Just as he was about to push the door a voice came out of nowhere.

'You are…erm... Master Hall's man?'

He turned to see a nun no more than three yards away from him. Her attire was pristine and white. She was, like her sisters, part of the Cistercian order who wore white to contrast with the black worn by Cistercian monks. He guessed that she was only about sixteen years of age and he also thought that she was very nice looking.

'Erm…yes. I have…. was…on the muddy track…' he replied.

'It is fine…meeting you...quickly…have you?' she said.

'My horse…right away'

Just as Silas was flattering himself that he had met someone that spoke the same gibberish, he considered that she may well have been nervous like he was but then dismissed the idea.

'Just a…' she said and wandered off again.

He took advantage of her brief absence and scurried around the cloisters. Beyond them, there seemed to be many cells although he had still not seen anyone else. He peeped behind a door that was slightly ajar and, in the dim light, saw some material that could have possibly been dresses, although they were incredibly ornate. There were silks and fine collars, inlaid jewels and sequins in all colours imaginable. He jumped as she returned. She stood at the end of the corridor with a small cart.

'Must hurry…' she said.

'Yes…' replied Silas and brought Annie alongside the cart where he unloaded the bundle.

'Goodbye and… erm… God bless you' she said.
'It was…good to...erm…nice…'
She leaned toward him and whispered,
'I'm sister Celeste' and then jumped back again.
'Silas', he replied.
'God be with you, Typhus' she said as he mounted Annie and turned around.
Silas didn't know what to think. Someone else has got my name wrong he thought. Bloody long way for one bundle he thought. Completed my mission well, he thought. That nun seemed scared, he thought. So much thinking had his mind blank for the next hour during which he decided to spend the night on the edge of a coppice, just at the entrance to the forest. Then, it rained and so he edged himself and his horse deeper where he found shelter in a small cave. So dry was the ground that he managed to start a fire and, in doing so, he realised that his last thoughts before sleeping were of Dunstan. Exhausted, he fell into a deep sleep and had a short, simple but memorable dream. In it, the devoted Dunstan simply said,
'Go straight home. As soon as you can, get straight home.'
And Dunstan repeated it time and time again.
Silas awoke refreshed, still proud of his successful errand. Annie easily found the road home. He must have travelled more than three miles before he recalled his dream but smiled presuming that it had no real meaning or significance. He was very much looking forward to seeing the Croppers again but was anxious to pick up Bolt first. Remarkably, he found his way to Isaac's house without getting lost only to find the dog outside but whimpering at the door to Isaac's home. Silas dismounted and, whilst Bolt greeted him as if he had been gone for years, he tapped on Isaac's humble abode. Eventually, the door was opened by a forest warden who abruptly questioned Silas.
'But where is Isaac…his family...is all well?' blustered Silas, increasingly nervous.

'This your dog? You were here yesterday?'
'Yes…erm…Bolt…I have been…the priory…Master Hall...'
'Yes. Been looking for you, I have.'
He walked out and slammed the door behind him.
'Wait here lad.'
He walked around the home and came back with another warden.
'Surrender any weapons. Tie your nag to his and follow him back to the city. You are hereby arrested under the king's law for the murder of the dwarf.'
'Wha...?...Murde…..he's…dead!...Oh…my!...Oh…oh…oh…no…you see'
Keep your drawbridge shut until we are back in York and then you can state your case,' said the warden.
'I didn't…wasn't…mmph…'
Silas was then well and truly gagged and the wardens were pleased of it.

8 York prison

York prison.
By the end of the day, Silas found himself in the smallest of cells at York Castle. Once a fortification that was the envy of all, the castle had now become run down. Since the development of explosive technology and in particular the advancement of cannon engineering, traditional castles began to lose their original significance and design. Like Warwick and many others, it was in a state of ill repair but worked fine as a prison and place of execution. Even for a skinny child, the cell was cramped. The rain flooded in and it was cold and riddled with bugs. There was no chance of him being fed either. He was a killer and, as such, had lost any rights. He attempted many times to put his case forward but not only was his account incomprehensible but neither was anyone interested. After spending his first terrifying, night there, the sheriff approached him.

'This yours?'

He waved Silas's axe in front of his face.

'Yes sir'

'Been used I see. Cleaned it did you? Get rid of the blood?'

'What blood? No sir…. tree…fallen in road you were…'

'See this nick here? Looks like that's where you were trying to hack through his neck. That's what I think. You're a bloody strange one, aren't you? Filth from down Dead Alley peacocking it around the city attracting all sorts of unnecessary attention. What had he ever done to you? You little bastard!'

Now, Silas was so frightened that he could not speak. His heart was broken. His friend had been brutally killed. How could anyone think that he could have done it? He wallowed in waste and pity for what seemed an indeterminable length of time and he was sure that no one would defend him so small was his world. Three days passed and his health was failing and he began to lose hope although during that same afternoon he heard a conversation that was nothing like the cries, groans and profanity of those similarly incarcerated. The voices came nearer and he was sure that Robert Hall's was one of them. He was right. As Silas struggled to stand up and clear his eyes he beheld his master. He was instantly encouraged although he also wondered why he had taken so long to get there. After all, it was only five minutes' walk away from his house. Of course, anyone else could have told Silas in a heartbeat that the reason lay in Robert's desire to keep his business dealings hidden.

He whispered through the grating on the door.

'I know you haven't killed anyone but…well, you see Silage, this is very embarrassing for me. No one is meant to know that Isaac was…well…helping me, you know? You might have to swing just to keep things stable if you know what I mean...'

Silas squealed and protested and made such a fuss that Robert Hall was desperately trying to hush him.

'Alright!' He whispered, 'I'll see what I can do.'

Two more days passed in which Silas sat in his own filth wondering if he could last out one more day. His wits, if he ever had any, had completely left him as had his employer. When he was calm, he thought and thought of a good argument that would vindicate him but he had none. If only Bolt could talk, he thought and in doing so realised how desperate his situation was. Robert was mortified. Almost all of his business dealings were arcane and he had also convinced himself that no one would miss the boy. After all, he was an embarrassment to the city. No one would ever know whether he was capable or not of seeing a child hang to cover up his business secrets but there was someone who wouldn't let him. There was one indisputable fact of life in the north of England that had been established for centuries and even defied the logic of the Bible itself. Men were in charge or, I should say that men have always appeared to be in charge but this was a counterfeit, a masquerade, a device to make society seem as though it had order and any married man from the north, from any generation, might well even whisper the truth after a few pints and that was that this apparent tradition had its limits and that included all decision making. The reality was and still is that women were the authority in almost every relationship and thank God too that it was always so. As soon as Robert's wife got a whiff of what he was up to he got a roasting. She not only rebuked him but shamed him and promised that she would have the boy released herself if he did not do it. Sixteenth-century wife-fright easily trumped any ideas of greed he may have harboured so he thought on the issue some more.

A day later, almost out of nowhere, the sheriff showed up at the castle again. He opened the door and said,

'Go on pudding prick, bugger off.'

He didn't need telling twice. As best he could, he ran out of the castle and straight to the river where he submerged himself just far enough to get cleaned off without drowning himself, something which was still one of the highest causes of death in the city. Almost every one of his dreams and desires had, once more, been shattered. It wasn't so much the incident itself but the reality that he would forever be England's whipping boy. Quite rightly, he thought himself innocent and could not understand why others hated him so much. He then went straight around to the Hall's residence but was turned away. Jenny told him to meet Robert Hall by the Merchant Adventurers' Hall at eight in the morning and make sure that he was well presented.

When he arrived, having had his first night's sleep in a week, he was directed into the chapel. Besides his guide, there was no one else in the building. He stood up as he heard steps approaching.

It was Robert who told him to sit and to be quiet.

'Isaac's wife, Geraldine, gave you an honest reference and told the sheriff that you had just left when she and her daughter left the home to go to the well and then collect mushrooms. Half an hour later he was killed. It makes sense that you couldn't be halfway to Rosedale Priory as well as being in Brint. Sheriff Hugh Hulley is now talking to the Galtres wardens! He also says that there are people at the highest level asking about this. Oh God...'

He put his head in his hands but suddenly looked up again.

'She also said that you left the dog there which, I should add, was meant to stay in York! If I ever consider employing you again lad, you must do as I say! Before you ask, I have no bloody clue whatsoever why he's been done in, but the family and the sheriff want an answer and they will have one. They have already worked out that I employed him so I am in a very bad situation. Very bad, I say. And then there's Mrs Hall...Did you speak about....' Robert started to whisper again,

'...the priory, to the sheriff?'

Silas shook his head.

'Or the payment to the dwarf?'

He shook it even harder.

'Bloody inconvenient Silage. Bloody inconvenient. I will have to be careful with my trade for some time but...you must...do...as...I...say!'

Silas began to tremble. He was now a wreck, fearful of his own safety and in complete despair as he had been so proud of his achievement.'

'You did leave the bundle at the priory?'

Silas nodded. He so wanted to tell him about the strangeness of the place and the seemingly diffident nun but could not speak.

'Go to your hovel, look after the mutt and the horse, both are outside the hall and have been well-tended. I will be in touch.'

Silas's expression spoke volumes.

'Oh, I expect I will use you again soon. Just wait for a message from me. Don't come to the house.'

And then, miraculously, he paid the boy and disappeared.

But Silas didn't go home, he went straight to the palace of the Queen of Sheba as he felt that he had recently neglected her. He tapped on the door several times and eventually heard a small voice answer. As he opened the door she was, as always, in her chair but looking frail. Despite it being a warm summer's day, it was cold in her house. This was unexpected. Silas had very few constants in his life and needed his queen to remain always as she was. She detected this and feebly commenced their ritual. A quiet voice announced,

'The Queen of Sheba...'

She could not take part in the ceremony as she was too weak to move so he did it alone and with a smile on his face. He then struck a fire and warmed a pot of stew that looked like it had stood for days. Then, he fed his queen. She smiled and placed her withered hand on his head.

'Tell me…tell me of your adventures, brave knight' she commanded.

Silas sat and told her the whole tale which was unquestionably somewhat cathartic.

'I will be better soon. Don't worry about me and come only when you are able. My stiffening is worsening…'

She had spoken a lot about her stiffening and, over the time he had known her, he had seen it take its grip on her. Stiffening of her back, her arms and her hands. Stiffening of her legs and ankles. He thought it to be a cruel demise but said nothing as she continued,

'How stupid of them to think that you would kill the dwarf. Be cautious of Robert Hall and his dealings, do as you are asked and no more…'

Then, she moved a little. Leaning into him she continued,

'There are many wicked things in this world young Silas,

I am sure your mother must have told you. But they rarely appear to be so. Be cautious of anything and anyone you don't know and even be wary of the ones you do. Do you know the quickest route to Hell Silas?'

He said and did nothing as he knew that she would tell him.

'Temptation. Priests talk so much about temptation because the pages of the Good Book refer to it constantly. It is how he gets you. Lurking. The Devil is forever lurking, cunningly beckoning you into his fold. Why did you approach the castle?'

He explained about the flags and the waving boy and, of course, insisted it was all innocent fun.

'But you were told not to go there. Not that I trust anything your master says either but you gave way to temptation. Of course, it seemed harmless, it always does. When you are an adult, you will be subject to so many more temptations and, believe me, they will never have the face of a monster.'

Somewhat anxious, Silas asked her how to know the difference.

'That little voice. Whilst we are in this world we are still connected. Connected to our Lord and all those who have gone before us. Do you often hear it telling you not to do this or agree to that?'

He nodded.

'Your conscience lad. It is most precious and all you have as you enter and leave this world. When you do leave make sure that, if nothing else, your conscience is intact. The Evil One awaits around every bright corner, at the end of each sunny path and behind many an inviting smile.'

It was a heavy sermon, particularly from a poorly old lady but all in all it made sense to him. He usually knew when he was asked to do things that weren't right and he was certain that all was not well at the priory.

He then told her about the jester as he had seen it in jail

as well.

'There you are, boy. He will forever seek you out. Deny him and he will go away for you have the power of the Holy Spirit vested in you, always.'

He mulled this over for a while but arrived at a place he had been to many times. Silas struggled to work things out and these could often be quite simple considerations. What she had said made perfect sense as did all the teachings of Christ. If people put others first, loved their enemies and forgave transgressions then what a wonderful, peaceful world it would be. But, they don't. They just don't, he mused. People went to church many times a week and then ignored most of what they had signed up for. At times like this, when he simply couldn't reconcile two truths, his head hurt trying to work out why it was so. This was one of the reasons why his default mode was to obey without question. She was right, there were to be many temptations in his life so it was as well that the queen's counsel stayed with him always only to be reinforced by his mentor, Dunstan.

He left her feeling much more comfortable and then made his way home to continue repairs.

For the next two weeks hardly anything happened or, at least, Silas wasn't aware of anything happening. He was certain that the murder had not been resolved but neither had it been spoken of. Hall gave him some modest errands in the city although Silas soon pined for the forest again despite the apparent danger. Robert had tasked Jenny with passing on messages to Silas and, to say the least, much of it got lost in translation. It also interfered with her ever-increasing duties. Initially, they were to meet outside the Adventurers' Hall but that wasn't working out either. Exactly sixteen days after he had been let out of prison, she met him along a snickleway that ran behind Robert's grandiose house.

The Prioress

'Too much for me lad. I have so many duties! How on Earth am I meant to even open the front door if I'm not there? What about the clothes? The washing? and then there's the silver!'

He desperately tried to get a word in but failed.

'This will have to do' she said, 'I just cannot be wandering back and forth between here and the Pavement three times a week and soon I won't be. Got plans of my own.'

She stopped, exhausted, clearly trying to remember what Silas's errand was.

'Now look what you've done! Can't bloody remember it now…'

'I think…' he said hoping to help.

'Yes!' she said, 'yes, that's it. This is a letter for the Croppers, Annie's mother and father…'

Silas could not hide his delight.

'Do not dally. Do not mention…erm…oh yes, Isaac. Do not go near the castle. Then onto the Priory. Hand in this and await a reply. Don't!... get the two messages mixed up and don't forget the reply from the Prioress.'

'But when I last went…'

Jenny was gone, disappearing in a cloud of haughty dust.

Within the hour, he was ready to set off, enthusiastic about his new adventure and almost dismissive of the recent murder. This time, Bolt stayed home and slept. Silas had left him enough food and water for a week.

With glee, he found himself once more at Bootham Bar, the northwest exit from the city but, as he looked up, there again was the jester. The same one he had seen hovering above his mother's bed that day. He had forgotten all about it until then. He thought about what he had said last time and what the queen had said about temptation. He looked up and simply said,

'I fear you not.'

He then closed his eyes and said,

'Fear not for I am with you.'

When he opened them he saw only clouds.

As he eventually settled at the Cropper's he noticed that the mood had changed since the murder although he was made welcome and he made sure to hand the letter over straight away. He wrestled with the obsession he had for Annie. With no point of reference or anyone in a parental role to guide him, he wondered whether he should just say how he felt. However, even during those early years, he was quickly learning that he was often ridiculed when he talked about what was going on inside him so thought better of it. He was more than satisfied with the smiles and quips offered by the girl for the time being. Cropper's brother was notably absent. On previous visits, he had always seemed to be lurking somewhere wielding his huge axe although his son, Arxe was with them.

This time, it just came out, even before Silas had intended it to,

'Where…is…how is the man…had an axe…'

He delivered this cryptic sentence so nervously that they all laughed, partly because they also knew exactly what he meant.

'He does not live here anymore' said Annie and, as she did, Arxe put his head down seemingly wanting no part in the conversation.

'Married now' said Annie's father.

'Ah…Aha…oh...' was all that Silas could offer.

'Married Isaac's wife, Geraldine. She's a Cropper now too' blurted out Emma Cropper and then everyone became silent.

Silas now had a thousand questions but, besides the certainty that he would remain incoherent, he could tell that it was a sensitive subject and said no more.

As he rode away, he just couldn't make sense of it. Why would Isaac's wife marry so soon and to the bedevilled axeman of Galtres?

The castle towers once more snapped him out of it. This time, the flags were still, although he stopped to study one that he hadn't seen before. This particular standard had a funny hat at the top although he also acknowledged that every creature and motif known to man seemed to be depicted somewhere on it as well. Now, something inside him was wishing that the small boy would, once more, appear atop the tower but he wasn't there and neither was there any movement. Proud that he had resisted temptation or, more accurately couldn't find what he was looking for, he heard what he thought was the wind.

'Shush! Quiet….'

He stopped, looked down and there at Annie's hind was Harry who then started to giggle.

'Harry, you will be in so much trouble!' said Silas fluently and with some authority.

'No, it's alright Silas, they don't know I'm here. Hehe'

'That's what I mean.'

'Come down and play'

Silas dismounted in the hope of sending Harry straight back. Looking at him he was struck once more at how fine his clothes were. Why was this boy living in a castle? Surely, he can't work there if he dresses like this? Why does he keep running away? Is he a prisoner or a guest?

Harry began to laugh so much that he rolled about on the ground. Unwittingly, Silas had thought all of those thoughts out loud.

'Will you be my teacher, Silas?'

'No…why...what are…'

'I have the worst teacher in all of England, Richard Croke, have you heard of him? The worst Silas, possibly in all of Europe. Bores me! Hehehe!….I like the jesters though…'

'You have jesters?'

'Ooo…yes…two. Watch'

Harry started to dance raising one knee at a time to shoulder height whilst his arms pointed in every direction imaginable. Silas laughed with him.

'You're so funny Harry.'

'I've been made to live here because I am...'

Suddenly the trumpet sounded and Harry needed no prompting, off he ran towards the bridge. Smiling, Silas went on his way, laughing at the silly boy from the castle.

Annie, the horse, took exactly the same route to Rosedale Priory shaving almost forty minutes off the original journey and, all in all, it was quite uneventful. His experience approaching the place was quite similar to the last time. There was no doubt that a large number of sheep were farmed there and they had all recently parted with their wool. However, this time he was sure that he saw more people but as he got nearer, they seemed to disappear once more. The weather was calmer and so he took his time climbing up to the priory entrance. The door opened. Celeste stood there with a smile on her face and a hand outstretched to greet him. Then, quite bizarrely, four other nuns came out and flanked her, two on each side.

'Prioress…' started Silas but was instantly interrupted by Celeste.

'She is otherwise engaged today; I am to collect Mr Hall's message on her behalf,' she said confidently.

He rummaged in his satchel, took out the message, checked to see that he had not given the wrong one to the Croppers and then stretched his arm out and looked her in the eye. But there, behind her, was an ageing man. Immediately, he came forward and he too smiled. He had a long white beard and hair to match. Silas thought of asking if he was Merlin but did not get the chance as he began to speak in a calm and friendly manner and Silas thought it wise to take in what was being said.

'Thank you boy. What's your name?'

'Typhus,' said Celeste.

'Silas,' insisted the boy, possibly for the first time ever.

'Ah, Silas,' said the old man, 'next time you come we will

have food for you. Today sadly is somewhat inconvenient.'

The nuns stood eerily motionless whilst this took place. The man broke the seal and opened the letter. Silas looked to see if his expression would change but, alas, he gave nothing away. Then Silas heard a clatter and, unwittingly, three of the nuns turned their heads in the direction of the sound. The noises became louder and there was no hiding the fact that a heavy-laden cart was negotiating its way downward but in the opposite direction.

'Off to the river' said the old man, 'much of it on its way to your master.'

This made sense to Silas. He was sure that Robert Hall was either trading with or having produce made by the nuns and he also knew that all sizeable cargo was always transported by water but he couldn't work out what a weird old man was doing in a convent. Once he took a closer look at him, he realised that he was no ordinary man and neither was he wearing ordinary clothes. They were not worker's or monk's garments. He had the finest decorated doublet with puffed sleeves which spoke of privilege. But, part of Silas's remit was not to ask questions, he knew his place and so waited patiently for a letter to be taken back.

'Seventy-five per cent' said the creepy, wizard man.

Silas still thought that Merlin might write this message down but, as he repeated it, he was sure that he could remember such a short phrase.

As he rode away, he would periodically look back but nothing changed. All six of them stood still as stone watching him retreat.

By now, the way home was becoming more familiar to him and, following a short rest where he fed and watered both himself and the horse, he saw the castle once more. It looked so very different from the north although still, awe-inspiring. Moving calmly through what he perceived to be a peaceful and benign part of the woods, he lapsed into default Silas mode in which his mouth remained open and he would gawp endlessly into the distance. However, once again, his dreams were to be shattered by the thundering hooves of many horses. He quickly pulled Annie off the track between two large hawthorns, readying himself for the race. This wasn't the same though. He heard trumpets and dogs barking, men shouting and the rattle of weapons.

It was a hunt and momentarily Silas delighted in the spectacle. The horses were better dressed than most people he knew and the riders, well, they were gentlemen. More than that, he decided that they must be noblemen. It took a few minutes for the whole hunt to pass but the biggest surprise? Harry was in the midst of it. Almost at the front and he was having the time of his life. This served only to confuse Silas even more. What an unusual treat for such a small boy, he thought.

As the last of the dogs disappeared into the dense and fervent landscape, Annie continued to amble but then suddenly and unexpectedly, came to a halt. Where her forehooves stopped, there was seemingly no change in the terrain and no reason for her sudden pause but, undetectable to the human eye was the edge of a swamp. Not only did Annie notice the swamp, but she also became aware of how instantly light she suddenly felt. Nonchalantly looking up, she saw a boy hurtling skyward, screaming and then landing in the pungent and ugly mush. Silas landed head first creating an awesome splash but then temporarily stopped sinking somewhere around his waist, leaving two very skinny legs and two worn, pointy leather shoes on the end, sticking up. This was Silas's first, and possibly last, experience of quicksand. He then started to sink at about an inch a minute and now and again one of his bony knees would twitch. Annie looked on wondering how long it would take her master to get out, unaware that he wasn't going to. Then, seemingly out of nowhere there was the sound of hooves, startling Annie so much that she was soon up on her hind legs. But this wasn't the hunt, this was a lone rider on a huge black steed. Everything he wore was black although he appeared little more than a streak as he sped by. As soon as he was alongside Annie, and without slowing, he grabbed the rope from Annie's saddle, threw it around the boy's legs and galloped by. Out Silas popped like a child pulling his finger out of custard and he flew forward a hundred feet. The dark rider dropped the rope and then disappeared.

As Annie approached Silas, he was barely breathing and barely recognisable. In an attempt to alleviate the situation, she stood over him and peed on him. As you might imagine, this was no light wash and it did help to quickly clear his airways. He vomited and coughed for another ten minutes and then, with no other thought as to what to do, climbed aboard his horse and made his way home completely ignorant of his saviour. Until the day of his passing, he would insist that Annie had thrown the rope to save him and, the horse never once contradicted him.

On this occasion, he chose not to write an ode.

One reliable element of woodland life was the clean spring water but did Silas think to clean himself up there? Of course not. He had his favourite spot via Castlegate in the city where he would douse himself when necessary. Your imagination will be sufficient to consider the many uses and abuses of any urban river in the sixteenth century but people did sometimes wash in there as well. Where he was smart was in his decision to enter the city via Walmgate where he managed to sneak down to the river relatively unnoticed. As he splashed away any remaining evidence of the quicksand, he turned to look at the sudden activity to his left. He was close to the Ouse Bridge but as one would walk away from it, there was clear evidence of new developments. There was nothing particularly striking about that in itself but one warehouse was clearly brand new and took up twice the acreage of any of the other buildings. Silas gawped at it for a while possibly admiring its construction as well as the speed at which it had gone up. He had little or no thought for his master awaiting an answer to the message he had sent to the priory. There were a few workers near the doors but, otherwise, there was nothing remarkable about it, Then, he saw a barge heading towards him. Relaxed, and grateful that he had lived through his ordeal, he watched on as the sun danced on the ripples of the Ouse. When he saw the boat near, however, he realised that the sackcloth around the bundle was exactly the same as the one that left the abbey. He gave no thought to whether it was the same one or just one similar but Silas needed no persuading that this had come from the priory.

As it was unloaded, the gaffer strode authoritatively toward him. Silas stood to greet him.

'What you doing here? Why are you spying on us lad?!'

This wasn't what he expected. He rambled but still did not manage to say what he wanted. He eventually blurted out,

'I work for Master Hall.'

This served only to further anger the man who told him to get on his way or he would end up in the river.

After a swift visit home to feed and collect his dog, he found himself waiting for Jenny in the alley behind the Hall's house. He waited and waited. Just as he was considering knocking on the door, she turned up.

'You have an answer then?'

It wasn't often that Silas stood up for himself but on this day, despite being nervous, he protested.

'…just not working…can't just wait…whenever you turn up…could take a whole day!'

And then he started to wobble and flap.

Jenny stood as a rock, hands on her hips.

'Well…you needn't blame me. Truth be told, it's his daft idea, hardly anyone is allowed in the house now. This is what I suggest. Come to the back door each time you return and knock like this…'

She tapped three times on a gate.

'…and do that, three times…'

Silas, confused, found himself both nodding and shaking his head although he was most satisfied that this was the first time in his life that he had managed to negotiate something.

'If I don't answer come back an hour later, and so on…'

He nodded.

'So, what did the prioress say?'

He paused for a moment and then confidently said,

'Twenty-five per cent…'

They parted company, both happy that a new arrangement had been made.

Silas was never to know it but only forty minutes later, Robert Hall was the happiest man in Christendom.

'Twenty-five per cent! Twenty-five per cent!'

He fell to his knees.

'Oh Lord! Thank you. This is so much better than I ever could have hoped for…'

9 The ambush

Silas would have moments where he would consider the many mysteries that had pervaded his little life. The murders around Coppergate and Dead Alley and his own mother's death, even his father's disappearance. He would even quiz what happened to his grandfather, the blacksmith. Added to this was the sudden death of a dwarf, and the even more sudden marriage with the sinister axeman of Galtres Forest, an afternoon spent in quicksand, an aeon spent in prison and then that encounter with the strangest priory in the land. He had almost forgotten about Robin Hood and those other men who were putting bundles on carts in the dead of night. Most of the time he convinced himself that it wasn't his place to have answers and little did he know that yet another conundrum would soon unfold before his eyes.

His knocking technique needed some work, to say the least but it did mean that he was now close enough to observe some comings and goings within the Hall household.

Weeks passed in which his errands became much more mundane although this did mean that he was at the house that much more often. One day as he waited for Jenny to open the door he pointed his little face toward the sun, breathing in the summer's morn. Bolt became agitated and started to offer muted barks. Silas tried to calm him but was soon distracted by voices within the house and, for the very first time, he attempted to eavesdrop. Despite Robert having access to state-of-the-art glass, it was still barely possible to see anything through his long, thin kitchen windows but Silas could see that there were many people in the house and Hugh Hulley, the sheriff, was easy to recognise. Robert appeared distraught but Silas could not work out whether he was in trouble or the sheriff was consoling him. Then, Silas saw something so unexpected that he pushed his face right up to the window. The sun's reflection was still hampering his view but he was certain that he could see the two girls, the MacManuses, the ones that sometimes played swords near the castle. Then, Mrs Hall bundled them behind closed doors.

The back door suddenly opened and Silas fell in.

Jenny grabbed him by the collar and escorted him, swiftly, out again.

'None of your business. Understood?'

Silas nodded and apologised. Apart from very soon learning that the girls were to stay there for a very long time, the reason why would escape him altogether until he was an adult.

'Yes, yes…' he said.

For a week or two, he persisted with more humdrum errands in which he tried and failed to establish himself as a person of importance in York city. He became aware that the queen was ailing and so he was glad to be able to call in on her daily. He sometimes pondered about Robert's business and the strange man at the abbey but did not dwell on it. And, he was missing the castle. He had found his paradise beyond the tree tops and curiously thought he belonged there.

As arranged, on a fine Tuesday morning, he returned to the back door of the Hall residence to await his orders.

'It is so very important that you don't get any of this wrong!' demanded Jenny.

He looked back at her expressionless which infuriated the girl.

'Well, at least say something!'

'I will not get anything wrong' answered Silas as monotone as possible.

She clasped her head in her hands.

'Sit down on the step. We'll go over this a few times…You are to take this seal to the river. Do you know where…'

'I have seen Master Hall's warehouse' he said.

'Good! Well, that helps. There will be a bundle to pick up and take to the priory. This purse has money in it. Put it under your saddle and don't take it out until you see the prioress...'

This was the point at which he really should have told Jenny that during his last visit there was no prioress but was so busy remembering the first bit that he didn't bother.

'...do not stop...anywhere! Do not go near the castle and do not visit the Croppers. Go straight there and come straight back. The prioress will have a message for you, it will not be written so you will have to remember it.'

Then, Jenny walked through it six more times. Although no two recitations were even similar, she was happy that he had got the gist.

'Oh, leave the dog at home...'

He had, at least, gained some confidence despite the obvious dangers associated with the forest so he took some time to check Annie's shoes and then carefully saddled her. He fed the three of them and left a little food for Bolt as he was sure that he would be back within the day this time. Hall's men were waiting for him at the river and one particularly angry-looking man with the smelliest of jerkins loaded the bundle behind his saddle.

'Thank you, kind sir, for I am, this very day...'

He'd gone.

The cargo meant a lot to Silas. It was one thing parading around York on a fine horse in clothes that didn't fit but something altogether different when it was clear that he was to bravely set forth on a mission that would change the course of history. By now, he had evolved an uncanny ability to deafen himself to abuse and so left York held high.

It was a hot, calm day and for a while, it seemed as though all was still. Even the flags at the castle at Sheriff Hutton clung to their masts. It was then that he realised that, already he was yearning for his little friend and even hoped to see what was inside. He shut his eyes as this was the only way he could block it out although the temptations would not stop there. He thought about what the queen had said and in doing so was determined to reach the priory without stopping. By now, Annie the horse did all the work and so he made very good time.

On the approach, he took time to admire the stone building set against the sprawling moors of Yorkshire, a bright blue sky casting mid-day shadows onto the courtyard. This time, he noticed a few people in the field tending the sheep but, otherwise no one else could be seen. There was a storehouse that was used for feed about three hundred yards to his right so he chose to tie up Annie there and walk the rest of the way. Something inside him told him that there would be less of a disturbance if he approached on foot.

This time, he managed to reach the door but then stood, staring at it. Silas's knowledge of everything and anything seemed to be like scraps of paper with nothing even coming close to a full page although he did know that as a boy, he should not be entering the domain of nuns. He turned around and spent some time admiring the buildings presuming that the strange old man had gone. Then, almost like an unexpected bout of wind, he started to remember his instructions. The bundle and the money were on the horse so he rushed back to get both. The bundle was soft and irregular like the first but this one was quite heavy and, as he wrestled with it, he was sure he saw something inside glint in the sun. He reached the door and it opened slightly without him knocking.

'Come on in. Do not make any noise' said a voice softly.

'You must be Silas' she said and put her finger to her lips, 'come with me.'

She took him into a small cell where there was a desk on which there was a ledger and some boxes, there was also a Roman chair and a stool.

'I am the prioress, Matilda Felton' she whispered, 'our business needs to be swift…'

As she spoke, she became suspicious, hunched over and constantly checking the door.

'Drop the cargo in the corner, Silas and give me the purse.'

She opened the ledger, started to count the coins and then took a quill ready to dip into ink when she suddenly stopped again.

'This isn't enough...' she said calmly but looking into his eyes, 'you haven't taken any?'

Silas dithered and protested so much that she can have been left in no doubt that the shortfall was not due to him.

'Let me see...did you take back the message to your master?'

He nodded.

'Can you remember what you said?'

Again, he panicked but eventually hazarded a guess at something to do with twenty-five per cent.

Silas was wondering when he would exist comfortably in a world where the said percentages also thrived. As he looked down, he could see that his little knees were knocking against each other now that the prioress had become silent.

'It is an error but a serious one. It needs to be corrected. I will write immediately to Master Hall to explain.'

Her head involuntarily swept to the right in response to a distant groan followed by a raised voice although that too was far away. Silas was sure that it was Latin but nothing like the Latin he had heard in York.

'Ignore it and go straight home. Here is my seal to confirm what you have brought today. Give it to Master Hall and tell him that I will write to him. You must go quickly.'

He didn't need to be told twice. As he mounted to leave, he could hear movement behind him and so took off at a gallop, her receipt still in his hand.

He had been sure that, on this occasion, he would return home triumphant. His master and Jenny would praise him for a job well done, for furthering the business interests of

Robert Hall and advancing his own position, ambassador to York. But, once more, his little heart was heavy or, at least something was. A lead weight hung on a sinew attached to his throat and it swung lower and lower and became even weightier. No matter what happened in his life, there was this certainty that he would always find himself back in the same place. He was worthless, many people knew it and many more would remind him of it. It seemed as though there was little on God's Earth that he couldn't bugger up and he just could not work out why he could not make himself understood. Is that why people dislike me? He thought. Or is it because I look and act so awkwardly? He had often thought to better himself but every time he did, things just got worse. He then wondered if he was the only one in England who felt so and then decided that it must be the case as everyone else seemed so confident. Gloom dominated for the next mile as Silas could think of nothing to look forward to.

Just as he hit his lowest mood for some time, he felt some movement in the trees far behind him but presumed that it was a breeze. But then, he became aware of a sharp punch in the middle of his back. Before he could turn to see what had happened, a sudden and fierce blow to his head felled him. Annie reared up and made an almighty fuss to no avail. Already, his head hurt so much that he could feel the pain spreading throughout his whole body, he was face down in the dirt and almost instantly restrained as someone had put their knee in his back. He was sure that these were adult men by how they sounded and also because of their brute strength and before another thought could enter his bloodied head, they began punching and kicking him and didn't stop until he was still. Annie had already taken flight, heading home in the hope of getting help. As the men ran away, he lay there lifeless with blood oozing out of his mouth, nose and ears.

Percentages

Two days later, Jenny handed a letter to Robert Hall.

'Aha! Will be from the prioress. I hope she can bloody explain why that scoundrel hasn't returned.'

He skimmed over it and then froze. He read it carefully once more and threw it down.

'Seventy-five per cent! Seventy-five! Do they want a foot and a hand as well? Here, take the bloody house! Nuns? Knaves I say!'

Jenny wasn't sure whether or not a nun could also be a knave but Elspeth, the blond girl in the corner was shocked. She had never seen him angry before and, as someone determined to enter holy orders, she was visibly upset by his rant and started to cry.

'Oh, there's no need' said Robert, '…oh there, there…oh there, there, there…'

Elspeth just cried louder.

'Oh there, there, there… Jane!' he bellowed, 'come and see to this child!'

'Any sign of him?' he asked Jenny.

'None sir. He has not been seen near Dead Alley but his dog has been wandering the city.'

'What's he up to?' he asked rhetorically and then as he sat, he became absorbed in calculations, presumably involving percentages.

Poultice

Silas had no awareness or feeling whatsoever until he heard the gentlest of groans which was his own voice although soon, he immediately lost consciousness again. Eventually, he heard voices which faded in and then faded out again and he found that, if he strained, he could just open one eye, slightly. So blurred and confusing was the sight before him that it took him a good five minutes to understand the silhouette. Looming over him was Mr Cropper's brother who Silas had referred to as the axeman and, he could see his axe too. The man placed his hand on his forehead and spoke,

'I think he's coming out of it and the fire in his head is cooling.'

Silas could hear another voice but not what they were saying and it would be another two hours before his eye fully opened. Eventually, he could see his arms and his chest but little more. His left arm was in a rudimentary splint and almost everywhere else was covered with poultices. He hurt all over and could not move.

'Take it easy lad. Be a long job this will but I think you'll be alright,' said the axeman.

Before he knew it, he was sipping a mushed egg. His wife, Geraldine, who was formerly married to Isaac, tenderly changed his woodland dressings.

'Don't move yet' she said, 'you will get better.'

Silas's first words were for his master but the Axeman laughed.

'He's the least of your worries. We'll get news to him soon.'

Silas realised that he was in a little shack and that the cot looked new. Eventually, they asked him what had happened but he could only remember the blows and the pain and after that, nothing. As he come around, they told him that they had to impart some bad news. As a boy, one of Silas's outstanding features had been his lively, flaming red hair. Although on top there was still a mass of wild curls, only patches remained around his ears.

'Might grow back,' said Geraldine Cropper. Silas raised his right arm as best he could but could only feel his scabby scalp in places. He didn't comment on it then or ever.

By the time he could start to walk, he had been there over a week in which the three of them, Mr and Mrs Cropper and their daughter, Maggie, looked after him. His son, Arxe, did not show at all.

He thanked them a thousand times but constantly worried about his employment. There was a part of him, however, that just wanted to give in to all the fuss and caring and stay there forever. It felt good that even for a short while, he mattered to someone and was worth fixing although he very soon decided that he didn't want young Annie to see him so. Silas also enjoyed the peace, no one seemed to bother the small population of Brint, certainly not this family but then, he remembered that someone had so recently been killed there. Soon, the peace was to be shattered anyway and, as horses approached, the axeman was the first into the clearing. Silas was rudely reminded of how damaged he was both physically and mentally as he struggled to hide inside the shack.

The axeman was very soon joined by his wife and daughter. His wife stilled his arm as it was clear that she recognised one of the riders.

'Master Hall' she said without emotion. Silas heard this and shrunk back into his bed.

'Aha! Isaac's wife' he said hoping to be diplomatic but reminding all that he didn't even know her name.

'Not any more sir. I am now married to this man here.'

Hall dismounted whilst the boy accompanying him stayed on his horse.

The axeman nodded and said,

'Geoffrey'

The mad axeman is called Geoffrey? Thought Silas.

'It is good to meet you. I come in peace; I am hoping…'

'He's here but in bad shape' and Geoffrey pointed at the shack.

He then explained how he had found the boy and, for his part, Hall seemed genuinely concerned. They told him to step in to see Silas who then did his best to sit up.

'No lad. Be still. What in God's name happened?' Hall asked looking at the splint, the injuries, the leaves and goose fat stuck all over him.

Silas started explaining about the meeting with the prioress and apologised although it was very hard to tell what he was saying. He said he didn't understand percentages although he couldn't pronounce it either and he apologised for almost getting killed. Hall selfishly listened intently to see if there was anything in there that might put himself in danger. He walked outside again and complimented Geraldine on how well she had tended to the boy.

'Not me' she said and nodded towards Geoffrey.

'Served the king I did. Fought the Scots at Flodden. Fixed up many a broken body, Scots and English,' he said in a matter-of-fact fashion.

'I compliment you' said Robert, 'I do not doubt that you have saved the boy's life.'

'How did you know he'd be here?' asked Geoffrey.

'Didn't. But his horse came back alone and...'

'What happened then?' shouted Silas realising that he was sounding impertinent.

'Well...there was...' blustered Robert.

'It took you a week to come look for him?' said Geraldine Cropper.

Hall turned around and looked to his companion for support. It was Daniel, the boy who had taught Silas how to ride. He said nothing at first but shrugged his shoulders until something suddenly came to mind.

'Your dog, Silas...he found his way to the stables. He sleeps alongside Annie. All is well,' said Daniel.

Robert Hall was to be saved from his embarrassment but soon other horses were approaching. They all swiftly turned to face the two huge horses that entered the clearing. Silas hobbled out, greeted Daniel and then marvelled at the heavy horses and then the riders. They wore leather skirted doublets and designs of lions and Fleur de Lys were embossed around the edges. On their chest was an emblem which entwined letters F and H. Their saddles were equally as ornate and rested on red velvet. Robert knew better than to try to pull rank so waited for them to speak.

'You are Geoffrey of Galtres? Woodsman?'

Silas was astonished at this rapid elevation of the axeman.

'Aye Sir'

'And this is your new wife, previously married to Isaac the Dwarf?'

She nodded.

It was clear that the questioning was to continue but the guard was rudely interrupted by a smaller horse pushing through which also revealed that there were more personnel behind.

'Where is he? Hehe!'

An imp seemed to appear from nowhere brandishing a wooden sword. He dismounted and approached Silas.

'Silas! Silaaasee! Hehe! Prepare to defend thyself!'

But then he stopped, shocked at the sight before him. No one had told Harry that Silas had been so brutally savaged. Everyone watched as little Harry thought about what to do next. He threw himself to the floor and shouted,

'I forfeit! My life is thine good knight.'

For the first time in a long time, Silas laughed and it hurt.

'I spare thee,' he muttered and that hurt too.

'Please your Grace,' said a very embarrassed guard out the side of his mouth.

Geoffrey leant into Robert and whispered.

'The bastard?'

'Aye, I think so,' he replied.

Harry walked back and mounted his horse.

'This is your errand boy?' asked the guard looking at Robert.

He nodded; mouth open.

He turned to Daniel.

'Can you walk back to the city, boy?'

'Yes sir,' said Daniel.

He looked at Silas.

'Do you think you can ride in that state?'

'I think so sir'

'Well…get all those bloody leaves off and get dressed.'

'Except for the young girl you are all to come with me, you are not under arrest. The woodsman and his wife may share a horse, we have one at the back for the merchant.'

Robert thought to protest but then thought better of it. Someone, if not all of them were in bother and there was no getting out of it. They checked for weapons and confiscated Silas's unused dagger, Geoffrey's axe and a dagger that Robert had concealed. For once, Robert Hall had been completely silenced.

10 The trial

Only Heaven would know why but Silas was shocked when they approached the castle. So sore was he that he didn't know what to think although he was sure of one thing, he yearned to see inside. If there was anything that was sure to raise his spirits it was this. Four yards behind him and on his own horse was Robert. He was terrified. Added to his somewhat less than enviable business practices, he had been involved with the long spate of murders that had taken place in York a few years earlier. He did not know who had summoned them to Sheriff Hutton but they were bound to have power and influence if they lived behind those walls and he was worried that they may know all of his secrets. Harry whooped and shouted as if he were invading the fortress whilst his guardians pretended that he wasn't there. As soon as Silas's horse set foot on the bridge, carrying him over the moat, he was feeling like his otherworldly self once more. They approached a portcullis which raised as they watched on, and beyond were two large wooden doors.

'Who goes there?!' came a voice from within.

"Lord Silas of York" was so clear in Silas's noggin that he was sure he had said it out loud.

'His Grace's sergeant at arms. I come with a party.'

Robert found some solace in his use of words, he could have easily said, prisoners.

Once through the doors, a panorama boasting a large courtyard opened up before them. In the distance, pigs were being slaughtered whilst further along the east wall was an oven being fired. All sorts of creatures and livestock were roaming about although it was those looking after the horses and professionally grooming and saddling them which attracted Silas's attention. A large trough was being fed by fresh water for the horses all of which were of fine breeds. People of different ranks and stations were busying themselves but few took notice of the strangers. Silas thought that there was colour everywhere, on the horses, on people's attire but more strikingly on banners and flags which sported various arms. As they dismounted, he noticed a long half-bricked building that had been built alongside one of the castle walls, he thought that it was something like the Merchant Adventurers' Hall in York and he was right.

Before they knew it, they were all ushered inside that same hall where they stood bunched together awaiting instruction. As they faced the front there were tiered seats and one, in particular, took precedence in the centre. Along the side were stalls, rows of seats that became increasingly higher as they went back. Silas was squinting and moving his neck as far as was possible and thought that it reminded him of a church, theatre or even a court although he had never been inside a court. The guards left as did Harry and a man rushed in wrestling with his dark cloak. Silas thought that he was dressed like William Fawkes and, yet again, was right as the man was a notary.

Just as they all thought to relax, the seemingly insignificant notary found a voice that belonged to a bear.

'Be upstanding!'

They all looked at one another puzzled as they were already standing.

'His Grace: The Archbishop of York, Lord Chancellor of England, Cardinal Wolsey.'

Robert felt ice permeate his bones. Surely this man was jesting? For, if there was one thing that the Archbishop of York was well known for it was for not being anywhere near York so, as he walked in, Robert thought that he may collapse so undone was he.

The man exuded authority. His chain of office alone spoke of almost unlimited power as the king's second in command and his bright red vestments also boasted of how close he was to the Pope.

They all bowed their heads.

Wolsey stood and prayed in Latin and then sat.

'What a bloody mess! As if I have nothing better to do…what a bloody mess!'

As he shuffled papers and made himself comfortable a horse stopped almost directly opposite the doorway. A valet rushed to help the rider who then came straight in. He apologised for his tardiness but the Cardinal waved it away clearly not bothered or interested. Just as Robert was presuming that matters simply could not get worse, Sheriff Hugh Hulley from York had appeared.

'I thank you for coming good sheriff. I understand that forest matters are beyond your jurisdiction so I will not keep you long.'

The notary had him make an oath.

Wolsey looked at Silas.

'My…you've had a beating lad. To start with, do you know anything of the child that rode out to meet you this morning?'

'He is called Harry, has…err fine clothes and is good with a sword' he said as best he could with such damaged features.

'Anything else?'

'No sir except I like him…very much.'

Wolsey laughed.

'He is an imp! A sprat! A free spirit and he keeps us all on our toes. A young city urchin and he is…the king's son!'

Silas was confused. Very confused. The king didn't have a son, he had a daughter, Mary. What did he mean? Robert meanwhile was thinking something entirely different. Silas enticing a royal out of his castle was treasonable and he knew that they both might very well swing for it. He so wanted to shout out that he had warned Silas against it but thought better of it. He also wanted to explain to Silas about the little boy called Harry and inadvertently, his mind wandered as he thought on it: for centuries, it was almost a matter of course that kings had mistresses and few people even batted an eyelid. Henry the Eighth happily picked up on this tradition and enjoyed a lengthy relationship with one in particular, Elizabeth Blount who gave him a male son. And, Geoffrey and Robert would have been right under any other circumstances, he would have simply been labelled as illegitimate, a bastard. The king however was already facing criticism about his ability to provide a male heir and that single issue would indeed become the most important one of his reign. Therefore, Henry happily recognised Henry Fitzroy as his and, in doing so, bestowed the highest compliment on the child as his surname literally meant "son of a king." It came with many titles and privileges including Duke of Richmond and Warden General of the Marches although these were probably somewhat misplaced in a five-year-old.

Wolsey was not only his godfather but was wholly responsible for him during his first few years although Harry had proved to be a handful. Despite the guards being fond of him, he ran them ragged. As he had told Silas, his forlorn tutor was called Richard Croke and so disobedient was Harry that he wrote to the king to complain that "he would spend time with jesters and go hunting rather than attend lessons." Fortunately, King Henry sent a Clerk of the Green Cloth to investigate who upheld the accusation.

Wolsey's voice snapped Hall out of it.

'Harry will be leaving Sheriff Hutton soon. You will not see him again and you must not try to,' said Wolsey. He then looked Silas up and down,

'Let him sit.'

And Silas was ushered to a seat in the stall to Wolsey's left where even through one eye he had a magnificent view.

'Let's start with the woman' he said swiftly changing the subject.

Throughout what would become a quite lengthy procedure, the notary made sure that everyone present swore an oath.

'You were the dwarf's wife?'

'Yes, your Grace.'

'Good, good…and who is the man next to you?'

'He is my husband now. Geoffrey of Galtres.'

'Ah, the soldier. Did you kill the dwarf?' asked Wolsey.

'No, your Grace, of course not. He was my best friend. We served together.'

'Mm. So you did. Feisty little bugger wasn't he. Haha!'

'So why did you marry her so soon…had you nowhere else to put it, man? I imagine it's lonely in the woods. You people have all sorts of desperate desires' said Wolsey.

'He had me promise to take care of her and the girl if anything happened to him. I'd say he knew that he was in danger, your Grace.'

'I'd bloody well say so too!' said Wolsey.

He turned to the sheriff.

'Why did you arrest the boy here?' said Wolsey who then turned to Silas who was now much nearer to him. 'God's teeth! What happened to you? Look like you've been wrestling with Norfolk!'

The notary looked once and then twice to read the Cardinal's mood. He chuckled presuming that it was the response he wanted.

'What you grinning at man?!'

The notary shrunk back into his dark shell.

Finally, the sheriff spoke.

'He was the last one to see the dwarf your Grace and he had an axe. Twas an axe that finished him.'

'So why did you let him go then?'

'I spoke to Isaac's wife who you have just addressed, your Grace,' said the sheriff.

'And…' He glared at Geraldine Cropper again.

'I found him dead long after the boy had left and he was known to be at the priory later that day and Silas did not return until long after my husband had been killed.'

Thomas

Then, two other notaries joined the proceedings followed by a much darker creature. He had a sense of purpose about him and, although he was seemingly late, the Cardinal did not bat an eyelid, in fact, he was pleased to see him.

'Aha! Thomas! My man…Thomas will get to the bottom of all this nonsense' and Wolsey sat back and started drinking wine from a silver goblet.

'You Grace' said Thomas ingratiating himself in a quite undignified manner.

This was Thomas Cromwell who would be referred to only as Wolsey's manager in 1525 and it was unlikely that anyone else present would have even heard of him. Nevertheless, he took over proceedings almost straight away and went straight for Silas who thought that this was a great show, possibly even better than those of Bayard and Dunstan.

'You are Silas Smith, son of Clifford of Dead Alley York?'

Silas nodded.

Then, Cromwell hesitated and looked at the sorry huddle of people gathered.

'You are in the wrong place. You should be standing to his Grace's right, not his left.'

En masse, they shuffled from one side of the hall to the other. From their new vantage point, they could clearly see the north wall of the castle and upon it were three heads. Swiftly they turned to face Cromwell again.

Snake-like he confronted Robert,

'You are Robert Hall, son of Robert Hall of Yorkshire gentry, member of York Corpus Christi Guild, member of York Merchant's Guild and you trade in wool, lead and glass?'

'Yes, my Lord' mumbled Robert.

'I am not a Lord, sir will do' snapped Cromwell.

Wolsey interrupted.

'Aha Master Hall I do believe you and I have common

interests today' he said pointing a heavily ringed finger at him.

'Is the boy yonder your employee?' asked Cromwell.

'Yes sir.'

'Was Isaac of Brint, this woman's husband your employee?'

'Yes, he was sir.'

'Did you have anything to do with his death?'

Now Robert was truly terrified. Was this why he had been brought to the castle? His mind wandered. At best, he would spend his days in chains, all his comforts removed, at worst? Well, he visibly shuddered at the thought.

'I thought highly of the dwarf he was….' He struggled to find any accolade for Isaac so little interest had he taken in his welfare, '…a valued worker. I did not kill him. I was in the city when he was killed.'

'Mm…of course you were…' said Cromwell and walked back towards Wolsey who was still quaffing.

Then, the notary once more found his voice frightening the living daylights out of everyone in attendance.

'Bring in the prisoner!'

'Bring in the prisoner!' shouted the guard.

'No'…said the notary, 'no need to do that…I say "bring in the prisoner." Not you.'

The guard apologised but looked somewhat chagrined, he had been waiting for such an opportunity for months.

Unsupported, a pathetic silhouette entered, head down. He was filthy and from his gait and the blood on his clothes, it appeared as if he had been tortured. He was thin and elderly with a long straggly beard, barely recognisable until Cromwell started to question him.

'You are Salvo, formerly Father Salvo of Whitby?'

'Yes sir' he muttered.

It was then that Silas realised that this was the man he had seen at the priory and before he knew it, was asked to confirm it. Just as Cromwell had everything in good order,

Wolsey stood up, toppling his goblet and completely losing his professional demeanour.

'Thou venomous monster! Devil's shithole! You will be shown today for what you are!'

Cromwell sat and waited until it was over.

'My very own trusted priest…friend even! Thou buggerer of mountain goats! You will pay!'

Wolsey looked around and, realising that he was embarrassing himself, sat and waved to Cromwell to continue and he faced Robert once more.

'Do you know this man?'

'No sir, I did not realise that there were any men at Rosedale Priory…'

'Bloody good answer Hall!' shouted Wolsey and turned his anger back toward the prisoner.

'What was I thinking of putting you in charge? You badger's bollock.'

Robert momentarily felt as though he may have gained some favour although, truthfully, he really did think that the prioress ran the priory, as anyone would.

'Call the next witness!' demanded the notary who also kept one eye on the guard at the same time in case he stole his act once again.

'Hic!'

Silas jumped and said, 'Ooh.'

Everyone else looked around.

'Hic! Hic!!'

It was Geraldine Cropper who now had hiccups. Her head went down and, no matter how much her new husband poked her in the ribs, she could not get rid of them.

Silas was shocked as he then saw the sad and downtrodden figure of the prioress enter. She took the oath and confirmed who she was.

Cromwell tried to remind Wolsey that he hadn't finished questioning Salvo but he ignored him.

'Do you recognise who this man is?' asked Cromwell of

the prioress.

'He is Father Salvo' she said'

'Hic!!'

'How do you know of him?'

'His Grace….' she paused and looked up at Cardinal Wolsey who nodded for her to continue, 'his Grace placed him in charge at Rosedale.'

Robert's mouth dropped open. Wolsey had interests at Rosedale? He then presumed that Wolsey may well have known all his secrets too. His anxieties speedily returned.

'To what end?' asked Wolsey calmly.

'We have farmed sheep for hundreds of years and, for the last hundred years have learned how to manufacture glass to a fair standard. Father…'

'You are not to refer to him as Father if you please, prioress' said Cromwell kindly.

'He was to organise us, the nuns, so that we could produce better glass…that is clearer, larger pieces of pane and even crafted goblets and…to be more business-like.'

'Hic! Hic!!'

'We bloody hanged the last woman to have hiccups in the courtroom!' said Wolsey.

Miraculously, they stopped. Then Silas's bad eye opened slightly so shocked was he to discover that he was in a courtroom. Cromwell suggested that Geraldine Cropper sat in the stalls next to Silas.

'Did he show any expertise in his management?' asked Cromwell of the prioress.

'Oh yes, sir. At first…'

'Go on,'

'At first, although we worked almost all day and night, we could see the improvements until...'

'That will do for now,' said Cromwell quite abruptly.

Murano

'Bring in the next witness,' he said.

Without any supervision, a young man walked in. He

looked as though he hadn't been fed properly in months and had grown a thin, wispy beard. Silas guessed that he might be in his mid-twenties but he was gaunt and his face was drawn. His clothes were unlike anything Silas had seen before. Although they were somewhat tattered and dirty, they were also overtly colourful and even each leg of his hose was a different colour, Silas decided that it reminded him of a jester from old paintings.

He was called Giovanni and spoke in Italian to Cromwell which further impressed Silas. Immediately, Robert was acknowledging that the young man was from one of the Italian states and that Cromwell and Wolsey not only spoke Italian well but they had many contacts there. After all, he thought, Wolsey is now a vicar of the Vatican and it is also where Cromwell had learnt many of his tricks from Machiavelli although, as yet, few would be aware of it.

Then, Cromwell asked him where he was from. His answer shocked Robert to the core.

'Murano, Venice.'

'Are you able to give testimony in English?'

'Yes sir,' he responded.

'Do you know the man standing next to you?'

Without looking he answered,

'His name is Salvo.'

'And how do you know this man?'

'I was on a managed and sponsored visit to the Netherlands when I first met him...' he began.

'Please…,' said Cromwell, 'in your own time and in your own words, tell the court the whole story.'

Giovanni said little about why he was in the Netherlands but said that he was introduced to a priest who had "common interests." Moreover, the stranger had information about affairs between the two countries, a trade agreement that could possibly avoid war.

'Which countries?' asked Cromwell.

'England and Venice' he answered.

A collective gasp momentarily paused proceedings.

'You do freely acknowledge that as we speak England is at war with Venice?'

'Yes, sir but…'

'Continue'

'This was before the war, six years ago.'

Cromwell nodded.

'He claimed that he was an ambassador for your king and that he had information that would sustain peace and trade between our homes.'

'Quite admirable,' said Cromwell now face to face with Salvo, 'please continue master Giovanni.'

'He bought…well, a feast. Fine wine and at first, I thought he was an interesting man. I also trusted him because he was a man of holy orders. Then, almost out of nowhere, he was joined by four other men. Rough fellows. He said they were his travelling companions, security but…'

'But they kidnapped you in your sleep did they not?' asked Cromwell quite dramatically.

'I thought I would die; I spent days on a small boat crammed into a cask and when we reached England, travelled over rough terrain.'

'What was your destination?'

'Rosedale Priory sir.'

All Robert could hear was his heart. He had almost stopped worrying about the murders in York for what the Italian had said already had him wishing that he had never heard of Rosedale Priory.

Murano was acknowledged as a quite exceptional place. Following the capture of Constantinople in 1204, there had been an influx of Byzantine artisans into Venice and, over time, skills, technologies and techniques evolved that were unique and renowned. The island of Murano was where the finest and most elaborate glass in the world was made and where the greatest masters resided and, stayed there for life. They were forbidden to leave or to share their secrets with anyone. Moreover, these masters were afforded special privileges which made them exempt from many laws and allowed them to carry a sword with them all the time. On rare occasions, masters would travel but only to boast of the rift between their work and that of the rest of the world or to promote their advantage. The bedraggled youth standing before them was one of those privileged and celebrated artisans.

Everything went quiet as the notary left and returned with a tray. On top was an object covered with velvet. He placed it in front of Wolsey who wasted no time in removing the cloth.

Almost everyone was aghast at what they witnessed.

'Do you recognise this?' asked Wolsey.

'Yes sir. I made it.'

Wolsey picked up the glass goblet which was huge, almost the size of his forearm. Where the glass was clear, it was completely clear but there were four snake-like coils which began at the stem and finished at the lip. These were perfectly spiralled but of a fine, milky appearance and, in between, were patterns of gold and rose gold. As he turned it, the glass was perfect from all sides. He showed everyone the base which boasted a lattice design, again without flaw.

'I must compliment you…and your fellow glass masters, signor. We rarely see the like in England except at court. Zanfirico filigree, I believe? We cannot make this in England, can we?' said Wolsey but then lost his temper again.

'Can we Salvo?! What in hell's name is this doing in Yorkshire?!'

Salvo fell to his knees.

'I only endeavoured to please your Grace. You had asked me….'

'Silence!' shouted Wolsey and slammed his fist into the lectern almost dropping the masterpiece.

Those who hadn't seen the goblet before stared and marvelled at it but very soon it was removed.

Wolsey nodded to Cromwell to continue.

'I thank you. I may come back to you although...he looked directly a Robert Hall...I think most thinking men will easily work out your role in these crimes and misdemeanours.'

'Next!' he shouted.

A guard accompanied the most bizarre-looking creature. It was a young woman wearing a dress that would not have been out of place on a nobleman's wife. It had a fashionable squared neck and pearls punctuated diamond patterns along its border. It was mostly satin with huge, billowing velvet sleeves and, around her neck was a large ruby. But, the bottom four inches of her dress were filthy almost dripping in fetid water and it was ill-fitting. It was, however, her head which had everyone in court staring at her.

The woman had no hair.

'What is your name?' asked Cromwell.

'I am Sister Marian.'

Geraldine Cropper crossed herself.

'And you reside at Rosedale Priory?'

'Yes sir.'

Cromwell unexpectedly turned to his boss, Wolsey.

'Is this how you expect ladies in Holy orders to appear, your Grace?'

Although he struggled somewhat, this time Wolsey kept a rein on his temper.

'I do believe that anyone in this room could answer that...you are a disgrace, girl and I fear for your very soul,' said Wolsey.

'I have no questions for you' said Cromwell, 'you will remain thus, a spectacle for all to witness.'

Silas didn't know what to think. He hadn't seen her at the priory and could think of no reason why she was dressed so.

Next, a young Englishman walked in. He removed his hat and bowed before Wolsey. Silas glared at his fine attire.

'You are Mark Walton, a musician?' asked Cromwell.

'Yes sir, I travel providing music for places such as this, halls, festivals and fine houses. I have even played afore the king...'

'Quite impressive, Master Walton. You must be good then? And...you employ other musicians?'

'Yes sir.'

'Do you know this man?'

Cromwell walked over and stood in front of Salvo who had his head down.

'I do.'

'Explain, in your own words, how.'

'I met him at Ripon Abbey sir. I was there on a commission from the precentor. I helped him with some new compositions...arrangements for the choir. He claimed.... he told me he was a bishop and that similar work was required at Rosedale Priory.'

'Did you think that unusual?'

'Yes sir. Men are not usually allowed in convents. I then met him at Rosedale when he told me of a private masque that was to be held....' he looked at Wolsey for permission.

'I give you permission to continue' said Wolsey intervening.

'A masque held in his Grace's honour...the Cardinal.'

'Did you believe him?'

'He told me that the nuns were on a retreat nearby...he made it sound if they were fasting, facing the elements as it were, sir.'

'How many times did you and your musicians play there?'

'Oh, just the once sir and then we left early.'

'Did he offer you recompense for your visit?'

'Oh yes, he paid very well.'

'Do you recognise her ladyship here?' asked Cromwell mocking the hairless woman.

Mark nodded.

'I thank you for your patience, Mark' said Wolsey, 'now, in your own words tell all present today what you witnessed.'

'Even allowing for the fact that this was a…somewhat private…party or masque. I was shocked to see so much wine and food. Having said that your Grace…sir…I believe that all those who had taken holy orders were not on the premises. Then, three other men besides Salvo entered, all seemingly prosperous and of rank and five women dressed as fine as any at court. One of them threw her French bonnet away and appeared…well…thus.'

'You mean that she had a shaved head?'

'Yes sir.'

'Carry on.'

'We played and they drank and danced but what began with much exuberance and gaiety soon become something else. The ladies began to…'

He stopped, acknowledging the prioress and Mrs Cropper.

'You must say it!' demanded Cromwell.

'They began to disrobe sir and then, the most ungodly acts took place before our eyes. We left. As we did, he threatened our lives if we spoke of what we had seen.'

Geraldine Cropper closed her eyes and genuflected so many times it was a wonder that she didn't fall over. The prioress took to her knees. Silas had no clue whatsoever what Mark was talking about.

'Then that is a very brave testimony Mark' said Wolsey who then turned to Salvo once more.

'Beelzebub has burrowed his way into your malodorous bowels! I so trusted you with the welfare of those good nuns and God's mission in Yorkshire…'

Salvo rolled himself into a ball, moaning and protesting and then suddenly yelled out.

'I was only doing your Grace's bidding. You…'

He was silenced once more, this time by a guard.

Although many were still confused, there was a story unravelling that made sense although everyone was still in the dark regarding Isaac's death. However, apart from Silas, there were few who actually believed that Wolsey was completely innocent of this corruption. Robert in particular had already worked out that Wolsey must have put Salvo at the monastery to further industrialise it. Was it likely that he knew nothing of Giovanni and the parties? He thought.

'For those of you here who may be perplexed' started Wolsey, 'I did indeed employ this man Salvo in whom I had faith and some high regard. He had shown himself capable of managing local churches; their finances in particular as I am soon looking to examine the efficiency of all our holy houses..'

Of course, he was. The writings of Martin Luther had already permeated most of Europe and not only had he exposed the corruption of monasteries, particularly the selling of indulgences (prayers that ensured that the souls of the rich took priority in entering Heaven) but he had also told the common man that he could access God directly. Wolsey had passionately denounced Luther but he and the king had agreed that many monks and nuns had been living the good life for too long so, yes, very soon Wolsey and his dark lackey would be running a thorough audit of all holy houses.

He continued,

'It is also true that I had instructed him to find means and technologies that would increase glass production including the sizes of panes and fine goblets. I would have even tolerated him travelling to Europe although it seems that as soon as he was let out of my sight, he gave himself up willingly to the devil himself. Under duress, the nuns worked almost every hour God sent them, eventually unable to maintain their prayers and other obligations. For the faithful, those like the prioress here, they were used as slaves whilst the more compliant enjoyed a life of debauchery and every sin known to man. Giovanni, the Venetian, was as much a slave as those nuns, death being the only alternative to submitting to Salvo's diabolical scheme. But you may ask, where do the lavish jewels and dresses come in? Where are they from? Perhaps you could assist Master Hall…' he said sarcastically.

Robert was grovelling even before he spoke. He was expecting this but was nevertheless unprepared.

'I…erm…I would get messages…often via Isaac. The prioress said that they would like fine dresses instead of money. Truth be told…'

'You profited that way?' said Cromwell.

'I suppose I did…yes. I know nothing of this…Salvo…person your Grace. I concur that trading in fineries is unusual but not unheard of. I would never...'

'Yes…very well Hall…that will do' responded an impatient Cardinal, 'bring in the ruffians…'

Even more guards brought in four men who were filthy and uncooperative. No two were the same size and they appeared unkempt and ill-educated. Cromwell addressed the biggest one.

'So, you know that man yonder?' he said pointing to Salvo.

He grunted.

'You must answer.'

'Yes sir.'

Cromwell persisted with some very basic questioning although it was proving to be hard work.

'The man is an imbecile, your Grace' Cromwell said turning to Wolsey who then spoke directly to him.

'Do you know of Isaac the Dwarf of Brint?'

'Yes, but I did not know his name.'

'Did you kill him?'

'He killed him, I helped' he said pointing to the imbecile on his left.

'See Thomas! We are getting somewhere,' said Wolsey.

'Why did you kill him or, if you like, assist in the killing?'

'Orders from the gaffer?'

'The gaffer being…?'

'Him as stands there.'

'Salvo?'

'Yup. We thought it was the right thing to do as the orders came from Father...'

'Do not call him Father' asserted Wolsey.

'Oh...'

'And your tired and overused "I did it under orders" will not suffice I'm afraid.'

He turned to Salvo.

'How dare you? Tell the court your reasons why you would have such a good servant put to death.'

Salvo said nothing.

'Mrs Cropper, come back down here, would you?'

She left her seat and stood in front of Cromwell who picked up the questioning.

'Do you know of any reason why Salvo would pay these men to kill your former husband?'

Sheepishly, she looked over at Salvo.

'He cannot harm you ever again,' said Cromwell.

'My dear Isaac knew too much. On his visits…on behalf of Master Hall…he would ask constantly about the prioress and why he could no longer speak to Sister Celeste alone but his size was an advantage, he would search the place unseen. He was so troubled sir. Didn't sleep at night and once the boy…Silas…started to work for Master Hall, he worried about him too. Anyway…he told Salvo that he would report him to the wardens and that was when he threatened to kill him. Soon after he gave notice to Master Hall that he would not work for him no more.'

'Any more,' said Cromwell.

'Pardon my Lord?'

'He would not work for him anymore and I'm not a Lo... oh, never mind. So, you are saying that he knew of his demise?'

She broke down, sobbing.

'That he did…sir…even asked Geoffrey to take his place

if he was killed. God bless him.'

'God bless him indeed' said Cromwell dramatically, 'I am certain that this brave man sits well with his maker as we speak and the court also acknowledges his part in uncovering this villainy.'

He walked over to one of the ruffians who was standing behind the other two and pulled at his disgusting jerkin. He walked back and held out his hand for Silas to see. He fully opened his good eye and then unwittingly, touched the side of his head, just above his ear.

Then, Cromwell showed Wolsey and the rest of the court. Clumps of Silas's red hair remained on the clothes of his assailants.

'Why didn't you kill the boy?' asked Cromwell.

'He wus a boy.'

'Yes, I know he is a boy! But why did you not kill him? You more or less left him for dead.'

'Couldn't kill a child,' came his excuse.

'And yet you did this...' he pointed at Silas, a sorry sight for even the hardest of hearts.

Wolsey once again addressed Salvo.

'You sad excuse for a man! Your greed has undone you. You are guilty of kidnapping a citizen of the esteemed island of Murano, imprisoning and enslaving that same man to produce the highest quality of glassware that neither I or Master Hall have ever seen afore, leaving me wondering who you sold it to.

In doing so, you have put the king in a very difficult position as kidnapping a Venetian will be seen as an aggressive act well before war was declared. In addition, you coerced women of God to work so many hours that they neglected their holy orders and the only way out for some was to give way to your extraordinary demands. Dressing up and whoring them whilst you drank and made merry through the night, believing that no one was the wiser. Arrogant enough to commission respectable musicians even. When someone was, at long last, able to confront you, you took his life, robbing a young girl of her father and a woman her husband. And then this. I have seen much, in war even, but to beat a child so is not only ungentlemanly but ungodly. Before you leave this world for the eternal flames, you will confess the rest of your misdemeanours as well.'

He then turned to Sheriff Hugh Hulley.

'Ah, sheriff...almost forgot you were here!'

'Will there be anything else your Grace?'

Robert's tired heart thumped away once more; he desperately wanted any testament of Hulley's to be over.

'Yes, return to York with my thanks. I will have a copy of judgements and sentencing sent to you as a matter of courtesy.'

And, with that, he was gone. Robert Hall exhaled so loudly that all heard it.

'There is much to consider here including his Grace, young Henry's escapades with this lad over here...'

He called over Cromwell and they whispered for a few moments.

'Sentencing will take place before the hour is out!' he announced.

The Dungeon

Cromwell walked over to the notary with instructions who then passed them on to the guards. Two of them herded together the prioress, Geoffrey, his wife, Robert, Silas and Mark the musician. They were taken outside and told not to speak. Mark was told that he was free to go and was thanked for his contribution. No sooner had the others blinked to acknowledge the sunlight than they were taken inside again, this time through an opening in the castle wall. They descended a spiral stone staircase and were put into a circular stone room. Then, one of the guards spoke,

'This is not a cell but you must await Master Cromwell here' and with that, he left.

Conditions were dreadful in that room. Rats ran around their feet and it was hard to find a place where they were not standing in the water. Added to that was the awkward silence. Arrogantly Robert thought to blame the prioress for Salvo's fallings and, no doubt, she felt the same about him. Geoffrey comforted his new wife but still, nothing was said.

Although it seemed like hours later, Cromwell returned in fifty minutes and, strangely, brought a stool for himself.

'Sentencing has concluded.'

They looked at one another. Were they exempt or was he about to read out their sentences?

'Prioress...mother, I must start with a question for you about an issue of some concern to his Grace.'

She raised her head.

'Do you think yourself capable of getting Rosedale back to what it once was?'

She looked shocked.

'Why...yes sir. With God's help, I am certain of it. If I could have...'

They heard footsteps. It was Celeste and other nuns from Rosedale who had refused to demean themselves for Salvo and who had consequently been ill-used as slaves. They were a shocking sight which impacted everyone in the room. The prioress embraced them.

'Does that answer your question?' asked Cromwell.

'Oh yes! Yes sir! We will make the finest holy house in Yorkshire. I give you my solemn oath that we will restore order and faith,' and the five nuns wept uncontrollably.

Quite sensitively, Cromwell gave them a few minutes to quieten and then asked them to be still whilst he continued. Rummaging in a small satchel he had worn throughout the trial, he pulled out a small piece of leather.

'Do you know what this is boy?' he asked of Silas.

'I... erm...I believe it is...part of...a nose brace.'

For the first time Cromwell smiled, the nuns were clueless as to what the object was.

'This is off Harry's horse. Yes, the nose brace or part of it. He is gifting it to you as a farewell.'

As Silas examined it, he could see those same designs: lions and a Fleur de Lys surrounded by embossed patterns.

'You cannot have the missing parts as they carry the king's coat of arms. That just wouldn't do, would it?'

Anyone who knew Cromwell either then or later on in his career would be wondering what was wrong with him. Maybe it had something to do with what the boy had been through. Cromwell had suffered a dire childhood much of it at the hands of his cruel father. Whatever it was, Silas welcomed it and thanked him a dozen times for the gift.

'Geoffrey of Brint and your good wife. You will be returned this afternoon to your home. We thank you for your testimony. His Grace will send one full sack of grain for you which will be paid out of Salvo's estate once dead' he looked around, 'none of you will be allowed to witness the executions.'

'Master Hall...'

Robert was now a shadow of that self which had earlier left York for Brint. He was drawn and pale, his clothes dishevelled and marked and there never can have been a man looking so frightened and, Cromwell knew it.

'That sir, is the look of guilt. Your greed has helped to put one good employee in his grave and another not far behind and....you had the arrogance to think that you had a monopoly at Rosedale. His Grace washes his hands of the place.'

Even the nuns looked shocked.

'He will shortly return to his other interests. He has granted permission for you to continue to trade with the priory.'

'Pardon...sir did you...'

'You heard right' said Cromwell, 'however, if it had been my decision, that would not have been the case...you will pay for the product with money...and nothing else! And, you will pay fifty per cent of their labour costs which will all go to running the priory, helping the poor and, of course, what is due to the Crown.'

Robert was dumbstruck, far from swinging on a rope he had ended the day better off than when he started. Minutes earlier he would have promised anything to secure the Cardinal's favour but now his arrogance was returning like an open tap as he considered future possibilities. It was then that it occurred to him that Salvo must have been selling to someone else besides himself and, if not Wolsey, who could it have been? He restrained himself for he was bursting to ask. Thankfully, Cromwell started to speak again.

'You will not speak of any of today's events. Not ever' he looked at Silas, 'do not come near the castle again. Do you understand?'

'Yes sir' replied Silas who groaned as he nodded.

Before they could think about what Cromwell had said they were on their way. Silas was still hurting and found it difficult to mount. Added to that was his realisation that no other horse was like Annie, he had to put some effort into riding the borrowed one. Nevertheless, he turned his head as best he could to get a final glimpse of that other world, one in which he was sure he belonged. For the rest of the journey, he turned the leather horse brace around between the fingers of his good hand, smiling.

Everything seemed to change once they arrived in Brint. The daughter came running toward them in tears and told them that she feared she would never see them again. Although Geoffrey offered to feed Silas and Robert Hall, there was an embarrassed silence. It would be a while before Robert's dignity would return and it made him uneasy.

'All has ended well and justice has prevailed!' declared Geoffrey and his wife kissed him.

'You will heal completely soon Silas. Be sure to visit.'

Geraldine Cropper gently embraced him. Robert still looked as if he did not belong there but then began to mumble.

'I... erm...I know a... erm...very good wood sculptor.'

They stared wondering where this was going.

'Ah, very good sir,' said Geoffrey.

'I would like to commission a memorial, here in Brint....of Isaac.'

Geraldine Cropper and her daughter both broke down. Geoffrey shook his hand.

'...and I will send a bag of grain. Anything the Cardinal can do...Haha'

They ignored his nervous laugh and accepted his generosity in good faith. He turned to Silas and pointed at the coveted nose brace.

'I will have that made a part of your colt's nose brace. You will not know that it came off another...'

Tripping over his words Silas politely thanked his boss and felt relieved as he was sure that once they had left the castle, he would find himself sacked. Robert then told Silas to rest with the Croppers whilst he rode back to York. On his return, he said, he would send Daniel with Annie.

11 The thieves and the poor

Whether Robert liked it or not, Silas was unable to work for a week or two so told him to stay home. Even his short break had left his home full of leaves, debris and wildlife but he cared not. Small as Castle Cooper was, he walked around in circles thanking God for all he had. Annie was happily grazing in a plot that was no bigger than she was and, with thoughts of further developing his humble abode, he lay back on his cot instead and reflected on what had happened. Curiously, apart from one or two events, he had not been the least bit scared in court, possibly because for the greater part of it he thought it was a show. Momentarily, he flattered himself that he knew something was wrong at the priory all along but then chastised himself for saying nothing. But the whole experience had thrilled him. It had shown him a new world and educated him about what important people did, how they sounded and how they dressed.

He had found a replacement for the old barrel that his mother had used for washing and, although it was full of rainwater boasting dead leaves and insects, he stripped off and cleaned his wounds and then the many layers of filth elsewhere on his meatless form. He then washed his clothes and hung them out in the sun but, as he looked up, naked, he saw two men scurrying away from the churchyard. Of course, he was worried that they had seen that which only his mother had previously set eyes upon but was more concerned that they were the men that he had seen putting bundles on carts in the forest at night. He was confused for, at first, he had presumed that it was them who had attacked him in Galtres Forest but they were not even mentioned in court. Perhaps this time I should tell my master, he thought.

As he put his clothes back on, he pondered once again about why they never seemed to fit but very soon that thought also ended up in the ether. He wandered through the city until Bolt chose to detour towards the Queen of Sheba's palace but as he approached the new church building near the Minster, he witnessed the end of one of Bayard's performances and loitered a while. Only the dedicated attendees would ever know how it had started but once Silas had arrived, he could see an actor dressed as Wolsey, drunk, groping and dancing with nuns, paint all over their faces and wearing fine dresses. A monk implored him to stop and then said,

'Your Grace...repent and show me the way to Heaven'

Wolsey belched, pointed at one of the painted nuns and shouted,

'Follow me, pilgrim!'

The crowd laughed. Silas didn't understand what was funny but otherwise thought it was a fine show and it didn't escape him that it had something to do with what had so recently been dealt with at the court at Sheriff Hutton. It didn't even occur to him that the coincidence was uncanny. Happy and healing, he looked down at his shoes, sure one was bigger than the other and remembered how many he had lost when he had worked for William Fawkes. When he looked up, Dunstan was there right in front of him.

'You will heal, Silas'

'That I will sir' he replied smiling.

'Just a few more years,' said Dunstan.

Silas did not know what this meant and so just ignored it, a strategy that had worked well for him many times in the past.

'Remember all I have taught you my young Silas, retain your good heart and do not let others change you, for you are blessed.'

For a moment, Silas thought that his friend sounded like a pastor so thought that he should pay full attention but that, seemingly is where the sermon ended.

'Why not help us pack up?' asked Dunstan.

'I would like to sir although...I am of... little use...' he smiled as he looked down at his many injuries.

Dunstan nodded and returned to his duties. Silas painfully waved to Bayard and then made his way to see the queen for it had been weeks since his last visit.

He knocked before entering but there was no answer. He pushed the door open as best he could and there, in the half-light, sat his queen in her chair although her head hung much lower than it usually did.

'All hail the Queen of Sheba!' he announced. She did not move.

He walked over and knelt by her chair. She was more than a stone lighter than when he had last seen her and her breathing was now laboured and shallow. He stood and scrambled amongst the objects on the table and, in doing so, had two mice scurrying for the door. He found some dry and partly mouldy bread and sniffed it, cursing himself for forgetting to buy her some. He then made a small fire and warmed the bread. She managed to chew no more than a couple of small pieces and then spoke for the first time.

'What...how?' she whispered as she touched his head where hair had been so viciously torn out.

'I am well' he said.

'Dear...boy...Silas. You have been...like kin to me. I have nothing to leave you but my love. Do not let...anyone...change you...'

He thought it curious that he had heard that twice within an hour. He then knelt and put his arms around her, embracing her twisted form and, in turn, she cradled her head on his bony shoulder. She continued to talk but he did not understand anything of it and he was certain that her end was near. Even at eleven years of age, he had experienced too much death and easily recognised its tricks and subtleties.

His ribs still hurt as did his shoulder and he so struggled to hold up her weighty head. Every fifteen minutes, the breaths became further apart until, eventually, they stopped altogether.

He stayed in that position for another hour when every so often tears would roll down his face though he chose to remain silent so as not to disturb her majesty. Silas was missing her already and he would never know for some years the immense value that he had added to the eccentric old lady's life.

Eventually, he stood up, faced the door and announced,

'The Queen of Sheba is dead! The whole nation mourns' and then he hung his head.

Silas went straight to the priest to tell him of her demise and begged the priest to inform him when she was to be buried.

Later that day, Silas decided to follow his conscience as he had so often been advised to do so. He urgently felt the need to report to Robert Hall's house and although he was unexpected, he banged several times on the back door until Jenny came.

'Lord in Heaven! He told me you have been battered but I didn't think you'd be so bad. Where's your hair?'

'Some of it is swinging from the battlements at Sheriff Hutton' he said thinking he was making a joke although Jenny was left clueless. She then reminded him that he wasn't supposed to be there but he told her that there was one more matter that his master should be aware of.

'I'll see but you know what he's like...' and she went back inside closing the door behind her.

Almost immediately, Robert Hall came to the door and surprisingly invited Silas in but deliberately shut Bolt out. He seemed quite cordial but was, yet again, wondering if Silas had something on him that would invite further trouble. Silas was instantly taken aback as Hall then asked him what was on his mind. Silas looked at Jenny, presumably for support.

'If there's something stuck in your pipeline lad, push it out; you'll feel better.'

Silas laughed. He rarely laughed or even understood jokes but this was a little rude and funny enough for him to react.

Even Hall stared at her astonished and it was then that she could tell that her master was wary of her and about to send her away. She was right and it was possible that he even considered sending the boy away too except that in the doorway behind him Mrs Hall appeared.

He looked around, turned back again and muttered, 'Checkmate.'

He wasn't getting out of it.

'Take it slowly,' said Mrs Hall addressing Silas.

Of course, his first attempt was almost unintelligible but eventually, he managed to get most of the tale out in one go.

'...heavy bundles onto carts and... I have seen them in the churchyard...'

For a man who had been brought down several pegs in recent days, Robert Hall suddenly found a renewed sense of purpose and confidence. He rushed out of the house beckoning Silas to follow him and Bolt tagged along too. Struggling to keep up, Hall marched him half the length of the city. Silas was mortified when he found himself in front of the sheriff once more.

'Judas's backside! Not you two again!'

Hall persuaded Hulley to listen as Silas's tale did indeed make some sense to him. The sheriff soon concurred with Hall's assumptions so much so that, Hulley and Hall, who possibly at some point in their career should have considered sharing a business name, stormed off and Silas followed, Bolt thinking it was the best game he had played all year. Silas soon found himself in Gillygate not too far from where the queen had lived. There, he could just make out a dark snickleway much narrower and much filthier than Dead Alley, somewhere he would not have gone alone. One man was keeping pigs but they were poorly looked after and almost emaciated. Others sat around in squalor and all the children were in rags. The buildings were in a state of ill repair, the street a quagmire and it was one of those places where people would not even bother to leave to relieve themselves and subsequently the stench was so grave that it almost deserved to have its own name on the map of York.

'What hour is it?' said Hulley.

'Four or Five' answered Hall.

'Then we shall meet back here at dusk.'

They both looked at the lad.

'I want to come,' said Silas.

Simultaneously, they replied,

'Leave the dog at home!'

Dusk came and the three of them found themselves standing at the opening of Gillygate observing the alley. They made a pretence of playing a game of jacks and kept their heads down, Hugh wore a hood and a cape that covered his sword and Silas found this incredibly exciting. Eventually, they heard a squishing sound coming from the alley which was nothing like anything they had heard before. Then they heard an argument brewing and as the quarrel became nearer, it was clear that the sound was coming from two men pushing a cart through the effluence. Hall put his head down so as not to be recognised and Hulley prodded Silas.

'That them?'

Silas nodded furiously. Not knowing what the plan was or even if there was one, he followed his master and the sheriff as, in turn, they followed the two men and the empty cart. It soon became clear that they were heading towards All Saints, Pavement Church although, as yet, they had not broken any laws as it was still before curfew. The men waited in the churchyard, one by the cart and one keeping watch. Silas was thrilled to be out beyond curfew and knew that he was only allowed to do so because the sheriff was with him.

The grave

For some time, nothing happened but eventually, the men took a shovel from the cart and started to take turns digging. Silas was so shocked that he gasped and so Robert instantly placed his hand over his mouth. As he still had not fully recovered, he was also finding it painful kneeling in the bushes and he wondered why they had not apprehended the men so he asked, his query distorted through Robert Hall's fingers. Quietly they told him that they wanted the unlawful act complete before they confronted them. A crime, intimated Hall, had to be witnessed.

Once the men were in the grave and attempting to exhume a corpse, Robert and the sheriff startled them. Hugh drew his sword and prodded the belly of the first with it whilst the other took flight. The sheriff's prisoner looked him in the eye certain that anything would have been preferable to being caught. His head cranked left and right contemplating escape.

'Up to you Banks, but be in no doubt that if you move, I will run you through where you stand!' Robert had made chase whilst Silas watched, unsure what to do. The second graverobber was swift, hurdling graves and monuments as Robert Hall ran after him. Robert tripped but, on hitting the ground made a forward roll and was soon upright once more. Along Coppergate, candles were being relit as people rushed to their windows to see what the commotion was. Halfway along Coppergate, the robber stopped in his tracks, turned and took a swing at Robert with the spade. Robert bent backwards as far as he could but the cutting edge still pierced his forehead dazing him momentarily.

Hugh Hulley had told Silas to run after his master but not to intervene as the boy would be a witness if he got away. Once Robert was upright again, his attacker took another swing but, as he did, Hall lunged toward him, grabbed the handle of the spade and then cracked his opponent's chin with it. Still, he tried to run but Robert overtook him, restraining him from behind, and putting a dagger to his throat.

'I'll happily do for you here, you creature of the night! Just give me an excuse...'

He then marched him back towards the graveyard where

he met up with the sheriff and his co-conspirator.

This was an altogether different Robert Hall to the one Silas had been used to and he was mightily impressed. He had pondered on how Hall had been so diffident at Sheriff Hutton. He is human after all, mused Silas and was certain that he had been employed by a secret adventurer and the tale of the grave thieves would be told, retold and embellished whenever he had the chance as, on this occasion, no one would tell him to keep the event quiet.

Hugh Hulley and Robert Hall watched over the perpetrators whilst they buried the body again.

Soon, Silas found himself back at York Castle although he was asked to wait outside. After an hour, Hulley returned to find the boy fast asleep. He shook him gently.

'Oh Annie!' he exclaimed in his slumber.

'Who the hell is Annie lad?'

'Oh... erm... tis my horse sir...' he said.

'Horse?'... The sheriff looked around and scratched his head, 'suppose it takes all sorts lad...'

Four torches lit the entrance to the castle, two on either side and they made erratic flapping noises as the wind picked up reminding Silas of the flags at Sheriff Hutton. Coming to his senses, he was suddenly aware of his recent incarceration at York Castle so it was with some trepidation that he followed Hulley back in once he had invited him.

'He's been dreaming about Annie! Haha' said Hulley to Robert Hall.

'I think that's what he calls his horse?' observed Robert.

'Wait a minute...' said Robert, 'isn't that the name of one of Cropper's children? The one with red hair?'

Silas said nothing although his face suddenly became the same hue as the locks in question.

'Well, well...you kept that quiet!'

Now he was truly embarrassed.

'Take it from me lad' said the sheriff, 'if you're sweet on a girl you should let on, after all, you could well be married within a few years.'

This was unwanted advice. They were now into territory that was unquestionably uncharted as far as Silas was concerned. He knew nothing of marriage except for that of his parents and the idea that he could have such responsibilities so soon, terrified him. Fortunately, they soon changed the subject.

'You have done a good deed today, lad. Been after them for a while but never once caught them in the act.'

Silas wasn't sure what the act was. He could think of no earthly or unearthly, reason why anyone would do such a thing. They could tell that he was bewildered and so Hugh Hulley thought to give him an explanation.

'You know that every man or woman deserves a Christian burial?'

Silas nodded.

'If you follow Christ and repent of your sins you will go to Heaven but that's your soul, lad. Even so, your body deserves permanent rest and respect. It is unlawful and ungodly to dig up someone's body. The king says that is possibly the worst of sins...'

His little face screwed up as best it could with so much damage to it.

'People buy the bodies, Silas. They chop them up...' continued the sheriff.

He looked horrified.

'They justify it by saying that we can cure more ailments, perhaps even the plague if we know what's inside us but, of course, any thinking man would tell you that you may as well butcher a pig! So, it is barber-surgeons, physicians and sometimes artists who pay such men to steal bodies but they are as guilty as the grave robbers themselves and I will be sure to find out who was giving those two demons money for corpses.'

Silas had, by now, changed colour. There was nothing about this revelation that was welcome.

Hulley continued,

'The king does at least acknowledge this so allows just four felons to be chopped up each year following execution.'

And then a huge smile filled Hulley's face.

'Might just have two here that he might be interested in Haha!'

Robert laughed along with him.

Silas had thoroughly enjoyed his evening escapade but now it was turning sour. Week by week he was learning about what adults got up to in their spare time and he didn't like it very much.

But he had also learned that when he opened his mouth and he made some sense, it seemed to be a good thing and he was even praised for it. The sheriff and Robert Hall then spent some time drinking whilst Silas sat with Hulley's dog in a corner. Around midnight, Robert jumped up,

'Let's be going lad, lots to do tomorrow.'

Silas was astonished that Hall cared enough to see him back safely to Dead Alley and impressed that he seemed to have the authority to be out beyond curfew. However, Hall stopped at the entrance to the alley and told him that he should be well to start work again in two days. Then, he pulled his cloak to one side revealing his dagger and underneath was his purse. He turned around so that Silas could not see the contents but then he held out his hand and the face of the king shone in the flickering light of his torch. He gave Silas two testoons, silver shillings, a currency so new that Silas had never seen one before although he knew what they were worth. Each was worth twelve pennies and Silas had only seen more when carrying out transactions for Hall. Neither were they clipped, a practice of gradually cutting off bits of coins in an attempt to make another, something that was altogether illegal and led to many coins that were incomplete.

'You needn't seem so surprised. I am always good at business. You'll still get paid whether you're in court or half-dead in the mud of Galtres. This is back pay owed. Silas started to kneel but Hall hurriedly picked him up.

'A thank you will do lad and I don't want you on your knees in front of me in the middle of the night, I've got enough problems.'

Not for the first time, Silas remained ignorant of his master's meaning but retired with a smile on his face. However, he could not sleep and although the antics of the grave robbers disturbed him and the chase excited him, it was something else that was on his mind. The alley from which the offenders emerged was probably the poorest Silas had ever seen. Squalid as it was, he could work out that people there had so little that they barely ate and that was evident in their outward appearance. On the cusp of his teenage years, he knew that he only understood a few things. Still, he could not read people's expressions, their responses and even their meaning. He also knew that he had maps in his head that were perfect but knew not why he had that gift. Added to that was his love and understanding of Jesus Christ and in very many ways, this guided and formed his judgements. Beyond all that, he was not allowed any feelings or opinions and neither did he want any. By now, there was a hole no bigger than a foot square, in his ceiling as the rest of it had been repaired. The stars danced and, as he looked down at his belt and open purse, so did the shillings. Then, he had such a good idea that he could not sleep.

Come six o clock, he was back at York castle. If it hadn't been for Robert Hall often lingering around that area, he would never have known that a new bakery had started up near the castle. To be more precise, Ryia Baker had decided to reopen her bakery some years after her husband had got up and left her. There was no question that it was quickly becoming popular. Like the Halls, she had a baby and she would bake with it by her side.

'Morning lad. What can I do for you?' said Ryia

'May I…I'd like…. when is bread ready?'

'I will have bread ready in half an hour lad…have you any money?'

'How many loaves can I get for this?' he asked fluently.

Ryia Baker almost fell over.

'Where have you got?..'

'It is back pay from my master. You have my word...'

Thank goodness this was Ryia he was talking to for many a trader would have loved to have got their hands on two faces of king Henry and would give him little in return.

'It will get you five loaves and two fish.'

Silas stared and then smiled.

'I'm teasing you lad.'

'If I had five loaves and two fish, could I make more?' he asked.

'No. But only because you're not our Lord... I can run to eight loaves.'

So excited was he that he flapped his arms for the first time in some time and was truly happy and almost ran away.

'Avoid the multitude' shouted Ryia.

She agreed to give him three fish and seven loaves and plenty of change, reminding him that if he bought too much from her that there would be little left for her other customers.

An hour later, eight bewildered families gave thanks for the young stranger's gift that would have lasted them five days. Moreover, he remembered what his mother had taught him about Christian charity. He would tell no one of his good deeds for, as he understood, boasting of it would simply serve himself and neither God nor his fellow man.

Given that he was still not working and even though he still hadn't finished repairing Cooper Castle, he was determined to travel into Galtres Forest to see the Croppers so off he went. It felt good to see the forest especially as he was feeling much better and much more mobile. He felt that some peace had returned and, on this occasion, he even chose to avoid any eye contact with the castle. But throughout, his emotions were like a brewing hotpot. Scared as he was to share his feelings, he was also excited at how delighted they would be on hearing his marriage proposal. Since first setting eyes on Annie, he knew that they were a pair. Whether it was the red hair or just how they had met or, even the fact that his horse had the same name, it no longer seemed to matter. Every time he visited, she would greet him with that warm smile and, over time, she had taken more interest in him than anyone else perhaps except for the Queen of Sheba. It was forever clear in his mind just like the maps and that alone confirmed it as a certainty.

As he neared, he thought about how his life would now change forever. He would have to make room for two at Cooper Castle and perhaps eventually even more for the children although he then acknowledged that he still had no idea whatsoever where he would get those children from. And, as it wasn't unusual for boys to be married as young as fourteen, he probably wasn't the only one in York with the same conundrum. As he tied up his horse, he paced back and forth a good two hundred yards from Annie Cropper's house. He muttered and mumbled, pontificated and persuaded, exalted, expressed and explained although little made sense even to himself. Then, the door flew open. It was Arxe, Geoffrey's son and he ran to greet Silas. He embraced him and told him that he was not only welcome but that his timing was perfect as they were about to feast. Silas attempted to share his intentions with Arxe but failed miserably as his friend was so enthused. He guided him inside where there was a full house. Geoffrey was there and he immediately stood to shake the boy's hand and then Annie's mother, Emma, kissed him. It was overwhelming not least in that they were all genuinely delighted to see him looking better. Geoffrey informed Silas that he had told the whole family of the boy's attack and his bravery afterwards but, of course, said nothing of the trial. Silas sat, quite embarrassed but delighted to be amongst good friends. Within seconds, a small wooden chalice, half-filled with wine was placed in front of him. When he looked around it seemed as though everyone was celebrating and then it dawned on him that they already knew why he was there and this gave him the mettle to make his announcement.

'My dear…dearest… why… I am… and without as much…' he began.

'Before you make your toast, young Silas' said Annie's father, 'you should share our news!'

Internally, he thanked God for Cropper was about to do the unenviable task for him.

If anyone, absolutely anyone, on God's Earth was in that seat besides Silas, they would have known by this point what was coming but not he. Ebullient and gaining confidence by the second, he smiled as Cropper stood, goblet in hand.

'So be it! Just eighteen months from this very day, my beloved Annie will become the wife of Arxe, and a finer young man she would not find within thirty miles of here!'

Everyone cheered. Everyone cheered except for one whose strained cry was drowned by the gaiety. Once more he felt that punch in his back, the one that had felled him from his horse, except this time no one had touched him. Then, every wave, cheer and embrace seemed to take place at an eerie slow pace. For a while, he heard nothing at all but watched on as yet again he was metaphorically punched, kicked, battered, berated, ridiculed, denigrated, spat at and tortured within an inch of his life except, this time, he wanted to die. At the same time as trying to make some sense of what had taken place, he was certain that this would have been his only opportunity to wed, ever. In his head, he had thought through his version of the future so many times that he simply could not comprehend any other. What could possibly have gone wrong? Frozen, he thought some more. He had never had one thought or premonition that Arxe and Annie would have anything to do with one other apart from being cousins and then he wondered if they were cousins.

Was he really Geoffrey's son? He pondered. Again, he challenged his thoughts and truths. Something was wrong, he told himself, as he was certain that she would have become his wife.

Then, absolutely everything stopped. The hat which Geoffrey had thrown into the air simply seemed to hang there and drops from Emma Cropper's chalice floated somewhere between its lip and the table. But nowhere were there any answers. Why can no one see what I am going through, he thought. They do not care for me after all. If I was being butchered in front of them, then surely, they would intervene but they are doing nothing. And then, that huge weight returned pulling his very being down into hell. No, he decided, not hell for this was far darker.

Without warning, their inanimate state ceased and they were suddenly all looking at him. There was a noticeable and uncomfortable pause.

'Oh...' he croaked, 'hoorah...um...hoo...hoorah, I say!'

Bless him, he had tried his best and, men being men, this was adequate for them but Annie's mother looked at him as if he was on fire and so rushed him outside.

'Oh, my dear Silas' she said powerfully embracing him, 'oh why, oh why have you never said anything?'

'Say...oh...about...err... what...'

Then she wept as she held him tight against her.

'I am so sorry. You deserve so much better and you are the finest of boys. This match was made long ago and... well... it is very complicated.'

As she pulled away, he told her that he was very happy for them and that he could not have had a higher opinion of anyone although it took him almost five minutes to say it. Mrs Cropper offered him endless reassurances but they were lost amongst the birdsong and his headache.

Sensibly, he asked to be excused and she told him that she would tell the others that he had an urgent errand. She also insisted that he continued to call in on them as he was dearly loved by the whole family. He nodded, mounted a horse that would forever remind him of his misfortune and rode away, never to return to their home again.

12 Sixteen years old
1530

In the months that followed, everything seemed to settle down. Whether it had anything to do with Wolsey and the prevailing fear of God should they mention anything about the trial or not, Silas's excursions into Galtres Forest became more and more infrequent and so banal that he even made up a story about seeing the notorious ghost. He had known since he had first set foot in forest mud that there was an exciting but somewhat tired fable that had started in 1283 when the Bishop of Durham had been frightened out of his wits. There are no records regarding his level of inebriation, if any, I should add. Nonetheless, he insisted that he had seen the spirit of Hugh de Pontchardin riding a tall white horse and, over the centuries, many others claimed the same. Silas sadly had forgotten this legend despite it only involving a handful of words and he had told Jenny that he had seen the ghost of the huge pond garden and nearly died in it. Robert never again tasked the boy with visiting any of the Croppers or the priory and this was possibly because of the expansion of his interests elsewhere and the employment of more, presumably cheap and gullible, staff. He certainly did not want to risk him mentioning anything about the trial. So, it wasn't so much that Silas had decided to snub Annie and her family but simply that any reason to call began to dissipate and after 1527, Silas rarely went in that direction again. He was proud of Robert's insistence that he was his only errand boy and messenger and remained obedient to his master.

At sixteen years of age, Silas was much taller but had hardly gained any weight. He was so skinny that of course, his clothes still did not fit. The attire provided for him by Robert Hall was more than he could have desired but his master could not have been held responsible for his physique and his gait. His neck protruded from a fine white collar; one of those he had been bequeathed when the Queen of Sheba died. To be more accurate, the sheriff had said that he could take anything he wanted from the old lady's house and he was delighted to care for those collars which he held in very high esteem. His legs were like two long branches of elm and that included the knots. Those legs did not, and never would fully feel at home within his hose and now, he had a codpiece, although he still did not know what it was for. This meant that often he would wear it in the wrong place and would wonder why people pointed and laughed. The hair that was so brutally removed when he had been attacked in the forest grew back in only a few places although there was still plenty on top. He had a few scars too but never wasted any time thinking about them. He rode well although all credit had to go to his horse. Although people still considered him a waif, a minnow in a smelly pond and a fool, he had his own home which was now complete although he had been the only person ever to set foot in it since that morning when Dunstan had suddenly appeared.

It was incredibly curious that he had never once queried the many strange aspects of both Bayard and Dunstan's existence. The shows continued and were so current and topical that you would have thought that they had been in the king's presence the day before. Often it was just Bayard performing although neither of them ever looked any older. Neither did their clothes change and they had this propensity of popping up and disappearing again. He had only spoken to Dunstan three times since 1525 and each time, Silas had either been in trouble or was feeling incredibly worthless. But to Silas, they were there and then they were gone and that was the top and bottom of it.

He had thought of Annie and often questioned why he had managed to make such a bad judgement. Nuances of conversation and relationships were alien to Silas and yet he still had the biggest of hearts. He did not necessarily long to be married but realised that more and more he was finding girls attractive although the idea of even talking to one was beyond him. The two girls that lived at Robert's house fascinated him and he would often strain to catch a glimpse of them. He had heard rumours that the eldest was to take Holy orders which left Silas certain that she would spend her life at Rosedale. The youngest one was spirited and a joy to behold and it was clear when he saw her together with Robert that she brightened up his days. This too was another measure of Robert's character for, to take on someone else's child and one who had a noticeable palsy would, in the sixteenth century, invite comments from friends and foes alike. There was no doubt too that Silas felt some affinity with the girl as she too had to suffer the derision of locals. But these encounters were evanescent as he was chastised for even going too near to the house let alone looking into it.

It wasn't as if those few years were without incident. He had once confidently and illegally scaled the city walls only to fall over the other side and, without Robert's seal on his person, could not get back in for another eight hours. As he grew, he started to fall off Annie regularly and so required Daniel's expertise for a while. He was also given to oversleeping in the morning and was chastised so often that in 1528 he considered joining a monastery but could not find one that would take him. His understanding of locations became better and better although his knowledge of trespassing seemed worse and worse so he had more than once been arrested and his familiarity with Sheriff Hugh Hulley became worthless as sheriffs changed almost every year in York. His comprehension of marriage, marital relationships and how babies seemed to appear out of nowhere caused ever-increasing anxiety for him as did how he should speak to girls and women. He had complimented himself on his most astute observation that ladies seemed to get bigger before a baby appeared but never once managed to work out that the bump and the baby were one and the same and his obsession with what he called "baby lumps" continued to annoy others for some time. At times, his increased nervousness led to his speech being confusing at best at an age when he should have been growing ever more confident.

All the same, there were great adventures and new friends ahead and he saw each day as a God-given mission that would put him that bit closer to the king and becoming a knight.

One winter morning at first light, he waited for his instructions and yet again decided to shuffle nearer and nearer to the back door when he saw something that he wished he hadn't. In a brief but heated conversation with Robert was what Silas would later refer to as "the courtier" except that he was dressed all in black from his cap to his boots. His cloak was black and he wore a black mask which covered his eyes and his nose. At that moment Silas decided that the stranger was very much like himself and this was solely because of his distorted sense of self, the one that thrived in his fantasy world. The stranger was indeed the same person who had saved him from the quicksand although it would be many years before Silas would find this out and uncover his identity.

Some days he would find himself staring at the forge that belonged to the Smith family: his grandfather, his uncle and his father. It had remained in the hands of a family by the name of Osborne and what an admirable success they had made of it. It was more than twice the size it was when Silas had been a small child and boasted eight workers. Silas wondered where that story had gone. The one that was his past. Why did so many, including both his grandfathers, his uncle and his mother, disappear so quickly? He thought. On those very rare occasions when he would speak with Robert Hall, that subject was abruptly dismissed but it would never leave Silas completely. Although he would get all those answers much later in life, that missing part of him would only contribute to his confusion and diffidence. Other times he would find himself gawping at the home that once belonged to the Queen of Sheba hoping that he might see her just once more although it was now much more desirable. The landlord had set to work on it as soon as she had died and was, no doubt, enjoying the increased income from it.

Annie and Bolt were fine although Bolt in particular was slowing down. On his few excursions to the castle area of York, he noticed that Ryia Baker's son was growing. Come 1530 he was six years old and Silas could not help thinking about himself wearing a very worn tabard and fighting dragons with his mother. How fleeting childhood is, he thought and how few of us realise this when we are so young.

His errands took him in all directions although, as yet, he had only ventured beyond Yorkshire once or twice. Robert had taken a fancy to some particular goods that were accessible from Tadcaster market and Silas had been to Loidis more than once. Daft as he was, Silas had few suspicions about these errands as it was clear that his tasks were solely related to the pricing and distribution of wool. Neither did it harm Robert to be known in Loidis as it was renowned amongst wool merchants. Eventually, it would grow exponentially and become better known as Leeds. The errands that most reminded Silas of Galtres, however, were those which took him as far as Knaresborough Castle in the Forest of Knaresborough. He seemed to spend half of 1528 travelling there and back and it was inevitable that memories of Wolsey, the Croppers, Isaac and, of course, Annie, returned. He still daydreamed just as much but had improved his skillset as far as keeping safe was concerned and, despite all of this, he thought that he had the best job in the world and was certain still that, one day, he would be knighted.

New horizons
Silas remained fascinated with the younger one of the sisters who had lived with Robert Hall possibly because he knew that the unwashed and unread of York sometimes made fun of her too but he never got to talk to either of the girls. He

continued to tithe to the poor but not through the Church and was gaining an admirable reputation amongst the very poor of the city who would have had little power in improving his status or reputation. Sometimes, no sooner had he been paid than he would get food and share it amongst those he believed to be most needy. He never once missed a holy obligation and remained way ahead of Lutherans as he had always nurtured a very personal relationship with God and would strike up a conversation with him whenever necessary or convenient and fortunately, God was fluent in Silas-babble.

January 1530 had Silas trying to work out how near his birthday was and whether anyone would be bothered. Poor people were not in the habit of celebrating birthdays as most didn't really have that many and someone of Silas's status would be lucky to live to thirty-five. Nevertheless, he was sure that he was born in February and he knew that he was already fifteen years old so was naturally worried about what being sixteen meant and the responsibilities that went with it.

The river was frozen and so it followed that everything else in York was too. Silas and Bolt only got through the nights by sharing each other's warmth as icicles had formed on the inside and outside of his humble abode. When it was noon, however, Silas construed that there could be no more beautiful place in the world than York, and the Minster itself looked like an iced cake good enough for the king and the queen to eat. When it snowed it was beautiful to witness although that truth did little to dispel the suffering that winter brought with it. It also made business that much slower for the likes of Robert Hall and much more difficult for errand boys. Silas had just returned from Loidis but it had taken him the best part of a week as even the best roads were impassable and he had to build or find shelter wherever he could on the way back. Whatever it was that he lacked, his sense of survival remained keen and if he could understand a map or a description of the same, he was sure that he could get anywhere.

Little by little, Robert was letting him in on some of his intentions although possibly only because it would benefit his endeavours. He had kindly told Silas that he could have two days respite whilst Annie was fitted with new shoes and a new blanket but that he was to report to the workshop that Thursday.

'I am not sure… where?'

'You have been to my warehouse along the Ouse?'

'Yes sir.'

'Same place…but the workshops are at the back. Ah, there's a treat in store for you lad! Take these with you.'

Robert handed over three parcels with names on and a small seal which was recognisable as his. By now, he trusted Silas completely and this was very likely why he kept him on, despite his flaws.

He now had a fine pair of boots. Not fine enough to keep out the cold but certainly sound enough to cope with snow so he happily crunched his way toward the river alongside a shaky, three-legged dog. As he neared the Ouse Bridge, he had the choice of steps or a slope to take him down to the docks alongside the river. For a moment he envisaged sliding down its length, coming to a sudden halt just before the jetty ended but then thought better of it as the possibility of him sliding all the way across the Ouse at an ever-increasing pace would make him late. It was, however, inviting. Many people were already playing and skating on the river as they had done for centuries. Further along, boats and ships had been halted in their tracks, going nowhere until the weather permitted them to do so.

After tiptoeing down the steps for what seemed like minutes, he could see the front of the warehouse and the ice had been completely cleared in front of it. He knocked on the door which was opened with some drama.

'If it is Master Hall's boy, let 'im in. I'm expecting 'im' came a voice from within.

Based on past experiences, Silas was not expecting a kind welcome and was surprised when he was summoned to the back.

'You're Silas, aren't you?'

He nodded.

'He starvin' you then?' said the man looking him up and down, 'come with me...'

This was a common first reception, people almost always thought that he was a starving waif from his appearance alone. The man was sleeveless on one of the coldest days of the year but had a neck to toe leather apron which had a few scorch marks on it. He took Silas right to the back of the warehouse and into a small tunnel. Off to the left was a small room in which there were a variety of personal possessions hanging from hooks of varying sizes. There were jerkins, tools, sticks, aprons, gloves and daggers and boxes with initials on but, in a corner atop a few burning branches, was a pot of lentil soup. For Silas, it was a treat just to get near to the fire but the smell of the soup made his day. The man was four times his size and yet he did not feel threatened by him. The giant lunged forward, grabbed a wooden ladle and scooped out a good measure of the Heavenly manna.

'Sit there, get warm and put a few pounds on lad and I'll talk.'

This was the best arrangement possible, thought Silas.

The lentils were so delicious and so warm that he could not avoid offering an unwelcome rendition of guttural song as he gulped it down, almost ignoring what this man was saying.

'I'm the gaffer here. My name is Jonks. You call me gaffer. We use this place to move around the master's goods to wherever they need to go, although all the work is done yonder...'

He pointed at the far end of the tunnel. This stopped Silas mid-gulp as he didn't know any work was done there at all.

'When you've finished, I'll show you but before I do...so

that we are clear, lad, the master means to involve you more in 'is glass makin' enterprise. Don't be alarmed, you won't 'ave to make anythin' but you will be expected to run errands to and from his clients and patrons. Just been to Loidis?'

Silas nodded.

'Well, that was one such contact. 'he thinks it would be better if you knew more.'

For a moment, Silas thought about Rosedale and the less than admirable practices involving glass that had taken place there. Perhaps, he thought, this is the master's way of showing me how it should be done correctly.

At the end of the tunnel was a thick wooden door giving no clue as to what lay on the other side. As soon as the gaffer opened it, a rush of hot air hit Silas. The world beyond was unlike anything he had ever seen before.

'This part is very important, Silas. This work is secret. You do not share anythin' you see 'ere with anyone else.'

Silas gave his assurances and, although Jonks wasn't to know it, they were the best assurances in the city as Silas never had, and never would, share anything of the trial at Sheriff Hutton let alone the secrets of Hall's glassworks.

The experiences that followed would be remembered by him for all his days and although it wasn't intended as a treat, he did indeed think it to be a marvel. As the door opened, his eyes were immediately drawn toward a man who seemed to be turning a long metal rod which had fire on the end. Jonks explained that it was glass, made from sand and ash but had no sooner said it than the man started to blow into the rod and in doing so began to shape the glass.

'That's muff glass makin' lad, when cooled it makes a cylinder…'

Silas screwed up his face so Jonks then demonstrated the shape of a cylinder with his hands.

'Then it's flattened to make a piece of glass. 'erbert, yonder, is usin' what we call crown method. As he spins it that bubble starts to become flatter.'

As Silas looked on in awe, he could see cooled pieces of glass in all shapes and sizes although few were very large and there was no sign at all of any goblets. Some of the glass had been coloured during the process and some of it appeared streaky but it was clear that he was not allowed a detailed inspection and the gaffer once again reinforced secrecy.

'You've been in the Minster?'

'Yes... err sir...the finest...'

'Indeed Silas. Some of the finest glass in England although it is a craft that is improvin' by the month. When you next visit, look carefully, it is lots of little pieces that make up the 'ole picture.'

By now Silas had a permanent grin which made him look almost catatonic. Jonks prodded him to leave and then the door was shut once again. There were two other doors in that tunnel, one of them slightly ajar but Jonks took care to close it. However, Silas stole a glimpse inside. It was a smaller room and it had its own opaque window through which two large draughtsman's desks were lit. On both were huge drawings although he could not make out what they were. At one, was an artist busily working in silverpoint and to Silas's astonishment it was not a draughtsman at all but a draughts woman no more than twenty years of age. He looked to Jonks for confirmation who looked back knowingly.

'All grand windows start with a drawin'. She's the best there is….'

Perhaps he should have added that apart from the obvious importance of the artist, it was often their instructions that dictated how glass should be made and how the final window was to be leaded and placed in situ. The artist was very important indeed and their directions were highly valued. Then, he put his finger to his lips and went on to explain how the glass was painted. Sixteenth-century glaziers had the benefit of diamond cutters which made the cutting of pieces much more precise and easier to handle. Using brushes of animal hair, they would apply painting techniques much like any other medium: shading and hatching and they even applied the skill of heating vitreous paints so that they would adhere to the glass. This was speedily becoming an art and science all of its own. Finally, strips of lead, known as cames would be used to hold the glass masterpiece together, although lead mining and production had already become an entirely separate industry. Finally, this was fitted into the ferramenta, the iron armature that would secure it to the window opening.

Was it any wonder that even in the sixteenth-century people saw York Minster's rose window as God-given? and it would remain a wonder for hundreds of years as well as an inspiration and a lesson in what could be achieved. The rose window at York Minster was quite new, designed and built to celebrate the end of the wars of the roses and the marriage between Lancastrians and Yorkists and was, in part, what had inspired Robert Hall. And, if it did not inspire him, it certainly inspired his purse.

Eventually, Silas was back at the front of the warehouse, his back to the severe cold.

'If you're still confused, the message is this…some of these people are very expensive to employ. Their skills are rare and the artefacts, from the drawin's to the finished window are very fragile. It's important you understand what you are dealin' with.'

Beatrice

Politely, Silas thanked him. He stroked Bolt who was delighted to see his master once again but on arriving home, he had remembered nothing of the walk. He was truly spellbound and there was no doubt that the experience had left him feeling suddenly quite important although twenty minutes later he also thought of the dangers that were ever-present with such practices. The following day, he wandered toward the now, half-built, St Michael Le Belfrey church in the hope of catching some entertainment but there was nothing there apart from swaddled individuals hurrying toward shelter and warmth. He turned into Stonegate to admire the buildings adorned with snow and became aware of an elderly man who could only walk using his stick. How he reminded him of the Queen of Sheba and, to his astonishment, he stopped Silas in his tracks, resting his hand on his shoulder.

'I know who you are.'

Silas had a default setting in situations like this, he panicked. He had an unwanted mechanism somewhere deep down that had him presuming that he was about to be ridiculed, insulted or attacked. Behind the old man was a young woman who stopped, presumably as she was intrigued.

'I wouldn't be here if it wasn't for you, sir…,' said the old man.

He pulled back a cloak so worn that there were more holes than there was wool. Underneath was a grubby and tired jerkin with a pocket. He pulled out a dry piece of bread and, as he did, Silas understood.

'I have a good life and good employment sir. It is nothing...' said Silas kindly.

'Saved my life lad.'

Silas was wearing gloves which he liked very much, especially on such a frosty day but as he looked down at them, he once again wondered why they were too big for him. It was at that moment that, possibly for the first time, he fully appreciated his employer and acknowledged that he had an older pair of gloves at home. He handed them to the man who kept refusing. The young lady stood in front of the gentleman and spoke,

'Thank God for this blessing. These may get you through another winter and I will pray that the frost abates.'

He thanked both of them and then limped away, disappearing down a nearby alley.

Silas gawped at the pretty young woman so long that it

was a wonder his tongue didn't freeze.

'You're Master Hall's lad?'

'Umph...'

'You recognise me?'

'Oh, yes,' he said rediscovering his voice, 'you are the master's woman.'

She laughed.

'Well until there's another word for it! I'll accept that gladly' and she laughed again.

'You are so clever' he said.

'Why thank you, young messenger, but...you never saw me...' she said winking.

'Oh...erm... of course ...yes...'

It was the young woman who had been drawing a stained-glass design in the workshop. She was seemingly an angel as well, deduced Silas.

Although it would have been very unwise of Silas to develop a crush on a young woman four years his elder, this chance meeting did affirm for him that, whether he liked it or not, he was changing and that included how things on his wonky body worked. Added to her beauty was the knowledge that she was an artist, one that Robert Hall had chosen over others and, this time, Silas very much doubted that it had anything to do with him saving money. Before she left, she reminded him once more to keep her existence secret then wished him well and then walked away. Almost unwittingly, he turned and so did she,

'Beatrice...' she said.

What a morning he had had. As he shivered, he considered that things could not have been better and was particularly happy that he had been shown the glass-making process. He never had, and never would as much as peek at any of the letters sent by his master and neither did he enquire about the detail of errands. Truth be told, he was genuinely honest and had no interest in any of it as long as he kept his job but now, he had become instantly fascinated with the industry.

Once home, he made a small fire and boiled some dried herbs in an attempt to recreate the soup. It was passable and he had a little bread left over to go with it which he shared with Bolt. For the first time in a long time, he thought about Annie the red-haired girl and tried to imagine what she would look like now at sixteen years of age. Moreover, he thought about how much he had been taken with her. If he had understood the meaning of the word obsession, he might have considered that too but instead he just mulled over the astonishing impact she once had made. Knowing full well that Beatrice was a woman and quite likely married, he also knew that she was beyond his reach but then started to ruminate over how he felt when he was near her. With no friends or family to speak of, such things would remain alien to Silas for some time.

The following morning, he was surprised to see Robert personally greeting him and very soon, he found himself in the kitchen where it became clear that Robert was also checking that they were alone. Quite fluently, Silas thanked him for the previous day's tour.

On the table were six small leather purses, each tied with leather string. A little piece of paper stuck out of each one and where the string was tied there was a wax seal. It was Robert's seal but a much smaller version.

'What a week you're having lad! Today you will go to the Minster! You know the new rose window?'

'Oh yes, sir...grand it is...in all its beauty…'

'Yes, yes.' He said dismissively, 'you'll need to listen. You will find six men either on scaffolding or looking up at the window. They distinguish themselves by wearing this guild badge...' said Robert showing him a drawing.

'You will hand one purse to each one of them but you are to wait until they are not busy. Understand?'

He nodded.

'You are to say: these are sent with the compliments of

your good servant Master Robert Hall.'

Silas repeated it correctly three times and then made to leave but Robert called him back.

'You will need this letter to get in and... don't take the dog.'

Silas was so enthused that he almost forgot the purses but soon found himself at the Liberty Gates which instantly took him back ten years to when he had worked for William Fawkes. Sure enough, he was admitted and so made his way to the south transept where the enormous rotund and colourful window shed pastel lights onto the Minster's intricate gothic designs. The six men were easy to identify but were much engrossed in their work. These were master glaziers and restorers. Any window, whether new or old, had to be constantly checked for integrity. Putty, lead and glass were all fickle and could easily fall victim to extreme weather so it was their job to ensure that the window was safe and that none of its expensive craftwork was lost.

Silas was quite good at waiting. There was always a fantasy or daydream ready to be completed so he was very happy to watch them at work and in doing so, drift off into a make-believe land where elves flew around large windows, painting, cleaning and perfecting them. An official came to speak to him and asked why he was there. As, for once, this didn't seem to be a secret, he told him that he had a message for the glaziers. The man politely responded on seeing Hall's seal and chatted to Silas for a while as if he was his long-lost friend although the biggest surprise of the morning was when he saw Daniel, Hall's stable boy, in the distance talking to a priest. He wasn't a boy anymore either. Daniel was almost twenty and for a moment Silas wondered why he had never been promoted or moved on to other employment. The Minster was a busy place and between one Mass and another all sorts of people of varying rank and occupation could be seen bustling about but a stable boy? Silas just could not see the connection.

Eventually, there was a natural break in the glass inspection and so Silas handed the purses over along with the message. One or two of them seemed confused whilst others thanked the boy and walked away with the purses. Inside was an invitation to visit Hall's workshops with a complimentary gift of twenty shillings each as Robert Hall was unquestionably going up in the world and wanted the best to work for him. If only one of the glaziers came his way, it would not only make a difference to the quality of his glass, but he would also be able to boast of employing the most respected glaziers in the north.

George Gale

Silas was rightly pleased with himself and, as he was so near, thought that he would see if Bayard had turned up. He could already hear the crowd as he exited the Minster although he was sure that this time there was some jeering as well as applause. However, as he turned the corner, he saw that there was no stage and that the crowd was in a circle, something he had never witnessed before. Whoever was providing the entertainment must have been at the centre of it all but he could not see anything apart from the backs of people. He presumed that this new style of show must have been very good if people were willing to brave such extremes so pushed his way through. At first, he smiled as he saw a young man on a horse although strangely, the horse was constantly rearing up. As the rider turned, he was seemingly shouting and the audience was shouting back. Trying to make sense of it, Silas pushed to the front. The first words he heard from the rider were,

'I am on the king's own business…I go to war!'

Everyone laughed, so Silas did too. Then someone shouted right from the back.

'I am a damsel in distress Lord Silas…save me!'

More loud laughter.

What did this mean? He thought. Horrified, he hurriedly

moved nearer to hear more.

The rider addressed his audience once more.

'I am Lord Sillyarse who cannot speak. I fall down holes that aren't even there and faint at my own stench!'

Uproarious laughter followed and seemed to last for minutes.

'I live in a shithole in a graveyard, Haha!'

Now, Silas understood what this was but didn't know why it was happening. He anxiously looked at the young man on the horse. He had purposely put on baggy clothes but otherwise boasted a fine physique so looked nothing like Silas. As he raised his head mockingly, Silas saw his scar. It was Jaxon who he hadn't seen in years and as if that revelation wasn't a deep enough wound in itself, it dawned on him that Jaxon was riding an aggrieved Annie. Then Silas became aware of some people starting to defend him, loudly berating Jaxon although it did not stop him. Silas simply did not know what to do although fortunately, the debacle was broken up in an instant. A constable from the Minster rushed out and grabbed the reins. Jaxon was instantly abusive and threatened the constable.

'You can't arrest me thou brainless ox! You have no powers out here.'

'We'll see about that; the sheriff is on his way.'

Jaxon tried to ride off and when he couldn't, he dismounted and tried to run but Bolt set upon him refusing to let go of his ankle. Then, others offered their support.

The sheriff announced to all that Jaxon Payne was being arrested for horse thievery, a very serious crime and where a small crowd had so recently stood there remained little more than disturbed snow. Jaxon had instantly lost his support and his efforts to kick the dog failed. He was dragged away by two of the castle's guards, the sheriff and the heroic constable.

In York, sheriffs came and went. They changed office every one or two years but make no mistake, they were very important. There were two sheriffs in 1530 and Silas's saviour that day was George Gale. He had been an alderman and was a member of numerous guilds like the esteemed Corpus Christi guild and was destined to be mayor. The parallels with the likes of Robert Hall were obvious. They drank from the same font and peed in the same puddles. Gale was a successful merchant and had plenty of money. Already, Robert Hall was wielding considerable power in York and had influential friends.

After having enjoyed a few good days, Silas was suddenly left reminding himself of his worthlessness and, on this occasion, felt the injustice viscerally. After all, he was obedient, worked hard and helped others without asking for a reward but he told himself that this reputation of being an idiot would never go away. He found it hard to accept and so wanted to stay home and never leave again. But later that day whilst he sat at home looking at the world's smallest and now, emptiest, grazing space, he heard a voice calling from the distance. When he made his way through the roughage to the exit to Dead Alley, he saw Gale standing there.

'Good God lad, you really do live in the graveyard!'

Silas explained that he had a home at the other end of the tunnel he had just emerged from.

'We'll be hanging him at first light, you need to come and get your horse. It's been looked after like one of my own so you needn't worry.'

He had been so worried about Annie, not even knowing whether she still belonged to him or not and he was sure that his master would be furious as he had been made clear that it was Silas's responsibility to care for the horse. The sheriff walked so quickly that he had to keep breaking into a little sprint to keep up and throughout that short journey he was nervous about being back at the castle once again. Entering the castle reminded him of the time when the grave robbers had been arrested although on this occasion, it was still light and the weather was completely different. Presuming that he was heading for the stables, his heart sank when he was taken down to the cells. At the bottom of the stone staircase stood Robert Hall who slapped the sheriff on the back who no doubt took it as a sign of close friendship. Hall didn't say a word but subsequently led Silas to the fourth cell along, so dark that it was hard to see what was inside. When he could make out a silhouette it was of a beaten and forlorn creature that could not have stood up if its life depended on it and his eyes were so swollen you could have believed that there were crab apples behind them. It appeared as if his right arm was broken and his clothes were now no more than rags. Silas was about to ask why he had been brought there but then realised that it was Jaxon languishing before him and, although he would never know why, he feared him all the more now he had been given a surname as well.

'Hanging or whatever you will,' said the sheriff.

Silas understood his meaning. Although for many crimes and misdemeanours there were set punishments, the lines were often quite fluid and the number of crimes for which you could be hanged was astonishingly high. To save time, and as Silas was the aggrieved party, they had brought him along to take part in the process.

'Not wasting court and lawyers' time and money on this filth so the penalty is up to you. He can rot here or he can swing afore the day's end.'

Silas was dumbfounded. He had no skills whatsoever that would inform him of what to do. He thought that the law was the law and that there were no grey areas to consider. The thought of someone hanging didn't entirely terrify him as it was so common but he did try to turn over in his mind the logic behind how England's laws worked. Then he wondered if they really were the same as God's laws. Hoping they would not mention it again, he said nothing but they told him once more that he had to make a decision.

'Are you saying I can do what I will with him?'

'Absolutely lad. It's only fair' and Gale held out a baton.

'Might feel better if you give him a beating yourself first, does wonders for me…he won't fight back now.'

'But sheriff…sir…I can… decide…truthfully.'

'Going round in circles lad…just get on with it.'

There was a pregnant pause although it did seem like quite a long pregnancy.

'Come on lad!'

'Please set him free. I forgive him.'

Jaxon's head moved very slightly whilst the other two huffed and blustered and further reminded the boy of his rights.

'I cannot think why, but he must have his reasons for hating me…,' said Silas.

Once more the sheriff tried to interrupt but fluently and marvellously, Silas continued,

'I cannot call myself a Christian and then make up my own rules. I am obliged to forgive him and forgive him I will… just…

'Yes'

'Please ask him not to go near my horse again.'

Silenced, the sheriff opened the cell door and told Jaxon he was free. He couldn't move, so damaged was his body, so the sheriff promised that he would be released once fed and improved. Silas hurriedly walked home before they could change their minds. Usually, he took the short walk along Castlegate and past St Mary's church and then into Coppergate. York had so many churches that anyone could easily map the city by their positions alone and often he would do that solely for fun although there was little joy in his heart on that day. Confused and morose, he took Annie's reins and decided to walk along the embankment towards the Ouse Bridge once more enjoying the blue sky and white landscape, one that stretched way beyond the other side of the river. However, no sooner had he caught sight of the river than he saw another small crowd.

'Oh no…please God…not again' he muttered to himself,

completely at the end of his tether. He took a breath, readying himself for what was to come but then realised that he recognised one or two of them and then they started to applaud. It wasn't uproarious, just gentle clapping and he remained suspicious of it for some seconds. Soon, it was clear that they were giving him their support, possibly in the only way they knew how to and then, without a word, they dispersed. His heart was pounding as his head tried to make sense of a difficult, confusing and emotional day.

As he meandered home, he recollected seeing a few faces of people he had given bread to in that small crowd. There were some he didn't recognise at all but at the very front was Beatrice. Buoyed by the experience, he welcomed fluttery thoughts of a life spent with the beautiful young woman and without anyone around to advise him otherwise, started to harbour improbable notions about her intentions.

13 Skipton castle

A new day offered him new thoughts and he happily waited for his instructions at the back of his master's house. Certain that he was to be sent to the workshop again, he was astonished to be told that he was to travel to a place he had never heard of. Names of places were slowly if slightly, changing as the lack of standard spelling and all manner of accents and pronunciations had led to any one place having three or four slightly different names. Shipton was one such town although already many had settled on Skipton. The former was much more accurate as it also simply meant sheep town which would have been satisfactory. Jenny sold him the mission by telling him that it had the finest of castles and that the castle was where he was bound. She gave him a package wrapped in hessian and tied with string, again with Robert's seal on it. Although it felt like a book, Silas had already decided that it was some of Beatrice's drawings and, as such, he saw these as his most important delivery to date. He was to wait for a reply and return without delay. She said,

'None of that nonsense that took place in Galtres Forest. Straight there and back! Daniel will tell you about the journey.'

Strangely, Jenny had her right hand clasped over the seal throughout that one-way conversation although Silas did not notice. Eventually, she removed her hand and gave it to him.

This would be his biggest challenge to date as Skipton was fifty miles away although Daniel did help to put his mind at ease. He advised him to get new shoes for Annie once he arrived and also told him that it was more or less a straight road although it would be very likely that he would have to confront some of the very worst elements especially when he hit the Yorkshire Dales. He asked Daniel why he had been in the Minster but not only did he seem embarrassed; he avoided offering an answer. Wisely, Silas left straight away and although he was optimistic that Annie could make the fifty miles in one day; he also knew that she would not make it before dark. He was now certain that he could navigate his way easily to Knaresborough and so planned to get as far as Blubberhouses that same day. There he would make camp for the night.

The temperature had risen slightly although the road if it could be described as such, was still hard in places and where it wasn't, was mired in slush and mud. Nevertheless, Silas was now a seasoned traveller and feared little apart from being attacked again. He wore a cloak which had become quite worn over the past three years but it gave him some protection and he had wrapped a scarf around his face. By the time he had pushed his cap down, all that could be seen of our hero was his watering eyes.

The journey was not only uneventful but he made Skipton Castle at midday the following day. This was quite unlike Sheriff Hutton, clearly having been built as a fort but looking very much like a place where a family of some significance would live and the foreboding watchtower and battlements had him wondering why anyone on Earth would ever consider attacking such a place. Once he had shown a guard the seal of Robert Hall, he found himself in the stables where an ostler tended to Annie straight away. He was then escorted through a modern courtyard and it was this that informed him that Skipton Castle was indeed a grand residence, the home of someone important. Soon, having passed the entrances to the beer and wine cellars, he found himself in familiar territory, the kitchen. There, he was fed in front of a huge fire where he trembled, steamed and made peasant gulping noises as he ate, occasionally glancing up at the young women who worked there.

Then, at the other end of the kitchen, a page appeared

and beckoned Silas over. Silas handed the package to him and the page then asked him to wait although Silas made a point of thanking him and telling him to thank his master or mistress for the food and warmth.

As he waited, he noticed a view along the corridor although he could not see what or who was at the other end. He had picked up from the kitchen maids that the banqueting hall was on the first floor and his heart bounced with delight at the sound of such a thing. This is the stuff of kings, barons, earls and knights, he thought, the brave deeds that must have been carried out by the owners of this castle in days gone by. Eventually, the page appeared in the corridor although Silas could hear raised voices beyond.

'Time is running out!' said a well-spoken gentleman, 'he needs to know, now!'

'But...the risks...it cannot be secure. Wait until we have someone suitable,' said a lady.

None of this made any sense to Silas and the page also looked both perplexed and mortified. So much so, that he kept turning back again and again until eventually, he disappeared altogether. So, Silas waited. Finally, the page reappeared with a young man just a few years older than Silas who, as he entered, was busying himself and dusting himself off. Slightly flustered, he said that he was "the Earl's man" and that he would accompany him. In no time at all, they were on their horses and heading east at some pace. John, for that was the only name he gave, spoke very little but assured Silas that he was shadowing him simply because of the importance of the package they were transporting which although partly true, did not inform Silas that the family were also testing his trustworthiness. And, to be fair, this was partly Hall's fault for there was little about his one and only emissary that spoke of wealth or status. When Silas had arrived at the castle, he looked more like a beggar than a messenger.

He certainly enjoyed John's company and remained in

awe of his attire and the beautiful horse which was several hands taller than Annie. When it went dark, they set up a small camp, lit a fire, ate and slept. The next morning, they arrived ten miles outside of York having made haste and John turned to leave.

'I will tell my master that you are to be trusted and that you can make the journey well.'

And then he galloped away.

'Ah... oh…alright... it was good…take...'

He was gone.

Silas took pains to tell Jenny about John and how important the parcel was and then took Annie home. The journey had completely drained him so he trudged wearily, guiding Annie by her bridle. He soon began to shiver so lit a small fire. By now, he knew that he could only sustain a fire for a short while as his admirable attempts to rid his home of holes meant that there was now nowhere for the smoke to get out. As soon as it was struck, it soon became too wet anyway and as he tried to sleep, he noticed that his head had started to hurt. Soon his sinews and bones hurt too, along with everything else within his meagre frame and he could not sleep.

Winter brought death to York every year. It was expected. Young children and the elderly were easy prey for influenza and smallpox and tuberculosis and dysentery were rife throughout the year. Each winter the populace would cry "plague" although there had been no plague in York for some time and winter was a time of year when deaths were so common that it would have been nothing to witness bodies being carried out of homes whilst people were going about their everyday business. Silas had been no stranger to illness or death and he knew that to live to sixteen was a blessing as child mortality was still so high. He also knew that what he was experiencing would not leave him within the week and that possibly, he could die.

He stayed where he was for it was only those who could

afford physicians who could get care, treatment and possibly even some sympathy. Throughout the next two days, his blanket would be wrapped tightly and then taken off again as his temperature went from one extreme to the other and then his throat closed up so much that he could not swallow, soon to be accompanied by an unproductive cough although, throughout his illness, he still ensured that Annie was grazing well and Bolt was fed. After day four, he could hardly move and became completely exhausted, the cough unrelenting. As Bolt sought to warm and console his master, he could feel his ribs, so thin was he now. The nightmares persisted and his woodland attackers, Salvo and Jaxon came to the fore as did others who terrorised the snickleways when he was a child.

Finally, so weak was he that he lost consciousness completely and, as he did, the now weak cough stopped as well. Bolt comforted his master knowing that he only had days left to live.

The Earl

Meanwhile, Robert Hall found himself pacing his expensive oak floorboards, kicking at the rushes and cursing as there was no one else around to hear him…'

'Dear God no! No, this cannot happen. I want no part in it!' He looked up, his mind spinning and considering the implications.

'But…it could raise me up in the scheme of things but…no, no…it is too dangerous...'

He had read the letter which Silas had brought back from Skipton Castle and was beside himself. What was meant to be a lucrative business proposition had turned into a request for help. He was to support a considerably difficult and dangerous cause and that had him thinking very carefully about which side to back. He was in no hurry to reply so hadn't even noticed that once again, Silas had not turned in for work. After much thought, he decided to ignore the request from Skipton Castle altogether and turn his attention to those matters which he believed were more important, namely making money. Later, having spent a morning looking over his most recent and most prestigious orders from Skipton, he called for Jenny.

'Where is he? I need him to go to Tadcaster.'

'I'm sorry, sir, I haven't seen him about in days and I have regularly checked the alley and everywhere else nearby.'

Disgruntled, he closed his ledgers and set about hunting for his errand boy.

Bogmorten

Silas had become so poorly that the cough had subsided completely and his whole being systematically began to fail. His body was now so frail that it was likely soon that he would succumb to the infection. However, he did eventually come around from his unconscious state, shivering and hurting so much in every part of his body that he could not have moved even if he had wished to. A flickering light teased open one eye and soon he was just able to barely make out a single, lit, candle. He presumed someone had found him and that he was still in his home but he could not raise any effort or interest in working out who that may be.

Then, a sinister and dark figure leaned over him and this confused him. Am I still in Galtres Forest after my attack? he thought. Is this Geoffrey the woodsman? As his vision cleared, he quickly came to learn that he was in a building he had never seen before and then, before becoming aware of anything else, the stench hit him. It was a heady brew of dead bodies and waste which seemingly had the previously unknown medicinal effect of bringing someone back to life.

'Drink this' said the dark figure and without question, Silas sipped at the cold stew.

'Thought ye dead thinks Boggy. Boggy knows and seen dead, a lot he has. Might be past the worst but Boggy will take care of ye until thy heals…'

Then Boggy coughed and a huge, sticky green and black projectile hurtled into the fire.

'Wh….where..?'

'With Bogmorten you is. Vermin catcher to kings and princes and shite cleaned wherever you will…'

Silas could not yet sit up but as he squinted, he recognised York's rat-catcher who, besides forever struggling to talk in the first person and sadly given to exaggeration, was very important in the city. He was as maligned as Silas was, both for his eccentric nature, his job, how he dressed and his unbearable aroma. Not surprisingly, Silas had previously become quite intrigued with the man who carried a pennant around York with pictures of his intended victims and his carrion on it. Fringes draped from his arms and his waist and he wore a large leather belt which had all manner of implements hanging from it. Neither was there anything random about his business as he had set fees dependant on the vermin in question and did indeed serve all levels of society except those who were happy to live alongside such creatures. And, the definition of vermin seemed to change depending on the client and ranged from hedgehogs and crows to moles and polecats. He would charge by the head and on the production of the same would get paid. And, he was the employer of the local gong farmer who would whistle as he cleaned any amount of human or animal shite if the price was right. As Silas looked upon him, Boggy had his full regalia on which included a sword. Eventually, Silas managed to ask him why he was there, somewhat concerned that he too had been caught for a fee.

'The lady was in such bad humours, and then she saw Boggy about his business. Kind sir, she says, I am in need of you. Bogmorten struck his colours and set forth to rescue thee!'

'What lady?' asked Silas.

'An angel from the very clouds says Boggy! A beauty for which the shittiest rat would not venture near, so fine was her aroma…'

Silas interrupted for it seemed as though he would go on all day.

'Does she have a name kind sir?'

'Aha! Beatrice methinks...'

Beatrice? Thought Silas. Beatrice rescued me. Bogmorten went on to explain.

'The dog found her. Twill be that kiss of hers that cured thee.'

She had kissed him? Beatrice had kissed him? Although it had been just a peck on his forehead, Silas concocted so many variations of what may have happened that he almost had himself believing that Beatrice spent all her days looking for him although he did not ask whether she had set foot in his home or not. Then, he realised that Bolt was sleeping by Bogmorten's fire.

Over the next day or two, the rat-catcher would keep a fire going and feed Silas. Then, he would go about his business until it was dark, returning home with a dripping sack full of assorted heads. During that time, Silas asked so many questions that it was no wonder Bogmorten boasted so much. Nevertheless, Silas came to like his fellow outcast and was in no doubt that he had saved his life although he insisted that he had no desire whatsoever to meet the gong farmer. Eventually, he was well enough to walk although he was still extremely skinny. He told his new friend that he would someday pay him back but that he had to go to find his master.

Somewhat recuperated, he made it outside and was immediately overwhelmed by the smell of crisp, fresh, winter air. He saw a small patch of grass where there was no ice and knelt to pray. He prayed for his recovery and his saviours. He prayed for his mother, his grandfathers, the Queen of Sheba, Isaac and even those at Sheriff Hutton Castle who lost their lives. He gave thanks for his position and his master and for meeting Beatrice whose influence was now looming large in his life. He gave thanks for the unkempt and unclean Bogmorten and he even prayed for Jaxon and finally, as all good citizens do, his king and queen.

With no thought of heading home, he hobbled towards Robert Hall's house only to see him in the distance hurrying in the direction of the warehouse and workshop. Hall opened the door almost as Silas had caught him up but his voice was so weak that Hall did not hear him so, naturally, he followed him in. Every one of the workers as well as Jonks presumed that Silas was with Hall and he continued to follow him as quickly as he could manage to the drawing room. Just as he was going to pull at his master's cloak, he saw that Beatrice was at work in there but then she stopped, turned and immediately embraced Robert. As if he wasn't feeling ill enough, Silas's heart almost stopped. He turned away and then waited in the corridor. Instantly, that display of affection haunted him as did the drawing he saw on the table. It was a magnificent design for a window over five feet tall and had the most dramatic image of a lady who appeared to be leaning on a cart. It was vibrant and impactful but not enough to take away the shock of seeing Hall and Beatrice together. He was exhausted, and upset and had to sit down. Hall and the girl then walked out together.

'Good God! There's nothing left of you. What have you been up to lad?!'

Beatrice intervened, explaining that Bolt had been roaming the alleyways whining and she had asked the nearest person, that being Bogmorten, to find the boy and carry him to his home. Hall looked at her wondering why she had not told him.

'I am...forgive me, master...I was...' started Silas.

'He was near death, as God will witness sir,' said Beatrice.

'Go to the house. I'll be there in ten minutes. I'll have Jenny provide you with some victuals and firewood. Get well and return Monday.'

He bowed and thanked Robert.

Grope lane

Come his sixteenth birthday, Silas was feeling much recuperated although he had forgotten all about the special day so it was celebrated by no one. Apart from what he had witnessed between Hall and Beatrice, he was yet again feeling more confident than ever and, without having any reason whatsoever, believed that all his past tribulations were gone. So much so, he told himself that he would no longer avoid parts of the city although, as you may already imagine, he would soon come to regret it. Grope Lane had a deserved reputation although a much more vulgar version of the name had been abbreviated to save some blushes for those of a more sensitive nature in York city. Even if Silas had had someone to talk to him about the birds and the bees, he would have been left wondering what birds and bees were doing with one another and why it mattered anyway. He had certainly learned that he liked young women and that, by and large, they were much better company than men and also that he, in addition to having had the flu, had developed a condition that seemed to affect his bloods, or one could say his circulation, when near young women. Beyond that, he was blissfully clueless. Regarding the notorious Grope Lane, like his dear mother, he knew that there was a lot of groping going on and that it was a lane although he did not know what groping was. He understood the grunting as he, and most other people did that when they wished to empty their bowels.

Yes, there was plenty of grunting in Grope Lane so, you can only imagine what was going on in Silas's mind when he had rushed by the entrance to it so many times.

Today he was confident. He was Lord Silas and people would make way for him. But as soon as he set foot in there, he was astonished at how many women, of all ages, were standing around, some in a state of undress. He averted his eyes but soon realised that there was nowhere to avert them to. Some were wrestling with men which he was sure must have been an unfair match as most of the men were bigger and there were all manner of noises echoing around the alley. He quickened his pace and then put his head down only to walk straight into someone. When he looked up again, he was wrapped in the arms of a young woman possibly in her twenties.

'What have we here then? You're a skinny thing, aren't you? Is everything skinny? Hehe! We'll see! Come here!'

She held him in a bear hug, his thin features now squashed against her ample bosom. He had no experience whatsoever in how to deal with such a thing so rested his head on her chest as if it were a pillow, hoping that the ordeal would soon stop. Then, she started to move her hands. They went up and down, around and about and then she giggled. They went to places even he didn't know he had and soon, he was panting for breath and praying that some of Wolsey's soldiers might come to rescue him.

Horrified, he realised as well that his circulation problem had returned and his ill-fitted codpiece began to twitch.

'Hehe!' she cackled, 'starting to come to life, are we?'

Now, he could not move even if he wanted to. On the cusp of shouting for the constable, he heard a coarse male voice above the caterwauling.

'Begone Delilah! Thou Salome! Jezebel! Boggy is fully armed and will do the king's duty!'

The girl became abusive. So much so that Silas thought she knew French as there were so many words that were unfamiliar to him. But Bogmorten was good as his word and drew his sword on entering the alley. She tried to laugh it off as did the others but she eventually released her grip due to the pervading stench. Silas escaped. Once clear of Grope Lane, he looked at Boggy expecting him to make fun of him as he was certain that he had made a complete fool of himself once again.

'Ye hath done none wrong boy. Her yonder is at fault and

should be ashamed. Boggy knows his commandments. Soldier of Christ is Boggy…'

Silas was thankful for Boggy's sensitive if not altogether brief, response, as there was nothing funny about what happened and neither had it done anything to educate him apart from now knowing that he should never enter Grope Lane again. It had also succeeded in further confusing him about all matters relating to the opposite sex or indeed any sex whatsoever.

The incident had unnerved him and so he rushed home. Once he had made his home frost-free and habitable again and ensured that his almost forgotten horse was good for work once more, he knew that he had to reset. He looked worse than he ever had done. The missing hair on his temples never came back and what was left was dirty and unkempt following his illness. He was thin and grey and still lacking energy. His clothes were baggy and unclean and he wouldn't have looked out of place in a mass grave. As it was, Robert had him carrying out some local errands for a while which gave him some time to get fit although he had been told that soon, he would be tested. He prayed that the tests would not involve percentages, quicksand, counting distances or travelling via Grope Lane as otherwise, he was looking forward to getting out of the city again.

14 The conspiracy

By the end of February 1530, he was again making his way towards Skipton Castle. Although still cold, the journey was easier and by now he knew how to find it. This time, he paused outside the walls and studied the coats of arms and those alone fed his fantasies. As he did at Sheriff Hutton, he could see Fleur de Lys but this time with flowers, a cross and a few circles and above it, a crown. He was shown into the kitchen once again but this time he was carrying a small letter. Very soon, a page came with a reply,

'Better get to your horse straight away. The earl is not pleased with how long your master has taken over this.'

'Earl?'

'God's teeth lad, you are in the home of the first Earl of Cumberland, Sir Henry Clifford!'

Seemingly John's mention of the earl on his previous visit had completely bypassed him. In awe and without hesitation, he ran to his horse. It didn't matter that he had never heard of Clifford or Cumberland but then understood the importance of his visit although it was never spoken of. On his return, he handed the reply to Jenny and immediately picked up more purses to be taken to the glaziers within the Minster. This time, the master glaziers seemed more grateful and one told Silas that he would consider meeting with Robert Hall soon. Silas lingered for a short while and wondered at how they had taken some small pieces of glass out of a medieval window to inspect in some detail. Yet again, he saw the same curate watching the glaziers and masons at work and Daniel was hurriedly leaving the Minster. Silas was possibly better than anyone in York at minding his own business but, on this occasion, could not resist following the stable boy who, not surprisingly, ended up at the stables and there was something there that shocked Silas to his wiry core.

On arrival, Daniel tended to a horse that was as fine as one could buy. It was grey with an ornate and expensive saddle and bridle but it was something else which immediately caught Silas's eye. Embroidered into the horse's blanket were the arms of Cardinal Wolsey, someone he thought he would never see in the north ever again. Then, Daniel unexpectedly turned around but Silas managed to make a clumsy leap backwards only to find himself in the manure dump. Up to his neck in it, the dung felt almost as bad as the quicksand and left him smelling worse than Bogmorten although he then managed to escape without detection. That was until the citizens of York saw him making his way home. To say the least, this latest faux pas did little to help his reputation. As he tried his best to get home undetected, he saw the curate from the Minster speed out of Monk Bar and beyond the city on a fine black horse.

The divorce
News about the king's quest for a divorce would trickle into York through rumour or sometimes even via Bayard's shows but often it was skewed. However, the king's desire to rid himself of his queen, Catherine of Aragon, made delightful gossip, especially the part where he had decided to marry his mistress. Most had remembered that when his brother Arthur died, it was decided that the ideal diplomatic solution would be that the new heir, Henry, should marry Arthur's widow, Catherine of Aragon particularly as the original marriage represented an ideal diplomatic tie. More importantly, it had been hot news that he had to obtain a dispensation from the Pope to do so. Now, having done some groping of Anne Boleyn himself, he wanted the Pope to reverse that decision so he could get rid of his queen and it was Wolsey who was tasked with securing it. As March arrived in York and the streets became free of winter's grip, Wolsey had been commanded by his king to return to his residence near York at Cawood Castle, although it would be

months before he would do so.

By the time April came, the king's obsession reverberated around England although it would be roughly translated and understood as it travelled. For most people, the idea that Henry would divorce without good reason to marry a lady's maid was a difficult concept not least as they had been taught that divorce alone was a sin and it was a wonder that every other marriage in the country was not in crisis so bad an example was he setting. Having a mistress was not so shocking so common folk needed a reason to grasp this relatively new concept. If he had wanted to keep his obsession with having a male heir kept quiet, he did a very poor job of it for it now seemed as though everyone knew. It didn't help that his mistress, Anne Boleyn was becoming notorious, much of it based more on fable rather than truth. It was no secret either that almost the full weight of finding a solution fell onto Wolsey's shoulders.

During the previous year, there had been an attempt by Wolsey to get Cardinal Campeggio to agree to an annulment of Henry's marriage although all his efforts failed. Increasingly, Wolsey was falling out of favour and England became divided over Henry's treatment of Catherine. So, instead, secretly, Wolsey began to build a case against Anne Boleyn presuming that if he could persuade the king of her unsuitability then the status quo would be maintained and he would be the king's favourite once more.

None of this was of any interest to Silas, mostly as he couldn't understand any of it. His world, for now, was big enough. He would lay on his bed looking at the ivy that had crept along his ceiling that previous summer and wondered why again he had been so fickle to give his heart to a young woman who he barely knew. It ached every time he thought of Beatrice who he now believed was one of Robert Hall's many dalliances. He thought of the curate who always looked suspicious and often loitered in the Minster rather than work in it and, how he had fled York on a horse. Then he tried to work out whether Daniel was his friend. He had certainly always looked up to him but what on Earth could he be doing in the Minster so often?

He then berated himself for having the same opinion as almost all of York about Bogmorten the rat catcher. What a kind soul he was and how I have misjudged him, he thought. Then, Silas did what he always did. He decided that it was not his position to even know about such things and went to sleep, his snores happily competing with those of Bolt's.

Temple Newsam

Not for the first time, Silas found himself bound for Loidis and to one of its finest Tudor houses, Temple Newsam. This was the home of Thomas, Lord Darcy who, in years to come would find himself in conflict with Henry Tudor although, in 1530, he was still very much in his favour. Silas was delighted that his career, if that is what it was, was heading in the right direction. Certain that rubbing shoulders with the high and mighty would lead to them recruiting him, he happily took on these more elaborate errands. His arrival at such grand establishments was never humdrum or for that matter, even the same. In an age where a person was a threat only when they were bigger than you, possessed better weapons than you, were a spy or had some emotional hold on you, Silas was seen as quite innocuous. That is why sometimes he was accompanied by guards and at other times was left to his own devices, few things could have looked less like a threat than our Silas.

So, as he waited in the grand chamber, perusing portraits, panels and poleaxes he soaked up the grandeur of its noble ancestors. A corridor led away to the east into which coloured, dappled light illuminated the floor and he found it irresistible. However, it was only when he sauntered in there to examine it that he could see that it was a half-constructed stained-glass window, the unfinished part covered with boards. Innocently, he tried to make out what the image was but it was the unusual wheel on which the woman was leaning that gave it away. It had unquestionably been made from Beatrice's drawing so, naturally, he presumed that the window was the reason why he was there and that Robert Hall had provided the service and materials.

'Tis a thing of beauty methinks. What say you? young ambassador,' said a voice behind him.

Silas whipped around.

'Oh no…sir…you see I h'am..'

'Haha! I know who you are. You are Master Hall's man…'

Silas was delighted as he had been flattered twice in less than a minute.

Lord Darcy introduced himself and Silas knelt.

'My Lord' he said with reverence.

Darcy looked at him wondering why he was so scruffy and also why he could not make eye contact with him but kindly said nothing.

'I declare that we should feed you! Yes! Feed you and show you the house.'

Silas gasped and then a smile appeared on his little face like a wave that started on the left-hand side of his mouth and eventually ended up on the right. Darcy stopped in his tracks and raised his eyebrows trying to understand what he was witnessing.

As he took Silas from room to room, he told him about the history of the house and the family and explained to Silas what the Doomsday Book was and how it referenced some of the oldest families in England. In one room there was a map of the estate and Silas studied it for no more than five minutes. After that, he was able to tell the erudite Thomas Darcy exactly which room he was and this adequately impressed him. Then, Darcy asked Silas about Hall's other clients but he honestly told him that he did not know their names and apologised. He pushed the issue for a while but then gave up and guided him back to the kitchen where there was a skinny maid with long black hair and she smiled at him.

Silas blushed and was once more in love.

The pledge
Meanwhile, Robert Hall had found himself under increasing pressure to collaborate with the Earl of Cumberland from Skipton. Certainly, he wasn't obliged to help him but someone with such status could have easily damaged the Hall business and reputation. It would not have been wise to cross a man with so much power and authority. Hall had held a lifelong policy of remaining neutral in all affairs unless it affected his coffers and that even included religion. The groat was his god and he worshipped at its temple daily. Neither was he interested in state affairs although, on this occasion, he could not wriggle out of it.

As he eventually agreed to help the Earl, he thought about continuing to use Silas as a go-between but despite the Earl's insistence that the boy was trustworthy, Hall thought it better to have Cumberland's man, John, transport the sensitive package to Skipton castle using one of his couriers. He did allow Silas to make the return journey with him when, once more, he found himself in the kitchen which was notably larger than the one at Temple Newsam. Silas was taken before an official and handed over what could only be described as a small note. It was opened and a smaller note fell out, the clerk picked it up, smiled at the boy and asked him to wait outside although via a different entrance, one behind his desk. There, Silas found himself looking at a stained-glass window and it was of exactly the same design he had seen at Temple Newsam and on Beatrice's drawing table. Understandably, he presumed that it was a much-desired image and chose to hover and simply enjoy it.

Soon, those exchanges came to an end and by the end of April 1530, Robert Hall had in his possession the very thing that Cumberland had spent months persuading him to handle, something that had more power and value than all his trading to date and he was not comfortable with it.

Arkwright

One morning, the rain was so fierce that it swamped Annie's minuscule grazing space and filled Silas's boots before he had even got out of bed and he realised once again that he was running late. Bolt sloshed through the ever-growing passage from his home to Dead Alley and ventured once more onto Coppergate. There before him, looking like his prey dragging itself out of the river, was the almost omnipresent Bogmorten. Silas was determined to talk to him although he was entirely engaged in the business of selling his trade.

An assortment of heads dangling from his waist, he waved his pennant whilst shouting,

'Bogmorten will rid thee of all thy woes and burdens! Dead in a day or thou doth not pay!'

You could well believe that such an irresistible offer would have had the witless of York queuing but on this dreary day, it seemed as though all were hurrying either to or from their shelter. Silas waited until he had his attention.

'I thank you sir for you saved my life...'

'Aha! Thou feverish soul! Boggy goeth forth with righteousness…'

Silas wasn't sure what he meant but could tell that his thanks were well received.

'If I can ever return your goodwill, please say so.' said Silas.

Bogmorten politely patted him on the head and went about his business.

The warehouse! thought Silas. He was meant to be there much sooner so turned and ran, Bolt a few paces behind him.

When he entered, dripping all over Robert Hall's precious factory, he found himself once more in awe of its industrious atmosphere not to mention the heat. Jonks ushered him into the corridor that led to the artist's room although before he got there, he witnessed an almost complete stained-glass window being constructed and yet again, it was that same image of the beautiful lady, now in bright colours and leaning on a cart. As he waited, he became aware of raucous laughter and amicable discussion and was thankful that his master wasn't angrily waiting for him. A door opened and a large man with a fine leather cap which boasted a large white feather came through it backwards. He was followed by Hall and the two of them were slapping backs, embracing and engaging in nonsensical banter.

'Ah, you're here' said Hall, 'this is my errand boy. Silas, this is my very good friend and business associate, Master Arkwright. He is of the finest gentry and is as much an expert on Yorkshire farming as any man alive.'

Silas was taken aback. This was the very first time Hall had used his name correctly and he had also introduced him to one of his peers. Appropriately, he bowed.

Seemingly out of nowhere, Beatrice appeared.

'He is Beatrice's father' said Hall and she hugged her father and then embraced Robert Hall.

Silas made a sound much like a pig's bladder being pierced.

'You alright lad?'

'Oh yes, sir. Oh yes…'

Delighted that Beatrice was no longer Hall's plaything, he felt as though he now had permission to look beyond them and at the drawings although the familiar design was nowhere to be seen. As Arkwright made to leave, Silas could just about pick up Hall's parting words,

'I simply cannot agree to send it the full length of England. It would be too dangerous…'

He turned back and spoke directly to Beatrice.

'Can you get this to Father Bartholomew via the usual route?' and he handed her a note.

'Yes sir, I can do that today' she answered.

Besides wondering why Beatrice seemed to be taking on errands, Silas thought nothing of his comment and went about his local deliveries. More and more, houses in York wanted glass upgrades and Hall was keen to be able to boast of that monopoly. Silas finished during the late afternoon and went to the house to report back. Almost two hours passed in which there were no signs of Jenny so he did what he always did and went to the door. Purposely, he pushed his nose up to the glass only to see a bereft Robert Hall. He was very troubled. Head in his hands, his wife was trying to comfort him. Silas had seen him in almost all moods possible in the time he had known him and it put him in mind of when Hall was at the trial at Sheriff Hutton.

'It will be alright my dear, you'll see,' said the doting, Jane Hall.

He raised his head and quietly said,

'I have just been threatened by Percy. I believe I am in mortal danger' he replied.

Lord Henry

Henry Percy was twenty-eight years of age, a knight, member of the Council of the North, deputy warden of the East Marches and the sixth Earl of Northumberland, not bad for a twenty-eight-year-old. As a boy, he had been a page to Cardinal Wolsey and many thought that Wolsey had been as good as a father to him. By 1530, Percy had already separated from his wife and previously had to be reprimanded by both Wolsey and the king for an illicit betrothal but remained a force to be reckoned with and by all accounts, much desired by the opposite sex.

Silas did not understand Robert's reference to Percy but left the alley concerned that his master was so very perplexed and feeling threatened. Did this mean that he too was in danger? he mused but believed that, following the convoluted and chilling events at Sheriff Hutton and Rosedale that Robert would protect him where and when possible. Perhaps, thought Silas, Percy wanted one of the many wonderful windows with the lady in it but could not have one. Reminding himself once again that not only was it not his place to think but that thinking also hurt his head, he chose to return to the workshop to see if he could leave his last reply of the day with someone there.

By now, those who didn't welcome Silas were either civil to him or just ignored him. The gaffer showed him to a secured chest whilst wielding a large key. He put the letter in it and locked the box. Noting his undying interest in the glass-making process, Jonks let him watch for a few minutes but not without thoroughly warning him of the dangers and reminding him that everything he was about to witness was secret. In addition to describing numerous injuries, including a lost eye and an arm from which flesh had melted, he took him on a tour of the current burns that were evident on the bodies of the workers. At the point of heaving, Silas said he would be still and quiet whilst he watched. Tired after a busy and very wet day, he slowly eased his backside onto a table behind him. Wondering what all the sudden shouting was about, he heard an almighty sizzle and all went quiet again although only for a second during which every single glass worker stood agape and motionless. Before they could express their horror, Silas leapt two feet into the air, screaming.

He had sat down on the cooling table although the glass bubbles that had been placed there were far from cool which meant that he was out of the building in an instant and down to the river. There was one very small patch, possibly only about four feet wide with a very shallow incline that ended in the water, almost like a miniature beach. There was nothing left of the clothing on his lower body and so he sank his frying backside into the now semi-frozen Ouse river. For passers-by, this would not have seemed out of the ordinary as some citizens would think nothing of emptying their bowels in the river even in bright daylight. Temporarily, it offered him some relief although he was not, as yet, thinking beyond his current situation. And then, as if things could not have got any worse, Beatrice walked towards him.

'What you doing? You having a shite, Silas?'

'Absolutely not!'

He was hoping to sound indignant but his voice was shaking and it was clear to Beatrice that he was in pain.

'Burn…burnt my arse…'

She put her hand to her mouth although her eyes were as big as planets. He stared at her awaiting a response.

'How long you going to stay there?' she asked whilst holding her breath.

'Until everyone has gone home. Feels very cold now…'

'Have you got any honey or…or snails?' she asked.

'Have I got any snails?'

This was practically a first, Silas did not do sarcasm and was rarely rude but as his only hope of finding both a long, and short, term solution to his predicament was standing right in front of him, he had hoped for better.

'Why would I have snails?' he grumped.

'Wait here…' she said.

As I if am going somewhere, he thought. Then, he remembered his manners and just nodded.

An hour later she returned with a shawl.

'I will hold this up and I promise I will not look. As soon as you are upright, wrap it around yourself.'

However, much as she tried not to, it was almost impossible not to notice how he could barely stand and he moaned constantly as he did. His legs looked like two long leeks dithering in the chilly water and it was then that she started to titter.

His head came up. He was astonished.

'I'm so sorry' she said feigning sincerity, 'I know you must be in so much pain.'

'I can't even feel my nether regions' he mumbled and then, at last, suppressed laughter burst forth from the pretty young artist.

'Thank you…kind…err…maiden. I will find my own…' he said haughtily.

'Listen. Please, Silas. I am ashamed. If you go home without any medicine you will suffer. Look, there...under the bridge....no one can see.'

He was both desperate and indecisive. He knew that she wanted to help but no one besides his mother had seen his secret parts. Then he remembered Jaxon. And his friends. Then Jenny came to mind as he recollected that she had bathed him. That's quite a lot, he thought. Reluctantly, he agreed but was clueless as to where such intimacy fit on the scale of male-female relationships. She told him to wait under the bridge with the promise of a return. As he waited, dithering and in pain, all manner of debris fell from the underside of the Ouse Bridge. As he looked up, he could see gaps in the boards and fetid water carrying all manner of waste dripped and spattered upon him. When she did arrive, Beatrice told him to stand with his hands on the wall as he faced it and then she gently smoothed a salve onto his wounds. He had an apple-sized crimson ring on each buttock and so similar were they that you may well have thought them placed there on purpose. He winced and howled as she carefully smeared it unsparingly. One or two onlookers nudged each other as they tried to comprehend what this most unusual and barbaric sex act was that was taking place under the Ouse Bridge. For her part, she was astonished at how thin he was, there was more bone than flesh and his real bum-fluff perfectly matched that which was sprouting under his chin. Every so often, she would stifle her laughter although it would have been adequately drowned out by his cries.

Then, he was sure that she had stuck something on him so he asked.

'I have put a snail on each cheek. They will roam around feeding on some of the ingredients and heal the damage.'

'I have to...I'm to walk home with...'

'Yes. You need to keep them on there.'

And, once it was dark, he did just that although it took

him almost an hour.

He paced the floor almost all night although the snails admirably managed to maintain their therapeutic grip. Eventually, he lay face down, naked, on his cot and wondered if he and Beatrice would now have to get married.

He was certain that he would never walk again and that she would tell everyone in York of his accident but he was wrong on both counts except that she did feel obliged to tell Robert who was left calculating the number of days that Silas had now taken off due to ill health.

Three weeks passed and he was more or less well once again although the snails remained traumatised for some time. The workers at the warehouse and workshop gave him a leather belt as a gift although they said nothing more about the incident and Silas avoided Beatrice as much as he could. But he had developed a walk, almost like he was still on his horse when he wasn't and it would never go away as he grew.

During that time, he had fostered a strange kind of friendship with Bogmorten and often they would greet one another although they would rarely converse. On morning whilst meandering along High Ousegate with the intention of catching one of Bayard's performances, he saw Bogmorten hastily retreat from a small house.

'What ails you Boggy?'

'I…I cannot say…most…unusual…'

His eyes were on stalks as he stared into the distance and it was several minutes before Silas got any sense out of him although what he finally declared could hardly have been described as sense. He told him that he had embarked on a most straightforward assignment, the owner had a solitary mouse which had taken up residence but when Bogmorten went to challenge it, the creature had told him to leave. Silas chuckled and thought it might well be a story silly enough to be included in one of Bayard's satires. Bogmorten remained bemused as they turned into Davygate where a figure rushed by so fast that he nearly knocked them both over. Silas could not suppress his inquisitiveness any longer and asked his friend who the ill-mannered priest was.

'That be Father Bartholomew. A curate, so Boggy believes. Works in the Minster no less. Lives in Lady's Row along Goodramgate'

Although it was none of his business, Silas could not help pondering over Bartholomew's strange behaviour. He did make the connection with his master though as he had mentioned the delivery of a message to Bartholomew via Beatrice. Perhaps Bartholomew works for Master Hall as I do, he thought. Boggy rambled for some time about indoor privies and how they were the filthiest idea known to man or woman.

'Who wants shit in their house?' he asked Silas.

Apparently, he was bound for a grand home along Petergate which had a polecat stuck inside the new privy. Although the owners were not the least bit amused that Bogmorten had pointed out that the polecat had actually defecated in there and that this was the sole purpose of a privy, they still wished him to remove it.

Silas was late for work and had already missed a performance although Bayard waved to him and Dunstan, yet again, seemed to appear out of nowhere.

'Do your master's bidding and do not get involved in the politics and schemes of his clients. You are blessed, Silas. Use your gifts wisely. These are very dangerous times.'

It would be some years before he would understand and value the counsel of Dunstan and walked away smiling as he was sure that he had no gifts, no real value and at times he thought, no purpose. Yet again, Robert tasked him with dropping off purses for the glaziers at the Minster which had Silas believing that his master was becoming desperate. But it was an easy enough task, he walked in as if he worked there and headed once again for the rose window. This time everything seemed different. He approached the same man he always did and passed on the purses with "Master Hall's good wishes."

The man kindly placed his hand on Silas's shoulder and told him that they were done. Everything had been examined and tested on the huge, round window and all was found to be completely sound. He then walked the lad over to a large table with so many items on it that it was hard to make out what was what. He pulled out a gold chain from the pile of objects.

'We have one of these each. Modest as we are, we are in great demand and we cannot work for everyone. All of these are gifts' he said pointing at the assortment on the table.

Silas was astonished although, on this occasion, he had something to reference. These men, he thought, were like the man from Murano in Italy, so gifted that they couldn't possibly share their skills with every patron who contacted them.

'Master Hall's money will be returned; with thanks' he said and then thanked the boy. He smiled, although as he turned to walk away, he saw amongst the gifts on the table an unusual jewel, certain he had seen it somewhere before.

As Silas turned to leave, he once more saw shadowy figures in the north transept and could not resist further investigation. There, huddled behind a stone column was Bartholomew although this time he was in discussion with Daniel and surprisingly, Beatrice too. He remembered what Dunstan had said, he was now meddling when he should have known better. Silas then headed straight for Robert's house. He knew that his master would be disappointed at the glazier's answer although he did not witness his response. Eventually, Jenny returned with some banal errands for the rest of the day and a message. From that moment on he was not to go to the house again. Fearful of losing his position he desperately asked her to elaborate.

'There is a new office beside the workshop. You will report there, sometimes he will be there or it may well be a clerk. There has been a door built so you do not have to go through the workshops or the warehouse. It has the number sixty-six on it.'

His face screwed up as he took this on board. Why would it be sixty-six when there were no more than eight buildings for a mile? He thought. At least it was a number he could remember and percentages were not mentioned.

15 The office

Although windy, the milder weather was welcomed by all. Silas had started to attend the office and sometimes his boss was there and sometimes Jonks issued instructions, usually when they were just straightforward local errands. Early one day, he made his way there as a matter of routine and spotted Mrs Tumble for the first time in many years. She was walking towards him arm in arm with a man and, as they became closer, he recognised him as the constable who had almost evicted his mother all those years ago. Mrs Tumble paused although only for a moment. Silas was sure that she was about to engage him in conversation but then she led her partner swiftly down an alley leaving Silas wondering why. In an instant, they were gone but it had a profound effect on him. Visions of his mother trying to cope with a small and curious child, waved over him and, as he walked, he thought about how far he had come and the many changes that had taken place in his life as well as the irritating realities of his existence.

He smiled for even though Bolt had slowed, he always led the way. He walked in front of Silas as his protector and was always first to greet others, friend or foe and often it would be Bolt making that choice. He barked at Bogmorten in the distance and he waved back. By now, Silas's trusted hound had become both an oddity and a celebrity in York just like his owner.

Even when criss-crossing the city, he tended to avoid the Shambles not least because of the mess and the smells but he had recently found cause to saunter past the high end of the alley as a girl was working there who smiled at him. He was at that age when a smile was enough, often more than enough. To be precise, he was overjoyed if anyone noticed him. A girl working amongst the slaughter and dismemberment of pigs was unusual but not unheard of and Silas presumed that she just did some cleaning work as that is what he had seen her do. But Agnes was the daughter of a prominent York butcher, one of seven children. She was slight in build and had a smile that was bigger on the left side of her mouth than on her right just as he sometimes had and she staggered when she walked. Silas had also noticed that when she smiled at him, her eyes were looking somewhere else and that she had only three teeth though it did not bother him. You may then wonder why he knew that she was smiling at him and the answer lay in the revelation that her behaviours were much like his. Although he had great hopes that he, and Agnes, were from some distant and exotic race, he could only think of one word to describe it and that word was odd for that was how he had always been, quite cruelly, described by others. Now and again, she would wave although her arm seemed to be flapping in all directions as she did. Nevertheless, it confirmed to him that there were people like him and that finding a lifelong partner would now be a priority in his life.

Eventually, he reached the office and the door was ajar so he walked in. There behind the desk was Daniel, Hall's stable boy.

'Kind of a promotion methinks, Silas. You'll report to me from now on…'

This wasn't a problem as far as Silas was concerned. Daniel had always been fair with him and often kind. Daniel began to explain what his next venture would be but Silas realised that he was also somewhat distracted. Dan kept looking at Bolt. Eventually, he expressed his thoughts,

'You know he ails?'

Silas nodded slowly.

'May I?' asked Daniel.

He nodded again. Dan knew everything about horses so it followed that he would also know a lot about dogs.

'You have felt these?'

This time when Silas nodded, a tear appeared in one eye. He knew.

'He has these growths in his neck and along his belly.'

Silas looked away.

'He is dying my friend and I think you know it. He is suffering although I know that he would follow you until his last breath. Tis unkind to keep him so…although I know you mean him no harm...'

Silas took some time to find his words.

'What can be done, Daniel?'

Silas already knew the answer although Daniel explained that it would be a great kindness to finish him where he lay. It was something Silas had known for a while but had ignored all winter. He would reassure himself that his beloved dog was simply getting old. It was the weather. He had caught his master's illness and it was lingering. He will be well tomorrow, next week or the week after. It was something he swallowed and will shit it out. There were only two of God's creatures on Earth that were dedicated to him and he could not even contemplate losing one of them even for an instant.

But reluctantly, Silas was glad of Daniel's consideration so he agreed and asked if he could have ten minutes or so to say goodbye and so Daniel left the room.

Silas lay down with his dog and held him tight. Soon, a limp and tired paw wrapped itself around its master's arm. Silas shed quiet tears and thought of that day when he first set eyes on Bolt in William Fawkes' office. Even with a leg missing, the dog had made straight for him.

'He used to be faster' Fawkes had said and Silas smiled as he remembered it. It was as if the dog had been waiting for its rightful master. He thought of how he had loved him from that moment on and how his indispensable Bolt had returned that love a thousand-fold. He gently lifted a long, scruffy wet ear and fluently whispered into it,

'Oh, faithful dog, my dearest friend and ally in all my

ventures. I have loved thee so and as you make your journey, Heaven-bound, my love goes with you. For there never will be a day when Annie or I will not miss you and think of you. How will I manage such challenges without my faithful hound? Our mother awaits thee with a warm fire and a cob dipped in broth and you will run alongside her as she skips to the market. Dear Lord, please take care of my beloved friend…'

He embraced him as if he would never let go but Daniel soon appeared and guided Silas out of the office and around to the front of the warehouse with the promise that he would bury Bolt as near to his mother as possible.

He could not find the strength to return that day and neither did Daniel pursue him. However, his duty was clear and so the following morning he was back at the office as soon as there was light in the east. Daniel sat him down and went straight to business taking care not to reference the absent Bolt.

'Your task is neither easy nor comfortable.'

'I welcome any and all missions' he said forcing a smile.

'You are to return to the castle at Sheriff Hutton. In Galtres Forest.'

Silas said nothing. A thousand ideas conflicted. He could remember the colours, the pageantry, how important people were and in particular the young and very silly Henry Fitzroy. But it had been a place of sinister revelations and danger and, he had been told never to mention any of those events again. Daniel prompted him out of his daydream.

'You need to go immediately and your errand is quite specific although it has to be secret. You must speak to no one about this brief before, during or after…you are to establish whether Cardinal Wolsey is in residence there. Nothing more, just that.'

Now his mind became incredibly busy. He had seen Wolsey's colours at the stable and wondered if he dared ask.

'I…erm…I was near to….one day…'

It took almost fifteen minutes for him to tell Daniel that he had seen a horse with Wolsey's coat of arms on it at his stables.

'That was indeed an equerry of the Cardinal's with a message for Master Hall although we know at the time that the Cardinal was still in London.'

'Oh…err…right…'

Silas was no wiser.

'Nothing else, do you understand? Use any means possible to see if he is in residence. Just because his colours aren't flying does not mean he is not there.'

Silas gave the appearance of being confident although he was clueless about how he would pull this off.

Reunited

He was away within the hour checking that he had some sustenance, his dagger, rope and his axe. He certainly enjoyed the journey. He loved the forest and the peace that came with it but it was marred by the knowledge that there would be no canine welcome for him on his return home. He reminded himself that nowhere else measured up to Galtres Forest. The winter behind him, the floor was becoming a carpet of green, branches even sprouted around the roots of trees and the forest took on a life of its own. This was possibly his first real taste of nostalgia as all the events of five years ago came flooding back.

He soon saw the castle's flags and his little heart danced as he saw the bridge and the familiar portcullis. He had with him a letter although the letter would only get him into the grounds, the rest he had to do himself. Very soon, he found himself standing outside the stables whilst his horse was being pampered by the ostler. He had no idea as to what would happen next so happily gawped at the ladies and young women who were working at tables outside the kitchen plucking feathers, churning cheese and slicing up a hog. It was all fascinating to him and he was as enamoured by the processes as he was by the maidens. Then one of them lifted a large cheese onto the table and in doing so, looked up and saw Silas. She let it drop onto the table with a thud but then stood speechless taking time to evaluate what she could see in the distance. Then, she started to walk at some pace toward Silas and the walk soon became a run.

'Silas! It is you! Silas…dear Silas!'

She was beautiful. An apron-tie accentuated her slim waist although she also had long legs. Her pretty face was perfectly framed by a mane of red curls and yet he was still clueless as to why she was addressing him.

'It is I, Annie…do you not know me?'

He gasped so loud that they could hear him in the kitchen but it was soon drowned out by all the other women cheering and laughing. He found himself, quite inappropriately looking her up and down, his brain trying to work out what happened to little Annie. More than anything, his eyes seemed to settle on her breasts. If this was Annie, who put all the other stuff there? he thought. Beatrice was a few years older but she didn't have as many bumps. Of all the situations in which Silas could have considered the greater mysteries of life, he chose this one. Then he quizzed why this plumpness happened to women and not men. Perhaps it was what they ate? He deduced. All in all, he considered, Annie looked delightful but nothing like the Annie he had left behind five years ago.

'You've changed too' she said, 'you're so tall now.'

Then, she embraced him and, although it took some time, he returned the gesture.

For a while, they both tried to talk at the same time and he did manage to tell her about some of his experiences and mishaps. Thoughtfully, he referenced Arxe and she told him that they now lived in Brint with Geoffrey and his wife and daughter.

'I have a child…' she said smiling.

He was shocked. He had known for years that she had

married Arxe and that it was only proper that he should forget about her but, he hadn't and it still hurt although by now he had learned not to show it.

'Why are you here?' she asked.

Without even thinking of whether it was a good idea or not, he just blurted it out. Annie didn't even ask why he wanted to know.

'No Silas...the Cardinal hasn't been here in the two years I've worked here.'

'Do you think it would be rude if I just left again then?' he asked.

'Not at all. Can you wait an hour? I finish then and Arxe would so like to see you.'

Silas became so flummoxed that all his words became mixed up. He wasn't sure he wanted to see Arxe at all but she insisted so much that he eventually agreed.

'I think the farrier is putting shoes on Annie so that will take an hour' he said confidently pointing at the stable.

'You named your horse Annie?' she said.

His mouth remained open and he went instantly pale. He had no idea whatsoever as to how he would avoid the question so Dunstan's advice came to the fore.

'Oh…Ah…. ell…. erm. Yes. Yes, I did. I named her after you.'

She kissed him on the cheek and said that she would meet him at the stable in one hour.

Silas didn't know what to think as they made their way toward Brint. Annie had explained that she usually walked but without warning jumped into the saddle behind Silas for the journey to Brint. She exuded warmth. Her touch excited every part of his mind, soul and body. He believed it to be like being in a blissful sleep but then he chastised himself for he knew it was wrong to have any feelings whatsoever for a married woman. Guilty, he picked up the pace which sadly only worsened the recurrent problem he had with his circulation.

Soon, Annie, Annie and Silas arrived and they were all sincerely overjoyed to see him.

'Why did you never return?' asked Geoffrey.

Silas explained that all his ventures had taken him everywhere but north and that there was no ill will intended.

'Come!' said Arxe, 'I have something to show you.'

As they walked into a nearby clearing, the statue commissioned by Robert Hall proudly stood as if it had been fashioned only yesterday.

Silas walked over and embraced it as if it were Isaac himself.

'I would not have missed this for a chest of gold' said Silas and, as he did, a little boy came running out. He had unkempt red hair, the same colour as Annie's. Immediately, Silas realised that this was their son.

'Hello fine fellow,' said Silas.

'Ullo…' said the boy and smiled. He grabbed a branch and thrust it at Silas. Silas found a stick to his left and played swords for some minutes only to, once again, tumble and admit defeat as the child giggled.

'Enough now Silas! Make your way in' demanded Annie.

Then, they all laughed at the confused look on Silas's face as he wondered why she was now ordering him about. Annie picked up the little boy.

'He is Silas too' she said.

'You…you…named…'

'Yes, we named him after you' said Arxe.

He then enjoyed one of the happiest hours he could remember. If only he had an inkling of the impression he had made on these simple folk. They laughed at his mishaps and all manner of emotions were exhibited as he told them of his treatment by Jaxon and the death of the Queen of Sheba and his devoted dog. For a young man who struggled so much to understand the nuances of people's expressions and moods, he was now left certain that others cared for him. He left with the promise of return although he could not say when. They had also given him an answer to something that had been on his mind for some time and left him respecting Geoffrey even more. At the Battle of Flodden, Geoffrey had tended to the injured on both sides and nursed an injured boy for days only to find out that he was orphaned. He took the nameless Scottish boy as his own and one day, settled and content as a Galtres Forest woodsman, he looked down at his axe and named the boy after it except his adopted son would never quite get it right. Annie and Arxe were not cousins.

As Annie the horse dawdled back towards the city, Silas remained buoyed and confident, a broad smile on his face. He thought for a moment about his first visit to the forest and how long it had taken him to deliver his very first message and then return. I will be back at the office early afternoon, he proudly reminded himself.

In the best of moods, he was excited to return to Daniel, his mission a success. As he walked past the front of the warehouse and turned to access the door to the new office with sixty-six on the door, he found it open. Happily, he marched in only to find Beatrice and Daniel in a fond embrace and kissing one another. His smile dissipated and his shoulders dropped. The couple did not know what to do. Of course, they were guilty, ashamed and terrified that they had been found out but both of them would have rather it have been anyone else for they knew that their secret would hurt Silas. For what seemed like an eternity, they were motionless, each waiting for someone else to speak. Eventually, Silas nervously broke the silence.

'I didn't…why did you not…I…'

It was clear to them both that already he had adopted their guilt, blaming himself for stumbling into a private liaison. Beatrice stepped forward and grasped both of his hands with hers.

'Oh, my dear Silas. Please do not think that you have done anything wrong and, although our love has been secret, we do intend to tell my father and Master Hall soon.'

Silas remained confused and hurt. He was also smart enough to work out that the incredibly successful and much respected Arkwright would probably not settle for a stable boy for a son-in-law whether or not he now sat in an office. He could not look at them so embarrassed was he. His brain was throbbing as it tried to make sense of what he had witnessed and that internal province that normally excluded any thoughts of interfering, temporarily lapsed as he asked them a question almost without thinking.

'Is that why I've seen you together at the Minster?'

Beatrice sat in Daniel's chair and sobbed.

'Bartholomew lets us meet in secret there. I do confess Silas, I also enjoy seeing the architecture, the windows, the bishops and others,' said Daniel.

'Father Bartholomew is my brother, Silas' added Beatrice.

His face screwed into a knot as he tried to make sense of the weight of new knowledge.

'Sometimes Bartholomew and his colleagues would ask to see her drawings so magnificent are they…,' said Daniel. Beatrice became very quiet in an instant and in that silence, all of them became aware of a creaking sound. It was somewhat like firewood crackling except much quieter. Then, dumbfounded, Silas pointed at the panel behind Daniel although both of them just stared at the end of his finger presuming that it signified something. Then, there was an almighty crunch and, where there had previously been just half panelled plaster wall, there was an opening, a small door and through it walked Robert Hall. All three of them jumped backwards in astonishment before he had even said anything.

'Think I've heard enough!' said Robert angrily.

Both Silas and Daniel had pondered for some time over the flimsy office that was no more than an add-on to the sturdy warehouse. Seemingly, Robert had set it up with the very purpose of espionage although, as yet, none of them knew why.

'You heard?' asked Beatrice.

'I did too. What will your father think?! So...you've been taking my drawings to the Minster?'

As she answered, she assured him that it was because she needed the praise, some acknowledgement although this seemed to make him even worse. Then, unwittingly, Silas asked something that would shorten Robert's inquisition by hours.

'Is it the drawings of the lady and the wheel, Beatrice?'

Robert's head spun around. She nodded.

'Is that why I see the same stained-glass windows everywhere I go?' Silas added.

Innocently, he had let the cat out of the bag. Although this made no sense to Robert or Daniel, they both thought that something was amiss. Sensitively, Robert Hall turned to Silas.

'What windows? Where?'

'At Skipton and at Temple Newsam they are all the same as Beatrice's drawing.'

Instantly, Robert understood and so started by explaining to Silas.

'I have no commission with either of them that would involve stained glass although I can easily understand why you would think that to be the case.'

He turned to Beatrice.

'Have you ever provided your brother Bartholomew with copies?'

She burst into tears once more. He awaited an answer.

'He told me...he said...as a woman...no one...would...would ever...take any notice. He promised me commissions and...status...he promised...' she blubbered.

'He promised you the impossible no doubt!' he shouted.

Hall was in no mood to be reconciliatory. He forced the girl into confessing all. They had used Silas, interfering with the messages that he had taken to Skipton and Loidis. They had ensured that small notes were included just behind the seal of Robert Hall's messages which invited the recipients to contact Father Bartholomew directly for quality windows at low cost. Bartholomew would then visit with the expert drawings and instructions and seal the deal.

Daniel was mortified. If it hadn't been enough that he was keeping his love affair secret, Beatrice was now confessing to theft, fraud and embezzlement that he previously knew nothing about.

'So, what of the manufacture?' asked Hall.

'I know not sir. I swear. I only gave copies of my drawings.'

'Does it have anything to do with the master glaziers working at the Minster?'

'I do not know, sir.'

Robert grabbed a Bible from the desk and gave it to her.

'Do you swear that you know no more than you have told me?'

'I do not although I fear that my brother knows all...'

Then, Hall's mood changed. He looked at his secret door and walked around the small office like a peacock, proud of his achievement.

'All of this will break your father's heart girl and as for you' he said turning to Daniel, 'do not harbour any desires or affections for that is now done!'

Then he paused and confronted Beatrice once more.

'So how do your small notes get into my letters unless... '

He looked directly at Silas who strained to hold in a fart but failed.

'No' said Robert, 'no, it cannot be you. I don't believe it.'

Then, trembling, Beatrice told him what he needed to know.

'Jenny.'

Robert Hall looked mortified. So many people so close to him had deceived and cheated him. Silas was also shocked to the core, aghast that Jenny could do such a thing as tampering with the messages that he had carried so far.

Robert thanked Silas, acknowledged that he had succeeded in his mission at Sheriff Hutton and assured him that he had done nothing wrong but then dismissed him. As he left, he heard his master send Jonks to get the sheriff and Arkwright as he knew he only had half a confession.

Nun Monkton

Of course, Silas's mind was a whirl and he was beginning to think that everyone was corrupt and, if not, a let-down. He struggled to work out how all this lined up with his faith. Am I the only one following the rules? he thought and yet that idea would still not puncture his values and eventually, he would have little trouble continuing to love his enemies. However, he considered, his friends were a slightly more difficult prospect. He knew in his heart that Beatrice was beyond him and now accepted that Annie was never his and always had someone else's heart. And, whatever happened in his life, he was still able to find that ray of sunshine, that drop of water in an oasis that made life worth living. For the time being, it was his horse, his job, his beautiful city and the toothless butcher girl from whom he was guaranteed a wonky smile.

It was two days before Silas was asked to return to the office and when he arrived, his boss was sitting at the desk and the secret door was impossible to detect again.

'You will soon be involved in a lengthy and dangerous mission which could have considerable consequences at the highest level... and... you might die.'

Silas only heard "mission" and was delighted.

'To save you any anxiety, I will give you a little task at a time although I will only ever tell you that which you need to know.'

He nodded.

They heard footsteps approaching, and as he looked, he saw that it was the sheriff who entered without invitation.

Silas made to leave but Robert told him to sit down.

'This lad has helped uncover this sorry mess and in doing so could well have saved me a fortune.'

'Methinks you are becoming indispensable, boy!' said the sheriff.

Silas was quite insulted but had heard worse. If only he had known what indispensable meant.

'I have news but it is not all good news Master Hall...'

Robert was anxious to hear everything he had to tell and was happy for Silas to hear it too. The sheriff told them that he had managed to track down Bartholomew and searched his rented house in Lady's Row. There, he found many copies of various designs created by Beatrice. There were also notes about materials, colours and so forth but nothing that indicated manufacture.

Unexpectedly, Silas interrupted.

'What is it?'

'What?' said Hall abruptly.

'The picture of the lady...'

'Ah that is a depiction of St Catherine of Alexandria and I have to say it is Beatrice's design alone!' Robert boasted.

Somewhat shocked that Robert Hall knew so much he asked what it meant and why there was a wheel in it. If Silas hadn't lit Hall's ego, he may well have stopped his enquiry there but, of course, he continued.

Robert told him that in the fourth century, Catherine had protested against the Roman emperor, Maxentius for how he persecuted Christians. Although she succeeded in converting many Romans, she was tortured and put to death on a spiked wheel, hence the term Catherine's Wheel. Instantly, the image meant so much more to Silas but then there was a deathly hush whilst the sheriff rummaged in his jerkin and eventually pulled out a piece of paper. He unfolded it and placed it on the desk for them to see.

'Aye' said Robert still proud, 'a copy of Beatrice's fine design.'

'Nay' answered the sheriff, 'a sketch of St Catherine of

Alexandria by Raphael Santi, one of Italy's greatest artists and a painting finished in 1508, twenty two years ago.'

Hall appeared hurt. Very hurt. How far did this deceit extend? he thought struggling to come to terms with the trust he had placed in the audacious Beatrice.

'For now, all we can presume is that this is a deeper intrigue than we first thought. I aim to track down this Bartholomew and I promise you Robert we will get to the bottom of this.'

'But he has gone into hiding!' said Hall.

'Rather clumsily, he had written down an address in Nun Monkton, just twelve miles away,' said the sheriff.

'Nun Monkton? There's nothing there but…' offered Robert.

'Nothing but a priory…,' said the sheriff.

'Not another bloody priory!'

'I know not why he would be living in Nun Monkton but I will get back to you once I know more,' said Sheriff George Gale.

The hideout

As the weeks passed and the streets of York dried out, Silas was tasked with local errands but was also tested on how quickly he could deliver them. Then, he was asked to travel further and return on the same day whilst his master timed him. Not once did he ask why or complain, for he knew something important lay ahead. He did not see Daniel or Beatrice again in York but this in itself was becoming a fact of life. People came and went regularly whether that was because of death or their supposed lack of worth. The crimes they had been accused of were severe and they may well have been languishing in a dungeon somewhere. Not that Silas didn't care, he simply knew that if he wished to keep his employment, he should not mention them again.

As June arrived, Robert Hall found an answer although it was not a welcome one. Bartholomew had been reluctant to admit to his crimes and was clearly covering up for someone else. The sheriff, to give him full due, had worked long and hard to get to the core of the mystery and that included visiting Skipton Castle and Temple Newsam. When Robert had been shown samples of the stained glass and lead work along with information garnered from those that had commissioned the windows, he acknowledged that they were of a fine standard and quality. Reluctantly, the sheriff had let Bartholomew run free throughout most of May but, as expected, the cleric could not resist renewed involvement with his clandestine and lawless employer who still remained anonymous. There was little to see at Nun Monkton even at the priory although Bartholomew's lone treks eventually took the sheriff's men as far as Tolerton which was in the province of Galtres Forest. On discovering this, he then had to liaise with Galtres wardens and other officials something which, in itself, informed the sheriff that Bartholomew was purposely attempting to throw the officials off the scent.

One day, at dusk, Sheriff George Gale, two wardens, a master regarder and two bowmen surrounded a small settlement outside of Tolerton. There, they discovered outdoor fire kilns dominated by a large building which was completely enclosed apart from the one door facing them. There was no indication whatsoever as to whether anyone was inside or not although, beyond was a newly built cottage and candles had been lit inside. Neither was there anything makeshift about the cottage, it was made almost entirely of brick with a fine chimney to match. The exotically coloured window spoke volumes especially as it too was made of stained glass.

'I will go in alone. The rest of you should surround the cottage…' whispered the sheriff.

Expecting a fight as soon as the cottage door was opened, the sheriff could only see two men by the fire conversing and drinking, oblivious to his entrance.

Instantly, he recognised Father Bartholomew but the

other, apart from striking him as quite strange, was unknown to him.

'In the name of the king you are ordered to open up yonder storehouse, forthwith.'

They jumped up but then seemed as though they did not know what to do. Seemingly they had no contingency plan for this eventuality so stood for a while looking back at the sheriff who had placed his hand on the hilt of his sword, ready to draw it whilst bowmen readied themselves outside.

Calmly, they told the sheriff that they would comply and then walked ahead of him towards the door of the larger building. The other officials were astonished that there seemed to be no greater threat apart from the priest and an old man.

Once the door of the large building was opened, the sheriff gasped. Inside was an arcane industry far greater than that of Robert Hall's. At least twenty workers were blowing and forming glass and others were either staining or painting it once cut. Gale demanded that they took him to the far end where there was a table strewn with designs, drawings and instructions, all copies of designs by Beatrice. At the centre was an excellent drawing of Saint Catherine of Alexandria which had been signed although the name on it was not Beatrice's

The arresting party were shocked at the scale and audacity of the enterprise. The sheriff told them all that they were to stop work immediately and it was only then that he realised that they were mostly women and young children, possibly peasants. As he further examined their condition, he was certain that they were being used as slaves although he acknowledged that there were bound to be expert glaziers involved as well but they were nowhere to be seen. In one corner were children crudely smelting lead and although in the sixteenth century the real dangers of lead were unknown, those children would have been lucky to survive their ordeal as daily it was finding its way into their pores, lungs and stomachs.

Suddenly, a row broke out between the priest and the older man.

'I haven't led them here!' asserted Bartholomew.

'It has to be you. You halfwit. See…the sheriff is from the city!'

'How on Earth did I get involved with you Salvo, you have led me on the road to hell' and as Bartholomew said this, he broke down completely and fell to the floor.

It would have been highly unlikely that anyone present would have heard that name before and it was also certain that Salvo would no longer have used it himself. However, one of the bowmen hurried over to George Gale.

'I know who he is sir. I was ordered never to speak of it but he was arrested by Wolsey some years ago. I saw his trial… he was meant to have been hanged…'

'That right?' said Gale addressing Salvo, 'you dodged the rope, you scoundrel?!'

'I am here with the Cardinal's permission and blessing and he will have your job and your head, thou motherless hog!' said Salvo.

'I very much doubt that!' said the bowman, 'though God alone knows why you still live.'

As soon as he had spoken, the bowman could see that Salvo was already glancing at the six horses tied up no more than thirty yards from where he stood. As the sheriff made to restrain him, Salvo turned and ran for the horse. Clumsily, he mounted, gasping for air and then drew a small dagger from under the saddle, hurling it at the bowman who had already drawn and deflected the dagger with the upper limb of the bow as it had already lost much if his momentum. The archer then let loose an arrow which struck Salvo in the throat. He dropped from his horse like a sack of lead. He was dead within minutes.

The bowman, concerned turned to Gale for approval.

'Apart from getting to the bottom of all this, I cannot

fault your action' said the sheriff, 'if there is any substance to his excuse that Wolsey is protecting him, your swift action may well be the only way in which we would see him dead. I believe you have saved a lot of good people some great expense and time.'

Bartholomew was terrified. He blubbered and trembled but said nothing at all worthwhile on the road back to York.

A week later, the sheriff sat down with an astonished Robert Hall and offered an explanation in the presence of a bewildered Silas Smith.

'His death was all fair. He resisted his arrest and threatened the life of a respected forest bowman who, in turn, told me of the whole debacle at Sheriff Hutton Castle,' said the sheriff.

'He was meant to be hanged!' said an indignant Robert.

'I hear that a lot. Apparently, at Sheriff Hutton, he managed to have one last meeting with Wolsey before he was to be executed. Rumour has it, and it is only rumour mind you, that he told Wolsey he had deposited written evidence in a secret location that would prove Wolsey's involvement in the illegal operations at Rosedale Priory. Seems as though the greedy cardinal may have well instigated his release and possibly even these further deceits and crimes,' said the sheriff.

'I can well believe that! So, he let him go free after the trial?'

'He was given a horse and told to simply enjoy a quiet retirement…'

'What possessed him to do the same thing all over again?' asked a furious Robert Hall.

'Bartholomew says that Salvo wanted to see you suffer. He was determined to take away your reputation and your stained-glass business which, I should add, he regards as quite amateur. He purposely targeted the Arkwright children as he knew that Arkwright was one of your closest friends.

Worst of all, Bartholomew has implicated the Guild of Master Glaziers although I have nothing to charge them with.'

'To think I offered them a small fortune as they worked in my Minster.'

Silas had adopted that expression. The one that looked like catalepsy, inviting the other two o prompt him.

'Well...out with it lad!' said Robert.

'It is...erm... in the... Minst...'

Robert Hall impatiently sucked in air.

'The master glaziers... they had that same jewel as the nun wore at the trial... at Sheriff Hutton.'

said Silas.

'You mean the one with the shaved head...who had a fine dress on?'

'Yes sir' said Silas, 'it was the same one, given to the glaziers in the same way you gave them purses.'

The sheriff glared at Hall. It was a look that was to remind him forever of how foolish he had been.

Robert stood and blustered for a while insisting that York was his to adjudicate, periodically banging his fist into anything he could find.

'Best artist this side of Florence...' he then said calmly.

It was then that the sheriff had to impart even worse news. Clearly Salvo had still maintained contacts, or perhaps even prisoners, from Italy. Beatrice had based her design on a fine copy of Raphael's painting. The copy was made by an artist from Venice.

'What effrontery' said Robert, downhearted.

'Well, I believe the priest to be the one that was the rot in the wood. If you want to know about the girl…' added the sheriff.

'I'm not sure I would…oh go on then…I suppose…no…oh yes…yes!' said Hall.

'She's in a cell fine enough for a princess. She has books and drawing materials. Up to you…'

'I thank thee good sheriff. Fine work. I will write to Galtres officials for they have given great service. I will think on the girl.'

'Did Bartholomew work for you?' asked the sheriff.

'It was one of the few times that I thought I would try someone different to the lad. I entertained the idea that he may be useful in establishing contacts within the Church as my glass interests expanded. I employed him partly because he was Arkwright's son...'

'Stick to the daft boy, methinks' said the sheriff.

The one good thing that came out of this sordid affair was that Salvo was dead. So certain was he of his power over Wolsey that he believed himself to be untouchable and, for a while, he was. If he had escaped once more, there would have been no doubt that he would have done the same thing all over again. As the aggrieved party, Hall was awarded all the resources that were found at Tolerton including the cottage which he intended to rent out. Whoever was managing and advising on the glassmaking process was never found and Bartholomew claimed he did not know although Hall would forever blame the master glaziers.

Eventually, Hall would make good all those illegal contracts for stained glass windows so that it did not ruin his business, Lord Darcy at Loidis was particularly delighted at getting his window free gratis. Although Robert was never to know it, since early 1529, Darcy had been plotting against Wolsey, even writing to the king outlining his failings and it was why he had questioned Silas about Robert Hall's clients and it was the sole reason that he pretended to take an interest in Hall's affairs. Ironically, he had ordered a window as a device to become closer to Hall unaware that it was being manufactured by Salvo and illegally designed by Beatrice and illegally sold by her brother, Bartholomew.

Jenny was sacked without further pay nor reference and Hall could not have cared less about what happened to her.

Although Robert was certain that his world was

imploding, he was pleased to get the matter resolved as much greater pressures were keeping him awake at night. He now had a bigger turnip to boil, one which was creating a stench that would have people pulling their faces as far away as Hampton Court.

16 Desperate measures

During that same month, Wolsey had all but given up on any attempt to secure a divorce for his king and so instead attempted to bring down Anne Boleyn. He was confident that he could solicit the support of Francis the First of France and Charles the Fifth, the Holy Roman Emperor but was left disappointed. Out of favour with his own king, he had been commanded to retreat to his residence south of York at Cawood Castle although the meagre reports that Robert Hall had commissioned about his whereabouts were either misleading or simply gave the impression that he wasn't there. For good reason, Henry Clifford, the first Earl of Cumberland wished to remain at Skipton although he felt that he had something valuable to offer in the matter. Reluctant to approach Wolsey directly, he had recruited the unwilling Robert Hall partly because no one at court would have heard of him despite his rising status in York. It was an appointment that Robert would have gladly refused for he could see the many dangers associated with the scheme. However, despite Clifford's somewhat cowardly efforts, Wolsey seemed to be hiding and the intelligence he was getting suggested that in all matters of state, Wolsey no longer mattered. Robert even considered hiding too for now he was being threatened by Lord Percy as well, someone with considerable power. His one and only confidante was his good wife Jane who failed to understand why they had been dragged into the intrigue in the first place. Wisely, she told him that if he wanted to be a man of significance in York and beyond, that he had to the bidding of his betters and he was inclined to agree.

If all he had to do was deliver a letter to Wolsey then he would have been fine, flattered almost but there was much more to those orders. Added to that was the reality that his one and only messenger, although as honest as the sun rising in the east, was apt to drop himself, and his master, in the cesspit at any point during the adventure.

Desperate to gather intelligence from others, Robert resisted saying anything at all as everyone was learning that their king would have his way in all matters and would happily cull anyone who stood in his way. However, Robert had one idea that would allow him to access the very latest news from court and so took a walk towards the Minster. The sun was now casting long shadows where there used to be none, for the new church of St Michael Le Belfrey was more than half-built. He paused to admire its designs and wondered if there was still time for him to be offered a contract on the building.

Before him, a crowd had almost gathered. He would normally have regarded the sight before him as beneath him, a spectacle for villeins and peasants only, although he was ready to admit that he had never ventured there before. Often, he had heard that the travelling bumpkin offered satire, poking fun at the likes of the king and Wolsey with no restraint. He was certainly impressed by the scale of the stage and the effort that had gone into the art of illusion. In the distance, he saw his errand boy sitting on the foot of one of the Minster's buttresses oblivious to the presence of his master and the hour as he should have already been waiting outside the office.

Today Bayard was using puppets. To begin, a puppet of the king walked on to a cheer from the audience. He had, in his hand, a hock of ham and to all purposes, the audience was led to believe that initially, he was talking about his food.

'God's breath! I am a hungry king! More! I say. My appetite is not satisfied!'

A puppet of the queen appeared and he kissed it.

'Mm…a mere entre! I must have more.'

Already the crowd understood where this was going and

so encouraged the nonsense. Robert was left astonished at the audacity of the performance.

Anne Boleyn appeared and Henry began to fondle her, telling her that she was his one and only true love. As she turned away to get some food, he detected a lady's maid behind him. His speech became drowned but as the audience fully engaged with the farce, even Hall chuckled.

Soon Henry was consuming vast amounts of women and disappeared amongst them. When the crowd saw Henry once again, he appeared much bigger and they roared.

Then, dressed from head to toe in red, Wolsey wobbled on admonishing the king.

'Your Grace! You may only have one woman at a time! Tis God's law.'

'That I have cardinal! I had that one first, then that one…'

Many laughed and others looked at one another so familiar was the trope.

As the cardinal persisted, Henry compromised and told him that he had decided to choose Anne Boleyn and that it was Wolsey's job to get rid of Queen Catherine. Here, the crowd booed which certainly gave Robert an idea of public opinion as many in York had continued to support Queen Catherine of Aragon. Then, some general silliness followed where Wolsey failed to give the king a divorce.

'I have to conclude!' said Henry, 'that cardinals know nought about women!'

The audience laughed, cheered and jeered.

'I'm sending you away. Get thee hence to thy castle at Cawood!'

The Wolsey puppet trotted to the apron of the stage and then whispered directly to the audience,

'I will go where I please. Methinks Southwell to be peaceful this time of year...'

Robert Hall gasped. Could it be possible that Wolsey has disobeyed the king and was hiding at Southwell in Nottinghamshire? he thought and, in thinking so, left him with a bigger problem as sending even as much as a letter to Nottingham would have been too much of a risk.

As the crowd started to disperse, Robert looked upon his lacklustre minion who was as much absorbed in the post-production work as the performance. He thought, as he always had, that Silas was a strange creature living in a world of his own. For an instant, he may even have considered what such a life was like and then hastily remembered his position. Somewhat perplexed, he turned to walk home but suddenly realised that Silas had seen him and was hurrying over.

'Master! Master…I am so sorry…the time.'

Hall swung around,

'You need not worry lad; I didn't come here to find you and you will not be reproached for a few moments' entertainment.'

'Thank…you…thank you sir. Aren't they excellent? Have you…?'

'They? There was but one man moving the puppets.'

'Surely sir?'

For a while, Silas insisted that two men were performing and that he knew both their names although Hall was certain that there was just one.

'I'll only need you in an hour. Come to the office then…'

Silas thanked him and dawdled for a while. Eventually, Dunstan approached him.

'Ah, Silas! The time has come don't you think?'

He looked at the weather and he also knew the time of day but he was clueless as to what Dunstan was referring to.

'I will be leaving you soon.'

Again, this meant little as he was forever coming and going.

'Heed my last counsel. Your greatest task is yet to come. Remember all I have taught you. In your daily life, chaos reigns. Inside, there is an order. It is pure and it dictates how you behave and how you react to and with others. That is your conscience, Silas and it is like no other, put there by

God long before you were made. It is precious like a jewel, do not let anyone take that from you. It is forged from love. You are blessed Silas, go forth in the spirit…'

Silas leaned in a little closer to see if he could detect alcohol on Dunstan's breath but there was none.

'Give love and take love when it is offered and where it is not, move on. In some years yet to come, someone else will replace me although, at first, he will need your help. He will be a stranger in your world and a stranger to his own body but he will come to honour you above kings and popes.

Soon, you may be asked to be part of a powerful intrigue. You will feel that you will have to choose between the will of earls, cardinals, kings and queens. Simply choose your conscience and all will be well.'

Following an embarrassing silence, Silas thanked him for his advice and his friendship and hurried towards the office by the river with lots of fancy new words ringing around his tiny cranium. By the end of the day, he would forget almost everything Dunstan had said but for some strange reason, his advice would return time and time again as the years passed.

Monasteries

For some years, Queen Catherine had been embarrassed by Henry's obsession with Anne Boleyn. By 1530, his intention to marry Boleyn was common knowledge although he had still not found a way of ensuring that it at least appeared legal. At the same time, monasteries and priories were already under inspection and for anyone who had previously felt secure within ecclesiastical life there was little doubt that a reckoning was coming. The king would have his will no matter what and via what route and those ripples of change were felt all across Europe. As Wolsey's light began to fade, Thomas Cromwell's somewhat warped brilliance shone that much brighter. He found himself much closer to his monarch and was very much involved in deciding what should happen to England's monasteries. In the first quarter of the year, the king had turned to his universities for a legal and intellectual solution to his marital status but, they too, could find no justification for it and there was little doubt that if there was just one person in England who could find this golden key, they would remain in his favour for years to come. By June, Henry had commissioned and bribed a small army of academics who could put forward a useful case for divorce, whilst for some years, Catherine had been pressurised to enter a convent and in 1528 was eventually separated from her daughter, Princess Mary.

Whether he intended it or not, Henry the Eighth had set on several courses of action that would soon divide England in two.

The fact that royal divorce in England was unprecedented left much of the population perplexed and rumours based on no factual evidence whatsoever began to spread about Catherine's nature and suitability as queen. In reality, she had been a model queen only guilty of failing to provide him with a male heir.

Almost simultaneously, people of rank up and down the country would either have been putting all their efforts into avoiding the issue or trying to do something about it. Henry Clifford of Skipton seemingly had something very important to say and Robert Hall, possibly for the first time, prayed daily that he would change his mind. Nevertheless, Robert was now deeply involved and his decisions over the next few months would affect his standing and ambitions for years to come.

The chimney

Although there was little need for Silas to visit Hall's house anymore, he would as a matter of business find himself in that area and early one morning in June 1530, he found himself rushing towards it as plumes of smoke filled the street and he genuinely feared for the life of his master and his family. As he arrived, almost sixty people were throwing everything they had at the burning building only half a furlong away from Robert's house. The more sensible ones were trying to access and use water although it would have been sparse as they were not near the river. Nevertheless, men were running back and forth to both rivers with buckets. Fortunately, it was a good six houses away from the Hall's but the fire was spreading fast. Silas dithered but soon found himself in the middle of a chain in which buckets were passed back and forth.

The development of the Tudor house was not, in itself, a tried and tested science. It would be reasonable to presume that the use of more brick and particularly in chimneys would have rendered them safer but that was not necessarily the case. Robert Hall was lucky, he had contacts in the trade and was, more often than not, offered quality work and materials although there were still no universal building regulations. The fashion of having a bigger, more ornate chimney than your neighbour was often a disaster in waiting. Many collapsed and others were built with a draw that was too small and this led to a fire within the chimney and that is exactly what Silas witnessed. Some bricks were also astonishingly explosive. This, added to a thatched roof, almost guaranteed a fireball.

As Silas strained his neck to witness the disaster, he saw Robert Hall and his wife close to the burning building exhausted but assisting. Heavy rain came as an answer to everyone's prayers and eventually, around six in the evening, it burnt itself out with little damage to neighbouring properties. Later, Silas was told that the house belonged to another merchant who was called Brumfield and that he was now completely ruined.

The effect on Robert Hall was almost as bad, as it was later reported that he was telling everyone he was cursed. He had certainly had a difficult year and he could not sleep at night wondering how he would release himself from the grip of Henry Clifford, Earl of Cumberland as well as the threats from Henry Percy.

In his worst nightmares, Salvo would laugh in his face as he stole away all his business and, as he turned away from him, it was the king who faced him, now on trial for interfering with his marital affairs. As he tried to reply, he found himself bound to a stake, the fire lapping at his feet. He awoke suddenly, sweating and desperate to locate Wolsey and have done at last with the demands of Henry Clifford.

Secret mission

Perplexed, Robert decided that he simply could not risk sending a message let alone dangerous information all the way to Southwell so, with no other sensible option open to him and some of the most important Englishmen on his back, he chose to send Silas to Cawood Castle to enquire about the health and welfare of his most gracious and benevolent Archbishop, as he put it. Even this was bold as Wolsey has been stripped of all significant political office and was out of favour with his king.

Silas was still somewhat ignorant of what he was becoming involved with and so gladly made the journey twenty-five miles south of York one warm summer's morn.

As he exited Micklegate Bar, head held high in remembrance of kings and knights that had entered the city there, he looked forward to a journey that would be in comparison easy to negotiate. He fancied for a few moments that he would have liked to go by boat for it was no coincidence that Cawood lay alongside the River Ouse but Hall had rebuked him and reminded him that he had gifted Silas a fine horse. It was, however, the first time that he really missed Bolt. He had been, where and when possible, his rock through all his adventures and it was so very different without him. Nevertheless, a mission was still a mission even if Hall said that it was an errand and it turned out to be one of Silas's more enjoyable journeys. Purposely, he followed the Ouse as best he could as previously, a map had been shown to him of that route. Etched into his mind, he took care to enjoy the Yorkshire countryside and small dwellings.

Crossing a bridge to approach the gate at Cawood, he could see no one so chose to knock on the door. By now, Silas had visited some fine residences which had even included castles but had been given no advice or training as to what to do when arriving. He carried the seal of Robert Hall and often that was enough to at least nudge the curiosity of someone within the establishment's hierarchy.

On this occasion, there was not a soul in sight so he knocked on the door again. Bizarrely, a small door within the door opened and a rotund, unshaven face peered through.

'Yes?!'

'I come with correspondence from York' said Silas perfectly.

'What for?!' came the brusque reply.

'Oh...I don't...there is a... letter...'

'Who is it from then?'

'Master Robert Hall of York member of...'

Then, the man retreated to blow his nose and for a moment, Silas thought he would not return. A minute later, his face appeared once more now almost all the way through the opening.

'Never heard of him...'

'I have a letter...see' said Silas trying to placate him.

'What's it say then?'

'I do not know...I am but a messenger. It is for Cardinal Wolsey...'

'Not here!'

And with that, he slammed the little door shut again.

Silas knocked a few times more without success.

He chose to return home straight away presuming that he had an answer.

When he returned to York, he was surprised to find out that Robert was quite happy with how the assignment had concluded and that was because he knew that Wolsey was not yet in residence at Cawood.

Silas more or less repeated the same journey and the same conversation three more times over that summer and on the last attempt the man took his letter and said,

'We are expecting him within the week' and then slammed his little door shut once more.

The flock
The relationship between Wolsey and the king had been anything but straightforward over the previous year. When it suited him, the king would draw his cardinal closer again and when it didn't, he left Wolsey constantly rethinking his position, particularly how he could permanently regain the king's trust. He would send gifts and that even included a fool. If there was ever a time in Henry's life when he needed a laugh it was now but it was unlikely that bribery would have swayed him so frustrated was Henry in every sense of the word; for Boleyn continued to keep the king at arm's length. Throughout 1530, Wolsey was certain that all would be resolved and his authority completely returned although he had not fully grasped the extent of the king's obsessiveness regarding the divorce. Eventually, his titles were restored to him although he had been replaced as Lord Chancellor by Thomas More who, in turn, would eventually have to face grave issues of conscience regarding the king's marriage to Anne Boleyn and the king's position within the Church.

Although Wolsey's return to Cawood was imposed upon him, he made it look as though it was an episcopal journey north. The Cardinal made a point of visiting people of influence as well as monasteries along the way and, by and large, people were honoured by his presence. He offered the ministry of a common priest including confession and blessings as he made his way and eventually settled near York. There was no doubt that the intended narrative was one in which an absent Archbishop had humbly returned home to his beloved flock.

When he arrived at Cawood, he immediately invested in repair, restoration and new builds despite being advised against it by Cromwell. He was no doubt turning the place into a palace fit to receive anyone and, in turn, find favour, support and admiration from the power base of the north. He was also continuing to scheme for he still believed that if the king could truly see the error of his ways, then all would be well again.

It was, therefore, with some considerable optimism that Wolsey had heard that the Earl of Cumberland, Henry Clifford wished to help. Such clandestine communications were so difficult that, until his arrival, he knew nothing of the detail of this support and that is why Clifford hastily desired to disconnect himself from the information he held. Long ago, it had come to Clifford's attention that Robert Hall, a merchant of York, owed Wolsey a favour. So thin was this thread of support that Wolsey did not even know whether it was evidence that would help to secure a royal divorce or something that would bring down 'The Crow' as Wolsey would refer to Boleyn.

Although by autumn 1530, they were both too deep in the hole to climb out of it, Robert Hall and his errand boy had become entangled in the most dangerous of schemes.

17 Cawood Hall

Delighted with the news that Wolsey was at Cawood, Robert Hall told Silas to meet him later in the day at the office. He sat him down and told him that matters were so important that he had to remember his orders word by word and that he was to speak to no one except the recipient.

After a while, the sheriff approached the office flanked by two guards which perplexed Silas as they were not accompanying anyone else. For a moment he even wondered if he was being arrested again but the sheriff and his master engaged in a whispered conversation ignoring him. Gale then looked at Silas and said to Hall,

'You sure he's your man?'

'Aye, spies will be expecting a heavily guarded wagon. I doubt they'll suspect a merchant's halfwit going about his business.'

Then, they stared at him and he began to grip the chair's arms tightly. The insult meant nothing but he was now sure that he was going to be asked to take on more than he could handle.

'Bring it in!' shouted the sheriff.

Silas jumped and then gasped as one of the guards brought out a plain wooden box so big that Silas alone could not have lifted it. They checked that there was no one around and that included the hidden door amongst the panels. Silas looked on, astonished, as they prised it open. One of them began to pull out seemingly never-ending amounts of straw from the box which landed on the floor becoming lost amongst the rushes. Then, he carefully removed a cask, beautifully formed although it was a miniature. No bigger than the guard's hand, the cask was in many respects the same as a full-sized barrel or wine cask although it was intricately detailed. Silas could not think of any connection between his current duties and this unique object but had learned to keep quiet in such situations and, before long, found himself included in the intrigue.

Along the length of the cask were ten raised squares of wood, five on the top row and five beneath. Each had a letter scribed into it. On the top was: A,Q,J,K,N and below: U,C,H,S,B.

'You are not to touch these. Do you understand?' said Robert Hall.

Silas nodded and wondered why he thought that he would.

'This is not for anyone else's eyes except those in this room. You will have to visit Cawood Castle again, possibly more than once but for the time being, this will stay here.'

The sheriff noticed that Robert still seemed to have quite low expectations of Silas although undoubtedly the lad would have taken any errand given to him, something his master should have grasped by 1530.

'I understand sir,' said Silas.

The guard went out and returned with Annie's saddle and threw it on the desk.

'It's ok lad, the horse is fine. We have something to show you...'

Between the skirt and the saddle flap, a support had been added that fit the cask perfectly. Moreover, it could hardly be seen once the flap was in place.

'Do not remove the cask until you are at your destination, you will have a letter explaining all.'

Silas nodded. Then, surprisingly, Hall let Silas examine the cask. It was light and had polished copper rings around it, into which all sorts of designs and emblems were engraved. He looked at it from every possible angle and yet there was no obvious way into it without breaking it although Silas had already presumed that the raised blocks with letters on had something to do with its operation. They all laughed as he shook the cask realising that there was nothing in there. Then, he noticed something scratched into one of the copper bands.

'Can you read it?' asked Robert.

'No sir.'

'It says, Dg cupe...'

Silas's eyes widened as he looked more closely at the marks.

'Doug Cooper? My grandfather?'

'Tis so!' said Hall proudly, 'this was made long ago for the old Archbishop by your mother's father...'

Silas was spellbound. With nothing left to remind him of his heritage, his eyes filled as he looked upon this masterpiece made by Doug Cooper. He wanted to keep it but for the time being, was content to hold and cherish it. As he turned the cask along its axis several times, he was left with no doubt that his grandfather would ride along with him on this new adventure. As he looked up, Robert, the sheriff and the guards were smiling at him like proud parents. That was until George Gale noticed and, in a clumsy attempt to clear his throat, snapped them all out of it. Silas never once asked how Hall knew of his grandfather although he would forever put great store in this treasured object that now linked him to another human being. However, Silas was to be disappointed. Although they had assured him of an errand to Cawood with the cask, he was to go at least once more with a letter.

The journey was now both comfortable and easily achievable and he wondered if on this occasion he would see the Cardinal at last. Without even thinking about it, he was soon three miles out of York. Again, he lamented the loss of his faithful dog and as he did, he heard the sudden screech of a tawny owl nearby. At first, he leaned backwards so much that he almost dismounted but as he straightened again, he found that it had rested on the pommel of his saddle. Silas chuckled as the owl then appeared to commandeer his horse and rode proudly for five miles before taking flight once more.

Silas's arrival this time was on a much finer day and he thought once again that it was the grandest establishment he had seen. The strange character that had confounded him previously was neither at nor behind the door. When he knocked, it opened and a man politely asked what his business was. As soon as Robert Hall's name was mentioned the door was opened and, on entering, Silas was astonished at the scale of the palace, there was so much more than could be seen from the bridge. Before him was a fashionable double courtyard and, to the right, stables for twenty horses. Annie was soon taken from him and he was led along a long hallway into one of the many chambers. Although he could instantly map the whole place in his head, he had also thought to count the number of chambers and then reminded himself of how poor his counting still was. Very soon, he found himself alone in the grand treasurer's chamber although after a short wait another official entered. He held the door open and a servant walked in and put down a plate with cooked eggs and fish on the table and then offered him some weak wine.

'Am I...should I go... is this?'

'It is for you. Eat whilst you await His Grace's response.'

And eat he did, it was as fine a meal as he had ever had and he devoured it all except for that which was left on his dusty doublet and hose. Soon the official returned,

He was dressed similarly to William Fawkes and others he had observed in various ranks of the legal profession. For once, Silas had been tasked with making a judgement. His master had been quite specific regarding the delivery of the letter. Whether or not it was because he wished to get away or that he was nervous but he handed over Hall's message there and then. Fortunately, he was being addressed by Wolsey's advocate and he gave Silas a reply immediately.

'You must remember this message. His Grace will not have it recorded. Do you understand?'

Silas had fully grasped the gravity of his errand and,

although he was still somewhat unsure of his ability to remember words, he knew he had to try.

'His Grace is well pleased. All those involved will be rewarded. The prize must be sent immediately.'

Silas stood then knelt, fell on his backside, stood again and quickly made for his horse. He had never seen her so well-groomed and, in less than ninety minutes Annie was boasting the shiniest saddle too. He made haste for York constantly reciting the words that Wolsey's advocate had trusted him with without pausing. He rode straight to the office near the river hoping that Hall would be there and he was not disappointed. Robert jumped out of his chair, locked the door and also checked the secret door hidden in the panels.

'Well?! How did you fare?'

Silas related the message perfectly and, as he did, Hall preened and grinned at this small but significant success, looking forward to the many honours that would be bestowed on him.

'I now must ask of you something extraordinary. It is well within human accomplishment although it is something that I have never before tasked you with. This is due completely to my good Christian heart and fears for your welfare.'

Silas was well aware of the term, horseshit, and although he had never used it previously, he was certain that it was now most applicable. Hall rambled a little more and then got to the point.

'I need you to travel through the night back to Cawood. Tonight, there is a half-moon and you are not, under any circumstances, to use a torch.'

He then stared at Silas wondering what his response would be. Silas was conflicted. He believed that Annie could make the journey blindfolded but he also understood that the worst of people were abroad at night despite curfews.

'Of course, sir. Do I take the cask?'

'Aha! You're learning Silas!'

He was astonished that he had used his name. Hall reiterated the details regarding the cask and its unusual lettered blocks which seemingly wasn't within the office. An hour passed when Silas sat alone in the office wondering why nothing was happening. Eventually, as the light was failing, he heard clanking and footsteps. Robert had returned with two armed guards carrying a plain box similar to the first one. The cask was removed inside the office which was now almost completely in the dark. Then, like last time, his saddle appeared again leaving Silas wondering where his horse was.

'Under no circumstances press these marked blocks. If anyone takes it off you besides Wolsey's men and they attempt to press even one of them, run. Once inside Cawood, hand it only to an official bearing the archbishop's arms.'

The Owl

After incessant nodding, Silas exited to find Annie ready outside and so he made way immediately. Navigating the city and finding his way to Micklegate Bar was easy as many windows along the way were still lit with candles. For the first half mile beyond the walls, he felt as though he was in complete darkness although his eyes soon adjusted. Relaxing into a steady pace, he was suddenly startled. He had fallen asleep and a screech had woken him almost four miles into his journey. It was the owl which then took up its accommodation on the saddle. As strange as this seemed, the creature gave Silas the confidence he craved although he knew not why. It hath a pair of eyes superior to mine and he can fly to our given destination! he told himself. Wherever fear encroached on Silas's peace and determination, his propensity for fantasy would soon take over and this journey would not be an exception. Half a mile later, he was convinced that the owl was a guardian sent by his grandfather from above. Even more curious was his certainty that every time the road, fields and trees merged into one blurred shadow, there was a lone dark rider ahead showing him the way.

After nine miles, he was feeling very sure of himself riding in the dark and certain that he had added a new string to his bow. But then, drowning out the natural sounds of the English countryside at night-time was the thundering sound of hooves. He looked in all directions but could see nothing. Both Annie and the owl turned and it was then that he could make out a horse approaching at a gallop from his rear. The rider howled out his battle cry which terrified Silas who then felt for his dagger and then thought to check if the cask was concealed but the man was on top of him before he could do either. Annie reared up in defence and Silas fell hard into the earth. The assailant's horse was huge and Silas could just barely make out that its rider was also a very large man wearing thick leather from cap to boot. Silas lashed out and caught the enemy in his midriff but it only injured his hand, the leather being almost as good as armour. A clenched leathered glove met with Silas's stomach and he cried out, winded and agonised. Then he rolled over. Hurriedly, the man started to search the saddle although Annie wrestled with him throughout each attempt he made. Then, she tried to race away but he grasped her reins. The owl gave forth an unearthly scream startling the man and then clawed his face. He cried out and with a fisted glove, grabbed the owl by one wing and then beat it into the ground. Silas was dazed and sore but managed to stand, dagger in hand, his worst enemy now his mind.

I must protect the cask and Annie. I must defeat him. I have a dagger. I don't want to kill anyone; it is a commandment. I might die. I should die…my master has explained how important this is. I am blessed, I am beloved and will be protected…'

And then so much of the words that had been offered by Dunstan came clearly to the fore and it gave him heart although soon he was again panicking and ruminating. He suddenly found himself successfully upright once more, dagger in hand but his opponent turned and kicked him hard on his shins. Silas howled and, certain that he was all but defeated, struggled to get up again. As he tried to straighten, he could see in the sparse moonlight that the thief had found the cask. He held it up to see its construction more clearly. Although Silas remembered that he was told to run, instead he lunged at the brute only to be thrown back down like a defenceless animal. Seeing that he was almost about to escape with the cask, Silas struggled forward one last time only to see that his opponent had suddenly slumped to the ground. Silas stilled himself and cleared his eyes as best he could although, as everything stopped, it was even harder to make out what was before him. Soon, he believed that he could make out a shadow flashing by so he moved closer and then tripped. He had fallen onto a third person dressed in a monk's habit who was busy ensuring that the attacker was no longer a threat. However, this monk was like no other holy man as he had successfully restrained the brute and had then plunged a knife into his heart. Following the sudden and shocking melee, apart from the shuffle of the monk's habit, all that could be heard was the bubbling sound of the menace's last breath and the owl's wings settling. Moments later, all was completely still. Traumatised, Silas tried to pull himself together. He checked that the man was dead as well as trying to see into the dark hood of his saviour.

'Oh... I thank thee...you do not know...please...who are?'

As the monk pulled away, the slender light of the moon caught his rugged features and Silas gasped as he recognised him. And, before Silas could utter another word, he was gone.

His next thoughts were for the owl. He scrambled around to find it and it was its weak flutter that helped to locate it. As he held the creature up against the moonlight, it started to beat its wings once again and Silas carefully placed him back on the pommel. Then he did something quite out of character. He started to kick the body on the ground.

'Yield ye knave! In the name of...and that...and the king! Haha! You have met your match this day... Lord Silas!'

And he felt that much better for it. He quickly mounted and hurried away just in case he wasn't dead after all.

Despite the ferocious assault and even that he hurt everywhere once again, little harm was done and the cask was intact. Within minutes he was back on course.

He then made great haste and his heart swelled as soon as he saw the village in the distance and the castle beyond but after journeying just a few yards more, he heard galloping hooves again and so took Annie into a gallop only to realise that this time, the assailants were in front of him. He halted to turn and as he did, one of the men shouted to him.

'We come in the name of his Grace, the Archbishop of York.'

In an age where people could be brutally tortured and seriously maimed in battle, where quartering was deemed sufficient punishment for treason and where men would kill for scraps, there remained codes of honour. An enemy of Wolsey's could well pretend to be one of his guards but it was unlikely. This greeting was assurance enough for Silas and he had worked out that even if he had been wrong that he was unlikely to escape a second time. His whole demeanour calmed as Wolsey's guards escorted him through the lit gates of the ever-inviting Cawood Castle.

Bed and Breakfast

The courtyards were lit by torches and Silas thought that the half-lit banners and pennants were awe-inspiring. He then decided to tell Wolsey's soldiers about the attack. Immediately men were sent back out to recover the body in the hope of identifying him although it seemed to be in vain as there was nothing about the man that gave anything away.

The farrier took Silas to the furthest corner of the distant courtyard where there was an aviary.

'Many of these are damaged and ailing' he said.

Before him were many species of birds, some that would certainly be used for hunting but others that were being cared for.

'Have him straight as a cross in the week' he added and the owl happily gave himself up to his care.

Silas was taken to a room and fed again although this time a sentry stood in the doorway and a guard took the cask away from him. Meanwhile, Wolsey had already left his sleeping chambers and met with his officials in the constable's chamber.

'Leave me be…guard the door,' he demanded.

Then, he carefully placed the cask on the table and took out the letter that Silas had delivered on his previous visit. Punching in just three of the protruding blocks, Q, C and A, he then let go of it and sat back. After a few seconds, there came a distinct whirring sound that changed in neither tone nor volume. If he hadn't been expecting that sound, there is little doubt that he would have found it both eerie and disconcerting and would have called for his protectors. He was delighted, for one mistake in the use of the blocks would have led to an almighty explosion and he knew it. As he looked at it sideways on, what would have been the top of the barrel was now to his left and it started to move outwards like a screw. The wooden lid had been attached to a long metal cylinder which stealthily made its way out as Wolsey delighted in its mechanism. Finally, it came to a halt and, once it was fully exposed, there was a sizeable gap in the cylinder large enough to secrete objects. In that space were crammed many documents and he deduced that it would have been impossible to get anything more in there.

Hurriedly, he lay out all the documents on his desk glancing up to make sure that no one else could see. Later, the constable waiting outside would declare that there was a good silence for almost forty minutes,

'At the end of which his Grace exclaimed so noisily that it had all surprised.'

On the other side of the courtyard, Silas could hear hurried footsteps approaching. Then, the door flew open.

'All is well' said the officer, 'you will stay 'til it is light. Follow me.'

He was taken to a small bed chamber with sparse furniture and decoration although it had a real bed with feather-filled pillows and blankets. As he looked closer, he found that blankets were on top of a mattress and he was astounded. After examining himself for injuries, he lay down on the floor next to the bed and started to nod off although his peace was short-lived as there was an assertive knock on the door. He was ill-equipped for such eventualities and so lay there waiting for something to happen. Then, the door opened slightly and a maid spoke,

'May I come in sir?'

Silas stood and looked around, then he looked under the bed and behind the curtains. Certain he was alone, he was left even more confused.

'Oh…sorry... only me here...' he said.

'I am speaking to you sir' she said, 'may I enter?'

'Why…yes...umm...'

'Here are some clothes for you to sleep in. There is a bowl set into that cabinet yonder and…you must sleep in the bed.'

His expression was so gormless that she giggled and that changed everything. He thought that, once again, he had made a complete tit of himself and so stood wobbling and feeling humiliated. She, in turn, became upset and started to apologise profusely. He stopped her immediately.

'No…no…you misunderstand…I did not know this was for me' and he offered her his wonky smile.

She smiled in return and left.

Before he did anything more, Silas floated around the room for a while. The experience of having a pretty blonde girl calling him sir had gone to his head and possibly other bits as well and by the time he had washed, changed and climbed into bed, he was ecstatic. Even so, he could not sleep for he was sailing on a cloud both metaphorically and physically. Then, he slept like a baby.

When he awoke, he could not believe what was before him. For Cawood, this was a modest chamber but to him, it seemed like a palace all of its own. He first contemplated the bed coverings which were embroidered with floral designs in bright colours. On the facing wall was a tapestry depicting a hunt and on closer inspection, Cardinal Wolsey could be seen in the centre. There was a miniature of the king on the wall and this in particular excited him for he had only seen his image on a coin before and that clearer image would stay emblazoned on his mind for many years to come. Birds were singing and he could hear that preparations were afoot at the stable and in the kitchens.

Just as he was about to go back to sleep, there came a knock on the door.

'Come hither!' he said now believing that he was Lord of Cawood and yet sure he could hear that same giggle again.

She was that much more beautiful in the morning light, made even more appealing by yet another tray of food. He pulled the blankets up so far that they covered almost everything except his nose.

She maintained her pose, posture and professionalism, wished him good morning and then delivered a message.

'Once dressed you are to walk to the office. The one which you frequented yesterday.'

'On my own?'

'Yes sir, alone.'

And then she left. Sadly, having fallen completely in love once again and sure that he would marry the girl, the door clicked shut and he never saw her again.

Astonished that he had been trusted to navigate Cawood Castle alone, he found it a very busy place and was surprised to pass Mark Walton, the musician he had seen at the Sheriff

Hutton trial. He seemed in a hurry neither acknowledging nor ignoring the boy. What was even more surprising was that large, burly guards patted him on the shoulders as he passed. Just as he was about to enter the office, he saw three huddled officers who applauded as he entered the room. Inside was the same official he had encountered on his first visit, seated and waiting for him.

'I am sorry sir…my tardiness...'

'Sit down lad. No apologies needed. You sleep well?'

'Thought my time had come and I was in Heaven sir.'

He laughed.

'You may go back to your master head held high. You have done well. Tell Master Hall that his duty is fulfilled and recompense will follow.' The official laughed as he had to repeat it several times.

On his way home, Silas raised his head proud of his greatest accomplishment. He imagined the young blonde servant at Cawood weeping into her gruel and pining for the crimson-locked knight in a matching doublet. People formed crowds along his way home and cheered for Lord Silas of York, of manly physique and handsome of face. Nearer, he thought. I'm getting nearer to the person I have always wished to be, the person my mother wanted me to be.

Halfway home and coming to his senses, Silas stopped at a still stream where Annie drank. Inadvertently, he saw his reflection for the first time in years and his recent elation dispersed as easily as it had arrived. He did not recognise the face before him. In many ways, he still considered himself a child although he knew that his body felt different. His hair was thinning although he knew not why, neither had it grown back where it had been torn out in Galtres Forest. He had wispy strands of red hair about his chin and under his now larger and more pointed nose. His skin was rough but he did, at least, compliment himself on his teeth as they were all still present. He contemplated the stranger before him and decided that there could not have been any maiden anywhere that would look at him more than once. Moreover, although it had been said so many times, he was shocked at how thin he looked. Following one of the greatest successes of his life, he was once again left completely demoralised.

Good news

He arrived in York later that same day and dutifully headed for the office. He would not have been surprised if someone had told him that Hall had in slept there for that is how it seemed. He jumped up both anxious and expectant.

'What news?'

'His Grace says that your duty is fulfilled and recompense will follow.'

Robert Hall jumped into the air and Silas laughed. Then Hall did a ridiculous dance and Silas laughed even more.

'This is the best of news, boy. You hath acquitted thyself of thy duty! Haha! The very best news but…you must not speak of this. It is between you, I, the Cardinal and the sheriff's guards. No one else…you understand?'

Silas nodded. Truth be told he was happy that his superiors were happy and, as always, was completely ignorant about what he had done although he would harbour a creeping interest in the clandestine journeys, the cask and what Wolsey was up to for some time. But for now, he remained silent.

'What happened to you?' asked Hall.

Silas rambled about the attack and how the assailant was confounded. He dramatized each breath and blow. Although Robert was both shocked to hear of it and delighted that he still managed to deliver the cask, he told Silas that that was not what he meant.

'No…why are your clothes a different colour?'

'I had a wash…washed these too…'

'Whatever for? Were you coerced?'

'No sir, I think it was…a treat.'

'Haha! The Cardinal rewards his supporters!'

He leaned in closer to Silas.

'Did he lay on any…extra…bedtime treats for you…hey? Haha!'

'Oh yes, sir. I have never known the like. Twas as if I was floating in Heaven.'

'Ha! Nothing like it, lad…made a man of you.'

Silas made his screwed-up face as he was certain that he wasn't much of a man when he had looked at his reflection but then added,

'A young maid offered treats afore and after I slept.'

Hall leaned in once more,

'It's a wonder you could ride home, Hehe.'

For a moment Silas thought that his master had lost his mind but then he settled and in a more serious tone asked him of the attack.

'Your saviour was a monk?'

'Aye sir except he wasn't…it was Jaxon.'

Hall didn't seem surprised.

'And he finished off your attacker?'

'Yes sir.'

Hall settled and took a deep breath.

'Well, well, well. Who would have thought it?'

Confused, Silas waited to see if there was more. Hall slumped back into his chair.

'Reap and sow. Reap and sow. Who would have thought it?'

And then he quietened. For the first time in many years, Robert Hall was contemplating his faith, something he rarely visited. He thought of whether he should tell Silas about what had happened to his lifelong nemesis beyond York prison but considered the most unusual turn of events that had taken place.

'When he was released, he struggled with what you had done lad. I'm guessing that he hadn't seen much kindness in his life so kindness had become a stranger as had forgiveness. Believe me, he almost begged the sheriff to hang him so insignificant was his existence. But so impatient did the sheriff become with his prisoner that he actually gave him choices…'

Hall put his head back and laughed,

'Ha…options…a sheriff giving options. What think ye of that? Nevertheless, that is what he did. The young man who had tried to make your entire life a misery chose to become a friar. He had sworn that day that he would travel the land, spreading the Gospel and changing the lives of those who had strayed from the path...'

'Why do you think he was on the road to Cawood, sir?'

'I expect he's been looking out for you. There can be no other reason… seems like your forgiveness moved something in him although I doubt that he will ever know that he may well have changed history in doing so.'

For a while, they both said nothing, somewhat dumbfounded by such a strange chain of events.

'I have an errand for you tomorrow!' said Hall jumping up and scaring the stuffing out of the lad.

'A treat for you…'

As Robert started to explain, Silas could neither see his errand as a treat nor could he fathom why suddenly, he was now sending him in the opposite direction.

18 The Cottage

Nonetheless, the following morning, he set off towards Nun Monkton, his destination being the deserted factory near Tolerton that had been so wickedly developed and managed by Salvo. Silas had been told that he had to first find the cottage and then go inside where there remained some keys. He was to pick them up, lock the cottage door and return. He had enjoyed the journey as well as the peace of mind as he was sure that the chance of any danger was less likely than during some of his recent assignments. The settlement was completely new to him and it was the large, characterless workshop that struck him first. There was a slight breeze and the door slowly swung open and shut, something he heard long before he had arrived at the enclosure. On reaching the door, he could see that there was hardly anything left within despite the poor light. The cottage was easy enough to find although its door was shut and it too was dark inside.

Casually, he opened the door hoping that he would find something more interesting there but instantly thought that there was some movement within. Without warning, the shadows turned around and it was soon evident that there were two people holding candles before him. Silas looked upon them in awe as words had completely escaped him.

'Welcome, dear Silas' said the female.

'Our dear friend, what a joy it is to see you,' said the man.

'But…I do not understand…I was meant to get…'

'Keys?' said the man.

'Yes…erm…yes keys.'

As he looked upon Daniel and Beatrice, he first thought that they must have escaped prison although there was nothing about them that would suggest that they were surprised to see him. The cottage was finely furnished and

Young Silas

there was a large drawing table to the left. The rushes on the floor were new and clean and they had furniture that would have been the envy of many York citizens.

'This is your surprise' said Beatrice as she sat Silas in a rocking chair in front of a burned-out fire, 'Master Hall thought you would be pleased…'

Then, it started to make some sense to him. As soon as she mentioned Robert, he was convinced that there was nothing underhand going on.

Daniel was very honest and told him that they owed everything to Master Hall and Beatrice's father.

'At first, he wanted me flogged and, no doubt, imprisoned although he could not bring himself to take Beatrice before the court. She persuaded her father of our genuine love for one another and I promised that I would, within a year, find a position in the house of an earl or baron, which I will.'

'No one knows more about horses than you do,' said Silas.

Then, he looked over at the drawings.

'All the work I do is for Master Hall and if that is for a lifetime then I would not complain. Soon I will be back at my desk near the Ouse in York. I am truly ashamed of my deception.'

He stared at them and they knew that what they had told him was not sufficient.

'Daniel knew nothing except for our meetings at the Minster, it pains me how I used him so,' said Beatrice, 'I was tempted Silas, the devil himself flattered me, flattered my work and because it was my brother who was telling me that the highest in the land would want to commission my drawings, my vanity then came to the fore. The only drawing that I copied for use in any window was of St Catherine of the Wheel. I made many more of my own designs. Originals, but they never saw the light of day.'

Silas tittered. He thought Beatrice was making a stained-glass window joke when she wasn't.

'I had nothing to do with the tampering of Master Hall's letters, it was Bartholomew who bribed Jenny.'

Changing the subject, she then asked him if he was comfortable in his seat and, for a moment, his heart stopped, nervous that she might mention her previous intimacy with his sizzling backside and that it would lead to Beatrice and Daniel having to get an annulment. He almost spat out his soup when she said that Robert had let them occupy the cottage rent-free but then remembered that, despite his many failings, his boss was given to random generosity now and again.

'Now to your surprise. Your reward for your success at Cawood.'

'You know?! You know about…'

'No, not at all' said. Beatrice. He just told us that you had an important errand as far as Cawood Castle and that he had no doubt that you would come through.'

This was a gift all of his own. At last, his master was starting to believe in him.

Daniel then opened a large chest and pulled out a blue blanket that appeared new.

'Ah, that is fine Dan, I'd love to see it on your horse,' said Silas.

'It is for Annie' said Daniel and placed it in Silas's arms.'

For some time, he was speechless and then began to thank him over and over.

'Thank your master, Silas. It is his gift.'

Knowing that he was under no pressure to return home, Silas enjoyed the finest afternoons since he had found the red-haired Annie once again. He beseeched Daniel to place the blanket on his beloved horse as he knew he would do it that much better than he could. Before he left, he quizzed them about Salvo although they assured him that they had no idea of the extent of their deceit and he believed that they had both sufficiently repented.

Purposely, he ensured that he arrived in York whilst there

was still plenty of light so that he could adequately exhibit his new blanket, something that would have been difficult to see except from a few angles but this did not deter him from parading for almost half an hour and, on this occasion, he was deaf to the cat calls and abuse. This, he told himself, was a day to celebrate.

Constable of York

The following day, Silas made his way into the city to find a small procession along Petergate which was heading for the Minster. You may well imagine that such a thing would receive quite a mixed reception although, on the whole, people enjoyed any grand spectacle, particularly one that distracted them from their humdrum lives for an hour or so. Silas pushed through the stinky shoulders of two loud men trying to sell sweetmeats and it was then that he recognised some of the well-established merchants of York as well as the sheriff. Walking formally and orderly, their heads were held high following a Merchant Adventurers' banner and they could not resist congratulating one another as they marched although it was the man at the centre who was getting all the attention. Silas would eventually come to learn that Robert Hall was being made a constable of the city. It was of course another honorary role but was, nevertheless, something to crow about. As he watched on, Silas revelled in the grandeur and flattered himself that he was an associate of the man in question although he could hardly have said so as his hat was soon knocked off and, in picking it up, he realised that he was yet again filthy. Very soon, the fuss was over as the privileged of York all disappeared inside the Minster to give prayers, presumably for themselves.

As he walked away, he was sure that he would not see his boss again that day as prayers would have been followed by copious amounts of mead and wine in the Merchant Adventurers' Hall. Neither did he deduce that this sudden promotion seemed to swiftly follow the delivery of the cask to Cardinal Wolsey.

With time on his hands, he wandered for a while avoiding the more odious parts of the city and that included Grope Lane. Not far from the walls of St Mary's Abbey, he heard the sound of gaiety, laughter carrying on the warm breeze and so he hurried towards the Minster precinct as he had almost forgotten that it was market day and that the great Bayard would be performing. It took Silas some time to find a vantage point but he soon settled on the steps that led to the city wall near Bootham Bar. He realised that true to his word, Dunstan, was no longer part of the show and then took some time to comprehend what was taking place. This, he told himself, was very clever. The king appeared with a switch and started thrashing it about. The crowd urged him to use it but, as yet, there was no one else there. Then, a second puppet appeared, this was Thomas More.

'Methinks I would be well advised to use my switch on you, my very good friend, Thomas. What think ye?'

Thomas More clasped his hands together and said,

'Do nought, Your Grace, until I have prayed upon it.'

The crowd laughed, already aware that this was More's answer to everything. He left the stage and Wolsey walked back on.

'Ay, to be sure, this is for thy ample backside!' shouted Henry and began to beat the Cardinal with it.

There were mixed responses from the crowd. Knowing that their Cardinal had joined them in the north once again, they weren't altogether sure they liked this portrayal but they did laugh heartily as other recognisable advisors and ministers were also given a beating. Suddenly, Wolsey returned alone with the switch and started to prowl about the stage swinging it wildly. The burly Duke of Norfolk appeared and the crowd beseeched Wolsey to go for him and, as he chased him, they cheered, jeered, applauded and laughed. Then Henry Percy, Earl of Northumberland wobbled on, announcing himself.

'But you are my friend are you not, Percy?' asks Wolsey.
'Why, yes you Grace...'
Then, the Percy puppet walked to the edge of the stage and said to the audience,
'But only as far as you can spit...'
Wolsey heard this and chased him off.

Wolsey returned once more looking extremely perplexed. He looked once again at the switch and threw it away saying,
'This is of use no longer. Let me see…'

He then turned around and picked up a puppet of his own which he bounced up and down and swung about much to the joy of the gathered citizens of York.

Silas could not believe his eyes. For a moment he cleared them and ran as close as he could to the stage to get a closer look at Wolsey's puppet. There was no question, it was meant to be Robert Hall and Silas wondered if everyone else had understood it to be the same. He had found this so disturbing that he had to leave without any idea of what to do with this revelation.

The plot

For a day he paced the city trying to make sense of what he had witnessed. The parody became as one with his memories of Skipton Castle, Cawood, Temple Newsam, the forest and even the trial years ago at Sheriff Hutton. He was rarely given to inquisitiveness, happy to follow orders and fulfil his errands but he was certain that he could have been killed on the road to Cawood if not for the much reformed and repentant Jaxon. With as broken a mental compass as one could imagine, he found himself unintentionally hovering outside the office. As he paced back and forth, the door opened.

'What you up to? You'll scare the swans. Last thing I need on such a jubilant day is a fine!'

Silas hadn't expected to see Robert in the office. He was with the sheriff and many empty and some half-full jars of sack.

'But! For my fine adventurer! Hehe! I shall make an exception…'

The sheriff giggled. They were both pickled as gherkins. Anyone else would have laughed but Silas, having still not mastered the art of human cues, just stared wondering what to do.

'What a day! Have jink!' insisted Hall.

Silas was given a watered wine and gladly accepted it. Fortunately, the sheriff seemed to be a lot closer to Terra Firma than his newly inaugurated and somewhat inebriated friend.

'Can I help?' said Sheriff George Gale grinning like Cromwell in a torture chamber.

'I thought…it was…then I saw…this very morning…I would like…'

'Shpit it owt lad!' shouted Robert Hall.

'I err… I want to know why I was in danger…the cask…Skipton…the Cardinal…'

Ecstatic and sozzled, there would have been few things that would have unsteadied Robert but this had him and the sheriff silenced.

'What for?' asked George Gale.

'It's all so very confusing for me. I need to know whether I am still in danger.'

'Danger! Danger! Ha!' exclaimed Hall, 'why, I will soon be the toast of Hampton Court!'

The sheriff then looked at Hall hoping to get some sense out of him but he had suddenly shut his eyes. Gale looked at Silas.

'I do not think it would do you good.'

'Ay!' said a waking Robert Hall, 'and some of it is not for the ears of someone so young…' he pushed himself up slightly and squinted at Silas, 'except I think you have recently joined the world of adults? Haha!'

He winked as he said it and then added,

'The maid at Cawood?'

Silas remained confused.

The sheriff grasped Robert's arm, partly because he was about to fall over but also to seek his permission.

'I can see no harm but the lad will have to swear an oath.'

In an instant, Silas had sworn on the weighty Bible that had been taken out of Robert's draw and the sheriff opened the secret door in the wall to check that there was no one else about and, in doing so, brought a chair for Silas. He then began to outline the whole plot.

'Twill be difficult for you…'

'Good at maps…he is…' slurred Hall.

'It may be better then, to think of the places I mention as much as the people? Do you know who Henry Percy is, boy?'

'He is the Sixth Earl of Northumberland and was trained in the household of the Cardinal.'

George Gale was so impressed that it temporarily silenced him.

'Do you know who Henry Clifford is?'

The sheriff was stunned when he said that he had met him at Skipton Castle.

'It gets a bit complicated so you'll need to keep up…'

The sheriff then went on to explain that Henry Clifford, the First Earl of Cumberland had once been married to a lady called Margaret Talbot, son of George Talbot who was the Earl of Shrewsbury but she died in 1515. Margaret had a sister who stayed close to Clifford even after Margaret had died. That sister was called Mary Talbot and she eventually married Henry Percy. Mary continued to write to her brother-in-law, Henry Clifford, throughout the marriage. Sadly, that marriage was a living nightmare for Mary. In her letters, she outlined how Henry Percy had never wanted to be married to her and how he abused and berated her. The sheriff then told Silas that Mary and Henry Percy had since separated

As fate would have it, Henry Clifford of Cumberland

married again after the death of his first wife Margaret, this time to Margaret Percy, Henry Percy's sister. Over time, she also confirmed the ill-treatment of Mary Talbot by her brother. Mostly in letters, damning evidence built up against Henry Percy but not enough to incriminate him of anything serious. That was until the king decided that he wanted a divorce from Queen Catherine.

'What did all that have to do with King Henry wanting a divorce?' asked Silas eloquently.

'You sure you are grown up enough for this?'

Silas wasn't sure but nodded anyway as the fog was already thickening.

'Henry Percy never wanted to marry Mary Talbot. Whilst he was still a page to the Cardinal, he secretly became betrothed to Anne Boleyn. As he had neither asked permission of his father nor the king, he found himself very quickly out of favour with both. It didn't help that Boleyn was also intended for another man.

'So, the king knows all about Percy liking Mistress Boleyn?' asked Silas reintroducing a modicum of innocence to the conversation.

'That he does and, between you and me lad, I think he chooses to ignore it,' said George.

'So…all those letters and documents…they tell of how Percy ill-treated his wife?' asked Silas.

'Yes…and the…err…ahem…. affair with Boleyn.'

'I don't understand.'

'That's because you have not heard all…'

Just when it all may well have made sense, neither the sheriff nor the tipsy Robert Hall were willing to give up more but surprisingly, Silas insisted.

'Alright! Alright lad. The documents you have been carrying include a signed oath from Mary Talbot swearing that Henry Percy had confessed….'

Silas begged him to continue.

'That he and Boleyn knew one another and had issue.

There. That's it, it is all out.'

But the sheriff was relieved for only a moment as both those phrases, although in common use by most adults, meant nothing to Silas so Gale tried again.

'They had a baby together but it died at birth!'

Silence.

'How can they have a baby if they weren't married?'

Gale looked at Hall.

'Told you,' said Robert.

'Come on lad…surely? take it from me, it is possible and, in this case, it was extremely dangerous because Cumberland knew of it and it is likely that others knew of it too. It has value because the Cardinal will show that evidence to the king. Then, the king will forget all about Anne Boleyn for the time being, get a mistress and restore good Queen Catherine to where she belongs.'

'Hurrah!' shouted Silas somewhat unsure of what he was celebrating.

George Gale slumped into his chair exhausted.

'But I thought the king wanted a divorce?' asked an increasingly annoying Silas.

Gale stood again and shouted.

'This is instead! Instead of a bloody divorce! The fat Cardinal did not succeed in getting the divorce so this is instead…better than! What you will!'

And he threw back his drink.

'Wouldn't she have had a baby lump?' probed Silas.

'A baby lump?! A bab….yes…yes of course but there are many ways in which a woman can isolate herself, wear larger dresses.'

Then, for a moment, both Gale and Hall wondered if they had been duped and looked at one another.

'Too much risk has been taken already for this to be a falsehood' said Gale and Robert Hall agreed.

Silas was wise enough to know when he had pushed things too far so said nothing more on the subject but was left wishing he had never asked. Ignorance, he mused, was much safer and easier to live with.

Tired and inebriated, silence reigned for a while and then the sheriff whispered to Robert,

'I had always wondered if Wolsey knew about Clifford Smith, this lad's father but he will not say anything now, I am sure...'

Hall grunted and thankfully Silas did not hear, although the events of his childhood would come back to haunt him again later in his adult years.

During the next half hour, the exciting intrigue and espionage had turned to silence but even that was not to last long. All three of them had fallen asleep and you could well have believed that there was a small band playing for as each time Hall snored, Silas gave forth a squeaky watery-wine fart whilst the sheriff mumbled the word 'Mabel' over and over. York was safe, England was safe and all was well with everyone. Or so they thought.

October 1530

The following month had Wolsey writing to his king. Strangely, he was seemingly the only person within courtly circles who didn't fully understand the extent of the king's disappointment in him and he was still expecting a grand enthronement as Archbishop within York Minster.

Excitedly, he crafted a letter in which he told the king that he and he alone had found a solution to the aching in his nether regions that would not go away although he wished to hold back the detail until Henry replied.

Certain that he would relent once he heard the full extent of Boleyn's looseness and debauchery, Wolsey was excited about his future role but he did not hear anything back from his king. His unfailing confidence told him that it was simply because wheels were turning. Those mechanisms that would damn Anne Boleyn and her family were being put into place without his evidence. The king was biding his time and would welcome his Cardinal back in due course.

And Wolsey did spend some time pondering about Henry Percy. Certainly, the king had already known that he had once been betrothed to Boleyn, it was his fury that stopped it. But would he look more favourably on Percy than Boleyn or would he punish him too? Either way, Wolsey simply could not leave him out of it for he was very much part of the case against Boleyn and so thought no more upon the matter.

By the start of November 1530, he still had not heard anything and so continued to build his popularity amongst his flock in the north and further develop his luxurious home at Cawood. It would be reasonable to say that he was blissfully ignorant, patiently awaiting his renewed authority and so it was with some degree of excitement that he received visitors of some rank on the 4th of November. At first, he was unaware of anyone arriving at Cawood but from his dining chamber on the first floor, he could see William Walsh, the Groom of the Privy Chamber. Excitedly, he ran to greet him, sure that he was there to collect the damning evidence and take it to the king under guard. When he saw Henry Percy as well, he was initially delighted to see him too, after all, he had been brought up in the Cardinal's home. He was also sure that Percy knew nothing about what he had to share with the king and so greeted him as an old friend.

Wolsey asked Percy to join him in his chamber before arranging a lavish dinner. The Cardinal remained pleased. It was Wolsey's gentleman, however, George Cavendish, who suspected that all was not well. As he stood by the fire, the twenty-eight-year-old earl seemed nervous and there was a tremble in his voice. Then, respectfully and quietly, Percy laid his arm on Wolsey's and said,

'My Lord, I arrest you of high treason.'

It is unlikely there can ever have been a more unexpected arrest in English history. Of course, he protested and asked if the king had received his letter. Wolsey put forward a reasonable and intelligent argument reminding Percy that he could not be arrested by any temporal power. In return, Percy ironically argued that when Wolsey had given him the title of Warden of the Marches, he had also invested in him the power to arrest anyone in the name of the king.

'His Grace could not be more injured than by your malicious and underhanded attempt to degrade Mistress Boleyn and take favour with the Princess of Aragon,' said Percy.

But Wolsey still believed that if the king was party to the pregnancy, then he would still win the day. He chose to say nothing as he was confined to his chambers in which he concealed the ominous cask inside his travel chest.

Two days later, he readied himself for the journey south, his destination the Tower. The king's men took his seal of office and removed any symbolism that tied him to Henry the Eighth. Still hopeful, he looked upon the entrance to his castle with affection and, as he did, his toe stubbed an object on the floor. It rolled forward and collided with the large oaken door which had everyone turning to see what it was. It was Doug Cooper's cask although it remained open and empty. His eyes came up, momentarily undisturbed as he had hidden the documents and then met those of Percy who held high the bundle of documents that would have damned himself and Anne Boleyn.

'I have found your secret, your Grace. Beneath your bed in your case. All is lost, give up any hope.'

A fire had been lit at the other side of the bridge and it consumed all manner of books, personal items and documents. Percy added Wolsey's cherished evidence to the flames although the cask lay where it had stopped in the doorway.

To this day, the citizens of Cawood commemorate Humpty Dumpty, the once beloved Cardinal that suffered the greatest of falls, all his attempts to secure support from the king and those around him failing miserably.

The fall

The first that Robert Hall heard of this was two days after Wolsey's arrest. The sheriff banged on his door and insisted on having a private audience. Hall was beside himself knowing that he was fully implicated in the plot.

'You have copies?' said the sheriff.

'Yes, we could still prove...'

'Burn them. Burn everything and, if possible, advise Clifford of Cumberland at Skipton to do the same. All is lost. Burn the code to the cask.'

At that stage, they were not sure what had happened to the cask. On Silas's penultimate journey he had taken a note with the simple code, Q, C and A for Queen Catherine of Aragon. Robert was even concerned about Doug Cooper's mark on the barrel and paced the room three times before answering.

'Yes, yes' said Hall manically, 'I will do it this day. Do you think the king knows?' said Robert

'I have it on good authority that news of this secret never reached the king. Only Percy knows and he won't be telling anyone.'

'Are we undone?' said Robert head in his hands.

'Keep a low profile. No boasting or peacocking about York regarding your new status. Mention it to no one. You will need to speak to the boy.'

'Yes', said Hall. 'Of course. I will see him today.'

Despite Gale's reassurances, Robert was terrified. It would only take one mention of his name and he would have been arrested. Any degree of protest would be useless as an arrest by the king's men was as good as a sentence and even the grim realisation that he would spend months looking over his shoulder had him running for his newly installed privy.

Later that morning, the sheriff caught Silas on his way to the office and told him that he had to go to Hall's house. Without question, he made his way there and only fifteen minutes later he was sitting in Robert Hall's drawing-room for the very first time in a seat as fine as he could imagine. Robert told him of the imminent danger three times over after which Silas calmly said,

'Mistress Boleyn won't get in trouble after all then?'

'Never mind that' blustered Hall, 'don't even mention her name again, did you hear?'

'Yes sir' he said calmly and then there was a pause whilst once more Hall rubbed his head with both hands. Then Silas had a question which he could no longer keep to himself.

'Did she have a baby lump?'

'What? No! Yes! How should I know… do not mention her name again!'

The more stressed Robert became, the more Silas glared at him.

'Can you tell me how women have babies?'

'What?'

'I don't understand about them not being marri…'

'God's blood! Forget about it. About her! Let it go!'

Silas complimented himself for, on this occasion, he had managed to work out that his master was angry so said no more.

From that day onwards, Robert intended to hide. He told Silas that he would write out instructions regarding his errands and chores and they would be read to him by Beatrice at the workshop. This was good news indeed and so he left with a further promise of silence.

Cumberland

The following day, Beatrice ran towards Silas when she saw him and then embraced him. Then she turned him around.

'How's your ruddy arse?' and she tapped him gently on the backside.

He could not reply. Of all the people who could have seen him so. He thought for a moment whether to ask her about babies but then thought it might seem rude especially if backsides were involved.

'I have read his instructions and you are to go today to Skipton Castle and insist that this letter is put in the hands of the earl and no one else.'

The journey was now very familiar and Silas thought little about his assignment and was looking forward to the maidens and fine food at Skipton Castle although he was to be very disappointed. On arrival, he was left in a cold courtyard and could almost immediately hear the Earl of Cumberland storming toward him. There was little doubt that the letter had come as a surprise. He hurriedly opened it and then as quickly destroyed it. In a fury, he raised his voice.

'You have never been to this place. Do you understand? We have never met!'

'Oh…err…I have been more than once my Lord, once…erm…the map…remember…'

'You have never set eyes on me boy!' he insisted.

'Oh…perhaps…have you forgotten?'

The earl drew back his hand and struck Silas so hard that he fell to the ground.

'Remembering yet lad? If you are having difficulty perhaps it would be best if you never arrived back in York?'

Silas was now beginning to get the gist but still could not understand why the earl would have forgotten him. So, he immediately got back on his horse and set off for home with little chance of making it home before dark. He stopped a few miles outside Skipton so that Annie could graze and drink and then made haste. The light was failing just outside Knaresborough and so he purposely slowed. On what had been a relatively uneventful journey, he suddenly became aware of figures shifting in the trees to his right. Then, he was sure that he could see an archer drawing his bow and aiming at him. Recent events had sharpened his reactions somewhat and he was certain that he was in mortal danger once again. There was no mistaking the swoosh of the arrow and it hit its target the first time, completely piercing the right lung. The victim slumped to the ground and died where he landed.

It was not Silas. Once again, Jaxon had been shadowing him and had saved his life. Silas dismounted to comfort his saviour but he was dead. A second arrow stuck into Annie's saddle and a third missed Silas's leg by an inch. A bit more meat on him and he would have been seriously impaired so he immediately leapt into the saddle, straddling the arrow and took Annie into a gallop. He turned once and once only and, in the half-light, could see Clifford's coat of arms emblazoned on the archer's doublet. Within a few minutes, he was amidst people again and confident that his attackers had retreated.

Shaken, he rode the rest of the way home in the dark and then went straight to bed.

The following morning, he sought out Daniel who was back at the stables and asked him to re-shoe Annie and repair the saddle.

'Say nothing to your master Silas. He is so terrified that he will not answer his door. If they were Cumberland's men, I do not think they will bother you again and I cannot see you having to make that journey ever again.'

Daniel's words were somewhat prophetic as Silas would only ever see Skipton again whilst on his way to Lancaster many years later.

The journey

Robert Hall need not have worried himself for things changed at some pace over the next month. The king had known for a while of Wolsey's allegiance to Catherine of Aragon and even if he had received the new evidence, it is unlikely that he would have believed it and turned against his beloved Anne.

Once Wolsey had been taken as far as Sheffield, he was met by Sir William Kingston Knight, captain of the guard and constable of the Tower of London. At last, reality hit home.

So much so that the Cardinal immediately became ill. By the 27th of November the Cardinal rested at the Abbey of Leicester where he became gravely ill and died. After all the intrigue, arcane plans and alliances, his story was over. Conspiracy theories gathered momentum over the centuries to come. Was it possible that King Henry wanted him silenced before he even reached London? That he wasn't even worth the effort of a trial or, even worse, that Henry believed Wolsey may still upset matters whilst he languished in the Tower?

Whatever the cause of his death was, the whole matter of Percy and Anne Boleyn was closed. At least for the time being.

December 1530

Bitter weather returned to York and even Robert Hall was confident that his association with Wolsey was secret and already in the past. Silas's errands became quite mundane and he was thankful for it. Via Beatrice, he had made a point of letting his master know that his life should have some value and, for someone who did errands for a local businessman, anticipated dangers should be less than they had been. In return, Hall managed to retrieve the cask and gave it to Silas for his efforts and he was also able to tell him that the owl had fully recuperated.

For the early part of 1531, many of his errands became much more local and this had him counting his blessings as he loved living in York. By March, Daniel and Beatrice had gone. Silas had heard that they were to be employed at Temple Newsam in Loidis although he did not know how her talents were being used. Now and again, he exchanged grimaces with the girl at the top of the Shambles and he could hold a conversation with the seemingly ever-present Bogmorten and so laid back were the following months that he finally completed all the repairs on his home, Castle Cooper.

In 1532, Silas was eighteen years of age. His hair thinner, his frame leaner and his nose a little more protruded and it would be impossible to confuse him with anyone else. Of course, some had nurtured some affection for him but the lampooning would never go away and neither would his desire to become a knight. As a young adult, he had even less confidence for he knew in his heart that almost all young men found a young woman and got married, something which seemed to forever elude him. And, he remained quite ignorant of those more vulgar details of life which only helped to feed his fantasies of becoming someone special. He certainly was special in a time when there was little or no toleration of such a thing but it could be fairly said that he remained true to both his conscience and his God throughout his life, something which even popes struggled to achieve. Since meeting Robert Hall, he had remained his one and only employer and possibly the only one that would ever put up with him.

However, as an eighteen-year-old, he was content with his lot, unable to decide whether to accept the dreariness of local errands or chase his dream and, in doing so, possibly risk his life. His best was, of course, ahead of him but, like all of us, he wasn't to know it. Neither did he realise how much he had learned from the first eighteen years of his life and how it would benefit him in future intrigues which would involve even higher powers.

19 Reflections

As spring arrived in 1532, one Friday morning he found himself with little to do so decided to amble. The sun was rising over Coppergate and, as he cleared his eyes, he saw the light dancing upon the waters of the Ouse. He stood, gawping into the distance and he thought for a moment of those days when it had frozen over. He turned to see the warehouse and glassworks of Robert Hall. Jonks was opening up and, smiling, Silas reminisced about when he had first met him. Then he thought back to when he discovered Beatrice proudly showing her magnificent drawings to his master, how beautiful she was and what a fool he had been for thinking she had become one of Robert's mistresses. He then smiled as he remembered getting drunk with his boss and the sheriff celebrating their great collaboration only to be left chagrined and deflated within days. As his head turned back again, he studied the quirky Ouse Bridge now becoming busy with morning traffic. All he could think about was that diminutive child being carried high only to be thrown into nettles and, as his eyes lowered, he chose not to think of the hour he had spent accommodating snails in the cold.

Somewhat melancholy, he resumed his journey and wandered towards York castle. For all its architectural beauty, it was also the place of nightmares and as he mulled over his imprisonment, he could feel its suffering viscerally. His own suffering and that of others. Of the grave robbers and, of course, Jaxon. Who would have thought that his life would have been saved by the person who had hated him most?

He recalled regularly visiting the nearby bread stall and giving bread to the poor and, at that moment, promised himself that he would never stop doing so. As he wandered, he soon found himself near his master's house. He chuckled as he remembered Jenny forcibly bathing him as well as the many outfits he had been given but not one that fit. Where there had been so recently blazing timbers, a new house had been built using tried and tested building techniques and boasting the finest of chimneys as well as the most advanced glass leaving Robert Hall of a mind to move, so envious was he. Along Goodramgate, Silas stopped to admire the old buildings in Lady's Row and wondered what had happened to Father Bartholomew, the priest at the centre of the stained-glass window fraud and who had lived there. For a moment, he was sure that he too would have escaped death and had simply been moved onto another parish where presumably, he could contrive further wicked deeds.

It was then that he pondered over the enigmatic Holy Trinity Church almost hidden behind Lady's Row. It sat quite dignified away from the attention of passers-by although it enticed them in as it did Silas. At that moment, he found an affinity with the small and unassuming House of God, sure that one day it would play a greater part in his life. Meandering, he soon reached the south entrance to Goodramgate, where he could see the top end of the industrious Shambles but the girl with the toothless smile was not there. Perhaps I will wander by again later and be rewarded with a smile, he told himself. Then, his deep thoughts were suddenly interrupted by a familiar sound,

'Rats, cats, all types of vermin, Boggy will rid thee of all thy woes! Why…ladies, I will even dispatch thy husbands if so desired!'

Those used to his mantra hurried on by although others offered a smile to his harmless wit. He waved to Silas as he passed and it was at that moment that he assured himself that he had a friend. But, when accounting for the recent loss of Daniel and Beatrice, he also acknowledged that Bogmorten was now his one and only friend in the city. Walking along Low Petergate, he did what every York citizen did day in and day out for all their lives, he stopped and marvelled at the Minster, sure once again that God alone must have built it.

He sat for a while admiring its contours and delighting in the expressions of those who had not seen it before. As he stood and walked beyond the south transept and towards the twin towers at the west end, he smiled at the tall trees that offered a natural backdrop for the cathedral and soon, he could see Galtres Forest beyond. What an adventure that had been, he mused. For a moment he could not remember how he first met Annie but then, he could see it clear as day. He had practically bumped into her in the woods, flanked by her father and uncle with no one knowing quite what to say. He sat again and, as he did, images of Isaac and all of the Croppers seemed to flash before him and so he paused and prayed for them all.

He then noticed that someone had arrived at the Liberty Gates of the Minster, showing their pass to gain access. Fawkes, he thought. What would I be without William Fawkes? That memory had become somewhat hazy but he smiled as he recalled the day that the man had first visited his mother which led to his employment.

'I would have been a waif, a beggar and outcast' he whispered and so counted his blessings. Then he wondered if any of it would have happened if his mother hadn't been so pretty. His whole body slumped as he once again felt the full weight of losing his mother so young and so wished to share with her his many accomplishments.

'Remember the good times, that is what you must do' he told himself and grinned as he thought of his scruffy childhood tabards, ragged hose and his fantasies which were, thankfully, still intact. He added Fawkes to his prayers and in those prayers, he promised that if he could ever help William Fawkes' children one day, he would do so gladly. Those memories and prayers deliberately took him out through Bootham Bar and along Gillygate. The house in which the Queen of Sheba had lived was now unrecognisable. A second floor had been added and it too had new windows. It was there that Silas understood that, as he walked, he too was being ministered to.

'God is reminding me of my many blessings' he whispered, 'the people who picked me up when I fell. How stupid of me to think that it was I who was helping them.' And then he afforded himself a smile only to become distracted by a stray dog that sat watching him before wandering off to look for scraps.

'Bolt, my dear companion' he muttered remembering his wonderful dog, 'the most faithful dog ever known to man, still, there is an emptiness to everything without you' and then he sighed. As his eyes came up once more and he perused the nearby squalid, snickleways, he thought of what he had witnessed that night when he had helped to capture the grave robbers. His mother would often remind him that no matter how challenging life became, there were always others worse off. How true that is, he thought and pledged once again to think less of himself and more of his fellow man and woman.

Showing the now worn seal of Robert Hall, he entered the city once more instantly finding himself standing where Bayard and Dunstan had performed so many times. The wind blew around the square ironically emphasising the emptiness without them. How at that moment he longed for many more shows to come although he was certain that he would never see Dunstan again and he knew why. He understood what Dunstan was and why he had become so very important in his life and so became resigned to losing him. His words and teachings had been etched in this young man's mind and would help him to navigate the rest of life's journey with or without maps. Then he remembered what Dunstan had said about someone, someday, replacing him but Silas could still not make any sense of it.

To his left was the overwhelming St Michael Le Belfrey Church, almost complete. Silas decided that it looked out of place and had robbed many locals of their view of the Minster. All the same, he decided, it was an architectural wonder and complemented the many other churches of York as well as the Minster itself.

Now, church bells throughout York became like individual members of a choir and they echoed around and around the square lifting the spirits of all who heard them. York was pulsating with life. Horses, oxen, pigs, hens, ducks and, here and there, many more of God's creatures that Boggy had categorised as vermin. People were walking, running, riding, ambling, standing still and gossiping. Others were shouting, selling their stock and wares and a few were even arguing. Seemingly, it was only rank that set them apart. Class, money and status were the things that dictated people's place in the world and Silas often wondered why. Emphatically, his faith taught that all were equal and that rich men could never enter Heaven but then he chastised himself for his ambitions and hypocrisy.

'I would accept a knighthood and live at court tomorrow if offered' he said to himself quietly and then felt very confused.

'Why do people always want more than they have and, even worse, what others have?'

He chose to think on it no more as his head was starting to hurt. By now, he knew every inch of wall around the city and he was familiar with every gateway. He clambered up steps and onto the wall at Bootham Bar finding a spot that was very rarely guarded. He was then bold enough to make his way to the top of one of Bootham Bar's towers and, from there, he happily surveyed his beloved home. People now seemed smaller, only distinguishable by the colour or complete muddiness of their attire. Yes, he mused, it is alive. York is alive. There lies drama and jeopardy, life and death, babies and corpses, rich folk and beggars, merchants and noblemen and noblewomen. Clever people and idiots. The brave and the diffident. They are beautiful but shitty, cultured and ignorant, fierce and tame. Some are artistic, some are scientific and some are both. People from everywhere would come to visit this very special place and that included kings and queens.

All in all, he decided, it was the finest place of all.

'Despite my trials, I have been blessed to find a home in God's own city alongside his chosen' he said out loud, 'this will remain my home, one in which I will no doubt be engaged in further, more demanding adventures and meet friends anew and…I promise mother, one day I will be your knight.'

Exhausted from his debut as a philosopher, he slumped backwards and fell asleep as York's beating heart found itself in very good health, ready to make history once more.

Epilogue

True to my word, I had completed my saga of Silas's adventures as a boy in just six months and handed it to Walsingham. When we met, he was as giddy as an infant. So much so, that he hardly made sense at times. And then, he started to question me about it incessantly.

'My Lord, please read it. Believe me, there is no gain in trying to prise parts of the story out of me, I doubt if it would even make sense! I do fear that you may not approve of it. Please, take it. Read it and we shall meet two weeks hence and, if you are not content with my toils, I will think on it again.'

'Oh yes… Hehe… oh yes indeed! Lord Sillyarse! Haha!'

He tapped his nose and winked as he said it as if awaiting a plethora of punchlines and anecdotes.

'My Lord…please read it.'

Calming slightly, we came to an agreement. I insisted that he should not show it to the queen unless he was happy with it as I was sincere in my attempt to get it right.

The weeks passed and we met again incognito, in the same pub. There, they had some of the finest ale I have ever tasted and we had both consumed three goblets of the stuff before we had started talking about the story. Then suddenly he started. It was almost as if he had just walked onto a stage. He feigned a mute expression and then burst forth with,

'Percentages! Ha! Percentages!'

And on it went. I tried to explain that it wasn't that funny but he would not desist. Five drinks in and he recited Silas's song about Annie over and over having presumably commissioned someone to write a tune for him in the meantime. Eventually, I told him that if he mentioned Grope Lane one more time I would leave but he was too drunk to hear.

'Do you approve of the story?' I asked.

'Snails! Hahaha! Bloody snails!'

'Do you approve, my Lord?!'

I had shouted so loud that everyone silenced. At last, he realised how much of a prick he was making of himself in a place where he didn't want to be recognised.

We parted amicably and I suggested that we should meet once more in York and he agreed. That was a month later. It was only as I saw him stagger over the horizon, that I realised that I had made yet another mistake as I didn't want to become Walsingham's personal tour guide to Silas's home.

Surprisingly, on that occasion, he had acquired the use of the Merchant Adventurers' Hall for the morning and, as he was not drinking, our conversation was much more sedate.

'Her Majesty was delighted with your history of the boy. Indeed…'

'I cannot offer more. Not yet at least. You of all people understand that I have many obligations and endless reports to write.'

As I looked at him, he made me feel as though I had told a child that they would never see sugar again so offered a compromise.

'I am collating some histories of well, everyday folk. What I mean to say is...'

'You mean that there are other commoners as comical as this boy?' he interrupted.

'It's not about being comical My Lord. Ordinary people have much to offer and in their own small way and still have an impact on national affairs….'

As I passionately tried to sell him my interest in everyday people he almost dozed off. Even when I reminded him that the Agents of the Word were all commoners, he seemed to just want more of Silas or, it could well just have been that the queen was so disposed.

Eventually, I agreed that I may be able to write more but

not for a while. Although I could not say so, I had a duty of care to many of my fellow Agents and I wasn't about to divulge every event, nuance and detail of their lives simply for entertainment purposes. Two of his guards accompanied him out of the building and I followed, smiling as Walsingham walked straight past a portrait of Silas Smith without even knowing that it was there.

Outside, I bade him a fond farewell and once he was some hundred yards away, he passed a limping, shadowy figure who watched him walk by and then offered me a wave and a familiar smile as he held aloft a small cask. I waved back and then he too went home.

THE END

ABOUT THE AUTHOR

Rob holds a degree in both History and Art & Design and for his postgraduate studies, concentrated on British History. He has taught both subjects for many years and his students have ranged from early teens to undergraduates. Later in his career, he specialised in the application of new technologies in special and alternative education.

He has written a number of plays and musicals and is the author of 'Be a Teacher!' in addition to the Micklegate series.

Facebook: The Micklegate Series
Instagram: micklegateseries

Other books in The Micklegate Series:
1541 The Cataclysm
1542 The Purge
1543 The Disfiguration
1547 Death of a King.

Printed in Great Britain
by Amazon